Vaporware

By
Richard Dansky

JournalStone
San Francisco

JournalStone books may be ordered through booksellers or by contacting:

JournalStone
www.journalstone.com
www.journal-store.com

ISBN:	*978-1-936564-77-4*	(sc)
ISBN:	*978-1-936564-78-1*	(ebook)

Library of Congress Control Number: *2013935627*

Printed in the United States of America
JournalStone rev. date: May 24, 2013

Cover Design: Denise Daniel
Cover Art: Vincent Chong

Edited By: Dr. Michael R. Collings

Praise for Vaporware

"Vaporware is life in the world of games, raw and real from a writer who did his time in the trenches - with a supernatural twist that'll make you think twice about late night log-ons and who is really lurking behind the avatar on your screen..." – New York Times bestselling author **James Swallow**

"A meticulous image of the real games industry so detailed that you'll just assume the supernatural must be part of it. So immersive it makes you want to go check on that video game your spouse is spending so much time with..." – **Mur Lafferty**, author of *THE SHAMBLING GUIDE TO NEW YORK CITY*

"Imagine you're sitting at a bar, surrounded by videogame industry veterans. They're telling war stories about their past projects, the kind of stories you'd never see repeated in interviews or online magazines, the kind that are insider legends. Everyone's laughing out of shock or horror at some of the stuff we go through to release a game before Richard Dansky launches into his tale. That's when everyone shuts up, because Rich is telling a story, and when Rich starts talking, you know it's going to be a hell of a ride...." – **Lucien Soulban**, writer, *Far Cry: Blood Dragon*

Praise for Vaporware

"Richard Dansky uses his background in video games to breathe realism into his characters, concepts, and environments. The result is a 21st Century techno horror story that manages the near-impossible: to be both geektastic and incredibly cool." – **Rio Youers**, author of *WESTLAKE SOUL.*

"Richard Dansky writes about passionate, complex, flawed, and completely believable people in this absorbing novel about the toll of caring so deeply about your art. Very highly recommended!" – **Jeff Strand**, author of *DWELLER*

"Nobody knows the messy collision of writing and game development better than Richard Dansky. And for anyone who's ever poured heart and soul into a creative project only to watch it die, Vaporware is hauntingly, and almost uncomfortably, familiar." – **Jay Posey**, Writer, *Ghost Recon: Future Soldier*

"Video game designer and novelist Dansky (*Snowbird Gothic*) uses his intimate knowledge of the gaming industry to create a believable background for his *Frankenstein*-like tale of creation gone awry. **VERDICT** Dansky's story of virtual horror is laced with quick wit and thoroughly grounded in the world of today. Sure to attract gaming and horror fans." – **Library Journal**

Dedication

To anyone who's ever crunched, fought feature creep, planted an Easter egg (or dug one up), playtested, playtested some more, killed bugs, done level reviews, checked in code after midnight, cleaned up after someone who checked in code improperly after midnight, watched their feature get cut or their project get killed and gone back for more because, damnit, we're making games—this one's for you.

And for the loved ones—spouses, children, parents, siblings and dear friends—who are there as we do it. It's for you, too.
Thank you.

Acknowledgements

This book would not have happened without the help of an awful lot of people:

First (and second and third and other bits) readers Ann Lemay, Leanne Taylor-Giles, Zach Bush, Erin Hoffman, Lillian Cohen-Moore, Michael Fitch, Crystal Muhme Fitch, Jaym Gates, Jay Posey, Mike Lee and Olivier Henriot, for their invaluable feedback and patience.

The late Janet Berliner, very much a mentor and very much missed.

The fine folks at JournalStone for taking a chance on something a little different.

The team at Red Storm Entertainment, as talented and dedicated a group of developers as you'll find anywhere. Special shout-out to the Design Department and all those who've been part of it over the years—someday, we will all meet at Circus Burger again.

The folks at Ubisoft Paris and all the studios around the world I've had the chance to collaborate with.

Patricia Pizer, Noah Falstein, Kevin Perry, Brian Upton, Alexis Nolent and the other experienced developers who were generous enough to take me under their wings and show me the ropes of game development when I was starting out.

The members of the IGDA Game Writers Special Interest Group.

Steve and Merrie Burnett and Luna Black, the home team.

Beverly Banbury, endlessly resourceful

My agent, Robert Fleck, for finding the book a home and regularly whupping me at Scrabble.My family, for encouraging me to write, even when it's books about scary blue people crawling out of monitors.

And most of all, my beloved and brilliant and patient wife Melinda, without whom this would never have been.

Chapter 1

The woman onscreen was blue. She was also faceless, lithe and predatory in her stance and graceful in her movements. Her softly glowing flesh was covered, barely, in what looked to be skintight body armor, beetle-black and iridescent. In her hand was a lethal-looking pistol, smoke drifting from the barrel as she gazed down upon her victim.

He lay on the floor, limbs contorted like overcooked pasta. A big man, he'd taken several shots to kill, as evidenced by the multiple scorch marks scattered across the surface of his powered armor. The faceplate of his helmet had been smashed in, revealing a dark and indistinctly bloody mess underneath. His left hand twitched once, then released its grip on the pulse rifle he'd been holding.

It clattered to the polished steel floor, and, casually, the faceless woman kicked it away. She stood there a moment, her head cocked to one side as if she were waiting for instructions from some outside voice, and then suddenly she moved. With serpentine grace, she swung one leg over the corpse and lowered herself onto it. Her movements were undeniably lascivious, her intent clearly to grind herself into the dead man's face in a way that wouldn't be allowed on basic cable.

Which is when I decided I'd had just about enough. I leaned over to the man next to me, whose eyes were plastered on the screen, and elbowed him in the ribs.

The wireless game controller he'd been clutching like his favorite teddy bear dropped down into his lap, and the shock of the impact straightened him up in his seat. "Hey! What's going on?"

I pointed to the television hanging on the wall, a 72" flatscreen monstrosity that cost more than some cars I'd owned. "What the hell are you doing, Leon?" Onscreen, the action was frozen, the female figure caught mid-squat. A blinking error message announced that the game had been paused and told us that we needed to press the X Button to continue; blorp-heavy dubstep played softly in the background.

Leon swiveled his chair around so that he could face me, his long legs kicking against the floor to speed the turn. "What's the problem, man? I was just doing what comes natural in multiplayer. You get a kill, you hump it. End of story." He held his hands up in a gesture of innocence and good faith. "You've got to admit, it looks good."

"Yeah, if you're fourteen," I said, disgusted. "Haven't we moved past humping animations as a feature by now?"

He grinned. "Only in games that suck."

"Yeah, yeah. Give me the controller." I held out my hand.

Leon shrugged and tossed it to me. "Suit yourself, man. Not my fault you're pissed off because you're old and whipped."

I caught heavy plastic and hit a button, quitting out of the action. Onscreen, the faceless female figure simply evaporated as I worked my way back up the series of menus to the main game shell screen, a throbbing azure logo that read Blue Lightning over a list of options. "I'm not old," I muttered. "Just a little more experienced than the XBox Live kiddies on daddy's credit cards." A thought struck me, and I looked up. "Where the hell did that animation come from, anyway? I never figured you for necrophilia."

Leon grinned, white teeth showing in a wide mouth that didn't seem to fit on his long, sharp face. "I stole 'em from the bar sequence in mission four. You remember the pole dancers you cut out of the level? The data's still in there, and one of the animators merged it into the main character's set. Pretty smooth, don't you think?"

I took a deep breath, opened my mouth to say something, and then thought better of it. Instead, I took a moment to rub the bridge of my nose in the hope that it was going to keep my brains from exploding out of my nostrils in sheer rage, and turned back to the television. "It's very cute," I said, smiling in a way that I suspected didn't get anywhere near my eyes. "And when you get back to your desk, I want you to disable the action and pull the animation."

"Aww, come on, man! It's beautiful. Hell, it's cool!" Leon was up and out of his chair, eyes wide, smile gone. Half a foot taller than me, he looked like they hadn't used quite enough material to make him and nobody had bothered to correct the mistake. Shaven-headed where I was dark-haired, bony where I carried a few extra pounds, he looked like he was auditioning for the role of the Scarecrow in a prog-rock *Wizard of Oz*. Everything about him except his mouth was vertical, from the way he held himself to the folds of his black t-shirt, a souvenir of a Rush tour from the mid-90s that was positively flaunting its age.

I stepped around him, and dropped into the chair he'd just vacated. "Look, Leon, the demo looks great. The physics rock. The particle effects are gorgeous. The gameplay is so goddamned there that it hurts, and we're not even at alpha yet. Do you understand what I'm getting at?"

There was a pause. Leon licked his lips and thought for a minute. "No."

I sighed. "What I'm saying is this: the game looks great. The game plays great. The game looks and plays well enough, as a matter of fact, that marketing is planning on leaving a copy of the alpha build with some of the bigger gaming sites and magazines so they can play with it on their own and really try to build buzz."

I paused, took a breath, and turned to point at the screen. "And what sort of buzz do you think we'd get the second someone took our game, a game with a strong female lead character, and made her hump a dead guy?"

Leon looked down at the floor. "It's not like we'd give them the cheat code."

I shook my head. "If it's in there, they'll find it. They found Hot Coffee in GTA, remember? And the last thing we need is for Blue Lightning to be known as the game where the hot blue chick dry-humps dead robots."

"But...but it looks awesome," he said weakly, even as the screen cycled into attract mode, a short movie showing the best carnage the game had to offer in an endless forty-five second loop.

"Come on, Leon, I'm not pissed. I'm just trying to look out for the game."

Leon blinked, and then nodded. "I know, man. I just thought it was cool, a little awesome for the multiplayer kids."

I grinned, to show him there were no hard feelings. "The kids are ungrateful bastards, and you know that as well as I do. But do me a favor and tell the rest of the guys in Engineering that it looks freaking brilliant?"

Nodding, Leon headed for the door. He reached it, leaned on the handle, and looked back at me. "Hey, Ryan?"

"Yo?" I didn't look back. I was too busy retracing the sequence of button presses that got me out of the game and up to the main menu. Too many, I decided. It needed to be trimmed down by at least two.

"I know there was a design reason for it, but I still don't get it. Why doesn't the lead character have a face?"

"Officially, it's to keep the air of mystery around her. Once you put a face on her, she's just like every other game character, and all the fanboys will be arguing over how hot she is and which celebrity we supposedly ripped off to make her."

Leon shook his head. "I know that. But we're not saving anything on facial animations, 'cause we need those systems for the NPCs, and I have to tell you, it's kind of creepy. So what's the real deal?"

I turned, frowning. It was one of the more controversial decisions I'd made on the game, and not everyone was on board with it, even inside the studio. "The real deal, and it doesn't go any further than this room, is that the publisher wants us to explore a custom facial construction system so players will be able to make their own face for the character, or scan in a picture from somewhere else, and really put 'their' face on the game."

Sputtering ensued, at least until Leon could get himself back under control. "That's stupid. There's already plenty of games that let you do face customization, and trying to add one in at this point in production is just going to make a huge freaking mess. You've gotta tell them no, Ryan. There's no way we can do it, not with the time we've got left, and not have it look like ass."

"Plus, there's always the possibility that fourteen year old boys will take pictures of their balls and use them for the facial image, which would cause all sorts of trouble." I made what I hoped was a calming gesture. "Don't worry, I'm with you on this. I'm not going to risk slipping on our ship date, or let anyone put a picture of their ass on our baby." I looked back at the screen for a minute, then up at where Leon stood, expectant. "Besides. I kind of like her this way. I like her this way a lot."

"Uh-huh. Do yourself a favor and don't tell Sarah that."

I shook my head to the negative. "Yeah, because the girlfriend so loves hearing about what I do all day."

"Then may that be your salvation, bro." Leon's tone was non-committal. "So you want me to take out those animations. Anything else?"

I thought about it. "Naah. Run the build past Eric, but I think we've got something we can send to HQ for pre-alpha milestone approval. It looks good, man. It really looks good."

Leon grimaced. "I hope BlackStone feels the same way."

"They're a publisher. They like making money. This game will make a shit-ton of money. Ergo, they're going to love it." I stood up, leaving the controller on the chair as the attract mode started again. On-screen, the main character poured herself out of a wall socket behind an unsuspecting guard before liquefying him with a lethal combination of firepower and kung fu. "New play mechanic, great graphics, and a strong lead character they can build a franchise on when they take the IP away from us down the road. If they market it at all, our baby is going to be a hit. A huge hit."

"Yeah," Leon said, looking less certain. "If." He shuffled out, the door slamming shut behind him, and then I was alone in the room with the game.

I watched the door for a moment, to make sure Leon wasn't coming back with any more questions. A ten count, and then another ten, left me sure enough, and I settled back in with the game. The attract sequence cycled through another time as I watched it, mentally ticking off features to make sure we were showing off the best of each one. Moving reflective surfaces to make characters literally gleam? Check. Advanced ragdoll physics to let bodies flail and twist as they flew through the air? Check. Destructible terrain and objects to let the player take apart the world brick by brick if necessary? Check. Independent muscular system animations, designed to make our models look like they were uniquely alive? Check. All present and accounted for. It looked good, it looked cool, and once we posted the attract mode loop online, it would get gamers salivating over the possibility of playing.

At least, that was the hope. But the attract mode was just chrome, a dog-and-pony show designed to encourage people to get their hands on it. The real proof was going to be in the game, as it always was, and that meant putting it through its paces without any of Leon's juvenile bullshit.

"Let's see what you've really got," I said to the screen as a new session lurched into its still-too-long loading process. "Let's see what kind of surprises you have for the guy who dreamed you up in the first place."

The loading bar reached the far side of the screen, blinked once, and vanished. In its place, the words "Press Start" throbbed, bright blue and white against the black background. I pressed the Start button. Somewhere in the virtual distance, alarms started going off. I caught myself grinning wickedly, and then the killing began.

* * *

"Blue Lightning," I said, standing at the front of the room, "is a first-person shooter for the next generation of consoles, with unique gameplay, a compelling story, and up to 32 player online multiplayer." I waved at the screen on the wall behind me, onto which had been projected an image of the game's central character standing in an aggressive yet faintly suggestive pose against a gunmetal grey backdrop. In the corner of the screen was the game's logo, a jagged affair that was mostly readable and instantly distinctive.

I paused for a moment, looking around the room to make sure that what I'd said had been given enough time sink in. There were six people in there besides me, all seated in various degrees of slouch in the black leather chairs around the room's central conference table. On the walls were posters and mounted blowups of magazine covers and articles, reminders of games that we'd made in the past. Normally they were bright and cheerful, a constant reinforcement of the quality of games that the studio made. In the dim, low light that the presentation required, however, they looked murky and a little old.

Down the long wall on the right hand side was a whiteboard, scribbled over in mostly orange and brown. One column held dates; another risks, a third names. Green lines were drawn back and forth from one list to another, establishing which names (hopefully) would be able to fix which problems (ideally) by which date in the development process. At the bottom was a single phrase, written and circled in red: "SUBMISSION SEPT. 1." It wasn't hard to notice that everyone in the room kept sneaking glances at it. That, after all, was the important information—dates and deadlines. I was just telling them what they already knew.

"Hold on, Ryan." Eric Jonas was long and angular, solidly constructed where Leon looked like he'd been made from scraps. He was the one sitting in the daddy seat; he was also the producer on the project, the head of the studio, and the ultimate in-house arbitrator of its progress and success.

Out of house was an entirely different story.

In front of him on the table was a tablet, its screen already covered with a series of scribbles. Next to it was a tall aluminum coffee cup stamped with the company's logo: A single horseshoe, or perhaps an inverted omega, with the legend "Horseshoe Games" underneath in simple block letters. The rest of the table was covered similarly, divided between identical cups and cans of beverages from the extended caffeinated family.

"What's the problem, Eric?" I asked, already cringing. I always hated looking down the table while the projector was going. It gave everyone on that end of the room the appearance of being ghostly shadow-figures, and it made their faces impossible to read. The fact that Eric was leaning over the table like a vulture in anticipation of its lunch wasn't helping.

"Did we scale back the MP numbers? I thought we were good with promising 32, and then maybe delivering 64 if we could work out the latency issues."

"Sure, that was the plan, and according to Tyrone—" Leon started in abruptly, then ended just as abruptly as Eric raised his hand for quiet.

"That's...not the point. Lights?" Aaron Shepherd, the QA lead who'd been sitting in his usual spot on Eric's right, scurried up to turn on the main overhead fluorescents. As they flickered into life, there was a groan from around the table, and the image of Blue Lightning onscreen faded into a dim outline. A faint, throbbing headache announced itself just behind my left eye; that meant that the full-fledged skull pounder was on its way as soon as Eric finished ripping me a new one.

Eric unfolded himself from his chair, leaning forward and resting his forearms on the table. "The problem we've got so far is that you haven't said anything."

"It's the first slide, Eric. I'm just defining the game." I snapped back, more defensively than I wanted. This wasn't a fight I could win, particularly not in front of witnesses. Yelling was just going to help me lose it that much sooner.

"You haven't defined the game. You've rattled off the same old back-of-box bullshit bullet points that we get on every project, that's all." He levered himself off the table and started walking around it, clockwise. "Come on. Immersive story? There are solitaire games that claim that. FPS? There's a million FPS games out there. 32 player multiplayer? Nice, but not unique. What we're missing," and by this time, he was within a couple of feet from where I stood, with only the still-visible projector beam between us, "is something that blows the doors off from minute one. Something that makes them know how amazing this game is, and why they have to publish. Something that says Blue Lightning, and not 'FPS with interesting feature set.'"

I tried not to glare at him. "Eric, you know these guys. If we don't come out and say it, they may miss the fact that it's an FPS entirely. Remember what happened when Virtual Vineyard tried to pitch that robot janitor game?"

Eric rolled his eyes. It was urban legend in the game industry, the story of a small dev team having basically shot its wad to present a pitch for a comedy platformer starring a wacky robot janitor to one of the major French publishers. Virtual Vineyard had pulled out all the stops, flown half their staff to the meeting in Marseilles, had put on a four-hour-long sell session that by all accounts had been legendary, and had been politely told thank you, but we're not interested.

Later, through back channels, the head of the studio learned that the word "janitor" didn't translate into French, and so none of the suits he'd been pitching to had the faintest idea of what he'd been talking about. And of course, none of them had, at any point during the process, bothered to mention this.

That was the scenario that every small development house lived in fear of, the thing they all took wild steps to avoid, and everyone in the room knew it.

"It doesn't matter," Eric said softly. "They know it's an FPS. They've been funding it for a year now. What we need to show them is why they've been funding it." He grabbed the mouse and started clicking through slides. "Here. What's this?"

I looked back. It was a screenshot, a moment captured from gameplay, showing the lead character essentially pouring herself out of a light socket in order to materialize inside a locked room. "It's wrapping up the circuit movement system. The player is jumping from inside the circuitry to the outside world and—"

"Exactly." Eric was nodding, the first hints of enthusiasm visible on his face. "Something cool that no one else has. Now, do we have a slide in here of the circuit movement?"

I nodded, my face hot and flushed with embarrassment. "We've got a capture of some of the gameplay, too."

"So you're saying we move that up front in hopes of giving the suits a stiffie?" The voice that came from the side of the room was the last one I wanted to hear chiming in.

"Jesus, Michelle, we're trying to save the presentation here." Inwardly, I groaned. There were very few women at the company, especially on the production side of things, which meant that even if Michelle Steiner had been the shy, retiring type, she would have stood out.

"Shy and retiring" was not how anyone had described Michelle, not now and not ever.

Eric looked over at me, his face an eloquent mask of "You deal with it." I shot him back a look that promised bloody vengeance, and then put on a grin as I turned to face Michelle.

She wasn't facing me, though. Instead, she was busy sketching something on a notepad, not looking at anyone. "What you want," she said, "is simple. We need to stop thinking of this as a project review and instead start thinking about it like it's a commercial. We need to use this to really get BlackStone fired up about the game, and that means showing them all the sexy stuff first to get them hooked."

She turned her notepad around, and on it was a rough storyboard for a new presentation, starting inside the machine and then exploding into the rough combat sequence that Leon had demoed to me the day before. "Something like this?"

Eric leaned down and grabbed the notepad. "Something, yeah." He looked over at me, then around the room. "Ryan, Michelle, why don't you sit down with this and try to rejigger what we've got. All the Powerpoint stuff is good, but if we can move this up front...will end of day tomorrow be all right?"

"Fine," I said, a little bitterly, and shut the projector down. The whirr of the fan filled the room, along with the scent of scorched dust. "When are we presenting this to the suits?"

"We're not," Eric said softly, accenting the first word just enough to let me know that all was not well. "We're just sending them the presentation, and their third-party group will be looking it over by themselves." There was a moment of quiet while that sunk in and he scanned Michelle's sketches. "That's why this thing needs to be kick ass all by its lonesome."

I could feel my eyes getting really big and my guts trying to drop into my shoes. If they didn't want to spring for plane tickets for us to present, that meant— No. I caught the thought, cut it off, and stuffed it away. No sense panicking the rest of the room, no sense freaking myself out, either. The game rocked. It was going to be fine.

So I just nodded and hoped like hell that I was keeping the panic out of my face. "I see. Michelle?"

She looked up at me, an unspoken question in her eyes. It translated roughly as "How screwed are we?" and I wasn't in a position to answer it here.

"My office, fifteen minutes?"

"Sure, if I can get my notepad back." Embarrassed, Eric handed it to her. "I'll see you then." She stood and, without looking at anyone else, left the room. The rest of the attendees followed, chattering amongst themselves, their low voices suggesting varying degrees of worry.

And then there were two of us, me shutting things down and detaching my laptop from the projector, and Eric standing there watching me. He waited until everyone else was out of the room, then crossed to the open door and shut it.

"You could have warned me," I said as I unscrewed the video cable from the port on the back of the projector. "Instead of hanging me out to dry like that."

"I didn't know what you had planned," Eric said, no apology in his voice. "If you'd nailed it like you usually do, I wouldn't have said anything."

"You could have asked for a preview." The cool-down light on the projector flashed green, and I shut it down. The fan whimpered into silence, leaving only the occasional thunks and groans of the building's HVAC system to fill the void. "If I'd known that wasn't what you wanted, I wouldn't have been here until midnight every night last week trying to finish the presentation."

Eric frowned. "It doesn't matter. Just work with Michelle and put the chrome up front, OK?"

I turned, and this time I didn't try to hide the fact that I was pissed off. "It's not chrome. It's the core gameplay loop, and it's what makes this game different. You know that." I'd said it, let him deny it if he had the balls to do so. He didn't, though. He knew it was good, too, that we had a chance for a real winner here.

"I know, I know. And I know how proud you are of it, and how hard you've worked on it. I know this is your baby, Ryan. But it's everyone in the building's baby, and I need to make sure that it's positioned best for the company." I looked up from wrapping the video cable into something vaguely knot-like and saw that he'd positioned himself in front of the door. That tore it. I wasn't going to be getting out of the room until we reached some kind of accommodation on whatever Eric had in mind, and God help me if I tried.

I picked up the laptop and tucked it under my arm. "What's the real issue, Eric? How bad is it?"

Eric looked away and flushed slightly. The admission that something was seriously wrong shocked me; I'd thrown the question out there primarily to elicit a denial, a confirmation that everything was in great shape. The fact that Eric wasn't denying anything was scary, a piss-your-pants bad warning sign that the storm was coming.

He finally looked at me but paused a long moment before saying anything. "I don't know. Maybe it's not anything. I've just been getting a weird vibe from BlackStone lately. They tell me everything's great, but when I ask about whether we're going to be showing at any of the trade shows they keep putting me off. And with the milestone eight payment coming up—the big one—it's just got a weird feel to it."

I stepped closer and shifted the laptop's weight. I'd dropped one once and still hadn't heard the end of it from IT. "Why would they want to kill it? It's great, it's as close to ahead of schedule as you can get, and it's going to be a hit. It wouldn't make any sense to kill it."

"Their decisions don't have to make sense to us, just to their bottom line. If they've got another shooter that's being done by one of their in-house studios, and they want to protect it, then maybe it makes sense to them to kill ours. Not that it's the case, mind you—I have no idea what they might be thinking, if anything. Like I said, I don't know. It could be nothing." Suddenly, Eric snapped back to himself. "All of this is between you and me, understood?"

I nodded, once. "Understood. Completely." We looked at each other for a moment longer, then Eric opened the door.

"Good luck with Michelle. Try not to kill each other."

I stepped past him, a tight grin on my face. "No worries. We got that out of our systems a while ago."

"Uh-huh." Eric sounded unconvinced. "That's not what half the office thinks. Or Sarah."

"Sarah knows better," I said, my words clipped. "And that's what matters."

"Whatever you say, Ryan," Eric said, and shut the door. From behind them, I heard a crash that sounded a lot like someone kicking a chair into a wall. I didn't go in to see if Eric was all right. After all, they were his chairs.

Besides, he'd told me to act like everything was fine.

Chapter 2

Michelle was in my office when I opened the door. More specifically, she was in my chair, with her feet up on my desk a series of rough storyboard sketches on the whiteboard. The air was thick with the scent of overworked dry-erase marker, and she was grinning.

I dropped the laptop onto what passed for a flat surface, then stopped. I looked at her, then at the board, then back at her. "Am I really necessary to this process?" I asked, "Or have you and Eric gotten it all doped out, and you just want me to do the typing?"

"Oh, relax." Michelle pulled her feet off the desk and scooted herself upright in the chair. "Most of what you've got is fine, I think. He just wants to start the presentation off with a bang, and I do bang better than you do."

"I think it's best if I don't respond to that," I said and sat myself down in the visitors' chair against the wall. It was a small office, cluttered with papers and empty game boxes, and nearly every square inch of wall was covered in pinned-up maps, charts, or other documents related to the game. On the door was the only personal touch I'd allowed myself, a poster of Charlie Chaplin as the Little Tramp. Someone had added a thought balloon over Chaplin's head that read "At least I'm not making video games." Everything else—desk, bookshelves, cabinets—was strictly functional and at least partially overwhelmed by the tide of clutter that the project had generated.

"I still don't get why you get an office," she asked lazily. "Is that my fault?"

"I don't know," I replied, flicking the door open a little wider so anyone passing could estimate at a glance how much physical distance there was between the two of us. "If you really want to know the truth, Eric insisted. He said he was tired of me not getting anything done before midnight because I was answering questions all day, so he wanted to put me someplace where I could shut the door and work uninterrupted once in a while."

"Which was conveniently located down the hall from his office," she said sweetly, without smiling. "And the fact that it happened right after we, you know—"

"Blew up all over the lunchroom?" I said it without rancor. "Don't ask me. I just work here. Besides, that was a long time ago, and we've got a presentation to fix." I looked across the desk at Michelle, the unspoken mantra of "eye contact, eye contact, eye contact" looping in the back of my head. She was short, and the way she sat, her feet dangled a couple of inches off the floor. Like everyone else in the office, she wore jeans, which she'd paired with a bright yellow t-shirt from a project we'd wrapped up three years ago. She cocked her head, and her hair, reddish brown and longer than she'd worn it when we'd dated, slipped down over one eye. Irritated, she brushed it away. No nail polish, I noted automatically. It went with the no makeup and the no jewelry. That was Michelle; there was never anything but Michelle, and if you couldn't handle that then God help you.

Back in the day, I hadn't been able to. But, I reminded myself, I was with Sarah now, and there was work to do.

"So how do you want to arrange this," I asked. I scraped my chair across the carpet to the whiteboard. "Are we going to start with a pure gameplay capture sequence, or do you want to see if we have time to do something pre-rendered?"

Michelle shook her head. "We don't have time for pre-rendered. The best thing we can do is a capture of you playing through the core sequence, then seeing if the sound guys can put some music behind it and maybe a little voiceover."

I nodded. "Embed it in the presentation, or run it separately?"

She rubbed her chin, then stood and walked to the board. "If we embed it, there's less of a chance of them forgetting to play it. Also, there's no time lost with a switchover. So that makes sense. What I was thinking," and she took a marker from the shelf at the bottom of the board, "would be that we'd start with the logo, then dissolve to the gameplay. Is there anything you think we need to show off besides the circuit runs and the combat?"

I grimaced. "Everything else is just FPS, remember." Michelle started to say something, but I interrupted her. "Seriously, that's our killer feature, and nothing else is going to look as cool next to it. If we want to have a wow moment at the beginning, that's it. Maybe pull in some multiplayer for later, but, no, at the start, we show that off."

"Show her off," Michelle disagreed, and sketched a rough female figure more clearly into the frames she'd made while waiting. "She's got to be a big part of this. She's important. Hell, she's the game."

"No, we're the game. Everything we've put into it. But you're right, she's a big part of it. Maybe if we—"

My office phone rang.

Instinctively, both of us looked toward the telephone. It was a sleek, black thing, covered with buttons and, occasionally, blinking red lights, and at the top of the keypad was a small LCD screen that conveniently showed the number of whoever or whatever extension was calling at the time. I twisted in my seat and leaned forward to get a better look at it, then realized that I knew whose the number was.

"Do you want me to get it? I'm closer." Michelle turned and took a step toward the desk. The phone jangled again.

"No!" I coughed. "I mean, no." Michelle shot me a quizzical look, and I wilted under it. "It's Sarah, and if you answer the phone, then I get to explain at great length what you're doing in my office, playing secretary."

"Jesus, Ryan, I wasn't offering to get you coffee."

"No, no, I know that, and she probably knows that, too, but, oh the hell with it. She just wants to know when I'm coming home, and the more time I spend talking on the phone, the longer it's going to take me to get home. If we just finish this, I can get home sooner and tell her that I missed her call. OK? Let's just get back to it."

The phone rang a third time, angrier and more insistent. Michelle gave a half-smile. "Lying? There's a great way to build a strong relationship, Ryan. I'm glad to see you haven't changed too much."

"Shared house payments are a great way to build a strong relationship. Everything else is secondary," I retorted. But I kept my eyes on the phone and my butt in my chair near the whiteboard and Michelle.

For a fourth time, the phone rang, then a fifth. Midway through the sixth ring, it cut off. I exhaled, only half-aware I'd been holding my breath. "It's kicked over to voicemail. We can get back to work."

I turned back to the board, pushing myself out of my seat, and a shuddering groan echoed through the building. The lights, both the dim wall-mounted fixture on the near wall and the harsh halogen floor lamp in the corner, flickered and dimmed. A quick look into the hall told me that the same thing was happening in the entire office. All the lights on the phone flashed red once and went dead, and my monitor and desktop system abruptly shut down with a groan.

"Brownout," Michelle said, looking under the desk.

"Hey!" I pushed my chair back and stood up. "What are you doing?"

"Checking to see if your UPS sucks or you just forgot to plug it in." She pulled her head back up. "Don't worry, that's all I'm looking at."

"Shelly—" I started, but broke off as the lights came back up. The computer rebooted with a ping, accompanied by the whine of an overstressed motherboard-mounted fan trying its best to catch up. The phone lights gave one final, desperate blink and then went out in unison.

"Huh. The brownout must have eaten her message. Oh well, I'll call her when we're done."

Michelle nodded distractedly, then glanced back at my monitor. "Hey, that's weird."

"What is?" I moved around to see, careful to maintain distance between myself and Michelle, who was still crouched half under the desk. After a moment, she uncoiled herself and stood up, about six inches too close for my comfort. I shuffled back, hoping she wouldn't notice.

She pointed at the screen. There was the first screen of the presentation I'd started giving in the meeting room. "I guess it didn't shut down completely. It's open to slide number one."

"Impossible." I leaned in for a closer look. "For one thing, I had the presentation open on the laptop,"—I paused to tap it, closed and hibernating on the opposite side of the desk—"not the desktop. For another, it did shut down all the way. We heard it stop and we heard it reboot. It should have gone to the login screen, not to Powerpoint."

Michelle looked at the monitor, a 36" flatscreen, then over at me, and then finally back again. "Huh," she said. "Why do you even have two systems?"

"Legacy. Eric likes keeping things old school. Doesn't matter," I said, a bit brusquely. "Now let's finish this, so for once I can get out of here on time."

"Optimist," she said and turned her attention back to the board. "So if we can keep this sequence to fifteen seconds, will that be enough time to show off the gameplay you want?"

"Twenty-five seconds, minimum. And that's if you want to do bare-bones, without any of the really cool route-mapping stuff that we've got in the UI."

"If it's really cool, we want to show it. Twenty-five seconds then, and then another thirty-five for the combat."

A line was clearly being drawn in the sands of time there, and I was almost sensible enough not to cross it. "Thirty and forty-five," I said, and then turned in surprise as the door to the office clicked shut.

"There are other people trying to work," said a muffled voice that was probably Eric's and most definitely on the other side of the door. "Unless you two are finished?"

"Just getting started," Michelle yelled, loudly enough that I winced. "If you're OK with that."

"Be my guest," maybe-Eric said.

Michelle turned to me and placed the dry-erase marker in my hand. "Shall we?" she asked.

I nodded and moved over to the board. "We shall."

* * *

Sarah's car wasn't in the driveway when I got home. In and of itself, this was not unusual. Sarah insisted on parking in the garage whenever possible, which was to say when the clutter from my side of the two-car space didn't spill over into hers. So when I pulled in at six thirty, there was no real proof that I was the first one home. There was no light coming from inside the garage, but that didn't tell me much. The internal lights only stayed on for two minutes after the garage door opened or closed, which meant that if Sarah had gotten home already, she'd gotten home a lot earlier than 6:28.

I pulled into the driveway, a concrete slope that angled uphill at just enough of an angle to scrape the undercarriage of my Mazda if I pulled in or out too fast. Killing the engine, I sat there, waiting for the last notes of the Who's "Eminence Front" to fade out before unplugging my iPhone and tucking it in my pocket. I always hated turning the thing on and getting the last few notes of a song. It did strange things to my momentum, or maybe I was just superstitious. Either way, now I made a point of letting the song run out before getting out. No musical leftovers—that was the rule—which meant that I'd sit there and just watch the house as long as necessary, in order to make sure I got to the end.

The house was nice. It was a nice house, in a nice neighborhood, with nice furnishings and neighbors, and if I had my way we'd live there maybe five years at most before moving to someplace with a little more character. It had a brick facing, or at least most of one, a rarity that was becoming increasingly commonplace in the Raleigh area as more and more carpetbagger types moved down. The sides and back were masonite, painted a soothing shade of grayish-blue that made the house look older than it was. There was a full-height window facing the walk, courtesy of the landing at the top of the stairs; Sarah had hung up a foot-wide stained-glass piece in the shape of an Amish hex sign there the day we'd moved in. "For good luck," she'd said.

"I thought they were supposed to keep bad luck away," I'd replied.

"Same thing," she'd told me, and then bounced off into the bedroom to make sure all the furniture there was situated appropriately. Not the same thing, I'd thought at the time, but I let it pass, and never mentioned it again.

That exchange had been a little over a year ago. The hex sign still hung there, the bedroom furniture had been placed in accordance with both feng shui and Sarah's steel-edged whims, and it was in all ways a most admirable and pleasant home to return to at the end of each day. This was true whether I was coming home at 6:00 (which never happened), 7:30 (more likely) or midnight, which happened more frequently than either of us liked to think about.

The walk from the driveway to the door was short, angular, and lined with shrubs that required a great deal more pruning than they were worth. The actual lot the house was on wasn't that much larger than the building itself, but it came pre-planted with a mix of highly aggressive bushes and Bradford pears to give the development an air of permanence. The dead-fish odor of the pear trees' many flowers still lingered in the air, with the last couple of blossoms hiding out in the thick leaves. Thin green shoots from the trees had started to poke up through the grass, I'd noticed, and for the umpteenth time I reminded myself to mow the lawn and do something about them. Saturday, I decided. If I'm not in the office, I'll do it Saturday.

I managed to drop my iPod on the welcome mat when I reached for my keys. Calling myself all sorts of names, I stooped to pick them up, even as Sarah heard the clatter and yelled "It's open."

"Thanks, honey." A quick check told me the iPod was still working, so I tucked it away and wandered inside, into what smelled like the lobby at an Italian restaurant.

"I'm in the kitchen," Sarah called out as I shut the door.

"I'm not," I answered, dropping the laptop bag in the atrium at the foot of the steps.

"I'm sorry I missed your call," I added as I stepped into the kitchen. "We had a brownout just as the phone rang."

Sarah turned from where she stood, coaxing steam from a pot of what looked to be multicolored wheat pasta. "That's all right. I just wanted to know when you'd be home, and I'd rather hear it in person than get a phone call at eight o'clock."

I leaned in and kissed her softly, mainly because I wanted to. She kissed me back, then returned her attention to the noodles. "Is that dinner I see in front of me?"

"Nope," she said with a smile. "This is for lunch for me for tomorrow. Pasta salad with sun-dried tomatoes, since I know you hate anything with vegetables in it. We," and she turned and gestured with the wooden spoon for emphasis, "are going out for dinner, because I have news."

"No hints?" I asked, wandering over to the refrigerator and taking out a can of Diet Coke.

"No hints," she replied, "And no snacking. You'll ruin dinner. And no caffeine. You'll never sleep tonight"

"Yes ma'am." I popped open the lid of the can and wandered through the kitchen to the den. "How much longer is the pasta going to take? If I don't spoil my dinner, I may resort to cannibalism." Saying that, I threw myself down on the couch—black leather, the only piece of furniture I'd contributed to the domestic arrangement—and took the master remote from its place of honor on the coffee table. The television flared to life, even as the clanging of pots in the kitchen told me that it wasn't actually going to be much longer. "Leon says hi, by the way."

"How's he doing? We should invite him over some time. And where's the colander?" Sarah's voice was muffled, due in large part to the fact that her head was tucked into one of the kitchen cabinets. "I can't find it anywhere."

"He's doing fine, and it's in the cabinet next to the dishwasher, inside the door," I replied, and scrolled through the DVR. "My God, it's all *Say Yes to the Dress.* What happened to my *Walking Dead* episodes?"

"Overwritten, sweetheart," replied Sarah in a tone that indicated that she didn't regret this in the slightest. "There was a marathon, and you set it to record all episodes of *Say Yes* for me like a good and considerate boyfriend would, and the rest is history. Besides, Netflix or something, right?" There was more clanging, then the sound of a cabinet slamming and something metallic landing in the sink. As if on cue, the stove timer went off, bleeping with self-importance as I cringed at the wretched sound.

"Do you need a hand in there," I asked half-heartedly as I turned the television off. "Or would I be in the way?"

"Just finish your soda and think about where you want to take me for dinner," came the response, and then the slosh of water being spilled out of a pot. "You've got ten minutes to come up with something dazzling."

I took a long swig out of the can and swallowed a small burp as I set the thing down on a coaster. "If I've got ten minutes, I've got time to do research. I'll be right back down with the golden ticket."

"As long as it's not the Golden Corral," Sarah's voice called after me as I bounded out of the den and upstairs to my office. One of the attractions of the house had been the multiple bedrooms on the second floor, two of which had been converted into offices. Sarah's was closer to the master bedroom, and with good reason; it was an actual office with an actual desk, filing cabinet, and so forth.

Mine, on the other hand, was something different.

I could hear the hum from my jacked-up Alienware gaming rig even before I opened the door, the blue light from the neon in the case lighting up the room as I entered. One wall was taken up with books, the other with games, and the floor held the papers that had yet to meander their way into the overloaded filing cabinet against the back wall. I'd hung up small but potent Altec Lansing speakers in each of the ceiling corners, while the desk and the desktop system dominated the space. No skimping on the chair, either—I'd gotten an ergonomic Herman Miller chair when one of the local middleware firms had gone belly-up.

"How's it going up there?" Sarah called as I opened up a web browser.

"Just fine," I answered. "Looking now."

My fingers worked feverishly on the keyboard. Just a quick email check, I told myself. Then I can find a restaurant.

I hopped to Horseshoe's remote mail server and logged in. There were twenty emails queued up, just in the few minutes since I'd left work. Some were spam, two were forwarded links to semi-humorous YouTube videos, and the rest were work-related from folks in the office who'd stayed even later than I had.

One was from Leon. It said "Hah! When was the last time you went home first?" He'd attached a gleefully obscene image to go with the note. I deleted it and moved on. There were other emails that were a little more pressing.

Where's the design for the multiplayer matchmaking? I sent the link to where the docs were sitting Horseshoe's internal server.

QA's saying that nobody's getting past the chokepoint on mission 4. I sketched out the alternate routes, then suggested moving a couple of the enemy units thirty meters back so that the initial combat wasn't quite as intense.

Some of the hand-to-hand combat combinations weren't flowing properly? That was a case of re-blending the animations, or maybe dropping certain combos that didn't work together, and I promised all fifteen people cc'ed on the email that I'd get with everyone tomorrow on it.

Sightlines on the first multiplayer map were too long? Put some crates in as placeholders and—

"Ahem."

I jumped in my seat as Sarah leaned in and cleared her throat, not particularly quietly, less than an inch from my left ear. "Nice research."

I swiveled the chair around, hoping the blue light from the case would hide the red flush of embarrassment in my cheeks. No luck; I could see in the reflection in her glasses that I just looked purple instead. "I was waiting for the search results to load, and—"

"And you decided to check work email, just in case the building caught on fire in the half an hour since you left it. By the way, you accidentally closed the page with the restaurant listings on it, too." She placed her hands on the chair and spun it back around so that I was facing the monitor. "Fortunately, I figured on something like this, so I already had a place picked out. Shut the computer down, put on a nicer shirt, and let's go. Oh, and you're driving."

"Yes ma'am," I said, and did as I was told.

* * *

"And what will the lady be having?" asked the waiter, who looked more like a barista with delusions of grandeur than the sort of waitstaff that The Magnolia usually employed. He hovered attentively over Sarah's shoulder, pad in hand and pen poised while I thought about glaring at him.

"The lady," Sarah said, "will be having the veal ossa bucco, and we'll be having a bottle of the Gaja Barbaresco." She set her menu down. "The 2001, if you please."

"Of course," the man said, raising his eyes fractionally. "And the gentleman?"

I scanned the menu, rejecting items sequentially as I came to them. "Chicken marsala," I finally croaked out, more out of desperation and a deep desire not to get red sauce on my shirt than anything else.

The waiter frowned, and I realized too late I'd picked a dish that wouldn't compliment the Barbaresco. The hell with it, I thought. I was this close to ordering a Diet Coke anyway.

"Will that be all?" the waiter added, turning back to Sarah. "We have some lovely antipasti, a superb selection of soups—"

"That will be all, thank you," she said, and raised her eyebrows to dare him to argue the point.

"Of course." The man backed away, bowing from the neck. "Your wine will be out shortly."

I watched him go. "Our wine will be out? What, is it tired of living the lie?"

Sarah shushed me. "Be nice. The wine will be."

"I noticed." I tapped the wine list. "That's beyond nice. That's positively saintly."

"That's because we have something to celebrate." Sarah smiled, and I immediately forgot about the waiter, the menu, and the price of the wine. Her smiles had that effect on me, particularly when she turned the full force of her attention my way.

I smiled back and straightened up in my chair a little. "So, are you going to tell me? Or do I have to guess?"

"When the wine gets here," Sarah chided. "It's the sort of thing you want to toast."

I nodded, then started ticking off guesses on my fingers anyway. "Let's see. You're drinking wine, so you're not pregnant. You let me drive, which means you want to have more than one glass, so it's really good news. I don't see a ring—"

"That's enough out of you," she said firmly. "Besides, the wine is coming."

And it was, and the waiter, who re-introduced himself as Andy, expertly displayed the bottle before cutting away the foil and pulling the cork.

"Sir?" Andy was waving a wineglass with a splash of red in the bottom under my nose. I fought the urge to throw myself backwards out of my chair and instead suggested that the lady was probably a better judge of such things. Andy nodded and passed the glass to Sarah. She glowered at me for an instant, then sipped, said "Excellent," and held out her wineglass for more.

"As you wish." Andy filled her glass, then looked to me with an expression that suggested I'd be better off drinking something with a screw cap, or maybe from a trough. I just nodded at him, and after a moment's hesitation he filled the second glass before leaving post-haste.

"So what is the big surprise," I asked, and raised my glass. "We have the wine, we don't have Andy—what more could I ask for?"

Sarah smothered a laugh, and raised her glass to mine. The two touched, rim to rim, the sound of crystal on crystal so faint only the two of us could hear it. "Well," she started, "for one thing, you are now looking at the newest senior account manager at Barnes, Derrick."

"That's great! That's fantastic!" I nearly went over the table to hug her, and I could feel how much of my face a grin was suddenly covering. "Honey, that's wonderful. I am so proud of you."

"Thank you," she said, and she was smiling, her glass still held up. "But there's more."

"More?" I paused with the wine hovering close to my lip. "What else could there be?"

She nodded demurely, smiling. "How about an office instead of a cube, and a raise, and all sorts of other compensation-type goodies that we can talk about later?" She took another sip of her wine before setting the glass down on the table. "Wow, I haven't seen you smile like that in ages. I'm really glad you got home on time tonight so we could share this."

"Me, too." I felt a warm glow suffusing my face and spreading down through my belly. The wine, I thought, or maybe just Sarah. She could do that to me even on days without earth-shattering good news. And on a day like today…

She took a sip of wine, then topped off her glass. "Which sort of brings me to the next topic, and it's not something you have to answer right now. I just want you to think about it."

"Is that the marriage conversation?" I made a show of sliding my chair back and pretending to bolt. "Should I start running, or—"

"You are impossible," Sarah said, but without heat or anger. She mock-glared at me, but she was trying to hide a smile, which killed the effect. "And don't you dare look relieved, mister."

I just pulled my chair back to the table, head down in contrition, as Andy set a basket of bread down on the table. "Anything I say now will just get me in trouble, so I'm just going to sit here quietly and gaze at you in adoration." I took a sip of wine. "And drink. But mostly gaze."

"That's a wise decision." Sarah's lips crinkled into a smile. "That makes two you've made tonight."

"Who's counting?"

She smiled for real now. "Me."

"Touché."

"Later," and the smile became a promise. "But as I was saying before we were attacked by delicious carbs—do you want some bread, honey?"

I unwrapped the napkin to reveal a steaming loaf of what looked to be unsliced semolina bread underneath. Braving the oven-born heat, I tore off a hunk and placed it on Sarah's bread plate. "You first, my dear."

She took up the butter and spread the faintest of schmears on the bread, then nibbled on a corner. "You're very sweet, you know that?"

I grinned. "Thank you. For you, I try. Everyone else thinks I'm a right bastard." I tore off a hunk of bread , then looked back up at her. "Anyway, you were saying?"

"I was saying that this is just something to think about, OK? There's no need for an answer any time soon, and certainly not until the game you're working on is done."

I felt myself stiffening in my seat, and in a decidedly non-erotic way. "Yes?"

She looked away for a moment, and it struck me that she was unsure of what to say next. That sent another jolt through me. Sarah was never unsure of herself, never at a loss for words. It was one of the things I found attractive about her, the ability to react to damn near anything and act as if she'd seen it coming all along. And now she was stammering, or the nearest thing to it. It scared the hell out of me.

The words came out of her in a rush. "Look, I did the numbers. You know how you're always talking about how, if you had the chance, you'd stay home and write? Work on your novel, really work on it?" She paused to gulp down a breath but plunged on before I could interject or affirm or do much of anything. "With my new salary, if you want to, you could do it. We could do it. We could afford it. We'd have to eat out a little less, and maybe tighten our belts in a couple of other places, but we could do it. If you want."

I opened my mouth to answer, but she shushed me. "You don't have to say anything now. You don't have to decide now. I know there's a long way to go on your game. But I wanted you to know," and she gave a little shudder, as if she, too, were afraid, "that I can do this for you. If you want."

"Honey, I..." My voice trailed off as my throat tightened. Words tried to force their way out but failed for lack of air behind them. "Are you sure?"

She nodded, not trusting herself to say anything. I closed my eyes and thought about what I was going to say next. This was serious. Anything flip or off-the-cuff was going to echo for a long time, and not in a good way. Sarah knew how much she was asking and how much she was offering. I wasn't—I couldn't—shove that offer back in her face.

But I wasn't sure I could take what she'd offered, either.

Deep breath in, deep breath out.

"Thank you," I said, and said nothing else for a minute. "And thank you for believing in me that much."

"You're welcome," she said, the words shuddering out of her. She took a gulp of wine, not a sip. "And again, you don't have to answer tonight, and if you say no it's okay, and—"

I reached across the table to take one of her hands in mine. "Sarah," I said. "I had no idea we could ever do something like this. I'll think about it, I promise. We're almost at alpha, so there's plenty of time. And if you change your mind, just say the word, and it will be like this conversation never happened. No hard feelings, no worries."

"I'm not going to take it back," she said, sticking her chin out for defiant emphasis. "You said you always wanted to write. Now we can afford it, and," she looked away, eyes shy, "It will be nice coming home to you, instead of waiting until the electronic gremlins let you go each night."

"That would be nice," I said, and I meant it. No more late, late nights, no more frantic rushes to publishers' deadlines, no more takeout Chinese in the break room because we weren't getting out of there until the deliverable was dead.

On the other hand, no more leading the team. No more being able to play something I'd dreamed up and see it live and on the screen, responding what I told it to do. No more making a vision become real.

No more making games.

It was a lot to think about.

I raised my glass. "To the decision, whatever it may be."

Sarah raised her glass to mine. "And to making it together."

"Together," I echoed. The glasses touched. We drank. And not another word was said about it that night.

Chapter 3

Not that long ago, I thought to myself as I stood in Eric's office, sending a vital message to Europe had been an occasion. It would have gone by clipper ship, with all sorts of fanfare and farewells, muttered imprecations of the importance of the missive and proud declarations that it would be delivered in good time—no more than a couple of months. Sending a message of that sort had carried weight. It had been an event, something of significance, something not undertaken lightly.

I thought about that as Eric hit a few keys on his Android and sent the presentation winging overseas. Attached had been a small note— "Hey, Phil, take a look at this and let me know what you think. We can do a polish pass before it goes in front of the board in London." I knew what it said; I'd helped draft it. Now, all we could do was wait, unless they asked for changes, in which case we'd make them and send them along, toot sweet. Privately, I expected we'd have at least four more iterations to go before everything was nailed down to everyone's satisfaction.

"That's it?" I asked, not expecting much of an answer.

"That's it," Eric confirmed, not giving me much of one. "He should still be in the office, so at least we'll get some kind of confirmation that he received it. Otherwise," he shrugged. "There's not a lot else we can do at this point."

"Do you want me to—"

"I want you to get back to work on the shell UI, is what I want," he said, almost gently. "There's a lot riding on this presentation. We both know that. But if you get wound up, then everyone you work with is going to pick up on that, and this place is going to turn into a psych ward." He coughed into his hand. "Hopefully, for no reason whatsoever."

"Gotcha." The word tasted unpleasant in my mouth. "So just go back to my desk and pretend it's all fine?"

Eric put the iPhone down on his desk and took a sip of coffee. "Go back to your office and stop being such a goddamned drama queen, if you can handle that. There's nothing we can do until BlackStone gets back to us, and for all we know they're going to double the budget and give us six more months."

"As if." I looked around, not wanting to meet his eyes. Eric's office was twice the size of anyone else's in the building, but somehow he'd made it look positively cozy. There were game posters on the walls—ours as well as ones from games he just liked—action figures on the bookcases, a lightsaber he'd gotten in trade from one of the guys at LucasArts propped up in one corner, and a general air of nerdly comfort. Not the desk, though. His desktop was orderly, neat, and polished to a terrifyingly bright gleam.

Once, back in the day, Shelly had half-joking suggested we break into Eric's office and have sex on his furniture. I'd refused, primarily because I was convinced he had motion sensors in there.

"Weirder things have happened," he said, breaking my train of thought. "If they like it, and again, there's no reason they shouldn't, then we should be ready to take advantage of it."

"And if they don't," I filled in, "then it's not like there's anything else I could be doing in the meantime."

"Now you're getting it." Eric raised his coffee in a semi-toast in my direction. "So get the hell out of here and get back to work."

"Yessir," I said, and put down the Transformer I'd been fiddling with. "Let me know if you hear anything?"

"Of course." His tone, if not his expression, was long-suffering. "You get to make all the changes they'll be asking for, anyway."

I didn't quite slam his door shut behind me as I went out. After all, I reflected, that's the sort of thing a drama queen would do.

Instead, I headed for the coffee machine in the break room at the back of the building. Watching Eric guzzle had reminded me of my own acute caffeine deficiency, which I resolved to remedy as quickly as possible. Without bean-juice-flavored rocket fuel, there was no way I was going to make a dent in the UI documentation that I needed to get on.

The break room was crowded, or at least the area around the coffee machine was. I waited my turn while turning over the UI issue in my head. Every screen between startup and gameplay was another chance for players to get lost and fail to find a way to play. By the same token, every screen players had to click through to quit was another exercise in frustration, one more likely to get the average users to turn off the console rather than quit out properly. That, in turn, could result in corrupted save data, which meant that the next time they played, they'd lose some of their hard-earned progress and get too pissed off to make up the ground. This was something preferably to be avoided. But at the same time, there were too many choices that players potentially needed to make before getting into gameplay that defined the experience, and all of them were important.

But, and this was the idea that was really starting to take shape, maybe we could move some of those choices into the game itself, so that the selection was an in-game process. In other words, the player character would make the choices in game, instead of the player doing it outside of the game world. That would save time and increase immersion, making the game flow better and more quickly. In my mind's eye, I could see the UI flow changing, screens dropping away and consolidating. It was too much to keep in my head. I needed something to write it down on before I forgot it all.

I grabbed a chair and started sketching on a napkin. Weapons selection could be integrated into the gamespace if you provided a suitable default. That chopped one, maybe two screens out of the flow, though it was going to mean a whole new ingame system, for which the engineering staff was not going to love me. But if we just moved those UI screens over...

A clank on the tabletop startled me, and the pen tore through the thin paper of the napkin, half-shredding the sketch I'd been working on. "Dammit!"

"Sorry, Ryan." It was Michelle's voice. I looked up as she slid a full coffee mug across the table at me. "Didn't mean to startle you."

"It's fine, it's fine," I said, clearly not meaning a word of it. "The important thing was that I got it down on paper, so I can reconstruct it when I get back to my desk."

"Be nice, and I'll tell you where we keep the pads with actual paper on them so next time you can use one of them."

"Thanks," I said, and tried hard to be actually thankful. "You didn't have to...the coffee, I mean."

"I know," she said, and slouched over the table. "But I saw you hand Alex the cup and figured you could use a refill. You're useless without your Jesus juice anyway."

"Just seemed like the nice thing to do." My efforts to reconstruct the napkin were shredding it with unerring efficiency, so I stopped trying and grabbed the mug. "You sure you don't want this instead?"

She shook her head. "I'm drinking water at work these days. So, drink up."

"Thank you," I said again, and meant it this time.

"Don't worry about it," she told me and got up. "I know where to find you."

"Everyone does." I stood as well, coffee in one hand, napkin in the other. "I'll catch you later."

"Maybe." And she turned, and was gone, and then someone was whooping over having found a hidden stash of cups in the cabinet under the microwave and I got the hell out of there before I forgot what I was working on completely.

Clearing space on my desk for the coffee was easy; finding a place for the napkin was harder. I ended up setting both down, one on top of the other, before kicking my desktop system out of sleep mode and pulling up the appropriate documentation for the stuff I was proposing to modify. The screen flickered and cleared as it woke up, and I found myself cursing softly. The same Powerpoint I'd been working on was up, despite the fact that I'd closed it before sending the final, Michelle-approved version to Eric for transmission to our foreign overlords. Changes had been made to it, too—I could see that much from the first screen. Somehow, the main character's pose had been changed to be more alluring. Her lean forward was deeper, the tilt of her head more, well, coquettish.

It was all very definitely come-hither, which I wasn't comfortable with. For one thing, the point of the game wasn't to come hither. It was to go thither, and then blow the living hell out of everyone you found there. For another, there shouldn't have been time for someone to change things up, not between when I'd sent it to Eric and when I'd come back from coffee. Someone would have had to sneak into my office, hack my password to unlock the system, load the presentation, replace the image, and then sneak out with enough time to spare for the thing to drop back into sleep mode, and I didn't think that was possible.

I stuck my head into the hallway and yelled. "Eric?"

"What?"

"Was anyone in my office while I was getting coffee?"

"No." He didn't look up, and his tone indicated that I was going to be in a hell of a lot of trouble if he did. "Why?"

"Someone screwed around with the images in the presentation. You may want to check the one we sent to make sure it's what we want them to see."

"Oh, for the love of—"

I didn't hear any more, ducking back into my office to see how much damage had actually been done. Flipping through the slides, I could see it—subtle changes here and there. A screenshot tweaked, a phrasing adjusted, a bullet point deleted. If you didn't know what had been there beforehand, you wouldn't know anything was different. If you'd sweated blood over each slide before turning it in, the alterations stood out like a full-grown tiger at a petting zoo.

Something blinked on the menu bar at the bottom of my screen. I glanced at it automatically. It was an instant messenger programming, proudly informing that someone wanted to talk to me. "Great. Just what I need," I grumbled and clicked on it.

A window popped up, dead center, with Michelle's username on it. "DID ERIC GET IT OFF?"

I typed "That's kind of a personal question," and then erased it. "He did. Did u make changes????" was what I finally went with.

NOT AFTER I SENT IT 2U

A pause.

Y???

"Something's changed," I typed in. "Lots of little edits from this morning, after we locked everything down. Check UR file."

OK.

There was a pause of somewhere between thirty seconds and ten years, and then she came back with HUH.

"Huh what?"

CHANGES YES I DIDN'T DO THEM BUT

"But What?!?!?!?!"

I considered marching down to her desk, considered picking up the phone, considered yelling really loudly. Instead, I waited.

R CHANGES I WANTED TO MAKE BUT HAD NO TIME 4

I sat there and digested that for a minute, even as I heard Eric's voice out in the hall. "Looks good from here, Ryan," he said. "Don't give me a heart attack next time."

"Sorry," I mumbled, not loudly enough for him to hear, and thought about it for a minute.

"If not you," my fingers tapped out, "then who?"

I paused a minute before sending it, hoping that Shelly would punch through something that would answer this, that would make sense. Maybe she'd made the changes after all. Maybe someone had 'fessed up.

No such luck.

I waited another minute, then hit Send.

Her answer came back almost immediately. DONT KNOW, she wrote, BUT WE SHOULD HIRE THEM LOL

Laugh out loud indeed, I thought. Very funny. I let myself cool down for a minute, then typed "Next time we check it in to the versioning software database so we can see who checked it out and made changes."

Yeah. There was a break, and then, But at least it looks good.

"Whatever" I sent. "Whoever it was could have stuck anything in there—porn or Hitler or whatever, and wouldn't that have been fun when Phil at HQ opened it up? Besides, someone hacked into your system, and mine, and maybe Eric's, and that bothers me. I really want to know who did this before they do something serious and nasty, and it's not just a case of a couple of GIFs being swapped out. If they start swapping out assets in the game, then we're really screwed." I slammed home the last period and hit Send.

The window blinked and spat back a "Too many characters" error at me. I watched it blink for a minute, then took a sip of coffee and closed the window. The hell with it, I decided and started working on the revised UI flow instead.

Shelly sent me a couple more messages, but I ignored them. The only logical solution to this little conundrum was that she'd made the changes, and if that were the case, I didn't much feel like talking to her. All she'd had to do was ask, and I would have gone along with them. I had to admit it—on the whole, the tweaks she'd made had improved the presentation. The points were clearer, the images more striking, the message stronger.

But there was no reason for her to have felt like she needed to sneak those in, or to sneak onto my system to do so. If anyone in the building knew me well enough to guess my password, she'd be the one. The coffee was probably just a way of distracting my attention.

I took a sip. It was cold and bitter. I could feel the grounds on my tongue. "Screw it." Shutting down the chat application, I went to work reconstructing my torn and tattered napkin, the road map of my revised inspiration.

At six, Eric left for the day. He stuck his head in my office as he passed. "Everything OK?" he asked.

I nodded. "I'm still not quite sure what the hell happened with that slide deck, but what the hell. As long as you're happy with it."

He scratched behind his ear. "Whatever. I think you just misremembered or something. It's off, and until we hear from Phil, there's no sense in worrying."

"We haven't heard from him yet?" I looked up in surprise. "I thought you sent it before he left."

"Yeah, yeah. He's not exactly the most punctual guy when it comes to getting back to us. You know that. Anyway, if there's nothing else?"

I grinned at him. "In other words, there had better not be anything else." With empty hands, I shooed him off. "There's nothing, I swear. I'll catch you tomorrow."

"All right," he said, and vanished from the doorframe. "Try to get out of here sometime," I heard his voice echo from down the hall as he walked away.

Try, I thought to myself. Try indeed.

Chapter 4

"Mmmm?"

"Shh, honey. Go back to sleep." I eased myself out of bed, one questing foot hitting the carpet before I dared move the second one. Beside me, Sarah snuggled close, maybe a quarter awake at best. I leaned over and kissed her forehead. "I love you."

"Mmmm," she said again, and then, in a small voice thick with sleep, "Hurry back."

"I will," I promised, and extracted myself from the bed. She rolled over, curling the blankets to her in a maneuver that I knew well. I stood there, watching her for a moment, my eyes adjusting to the darkness of the bedroom even as the klaxon of NOT TIRED NOT TIRED NOT TIRED echoed in my brain. I'd been in bed for a solid hour, lying as still as I could in the dark so as to avoid waking Sarah, eyes open and staring.

Eventually, I'd decided that sleep just wasn't in the cards and thought I should do something useful instead. First, though, I waited and watched until Sarah's breathing grew regular and she'd bunched a pillow up to curl herself around. I pulled the sheets up to her chin, resisted the urge to kiss her again, and shambled off to my office.

The night was warm enough that I didn't have to worry about a bathrobe; stripey pajama bottoms were good enough. I sagged into my chair, making sure the office door was shut behind me, and fired up the computer. A quick email check, I decided, and then some useful competitive analysis, by which I meant playing a game for a while. I thought about working on my novel—it had been sitting peaceably at a cool fifty thousand words since National Novel Writers Month ended—but decided against it. Too tired, I told myself. Whatever I wrote wouldn't be any good.

The company email page took forever to load, grumbling along like it was dialup. Someone at the office was downloading something big, I decided. Probably porn, or maybe BitTorrent movies. Either way, I didn't much care. I just tapped the desk with my fingers until, one by one, the screen elements popped in. I checked the clock. 3:30 AM. I'd been counting sheep longer than I'd thought.

"Just a quick mail check," I repeated, and scanned the list. One item caught my eye. It was from a BlackStone address, a familiar one.

When Eric had sent the presentation over to Phil, he'd cc'ed me on the message. I'd paid no attention at the time.

Phil apparently hadn't paid any attention either. He'd hit Reply All, not just Reply, which meant that I could take a look at his thoughts on our presentation. With luck, he wouldn't be asking for major changes, and I could spend minimal time making his requested tweaks. BlackStone was funny that way, constantly moving the target that the third party studios were supposed to hit. Michelle had voiced her suspicion, more than once, that they were just doing it so they could call "breach of contract" whenever they felt like it. I'd been more generous—I'd said that they didn't know what the hell they wanted, either.

I clicked the link. Phil's email opened up.

The third time I read it, it finally sunk in.

Eric:

Thank you very much for your presentation. I'm sure it is excellent. However, it is my understanding that the Executive Board has decided that it is not in BlackStone's interest to pursue the Blue Lightning project at this time. This is not a formal announcement, of course, but I wanted you to be aware of the way the wind was blowing. I do know that they are very pleased with your studio's work and plan to offer you something else to make up for the disappointment.

I am sure we will be in contact soon.

Best Wishes,

Phillip

I stared at it for a while, then stared some more. There was a soft ping, the sound of new mail, and I looked down.

It was from Eric. Apparently, he'd been having trouble sleeping as well. I opened it up.

> Not a word to anyone.
> -Eric

That was all it said. That was enough.

I shut down the computer and walked out of my office. The bedroom was to the right, warm and inviting.

I turned left, went downstairs, and spent the rest of the night sitting in a kitchen chair, staring at the wall.

* * *

Sarah was her usual bustling self in the morning. If she noticed that I hadn't come back to bed, she didn't say anything about it. For my part, I didn't say anything about the email I'd seen. I had a bowl of cereal; she had an egg-white omelet with low-fat cheese and a precisely measured pinch of parsley, and then she was off in a whirlwind of newly promoted efficiency.

I stood at the front door and watched her go. It wasn't until after her car's taillights had faded into the distance that I dragged myself upstairs and threw myself into the shower.

Maybe it was a mistake, I told myself. Maybe Phil jumped the gun. Maybe I didn't actually read what I thought I read. Maybe, maybe, maybe.

But in my gut, I knew it was bullshit. I knew the project was dead. Maybe it didn't know it yet. Maybe I wasn't allowed to tell anyone that the sentence had been passed. But it was over.

Hot water sluiced over me. I stood there, letting it run down my back, and leaned into the wall. It should have been no big deal. Projects got killed all the time. There were guys I'd met at Game Developers' Conference who'd been in the industry ten years without ever shipping a title, because the games they were working on always got axed or handed off to another studio or otherwise taken away.

But this was going to be the one. I'd felt it. So had the team. There was something magical in the game, a real sense of something new and exciting and cool. This was going to be the one to really make us as an independent studio.

I was the creative director, and it was going to be the one to make me. Now, for reasons that would never be explained and that I would never comprehend, it was dead.

Just like that.

I sank down onto the floor and let the water flow over my skin until it was freezing. I was thirty-five, positively ancient in game-development terms, and I'd just seen my best shot go bye-bye. Maybe Sarah was right. Maybe it was time to let her pay the bills while I tried to do something else, something that didn't rely so much on so many other people, so far away.

Eventually I turned the water off.

* * *

Eric was waiting for me when I walked in the door. "My office. Now."

"And a good morning to you, too, Eric." I dropped my laptop bag on the floor outside my door. "Is this a before-coffee or an after-coffee conversation?"

He glowered at me from behind his desk. "It's a now conversation."

"Right, then. No coffee." I was already headed toward his office as I said it, any cheap bravado I'd felt draining away.

"Shut the door."

I did.

"Sit."

I sat.

He leaned forward over his desk, looking tired. Looking beaten, for lack of a better word. There were dark circles under his eyes, which were reddish in the way only a sleepless night or a long drinking binge can bring. There were lines down his face, and his hair looked like he'd done the five-finger brush job instead of his usual immaculate grooming. There was stubble on his cheeks.

I was shocked. There was never stubble on Eric's cheeks. Other times when we'd had contracts pulled, other times when it looked like the entire company might go tits-up, he'd always managed to maintain a positively respectable appearance. I'd asked him about it once, and he told me it was simple—if he looked like there was nothing to worry about, then other folks would figure there was nothing to worry about. Look like the world was caving in, and there would be panic in the streets, which would then make his job that much harder.

Today, he looked like crap.

"So," he said, "you saw the first email in that chain. Would you like to know the rest of it?"

"I'm not sure," I said cautiously. "Should I know this stuff?"

He rubbed his eyes. "You're going to have to, sooner or later, so you might as well. The short version is that there were about fifteen more messages back and forth last night after I chopped you out of the cc list. Some was with Phil, some was with the higher ups, but none of it was what you'd call good."

"So we're screwed?" I felt myself deflating, even as I asked. There had been some tiny particle of hope that the email I'd seen had been incorrect, that Phil had gotten his wires crossed or had been since overruled. Now, it was snuffed out.

"Blue Lightning is screwed," he clarified, and looked at me through his fingers. "That's why I called you in here. As for the suckage, it's real simple. Their marketing department 'no longer has confidence' in Blue Lightning, and are no longer supporting the project. We are to stop working on it immediately, if not sooner."

Feebly, I protested. "But...we have a contract."

"In theory, we'll get a kill fee."

I blinked, suspicious. "In theory?"

Instead of answering, Eric stretched out in his chair and stared up for a long moment at the ceiling. "In theory," he finally said. "In reality, I expect that trying to recoup it from them will take somewhere on the order of five years, and cost us a half a million in lawyer's fees."

"We can't afford that," I blurted out. The pressure in my chest eased infinitesimally. As dire as this seemed, the fact that Eric was talking to me indicated that he had something else up his sleeve. If he didn't, he probably would have been setting the place on fire for the insurance money. He was a practical kind of boss; that was one of the reasons everyone liked working for him. Still, having Blue Lightning cancelled was a kick in the creative crotch. To lose it now, well, that was a lot of work they were asking us to throw out. A lot of late nights and passion and skull sweat, a lot of weekends blown to make milestones and self-imposed deadlines, a lot of hours spent as a small part of a medium-sized team trying to make something big.

A lot of love.

"No. We can't," he agreed. "Which is what they're counting on." He left the sentence hanging, as if daring me to finish it.

Another bout of panic seized me. "Do they want the assets?" If they did, we'd have to bundle up every bit of work we'd done—art, code, design, sound—and hand it over, never to be seen again. BlackStone could then theoretically turn the project over to someone else to do whatever they wanted with it, or they could sit on it, or they could just use the discs we'd backed everything up onto for coasters. Every trick that we'd come up with over the course of the project would be theirs, never mind that we'd done a lot of the heavy lifting before they sent dime one in our direction.

Eric waved off my concern. "No, they're not asking for that, at least. They just want us to stop working on it." He gave a wan grin. "I don't think they particularly want the IP, to be honest, which tells you how little they think of it."

I tasted cold vomit in the back of my throat and swallowed hard, trying to clear things enough that I could actually speak. "And those guys want everything. Wow. They must have really hated it if they're willing to let it go."

"They don't think it will come back to hurt them," he said. His fingers drummed the desk. "The really angry-making part of this is that they're probably right."

I stared at him, suspicion beetling in my mind. "There's something else going on, isn't there?" I leaned back in the chair and tilted my head back toward the ceiling. "OK, I'm not seeing it."

Sound, rather than sight, told me that Eric had gotten up. "What the hell are you doing?"

"Looking for the other shoe," I replied. "Any second now, it's going to drop."

He laughed despite himself, and came around to the front of the desk. "I hate to say it, but you're right. There's a one-two punch here, and there's no way to duck."

"Part one is killing our project. Part two is…"

"They've offered us something else."

My head snapped down so fast I could actually hear my neck crack and feel my molars bounce off one another. "Something else?" My eyes narrowed. "Like what?"

He held up that damnable piece of paper. "That's the bitch of it." Someone knocked on his door, and without turning he called out "In a meeting. Come back in five minutes."

I raised an eyebrow. "Five minutes? You're an optimist."

He fixed me with a decidedly humorless stare. "I don't think either of us will want to continue this conversation past that point. Look, here's the deal." He started pacing, ticking the points off on his fingers as he did so. "They want us to do an old-gen port of their new FPS project. Maybe PC, too, if we look like we can handle it. They're offering acceptable money and a longer contract if we just roll everything off of Blue Lightning and onto this new thing, which they've code-named Salvador."

"That's nice and humble," I said, but he waved me to silence.

"If we say yes, everyone keeps their job. We might even need to do some hiring. We get steady work for at least another ten months and at least one SKU on a project that they're going to be devoting a lot of time and money to, not to mention a major marketing push. We're talking TV, print ads, serious viral stuff online—something they weren't going to give Blue Lightning."

"Because they didn't own the IP," I said softly. Eric's voice had the strangled sound of a man trying to convince himself it would be better for everyone if he murdered his wife. Including, I might add, the wife in question. "And in exchange…"

He sighed. "You know what the exchange is." He stopped and turned to face me. "We kill Blue Lightning, at least for the duration of this project, and with the way the tech is going, that effectively means forever. That's why you're in here and we're having this talk."

"Is it?" I couldn't meet his eyes. There was a very interesting patch of carpet near his left foot, however, and I studied it intently. "You're the boss, Eric. If you say we're doing Salvador on an Etch-a-Sketch, I'll go make it happen. You know that."

"Yeah. But that's not the point. You know exactly what's going to happen when I announce this."

"If," I corrected him. We both sat there in silence for a second. "OK, when. You're right. Your job is to make sure everyone else has a job, and that means you have to take the deal."

He nodded. "But it's going to be ugly. We're going to have people at least think about quitting. We're going to have a lot of yelling and screaming and anger, and we're going to have a lot of resentment toward whatever project comes next. And depending on what you do, it could be bad, or it could be bloody awful."

I blinked. "Me?"

"You. You're the creative director on the project, the leader of the team. A lot of people around here, for whatever reason, regard Blue Lightning as your baby. If you put up a fuss, they're going to rally behind that and make the next year or so miserable. Even if you just drag your feet on the new project, a lot of people are going to be following your example."

My throat, I decided, had done enough involuntary tightening for one day. It needed to relax and let me breathe. That was all I really wanted from it.

"On the other hand," Eric continued, "if you dive into the new project with something approaching enthusiasm, anyone who dogs it is going to look like a bit of a tool, which is going to make getting up to speed on Salvador a whole lot easier."

Suddenly, my chair felt too confining. I stood, fighting the urge to put something solid behind my back as a psychosomatic itch popped up between my shoulder blades. "So let me get this straight. You're asking me to smile and play nice when you tell everyone out there that the project we've been sweating blood over for the last two years is in the crapper? What happens if I don't? Do I get fired? Or do you just make my life miserable enough that I quit and you can bring someone else in? Wait, is there a bonus if I play along? Because I think I see where this is going, and I don't like it."

"Knock it off, Ryan," he said, sounding tired. "I'm not making any offers, and I'm not making any threats. You can do whatever the hell you like. I'm just telling you what I see and where I think you fit into this, because I need your help to ride this one out without someone getting damaged. Like you said, my job is to make sure everyone else has a job, and taking the deal seems like the best way to ensure that. If I try to fight this, God knows when we'll see the money from the kill fee and we've got no line on the next gig. If we try to do Blue Lightning in the meantime, we'll run out of cash in under three months. Any other publisher we talk to will know we're over a barrel and will screw us that much harder."

I wanted to get angry, to get indignant on behalf of our work and our integrity, but all I got was a hollow feeling. "I know," I said, and it came out like I'd been gut-punched. "It's just…"

"It sucks." He took a few steps closer and put a hand tentatively on my shoulder. "It sucks a lot, and I know this is a lot to ask. But, if you understand why I have to make this decision, you can help make it easier for everyone. I don't want people hurting themselves, Ryan. I don't want anyone cutting their own throats because at the end of the day, this is a job. It's a job we all love, but it's still a job, and the paycheck is what covers the rent, not artistic integrity or anything else. If you want, I can see if I can find something to tuck into your envelope to make the medicine go down a little easier, but I don't think that's a good idea."

"Cheap bastard," I said weakly.

He shook his head. "No. I just think that if I do that, in about two months you'll decide that you were bought off and will work yourself up to doing something really stupid, like quitting, in order to make your conscience feel better. I'd rather have you here, without any more self-inflicted holes in your stomach lining, and feeling all right about what you're doing. If this works out the way I hope it will, there's going to be plenty on the back end for everyone, anyway." Abruptly the pressure of his hand left my shoulder, and

Eric turned to look away, a tired scarecrow who knew the big black birds were coming. "So make up your mind," he said. "I'd appreciate your help with this, if you want to give it. If not, I understand. You've put in a lot of time on that project, and put a lot of yourself into it."

I put my hand on the doorknob. "I'll think about it," I said thickly. "That's all I can promise."

"I know," he said. "That's all I can ask for. Now get out of here, and I'd appreciate it if you didn't talk to anyone else about this. I'll be making the announcement today, but I have a few other folks I need to sit down with before the shit officially hits the fan."

Pithy comebacks came to mind. "It already has," maybe, or "I'll go get an umbrella." None seemed worthy, and instead I just let myself the hell out, leaving the door slightly ajar. I had a feeling that I wasn't going to be the last one in that office this morning, not by a long shot.

Chapter 5

My email app pinged. Eric's note announcing the unscheduled company meeting had just come in, setting a time down to the minute when he'd be forced to lower the boom.

It was a nice piece of business writing, clearly designed to foster the impression of honesty and open communication while mitigating the knee-jerk panic that always accompanied something like this. I wasn't sure how much good it was going to do, but the attempt, at least, was praiseworthy.

I remembered the first time I'd been laid off. The company president had sent an email calling a company meeting in the parking lot outside the office. The last time he'd done that, there had been an ice cream truck waiting as a reward for our hitting a milestone. This time, he told us that we were all fired, and the VP of marketing locked the doors while he was making his speech. It was two weeks before we were allowed back inside to get our stuff.

Out in the hallway, I could hear the rising buzz as people reacted. At some companies, I knew, they'd preface something like this by cutting net access or taking down the mail server, pulling the plug on the phone system, and maybe locking the doors, never mind that it was a fire hazard, all to keep word from getting out a half-second faster than it might otherwise. Eric didn't bother. Enough people had net access through their phones that trying to shut down the lines of communication was just going to look stupid and out of control.

So I applauded Eric for playing it straight, even as I checked the clock. The meeting was scheduled for eleven; it was a few minutes after ten now. There was plenty of time to prep for whatever I intended to do, as soon as I figured out whatever the hell that was.

The cell phone fell into my hand as if by reflex. Yeah, I thought. Calling Sarah would be a good start.

She was at her desk when I called her, the phone ringing precisely twice before she picked it up. "Sarah Bogdan." It was an announcement.

By calling her, I'd come into her place of authority, seeking an audience. Or at the very least, that's what it felt like.

"Hi," I said. "Do you have a minute to talk?"

"Ryan." She sounded exasperated. "I thought if you were going to call me during the day, you'd use the landline so we didn't use up minutes."

"Sorry. I just hit the first number I had for you."

She paused for a second. "Are you all right? You sound funny."

I pulled the phone away from my face for a moment, so the explosive sigh I'd been holding in didn't deafen her. "No, I'm not all right," I said. "Remember that offer you made last night?"

"Yes?" She drew the word out until it was begging for a few more syllables. "Why?"

I pressed on. "Remember how we said there was going to be plenty of time before I needed to make a decision?"

"What are you getting at, Ryan? I'm kind of busy, and I'm sorry, honey, but I don't have time for guessing games."

The urge to hang up came and went, just like that. Calm, I told myself. Be calm. She doesn't know. "You said when my project's done, right? Well, that's going to be in about an hour."

There was a pause which I put down to either confusion or elation. "I don't understand. I thought you weren't at alpha yet. How can you be done...oh. Oh, I'm sorry, honey. That's terrible news."

"Yeah." I kicked the floor experimentally, sending my chair spinning slowly counterclockwise. "So, anyway, I, um, I just wanted to let you know. That maybe, there'd be a change coming sooner instead of later. Or maybe not. I don't know. It all depends. I just wanted to let you know, if that makes any sense."

"Of course it does." Her voice was calm now, soothing. "Look, sweetheart, I really have to go. First day in the new position, and they're watching me like a hawk. But we can talk about it tonight, OK? Just don't worry and know that whatever happens, I love you."

"Love you too," I said and broke the connection. My office felt stifling and dim, the tasteful light from the wall sconce barely enough to illuminate the papers on my desk. I looked at them. Design specs for Blue Lightning, sample promotional material, a list of basic interview questions from BlackStone PR that they'd been planning on feeding to magazines and websites once the game got a little more play—all of it worthless. I stacked them next to my monitor and headed to the conference room. As far as I knew, there was still a version of Blue Lightning set up in there, minding its own business. In under an hour, it would get shut down. The debug kit, a sample version of the finished console hardware, would get its hard drive wiped, and the equipment would get assigned to another project. The television would get something else jacked into it, the controllers would go back in a box somewhere, and the code that made up Blue Lightning would get backed up and hidden away.

If I was going to play, this was going to be my last chance.

I stalked down the hallway, nodding and smiling and minimally waving to the folks who said hello as I passed. A couple shouted out questions—had I seen Eric's email, did I know what was going on, did I have time to talk? I gave a shrug for an answer, or a "Dunno" or "I'll catch you after the meeting, OK?" Stopping seemed like a bad idea; I'd get swamped and never get started again. No one was working. Everyone was talking, huddled into clumps or jabbering excitedly into smartphones. A couple of the younger kids just sat there, staring at their monitors with looks of dread on their faces. They hadn't been through it before and probably thought that they might never get another job in gamedev. Someone else would set them straight, I was sure. Someone always did.

The clock on the wall of the conference room read 10:30 by the time I made it there. Half an hour, then, to get in my last licks. I shut the door, debated going back out for coffee, and decided against it. Instead, I booted up the debug kit and killed the lights. The room went dark for a minute, then went electric blue as the game's load screen flared out from the television. The placeholder logo was there, bright and jagged, and next to it…her.

She was crouched, predatory, one hand cradling a smooth, streamlined pistol, the other held up so that electricity could drip off her fingers like water. Sparks flowed down and puddled at her feet, while the blankness where her face ought to be was turned to the camera, its challenge implicit. She was almost too bright to look at, the sheer intensity of her coloration illuminating the room even as it faded everything else onscreen to insignificance. Below her, the words "PRESS START TO PLAY" throbbed slowly, fading in and out in time with what might have been her imaginary heartbeat.

I picked up the controller. It was warm, as if someone had just been playing it. Thumbing it on, I walked over in front of the television and braced myself. There was a chair behind me, but I gave it a little kick and it skidded off. Standing would show respect for the game, and I was too wired to sit in any case. As an afterthought, I found the remote for the

TV and thumbed up the volume. Let her go out with a bang, I thought. A bang, and a crash, and a couple of big-ass explosions.

A couple more button presses and the action screen faded in. I recognized the space, a futuristic library. Multi-leveled and chopped into innumerable small rooms, it was a claustrophobic nightmare generously stocked with hunter-killer robots, alien nasties, and human commandos intent on wiping the player avatar out. There were no bookshelves here, just gleaming rows of data banks and helmets that users could jack into. These were conduits the player avatar could disappear into or pop out of, giving the player one advantage over the insane numbers being brought to bear against him. Her. Us.

I considered it an almost fair fight. In the single-player game, the plan was for this to be the penultimate level, where the player would face off against an evil version of their character. The evil twin could also go circuit-riding, negating that player advantage, but we hadn't even gotten to the point of designing the AI necessary for that. It was, and would remain, a dream.

This, on the other hand, was just pure hunter-killer mode. There were lots of bad guys, one me, and a time limit, nothing more.

I checked my weapon. It was the basic blaster pistol, blessed with unlimited ammunition but not much else. That was fine. Other weapons would be coming available shortly.

Sighting down the barrel of the pistol, I put one round into the floor to blaze my trail. In front of me was a closed door. I opened it and started running.

* * *

It wasn't the shouting that got me out of the game, it was the heavy pounding on the door, which only slowly distinguished itself from the sounds of onscreen carnage and destruction. Then and only then did the words become clear.

"Come on, Ryan. Open up. The meeting's starting. Get out here, man." The voice was Leon's. I checked the clock, which read 11:04. For gamer time, that was pretty punctual.

"Coming!" I shouted, then turned down the volume and repeated myself. Onscreen, Blue Lightning stood frozen, paused mid-kill with an explosion blossoming behind her. Dead bodies, broken robots, and shattered crates were everywhere, a more spectacular method of marking progress through the level than shooting the floor. A blaster bolt hung, suspended in midair. It would never reach its target.

I tossed the controller onto the table but didn't shut off the console. Let someone else do that. I wasn't going to be the one to pull the plug on my baby.

The common area was full when I stepped out of the conference room. People stood or sat, clustered by department or temperament. Leon stood by the door, fist raised to knock again, but most of the rest of the engineers were huddled at the back, arms folded across their chests and looks of disbelief on their faces. Alex, the guy I'd beaten for the last coffee cup the day before, was pontificating about something; three or four other engineers stood in a circle around him and nodded enthusiastically.

"Hey, Leon," I said. "Thanks for getting me out of there. I just got sucked into the game."

He nodded. "I know how it is, man. Even without the real polish, she's a beauty, huh? Just wait until we get a chance to really make her sing."

I bit the inside of my cheek, hard, to avoid saying something, and instead found a spot strategically located near the rear. It was close enough to the engineers that I wasn't isolated, far enough away that I didn't actually have to listen to them. Leon looked around for a minute, then decided to stick with me.

"So what's this about? You know?"

I shook my head. "It's Eric's show. Let him tell you."

"OK." He sounded dubious. "I just thought since you were in there this morning…"

"It's Eric's show," I said firmly. "Let him tell you."

A quick look around the room told me whom Eric had already spoken to. Those were the guilty faces, the ones with eyes pointed at the floor and mouths kept resolutely shut. I counted four in the room. Eric had been keeping this one close to the vest all right, not that it would matter now.

And he had in fact been waiting for me, because as soon as he saw Leon and me at the back of the crowd, he started waving his hands and shouting for quiet. "People, people," he said, and the hubbub cut off like it had been sliced. Faces turned to the front of the room. Silence fell. Someone coughed expectantly. Somewhere up in the rafters, the HVAC thrummed to life, then thought better of it and shuddered to stillness.

Eric scanned the space, hands held out like an orchestra conductor trying to put down a mutiny from a well-armed brass section. For a long moment, he said nothing, and as he didn't, neither did we. Here and there, you could see heads turning, people looking away as if doing so would somehow prevent Eric from saying something bad.

I just stared at him.

"I want to thank everyone for coming," he said, then coughed into his hand. "No. That's not right. I want to thank everyone for listening, and for not jumping to any conclusions before I had a chance to talk to you." He scanned the room, locking eyes for a moment or two with those who'd look at him, passing over those who wouldn't. "And before this goes any further, let me state one thing right off the bat: Everyone's still got a job. We are not closing, we are not laying anyone off, and we are not going out of business."

Eric paused to see if what he'd said had produced the desired effect, but there was no need to. There was a rush of air as half the company let out the breath it didn't know it was holding, conversational flotsam like "I told you so" and "Thank God" bobbing to the surface of a sudden buzz of discussion.

Again, Eric held up his hands for quiet. This time, it took him a few seconds to get it. "If you don't mind, I'd like to keep what we discuss next in-house until everything is said and done. I've always tried to be open with you about the business side of things, and that means trusting you to keep information inside the building. Again, I'm sorry if it seems like there's a lack of trust on this one, but I just learned most of this myself this morning, and what we're talking about is so big that I couldn't take any chances."

He looked around the room, letting those words hang there in the air while he crossed his arms over his chest.

"What the hell?" Leon whispered, and dug an elbow into my ribs. "What's he talking about, man?"

"Wait for it," I told him sotto voce. "You're going to love this one."

Leon turned and looked at me quizzically. "He told you? Why'd he tell you?"

"I wouldn't dream of spoiling the surprise," I said, not without bitterness, and turned back to the front of the room. "Come on, man," Leon muttered, but after a moment he did the same.

"As you know, we've been working with BlackStone for the last year to publish Blue Lightning. Everyone here has put a lot of time and energy into that game, and I want to thank you for everything you've done, but unfortunately, BlackStone does not want to continue funding development for Blue Lightning at this time."

"BS!" someone shouted, an old joke from the team rooms that suddenly wasn't funny. "So we're going with another publisher, right?" someone else called out, a female this time.

"They can't do that!"

"Why do they want to kill it?"

"Are they crazy?"

And finally, the question Eric had been waiting for, "What's going to happen to us?" It came from up front, from an engineer named Terry Lee who put the "er" in "nerd," a quiet guy passionately devoted to his work and his gadgets and, near as anyone else could tell, not a hell of a lot else. "What's going to happen to us?"

Eric smiled, an "everything is going to be all right" grin that didn't quite make it to his eyes. I could feel my hands curling into fists as I saw him do it, knowing that the whole thing had been choreographed so neatly that Terry didn't even know he was part of it. In a couple of seconds, Eric would look sad and tell everyone that Daddy had a new girlfriend now and that we should be happy to meet her. And the whole thing was so smooth that they'd all go along with it, be on their best behavior and spit-shine their virtual shoes in order to make a good first impression when the new project came down the pike.

The fact that he was right to do it didn't help me feel better, not one little bit.

"We," he said, and I winced in anticipation, "are going to be doing the current gen console and PC ports of the project they call Salvador. That means that we're going to be on a tight schedule. It means we're going to be busy. It may even mean that we need to do a little staffing up, but," and he paused for effect, "if we do a good job on this, there could be more work coming down the pike. A lot more."

Pandemonium resolutely failed to erupt, just a low rumble that was half grumble, half excited whisper. Leon made a noise like steam escaping from a busted pipe. "Man, that sucks. Blue Lightning would have kicked ass."

"I know." Something in my tone made him look at me speculatively. Up front, Eric was answering questions, each one no doubt of vital importance to the future of the studio, but I wasn't listening.

"Shit. This has got to blow big time for you. I'm sorry."

I hitched my shoulders. It might have been a shrug. "At least he let me know first."

Leon shook his head. "Yeah, like giving you the blindfold and cigarette after he shows you the bullet with your name on it. That's cold, man. That ain't right."

"It's the publisher, not Eric. He's just doing his job," I said, but it sounded hollow, even to me. Leon said something that might have been "Wait here. I'll be right back," and slid off into the crowd. I watched him go for a moment, then turned my eyes back to the front of the room.

As I did, the lights flickered briefly, never quite going out, but dropping to a definite dim for a good half-second or so. People looked at the fixtures, worried for that split second until the roar of the air conditioning unit reawakening confirmed that we did in fact have power.

"No big deal, just another brownout," someone ahead of me explained, and woman standing next to him—a new hire, I thought, a younger woman who'd just graduated from one of the video game degree programs popping up like mold in a bachelor's fridge—nodded, relieved to know that we weren't getting a flyover from a UFO and instead were just teetering on the edge of a blackout because too many people in the local grid had cranked their HVACs too high. Behind her, I could just make out Leon talking excitedly to someone, but from where I stood, it was impossible to see who.

Eric took that opportunity to wrap things up. "That's all I've got," he said. "I know it's a lot to digest, so I'm going to unofficially shut down production for the day. If you want to stick around, play games, talk, whatever, I'll be here in my office until six. Otherwise, if you want to get out of here, go ahead. We'll get a fresh start on Salvador tomorrow."

He turned and walked slowly toward his office, trailing would-be questioners like a celebrity trolling a string of reporters. By the time I looked away, the rest of the group had already started to break up, drifting into clumps mostly broken down by department. In ones and twos, people were straying back to their desks, far more than were headed for the door. I stood and watched, shaking my head.

"Pathetic, huh?" said a familiar voice at my elbow. "Give them the day off and they still head right back to their desks."

"Maybe they're just packing up, Michelle," I said stonily. "Or they have other things to do."

"Uh-huh." She sounded unconvinced. A hand, which I was reasonably sure was hers, latched onto my elbow. "Leon and I are going out to Montague's so we can get properly drunk and pissed off about this whole thing. Are you coming?"

I turned to face her, brushing her hand off my arm in the process. She stood there, her arm half-poised in midair to try to tug at me again, face caught in an expression that I'd long since grown familiar with, then gotten weary of. It was the look of "What am I going to do to Ryan for his own good," as portrayed by widened eyes, a mouth turned down into a concerned frown, and an ever-so-slight head tilt to the right.

"You go," I said, feeling myself falling into the steps of a familiar dance. "I want to see if Eric's got any docs on the new project I can look at. You know, get a head start on tomorrow."

"God, you're bad at this corporate rah-rah shit," she said, gently re-attaching her hand to my arm and then closing it in a grip that told me she'd been studying with fiddler crabs. Not-so-gentle pressure drew me down the hall and toward the door. Leon was already there, holding it open and blessedly doing so without comment. "We can do this one of two ways. Either you can say something stupidly noble, which will piss me off enough to argue with you in the middle of what is really looking like a shitty day for everyone, or you can just let me drag you off peacefully."

"Those are my only choices?" I asked, barely bothering to try to slow the pace. Honestly, there wasn't much point to it.

Michelle shook her head, hair going everywhere. "Not much of a choice, to be honest. Either way, you end up at Montague's, completely shitfaced, before lunch. The only question is, how long is it going to take to get you out the door?"

I looked at her, bemused. "Yeah, whatever. I'll be fine."

In response, she spun me, shoving far harder than someone her size should have been able to and slamming me up against the wall. My head hit maybe an inch from a framed poster celebrating one of our early games, a misbegotten platformer starring an anthropomorphized vulture named Varney. It had tanked. I had about six-tenths of a second to consider that before Michelle was up in my face, furious with me. "You listen to me, Ryan Colter. You will not be fine. You are not fine right now. You are having a really crappy day, and the best thing I can do for you, as a friend, is take you someplace where you can shut your brain off for a couple of hours and tell everyone how you really feel about what just happened, because today you get a mulligan. Today, you can be a dick and no one will call you on it. So even though you'd rather pretend to be noble where everyone can see you, you might as well take advantage of this one time offer and the fact that you actually have people in this office who care about you." Her volume had been rising as she went along, until by the end it was a full-fledged shout. She stood there, red-faced, and glared at me. Somehow during this exchange, her hand had moved from my arm to the front of my shirt. It looked for all the world as if I were being mugged.

"You're not supposed to care about me anymore, Shelly," I said. "It's very sweet, but—"

She slapped me. The crack of skin on skin echoed like a pistol shot, deafening in the enclosed hallway. "You stupid son of a bitch," she said, and took a step back. "I don't. Leon does."

And she turned and walked away, out the open door, while I stood there and felt all the eyes on me. Leon shot me a glance that said everything that needed to be said, then let the door swing shut and walked down to the parking lot, a few steps behind Michelle.

"Ow," I said to nobody in particular and rubbed my cheek. It stung where she'd popped me, and I was quite certain that the left side of my face was now fire-engine red. "Brilliant," I muttered and headed for my office. There was no sense in heading home, not until my face got its usual pasty sheen back. With my luck, Sarah would decide to come home for lunch, and explaining to her that I'd been slapped at the office by an ex-girlfriend was simply not something I really felt up to doing.

Instead, I figured, I'd get a head start on tomorrow's work. I'd archive all of the Blue Lightning documents and prepare the closing kit, the virtual steamer trunk full of everything related to the project that would get tucked away into a virtual attic in case anyone ever wanted to see it again. The decks would be cleared for Salvador, assuming I stuck around long enough to work on it.

I'd been at it for all of ten minutes when there was a knock on the door. I looked up to see who it was and spotted Terry, half-leaning around the corner. "Can I come in?"

I nodded. "Sure. Have a seat. I wasn't doing anything important, just cleaning up some old files."

He blinked, then ambled in. Terry fit the first half of the old saying about game developers, "rail or whale," and he looked like turning up the HVAC would blow him clear out of the building. He was tall and skinny, with a shockingly round face and black hair that was maybe ten bucks' worth of trimming away from being done with a Flobee. As he folded himself into the spare chair, I finished packing files into the archive I was building and waited for him to speak.

"So, uh, what do you think?" Terry's eyes were focused somewhere about a foot above my head and to the right, which was as close as he was likely to get to looking me in the eye.

"About this?" I shrugged. "It's business, Terry. Eric did a great job taking care of everyone."

He leaned forward, his arms resting on the edge of my desk. "But he didn't take care of everyone."

"Hmm?" I shut down my web browser and chat programs and glanced in Terry's general direction. "We've all got jobs, don't we? That's what's important."

"You don't sound like you believe that."

I shook my head. "What's not to believe? Who didn't get taken care of?"

He blinked, then said solemnly "Blue Lightning."

"Blue Lightning?" I laughed. "I'd say Blue Lightning got taken care of once and for all."

He snorted, his face turning red. "Blue Lightning's a great project. They should have let us finish it."

I nodded. "Thanks, Terry," I said softly, then got a hold of myself. "I think so, too. But it's out of our hands. If we want to have jobs tomorrow," —And do you? my subconscious kept asking— "then we have to wave goodbye. I don't like the decision, but I can't argue with the logic. Besides," and the words tasted like the inside of an ashtray as I said them, "I hear some cool things about Salvador."

Terry looked crestfallen, and his face went from red to white. "I thought you'd be the one person to really stand behind the project, Ryan. It was your vision. You've been on it longer than anyone else. Why aren't you trying to save it?"

The shutdown sequence on my system started, I spun in my chair. "Because there's no way to save it. I can't fly to BSoft headquarters and convince them to fund the game when they've made up their mind already. I'm not going to drag my heels and screw up the next project, and get people fired. What exactly do you want me to do, Terry, because I don't know what it is that I can do? Hell, I don't even know what I want to do, not that it actually matters worth a damn."

Terry's eyes opened wider, and he rocked back into his chair. "Jeez, man, I'm sorry. I know you're upset about this—"

"I'm not upset!" He stared at me. I coughed into my hand. "OK, maybe I'm a little pissed off. Not at you, Terry. But Blue Lightning is going away whether we want it to or not, so I can't—we can't let ourselves go crazy over it." I tried to smile. "You did some really great work with the AI. Did I ever tell you that?"

He nodded. "Yeah. A couple of times. You said you liked the detection algorithm that would chain the state changes through the guards." He looked pleased at the memory. "And I really hate to throw away that work."

"It's not getting thrown away," I told him as I stood up. Ideally, Terry would get the hint. "We're keeping all the Blue Lightning assets."

"We are?" Terry's face lit up with hope. "Are they staying on the network?"

I thought about it for a minute and took a couple of steps toward the door. Coincidentally, this took me a couple of steps closer to the still-seated Terry. "I don't know. Eric didn't tell me how we're going to handle things, though I think we might just back up the database and pull it off Perforce. But BlackStone isn't taking the assets. So who knows? Maybe someday we'll be able to resurrect the game and do it properly."

He nodded, a little too eagerly, and uncoiled from the chair in a cloud of knees and elbows. "That would be great," he said. "If we could work on it again someday. Thanks for your time, Ryan. I really appreciate it." He grabbed my hand, shook it, stood, then shook my hand again and walked off with a particularly energetic, stiff-legged gait. Just watching him go made me nervous. It reminded me of water striders and Daddy Longlegs and things that live under the bed when you're six years old.

A ping from my system told me that it had finally finished shutting down. There was no reason to stay in the building, not any longer. I might have given Terry the party line, or at least some of it, but there was still a lot of thinking I had to do for myself.

The lights in my office suddenly seemed much too bright. I turned them off and left.

Chapter 6

I'd made it almost halfway to my car when my iPhone started blowing up with text messages. A quick look told me they were all from Leon, and all variations on the theme of MAN WHERE R U?

GOING HOME, I texted back, and made it maybe ten feet further toward my car before the response hit. "WRONG ANSWER. EVERYONE @ MONTAGUES. WAITING ON YOU." Then, a second later, "RUNNING OUT THAT FRUITY BELGIAN CRAP YOU LIKE. HURRY."

In spite of myself, I laughed, then sent back a response. "NO THX—MICHELLE." It zipped into the ether with a ping, and I crossed the rest of the distance to my car.

It was silver (mostly) and looked new (mostly), at least until you peeked inside and saw the impressive amount of crap strewn around the back seat. Fast food wrappers, abandoned electronics packaging, unopened mail, dog-eared books, and more rattled around back there, accurately reflecting my state of mind most days.

The phone rang as I was swinging myself inside. "You're kidding, right? Nobody uses phones to actually talk anymore, Leon."

He snorted. In the background, I could hear yelling and the clatter of glasses, overlaid with a thin coat of jukebox George Thorogood. "You text too slow. Shelly said just call you and end the drama."

I shut the door and pulled my seat belt on. "You seriously think I'm going to swing by so Shelly can take another swing at me?"

He laughed. "You asked for that one, Ryan. But if you apologize real nice, I think she might let you buy her a beer and tell her you're sorry."

"I'm not supposed to be buying my ex-girlfriend beers, Leon," I said, hitting the ignition button. "Or had you forgotten that?"

I could almost hear him shrug. "Details. Just get over here, all right? I'll see you when you arrive."

"Sarah—" I started, but he cut me off.

"She knows. I called her and told her you needed to get pissed, and she gave her blessing after I promised I'd get you a ride home." He paused. "You got a smart woman, bro. Now come on over to the 'gue, get stupid, and get it all out of your system before you go do anything stupid. No argument."

He cut the connection before I could protest, and I flipped the phone onto the passenger seat. I thought about it and decided that if Sarah was good with it, I'd better be good with it, too. Besides, Leon was right—better to talk things through with people and maybe come to an informed, reasonable decision before talking to Sarah about the future.

None of the other folks walking across the parking lot waved as I pulled out, but that was all right. I didn't wave to any of them, either.

* * *

Montague's was not technically what one would call an Irish pub, not in this day and age. For one thing, it was most emphatically not decorated in chintzy pseudo-Celtic knickknacks, black and white pictures of James Joyce, or huge reproductions of classic Guinness posters. The old-school jukebox—which meant that it wasn't digital—featured precisely one Chieftains CD, and every time someone tried to play a track off it, the bartender cut the feed to the speakers in under thirty seconds. They did in fact serve Guinness, as well as Harp and Magners and a number of more obscure brews that originated in Ireland, but this was a matter of customer preference and not part of any horseshit prefabricated theme.

By the time I got there, the drunk was already well underway. Shelly and Leon may have led the charge, but several other folks had gotten the same idea, and the center of the bar was a knot of grumbling game devs pondering their next move. There were already enough in place for the central table amoeba to have formed, with numerous smaller ones pushed together to make one contiguous, oddly-shaped seating arrangement.

I stood there, framed in the doorway for a moment while my eyes adjusted to the light, or lack thereof. The board at the end of the bar announced the day's specials. There were $2.50 drafts for beers I'd never heard of, a burger with stuff on it I'd never eat, and a mixed drink called a "staggering squirrel" that sounded like a third-string Batman villain. The televisions over the bar were on but muted, two showing soccer games and one showing a combination of stock tickers and talking heads.

When my vision cleared, I could see Leon at the far end of the mass of tables, an empty chair next to him. A purse hung over the back, and a half-empty beer sat on the table. For a moment, I thought it must be Michelle's, only to my knowledge she'd never left a beer half-finished in her life.

"Dude!" Leon had spotted me, half-rising out of his seat and waving me over. "I didn't think you'd make it."

Heads swiveled and a couple of beers were raised in my direction as I made my way over to the table. "Hey, folks," I said, and pulled up a chair on the other side of him from where Michelle's stuff lurked. "What we have here is a failure to lubricate."

"That should be taken care of immediately," he said and raised an arm for a waitress. "This man needs a beer, bad." I cringed, but the server, perhaps recognizing that this had been One Of Those Days, just nodded and vanished into the darkness behind the bar.

"So, man, like what the hell?" Across the table was one of the character artists, a skinny little guy named Gordon who'd just started six weeks earlier. He'd been with EA and a couple of the other big companies, and everyone on the team had been blown away by his portfolio. We all thought we were lucky to get him. "I mean, I came out here to get away from all that political bullshit killing projects, and here it is all over again."

He took a swallow of beer for emphasis, then looked at me like I might have an answer. I didn't have one, so I grabbed a couple of peanuts out of the bowl in the middle of the table and popped them in my mouth.

"You work for BlackStone, you ain't getting away from the BS," Leon chimed in, to a general round of bitter laughter. "Man, I am so pissed."

I put my hands on the table. "It could be a lot worse," I said. "Nobody's getting laid off, we've got work on a title that's going to make some money, and..." My voice trailed off as I tried to think of a third good thing.

Gordon didn't let me twist in the wind for more than half a minute, which I thought was kind of him. "We're working on a port," he exploded. "Ports suck."

"Ports are easy," I argued back.

"That's because they're shit work," he replied. "We're going to be scaling down next-gen stuff for old-gen consoles, which means it's going to look like crap. Plus, we won't get enough time to do it right because hey, it's just a port."

"They're going for simultaneous release—" I started, but he waved me off.

"Whichever team is doing the lead SKU is going to have bigger problems than getting us assets on time." He sat back in his chair and drank angrily. "And the worst part is, once you get a reputation as a port house, nobody ever looks at you as anything else, ever again. We're screwed."

And here it was, the very thing Eric had mentioned. Gordon was going to jump ship. Whether or not he already had lines in the water was immaterial. It was clear that he'd made up his mind, and was trying to make up everyone else's for them. If his arguments got a foothold, there'd be a stampede out the door. That would leave the folks who stayed short-handed and force us to hire any warm bodies we could find, and that meant the chances of the game being crap would go from 98% to a cool one hundred.

Michelle picked that moment to return, sliding bonelessly into the chair. She shot me a quick look, then planted her elbows on the table and leaned forward. "Come on, Gordon," she said, not taking her eyes off him. "It's not going to be that bad. Right, Ryan?"

The look she gave me this time was fraught with significance. It said, Here is your moment, which I am giving to you. Do with it what you will, but you owe me.

The beer finally arrived—Guinness, of course. I took a sip. "Shelly's right," I said. Gordon snorted in disbelief, but I didn't let him start up again. "Look, losing Blue Lightning sucks. Trust me, it sucks worse for me because I knew about this before you guys did and had to sit there and take it while Eric said he was going to kill my baby." I took another drink, and corrected myself. "Our baby."

There were murmurs of agreement around the table, and I pressed on. "I don't necessarily like the idea of working on a port, either. But if it's going to be a port, at least it's a port of something cool, and something that's going to sell. And when we come through, we're going to be fucking ninjas and we'll write our own ticket."

The words were coming fast and easy now, and they were having an effect. I could see a few heads nodding in agreement, the guys who were looking for a reason to stay. Next to me, Leon was a statue, staring into his beer. Michelle kept her head on her hands, looking everywhere but at me with a tiny half-smile on her lips.

"We're keeping the code base. We're keeping the assets. Blue Lightning is still ours, not theirs. So we do this, we make our cash, and then we flip BS the bird as we sign on with a new publisher and make something that will ensure they piss themselves with envy." I didn't know where the patter was coming from, but it fell into that old rhythm that I knew from a thousand feature meetings, the one that let me take everything everyone had said and weave it into a simple, single vision that everyone recognized as something they'd helped make.

Something they could believe in. Something they could make real.

"Besides, it's going to embarrass the hell out of their internal teams when we do an old-gen version that plays better than their next-gen ones. You know we're better than they are. Give them a head start, give them twice the team, I don't care. We're going to play tighter and better on old-gen because we know our shit, and there's still a lot more people with those consoles than with the next-gen ones. We'll get better scores, we'll sell more, and at the end of the project, we cash the check and give BlackStone a big, fat fuck you."

I took a long drink of Guinness, which under normal circumstances would have been a mistake. Screw it; these circumstances weren't normal. If Eric knew what I was saying, he'd probably have a heart attack—the bill on all this anti-BStone sentiment was going to come due sooner or later—but he'd asked me to get people to rally 'round, and that was exactly what I was doing.

Slowly, across from me, Gordon shook his head. "Believe that if you want," he muttered, but that was all. It was over. The table broke into a dozen small conversations, or at least the people sitting at it did, and I felt the tension leak out of me. Michelle was still sitting there, smiling, which I wasn't sure I liked, but Leon was thumping me on the back like I'd just taken down Apollo Creed without crapping thunder in my shorts.

Since Leon's built like a telephone pole and I'm built like a fire hydrant, this didn't quite result in my spraying Guinness all over the table, but it came close. "Easy, Spartacus," I told him and got a laugh in response.

"Good stuff, man. You know, I was real worried about you at that meeting, but it looks like you're OK. I'm glad you're cool with it."

I took another sip of dark foamy goodness and found to my surprise that I'd nearly emptied the pint glass. "It is what it is. You make the best of what you've got and try not to screw anyone else in the process." I killed the beer and started looking around impatiently for the next one. Someone else patted me on the shoulder and pressed a full glass into my hand. I took a sip, looked around to thank whoever had given it to me, and found they were gone. What the hell, I told myself, and raised it high.

"To Blue Lightning!" I said. "Blue Lightning!" the rest of the room echoed. "She was gonna be beautiful," I said. "And we're gonna miss her."

I called Sarah as another beer arrived and told her that I was still at the bar. She told me to take my time, and then asked me to hand the phone to Leon. I did, and after that, things got a little blurry. Loud, too, but they'd been loud before that. Lots of people being loud, either talking about what had just happened or aggressively not talking about it in a way that said they were still stewing over what had happened. For my part, I just tried to keep everyone laughing. In the end, the noise and the light and the laughter all blurred into one, the wake for the game we'd all slaved on and loved and would never see again.

* * *

I'm reasonably certain I didn't go face-first into a beer. That's because when I woke up, I had marinara sauce on my nose, and that told me I'd gone down into one of the plates of fried cheese sticks instead. Slowly, I wiped it off, and tried to synthesize the sounds I was hearing into something that might or might not be words.

"I'll take him home." Michelle's voice came from someplace far away and to the left, and I tried to turn my head to get a better idea of where it was coming from. After a moment of this, I realized that opening my eyes might help, though the significant effort required might be beyond me at the moment.

Leon, or someone who sounded a lot like him, answered. "You sure? I can take care of it. It might be easier, 'cause I can carry him better."

"I'm OK," I heard myself announce. "Just gimme coffee. Gonna be fine."

"Oh, no, you're not." I knew that tone of voice. "Leon, get his keychain before he tries to do something stupid." I felt fumbling hands go at my jeans pockets and tried to slap them away. "Come on, man. I don' like you like that." Sensibly, Leon ignored me and fished out my keys.

"You're positive," he asked, before dropping them with a jingle into Michelle's outstretched hand.

"Yes," she said. "It's the opposite direction for you, not for me. Just help me get him out to my car and I can take it from there."

"Gotta pay my tab," I protested. "Can' go home 'til I do that,"

"We covered you, Ryan," Michelle said without breaking stride. "And since you can't drink anything else without dying of alcohol poisoning, it's time we cleared out and let the nice people at the bar have some new paying customers."

"I'll pay you back," I promised, my head flopping down and my chin hitting my chest as Leon hoisted me out of my chair. "Hey!"

"Easy, man. Just helping you get out to the car." He slid one arm under my shoulder and wrapped it around me, yanking me up and toward him so that my constant collapse could be translated into forward motion by his direction. We played table slalom as we lurched toward the door, Michelle presumably following, as I didn't see her in my admittedly narrow field of vision. Behind us, I heard the waitress who'd served our end of the table call, "Have a nice evening!" over the clank of glasses.

Evening? Jesus. How long had I been there?

Outside, the sky was dark, or nearly so. As I gaped at the few visible stars, Michelle came around and got her weight under me. "My car's just over there," she said. "Help me dump him in the passenger seat and I'll take care of the rest."

"My car's right there," Leon answered. "Last chance—"

Michelle tensed. "Look, Leon, if you want to say 'Sarah's going to be there,' go ahead and do it, and I'll still say the same thing. I've got no problem with Ryan, or with Sarah. If she's got a problem with me, that's her issue, and if she'd rather Ryan wrapped himself around a tree instead of having me drive him home, then to hell with her." As if to emphasize her point, she dropped her half of the dead weight that was yours truly and headed for where she was parked.

"Michelle, wait. Oh, man, I didn't mean—" Leon's excuses trailed off into muttered under-the-breath frustration, and he followed after her as fast as my limp presence would allow.

She was already in the car, windows down and engine running. "Door's open," she said, not moving to help. "Just open it up and dump him in."

"I didn't mean that, Shelly," he said, propping me against the side of her car as he yanked the passenger side door open. I slid a few inches but stayed mostly vertical. Don't drool on the window, I told myself. Surely you can handle that much. Then Leon was grabbing me again and shoving me inside. A dangling arm was pulled out of the way and thrown into my lap, and then the door slammed shut. "I just don't want you doing a nice thing to become a problem, you know?"

She shot a withering glare past me, one that gentled a bit after a moment. "Silly man. Nice things always become problems. I'll see you tomorrow."

"See you, Shelly," he answered, and then turned and trudged off. We sat for a second. Michelle put it into gear and the crunch of gravel announced that we were leaving. Cool air slapped me in the face as we picked up speed, and I could see my car, tucked into the corner of the lot, as we turned out into traffic.

"The windows are down so you can puke if you want," Michelle said conversationally. "I'm not going to slow down, though, so be careful where you aim."

"Don't need to puke," I answered, and then pressed my gut experimentally with my fingers to test the hypothesis. "Just sleepy."

"Uh-huh." She spared me a glance with all the leftover scorn she'd pulled from Leon. "You need coffee, and a hot shower, and a lot of water, and maybe a B complex vitamin, and then you need to sleep."

"Sorry," I said, and turned my face to the cool plastic of the seat. "Didn' wanna be a bother today."

"Today you're entitled," she said, a little more gently, as she made a left and went around a minivan doing a leisurely cruise in the passing lane. "Tomorrow, God help you, but today, you get a freebie. What Eric pulled on you was a dirty trick."

I shook my head, or tried to. "He's right. Gotta take care of everyone."

"Including Eric," she said. "He just killed your baby. You should have had some time to deal with that before he asked you to play rodeo clown." I got another look, longer and more searching. "You did a great job back there, but I could tell your heart wasn't in it. Blue Lightning was going to be a great game. If you'd called bullshit, a lot of people would have followed you right out the door, you know."

Including you, I thought, but didn't say. We went past trees, past new housing developments with names like "Kirkwood Highlands." past strip malls at a steady rate of one supermarket per. Somewhere in my cerebellum, drunk was fighting a holding action against coherence and losing. "I was being selfish, Michelle. I love Blue Lighting. I love having a job better. And if I walked, Sarah wasn't going to let me get another job in games. She hates me doing it, you know. And I didn't wanna go out the door 'cause I was being an artiste." I tried to bring my hand to my forehead in the time honored "sensitive artist" pose, but just succeeded in slapping myself instead. "Ow," I said, and stared at my traitorous hand.

There was silence for a couple of blocks before she answered me. "You might want to think about who's being selfish there." And then, "Give me your cell phone."

I reached into my pockets to haul it out. "Why?" I asked stupidly.

"To call your girlfriend to let her know you're safe and on your way home. That's why."

"Oh," I said, handing it over. She fumbled with the autodial for a second, then put it to her ear.

"Hello? Sarah? It's Michelle. Yes, I'm on Ryan's phone. He's fine. Just had too much to drink. I'm bringing him home. Leon was headed the other direction, so…no, no, it's no bother. Yeah, there were lots of people there. He just drowned a couple of people's sorrows with one too many. Yeah, I will. Don't worry. I'll give you his keys. Bye now."

She flipped the phone closed and tossed it into my lap. "At least she had the good grace not to ask if you'd gotten wasted over at my place."

I protested. "She's not like that." A pause. "She likes you. She told me."

Michelle laughed, short and sharp and bitter. "Oh, God, Ryan. She may say that. She may even want to think that. But she doesn't and she never will. It doesn't matter that we're ancient history. She'll always worry."

We coasted to a stop at a red light. I recognized the intersection. We were maybe six blocks from home. "Why?"

"You'll figure it out one of these days. And in the meantime, if I do enough stupid things like this, maybe she'll finally unclench her hair." Grinning, she looked over at me. "God, can you imagine if I did take advantage of poor little drunk you? She'd have a heart attack."

My expression must have said volumes, because Shelly just laughed. "Easy there, tiger. I'm not interested."

I slouched back in my seat, a half-dozen responses coming to mind. She doesn't like you because I was a wreck after we broke up, she does like you but thinks you're keeping me in video games when I should be moving on to something else, she wants me to get a better-paying job that doesn't work me so hard—all of these came and went. Instead I just said, "So are you going?"

Michelle shrugged, then took the last right before the turn onto my street. Mini McMansions rolled past, anonymous and identical. "I don't know. My headhunter texted me a couple of times today with some stuff. Word's already out somehow."

"Gordon?" It didn't really matter. All it took was one guy barfing something onto Twitter and word would spread, and then the vultures would start gauging their chances.

"Maybe. Don't know, don't care. We'll see if any of the offers look interesting." She turned left without signaling onto Cordero, my street. The house was three blocks down.

"I'd like it if you stayed," I mumbled, then leaned my face out the window. Maybe I'd been too hasty with my assessment of my gastro-intestinal state.

"That's sweet, Ryan," she said in a low voice. "Thank you."

"Welcome," I muttered thickly. "I'm still pissed off about this whole thing, you know."

I felt, rather than saw, her nod. "I know. That's why I wanted to make sure you came out there today. I figured you could get some of it out of your system. I didn't know then that you'd been co-opted."

"Leon tell you?"

"Leon has a hard time keeping his mouth shut," she agreed. "And he likes you. So if you want to do right by him, figure out how you really feel about this and deal with it. Even if it does mean moving on. Because otherwise, you're just going to drive yourself nuts, and I won't always be there to take you home."

"We'll see," I said, as the car glided up to the curb. The front door was open, and, at the sound of the engine, Sarah came outside to the curb.

Michelle cut the engine. "This is your stop, sailor," she said, and unbuckled my seat belt before getting out of the car. "Sarah? He's fine. His car's at Montague's." My keys dangled from her hand.

Sarah was smiling, mostly. "Thanks for taking care of him, Michelle. I owe you one." She took the keys, even as I fumbled with the door handle and let myself out.

"Sounds good," she said, instead looking back at me as I wobbled to my feet. "Really, though, it's no big deal. Leon would have done it, but like I said, he was headed the other way."

"Leon's a good guy," Sarah agreed, walking past Michelle to where I was taking cautious steps house-wards. "Honey, let's get you inside. You've had a rough day."

"I'm sorry," I said to her. "Was just going to go for a little while and—"

"Shhh," she said, even as we walked past where Michelle stood. "I understand." Small steps, all uphill, carried us toward the door.

"Let's get you some water and some aspirin, and when you feel like it, we can talk about what happened and what happens next."

"Thank you, honey," I said, and felt myself close to tears for some inexplicable reason. "You're good to me."

"Most of the time, you're worth it," she said, but she was smiling. Then we were on the porch and she was opening the door. When I craned my neck back down the hill to thank Michelle, she was gone.

Chapter 7

Much later, we lay in bed, neither of us speaking. I'd been dosed with multiple applications of hot water, cold water, coffee, and stern glances until I'd reached a reasonable approximation of sober, and then poured in between the covers with stern admonitions not to do anything except sleep.

Sleep, of course, proved impossible.

The venetian blinds sliced the streetlight outside into thin, neat strips that ran across the ceiling. Occasionally, a car would go by, its stereo almost loud enough to be heard. After a while, Sarah came to bed, undressing without a word and climbing between the sheets. I'd set Linus, her favorite teddy bear, on her pillow before my last attempt to shut my eyes and force myself to sleep. She held him up for a moment, then gently set him on the floor and lay back, inches from me.

Outside, a neighbor's cat got into it briefly with something or another, One yowl, then another, then that was all she wrote. I found myself hoping the cat was all right, then wondering where the animal's owner was before finally giving up and not caring. Next to me, Sarah's breathing was deep, slow and measured, the sound of someone trying to go to sleep.

Trying. Not succeeding.

"It would have been a good game." I said finally, into the stillness. "It really would have."

"I know, honey." She didn't move. "I know that one meant a lot to you."

I let out a long breath. "You don't understand. It really was going to be good. We had something different. Something really cool."

"I'm sorry," she said. "I really am, Ryan." Then she rolled over, propped herself on one elbow and looked at me. Her hand reached out to take mine and hold it, tight. "I wish it hadn't happened, and I'm sorry if it didn't seem that way."

"No, no. It's not that at all." I raised her hand to my lips and kissed it. "It's just…hell, I wanted to see it. I wanted to play it. All those games I've worked on and there weren't a whole lot I just really wanted to play, you know? They were work, and they were kind of interesting to do, but this was the first time I really felt like we were doing something special. Like I'd finally done something worthy with a design, something memorable and new. And now it's gone."

She didn't say anything for a moment. "Is there any chance…" The words just trailed off, and I let them.

"In theory? Maybe. In reality? No." I laughed, surprised by how bitter it sounded. "By the time Horseshoe's next project wraps up, the tech will be outmoded, or someone else would have thought of it. It's just not going to happen."

"Horseshoe's next project…" she said. "Does that mean it's not going to be your next project?"

"I don't know. I need more time to think."

"How much time?"

"I don't know," I repeated, a little more forcefully. "Jesus, Sarah, it's so tempting to just walk away. Eric laid this guilt trip on me this morning, about how everyone's going to follow my lead, so if I go it's all going to fall down. Like I'd be screwing Leon and the team if I left."

"That's not true, and you know it," Her voice was right by my ear, her body pressed up against mine. "And that's not fair of him. It's not your fault the game got cancelled."

"No. It's those bastards from BlackStone." Pulling my pillow out from behind my head, I gave it a couple of punches. The gesture felt weak and empty, and after a moment, I let the pillow drop. "And now the next project will be with them, so every day the knife gets another little twist."

"So leave. Walk out. You don't have to find another job. You could stay home and write—you could stay home and not write if you wanted to. But I don't want you beating yourself up every day."

I swallowed, surprised at the sudden presence of what felt like a dagger in my throat. "It's not even that," I croaked.

Sarah's hand clenched for a second, then relaxed. "Honey? What is it? Don't tell me you're still thinking about going back." She said it without hope, without judgment, without anything at all.

I nodded, afraid to speak. "Thinking about it."

"Why?"

Something grabbed my guts and twisted them, even as I tried to answer. It was obvious, it was simple, it was impossible to put into words. I opened my mouth and nothing came out.

"Honey?"

I swallowed, closed my eyes, and tried again. "It's hard to explain." A deep breath later, I gave it another shot. "There are people counting on me. If I quit over this, it's going to look bad. It'll look bad to whoever I interview with next, because I cut and ran."

She took her hand from mine and patted my cheek. "Funny, I thought the time in between projects was the best time to switch jobs. And if you're staying home, it won't matter, anyway."

"Yes. No. I don't know. That's not it, okay?" I rubbed my eyes, covering them with my hands. "It would be like I'm being driven off, like I'm taking my toys and going home."

"Maybe you're too big for toys."

I kissed her gently. "Are you saying it's time to be a grown-up?" I asked when we broke apart.

"I could be. Being a grown-up has its benefits." She draped one leg over me. "Just thought I'd mention it." My face rose up to meet hers and we kissed again. My hands found her back and roamed over it, pulling her to me.

And when we broke the kiss, she looked into my eyes, and said, "You're still going back in tomorrow, aren't you?"

I looked away. "Tomorrow? Yes. Beyond that, I don't know. It's what I do, honey. I make games. Without that..."

She sighed and dropped her head to my chest. "I know you love your work, Ryan. I just hate how you have to do it."

"This one's a port. They've already done most of the heavy lifting on the design end so it should be a pretty easy development cycle for me."

Her chuckle was a felt thing, not a heard one. "Oh, come on, love. We go through this on every game. There's always a reason this one's going to be easier, and there's always a crisis and a deadline and a milestone and you're there until two in the morning every night for a month."

"It's not—"

She put a finger to my lips. "It is. Every time. And if this is what you still love and still want to do, I understand, and I won't make you choose between it and me, because I lose that one no matter what. But it's not what I want for the rest of our life together, Ryan, and I keep hoping that you're going to get as tired of it as I am."

It took me a moment to realize that the strange warmth I was feeling were tears, her tears, and that she was shaking. "I'm sorry, Sarah," I said, knowing it was inadequate, knowing I hadn't explained anything at all. "I just can't. Not now. Not yet." I wrapped my arms around her, and buried my face in her shoulder, even as she buried hers in mine.

"I know," she said, and we stayed like that all night, not speaking another word, until morning.

* * *

Breakfast was mostly silent. Sarah offered to drop me off at my car. I thanked her, and then we both concentrated on eating. Last night's words hung heavy in the air between us. At one point, she asked me to pass the orange juice. I did so without comment.

The drive to my car was nearly as quiet. It wasn't until Montague's was visible ahead of us that she turned to me. "Are you going to be home at a reasonable hour tonight?"

I shrugged. "Most likely. If I'm going to be late…"

"…you'll call," she finished. "I hope you won't be," she said a moment later. "It would be nice to have an evening together."

I nodded. "I'd like that." We pulled up at the curb by Montague's. "I'll get out here. No sense making you pull into the lot. It's a minefield."

"OK." She leaned over and gave me a peck on the cheek. "Have a good day, Ryan. And I really am sorry about your game."

I got out. "I know. Love you too." I shut the door and she peeled away, trying to catch the light at the end of the block while I walked across the lot, dodging potholes and puddles. The car was right where I'd left it, which I appreciated. A few bars I'd known would tow vehicles left there overnight, but Montague's would give you until five PM the next day to come get your car. The sole exception was if you just went back into Montague's and started drinking all over again. Then you got an indefinite stay of execution.

Looking in the window, I could see that my laptop bag was still safe and sound on the passenger seat. That was a relief. I'd half-expected it to be gone, courtesy of a broken window. Muttering silent thanks to whoever watches over drunks and their stuff, I climbed in. Plugging my phone into the aux cable took a second—old school hardware, I know, but some habits die hard—and punched up a driving mix. God knew something had to psych me up for going in to the office, and caffeine wasn't going to be able to handle the job on its own.

The first track that came up was some AC/DC, a version of "Thunderstruck" off a live album. Good stuff to start a day with, I decided, enough to get the blood pumping. Slamming my hands on the wheel in time with the beat, I rolled down my window and started howling along with Brian Johnson. Other drivers shot me Significant Looks, which I mostly ignored. Let them get their own AC/DC, I thought.

Three choruses in, the song started skipping. A steady pulse of "THUNDATHUNDATHUNDATHUNDA" hammered at my ears until I hit a red light and was able to pause the damn thing. A skip was bad news—it meant either the file was corrupted or the hardware was, and as "Thunderstruck" had played just fine earlier in the week, the odds were I was looking at a trip to the Apple store.

I clicked through to the next track. Maybe it was just the one song that was corrupted, or the thing was still warming up. The dulcet tones of Mama Young's best boys cut off abruptly, replaced by a random Yes album cut. It lasted maybe thirty seconds before it started sputtering, and I took the opportunity of another red light to stare at the thing in disbelief.

"Oh, no you don't," I told it and clicked through again. It got halfway through the intro before REM's "Driver 8" was choking on itself. "Crap, crap, crap," I said to no one in particular and tried again.

It was an instrumental this time, heavy synth lines with a weird contrapuntal thing going on in the guitar part. It took me a minute to recognize it as one of the sound files we'd commissioned for Blue Lightning. The track was rough—the percussion line was way too over the top, and the main riff wasn't quite there yet—but we'd been talking about this one as the main "alert state" loop, the one that would play every time things started to go to hell for the player. I'd dumped all of the rough music cuts to my iTunes so I could give them a few good listens before sending notes back to the sound studio in New York. I hadn't had the chance to do it more than once, though, and now it didn't seem like there was any point.

Still, the song was catchy, and it wasn't skipping, two points in its favor. I let it go and got into it a little bit as I drove. It was too short to be good driving music—loops like that rarely get over two minutes long, or they don't work for in-game—but it was fun while it lasted. Finally, it faded out in a crash of major-chord synths, and the too-familiar intro to "Baba O'Riley" started in. "Come on," I encouraged it. "Get to the vocals. Just make it to the vocals. You can do it."

Instead, it tripped over the first guitar riff and kept stumbling through it, replaying a half-second of Pete Townshend windmill for as long as I could stand it.

I did a quick location check. Five more minutes to the office. All I needed was one more song to get me back into a good mood, and I'd be able to tackle the day.

I clicked forward on the playlist.

Garbled sounds that could have been something off the new Dave Gahan album.

Click.

A few bars of an acoustic Richard Thompson performance from Newport, jangled up with one another into an impenetrable mess.

Click.

Some Elvis I'd thrown on there as a joke, "Love Me Tender." Only this time, it jumped straight into the middle of the song, letting the King beg "Love me/Love me/Love me/Love me—"

"Sorry, Elvis, you're not my type." Click.

Roxy Music, telling me what lived in every dream home, or at least trying to before their own noise overwhelmed them.

One more, I told myself. One more, and then I'd shut it off. After all, I didn't need music, I just wanted it.

Click.

There was nothing for a moment, then up came a swell of strings with that voice-of-God, O Fortuna chorus chanting over them. I felt a chill run down my spine as the brass came in, jagging along in an unresolved chord while the vocals thundered over it. It felt majestic, like the soundtrack to the end of the world.

Which it had been meant to be. Even as the first chords came up, I realized that what I was listening to was supposed to be the music for the intro cut scene of the game, the quick cinematic sequence that laid out how the world had fallen apart and what you, the player, were expected to do about it. In other words, more Blue Lighting. That made two tracks out of the first ten that the randomizer spat out, an impressive feat considering I had over six thousand songs on there.

Then again, they were both playing when nothing else was, so I didn't feel like complaining too much. Odds were that they were on an uncorrupted segment of the hard drive, and that's why they were fine when other stuff wouldn't do more than burp. That might have explained the frequent plays, too—other sectors just weren't reading as there anymore. It sucked, but it made enough sense to calm whatever paranoia I had, and let me enjoy what music I heard.

Two minutes out, and the song ended. No doubt I was now due for more mangled songlets, if I bothered to listen. Two minutes. I didn't have to listen to anything else for two minutes. For crying out loud, I told myself, I could turn on the radio for two minutes.

Instead, I let it play. No music came out, just some clicking noises, and then those same familiar strings, this time matched to a thudding bass line. This time, I recognized it instantly as the music for the shell user interface, the stuff you'd hear when making your way through the menus.

It was still playing when I drove up to the office. It had ended and started itself again, and I just didn't have the heart to cut it off. Instead, I parked and sat there, listening, until the last notes faded away.

I hit Stop, pulled the cable out of the phone, and stuck it in my pocket. "Well," I announced to myself, "that's two things that are really messed up already today," and headed toward the front door.

Chapter 8

The game company offices you see in movies look like dot-com heaven. Chrome, glass, light, air—they're where the cool kids work, laughing all the way.

Our offices were not like that. They were set in an office park, one floor of fire hazard-filled office space behind a glass door with our logo.

Inside was dim and vaguely warm and not-entirely-good-smelling, the scent you get from too many people sweating too many deadlines in too tight a space. The funk had settled into the building a couple of projects back, gotten itself into the mud-colored carpet and the slightly paler mud-colored walls, and had lurked in there ever since. My office was better, but not much, and not always.

There was a pile of documents on my desk when I got in that morning, which I completely ignored until I'd inhaled a cup of coffee and chowed down a strawberry frosted Pop-Tart.

Only after my blood chemistry had the right mixture of agitated and frosted did I pick up the top page and start reading. It was the vision statement for Salvador, the overview of the game's core boiled down into a bite-sized nugget that could be communicated equally well to the team, to marketing, and to the public. Here, then, was the essence of Salvador, the foundation that everything else would be built upon. This what I was supposed to take, to breathe life into and use to inspire the rest of the team to chain themselves to their desks in order to meet the euphemistically phrased "aggressive schedule" that we'd be getting from BlackStone.

I read it and blinked. The game, which preliminary hype had suggested was going to "reinvent the first-person shooter," had been summed up by its creators as essentially "You shoot people, and they blow up real good."

I closed my eyes, clenched them shut for a minute, then opened them again. No good. The words on the page hadn't changed. Oh, sure, there was some stuff in there about setting ("gritty and urban") and tone ("futuristic"), but mostly it was buzzword central. First-person shooter, strong multiplayer component, microtransaction content, destructible terrain—all the usual suspects lurking in the woodpile for a game that would be technically polished but utterly generic. Run around, shoot aliens, get a bigger gun as a result—it was nothing the average gamer hadn't seen a thousand times before. Oh, sure, it would be pretty. Gorgeous, if the guys in the art department had anything to say about it. But the gameplay would be the same old same old. There was nothing new here, nothing to grab a hold of and say "this is what's going to make this game cool." For all that the pitch hit all the right notes for the suits, it didn't have anything in it for the devs, the guys who'd actually be making it. It was empty. Soulless, even.

I thought about that for a second, then said it out loud. "This game has no soul." The words felt right. Look closely at Salvador, and it was a Frankenstein monster of a design, features ripped out of a dozen other games because they'd sold well, not because they belonged together or said anything new. The vision was a masterpiece of cynicism.

Not like Blue Lightning.

Abruptly, the air conditioner cut out, and the lights fluttered then faded for a moment. I could hear a loud popping sound coming from under my desk as the surge protector failed to do its duty, and then the light on the monitor screen flared white and died. Out in the hallway voices called back and forth, each confirming to the other that it wasn't just them and that we were in fact getting hit with yet another in our regular series of brownouts. Most were just long enough to chow down on unsaved data; a few turned into genuine blackouts. Each time one hit, it was the signal for people to start counting down until the power outage was long enough to justify everyone going home for the day. In the meantime, people went outside, people pulled out their tablets or Magic cards or smartphones, or people stood around and bitched.

For my part, I kept on reading, mainly because there was enough light for me to do so, and waited for the power to come back up.

Five minutes on, the brownout had officially faded to black and people were streaming outside as the heat built up inside. As I swapped the core vision for the feature list, I saw Michelle headed through the door at a fast trot, across the parking lot, and out of view. I could hear laughter drifting faintly back. There were worse things than sitting outside in the sun while on the clock, or at least that's what it sounded like.

With that cheerful thought, I went back to reading. I'd made it six whole bullet points in before someone knocked on the door.

"Hey, Leon," I said without looking up.

He stepped into the office, blinking. "How'd you know it was me?"

I shrugged and kept trolling through the proposed game features. They were really big on wide-scale destructible terrain, the ability of the player to basically cause property damage inside the game world. This was tricky for a whole host of reasons, not the least of which being that characters controlled by the game's artificial intelligence generally weren't very good at dealing with changes to their world. When the world changed, your average AI would make characters walk into large pieces of rubble in best wind-up toy fashion, which rarely made for challenging gameplay. Throw in the ability to clamber over obstacles, which was tucked in a couple of bullet points down, and the game had the potential to be a physics-AI steel-cage-match nightmare. "Michelle's the only other person who'd actually come looking for me right now, and she's already outside. So it was either going to be you or the ghost of Duke Nukem."

"The new Duke Nukem came out last year," he corrected me. "So what are you reading?"

I tried to read another line, then gave it up as a bad job and put the paper down. "Design docs on Salvador. This one's going to be a bear."

Without asking, Leon crossed to my desk and grabbed a sheet of paper at random. "Let me guess—too many features, not enough time, too many external dependencies, and the assets we're getting are crap?" He settled into the much-abused visitors' chair and put his feet up on my desk. "Did I miss anything?"

"I can't vouch for anything except the feature list, which reads like a fanboi's three-legged wet dream."

"Tentacles?" he asked. I threw a wadded up ball of paper at him, which bounced off his shoulder and into the trash can. Stoic to the last, he ignored it, and grabbed another paper from the stack. "Man, you're right. This is a recipe for crunch time goodness, starting tomorrow. Still, if we can pull it off..."

The heat in the room was suddenly oppressive. I was acutely aware of the silence where the clunking sound of the HVAC normally was, the higher-pitched whine of my machine's CPU fan on top of it. The voices of our coworkers were a muted buzz at best. Leon looked at me. "Dude, are you all right? You look kind of pale."

Not trusting my voice to say more than "I'm fine," I nodded. The sweat rolling down my face was oddly warm, and I could feel more of it trickling out of my armpits and down my sides. "Just got hot all of a sudden," I gasped.

"Maybe we ought to go outside." He offered me a hand.

I waved him away. "No, no, I'll be fine. Really. Just need the AC to come back on. And as for the game, I don't know."

Leon blinked. "Don't know what?"

My fingers drummed the stack of documents. "I don't know about it. If we pull it off, it's going to sell, no doubt about that. It's going to have chrome out the yin-yang, assuming we don't start cutting too many features to fit it on an old-gen box or killing ourselves to meet milestones and implementing stuff half-assed."

"But?"

"But there's nothing at the heart of it. It's like someone saw all the cool stuff that other games are doing and said 'We want that and that and some of that,' and never mind actually coming up with a game concept to hang all this crap on. There's a hole in the middle of," and I tapped the doc pile, "this." The words were forcing themselves out, like I had to say them while I still felt brave enough to do so. My head was throbbing, and I found myself wishing for a glass of water.

Leon sat back down heavily. "So you're saying we're screwed."

I shook my head. "No. That's not it at all. Like I said, it's going to sell. It's going to be shiny and pretty and cool, and if we get it out the door it'll sell like crazy for about three, four weeks. But it's missing something. It's missing that thing Blue Lightning had, where all the pieces fit seamlessly because there was a game there, and the features were just aspects of it. This is just...features riding the bus together." I wiped my brow with my forearm. It came away wet, and an instant later I could feel the slow, fat drops of sweat rolling down again. "Blue Lightning might not have sold as well, but it would have been a better game."

The words came out slowly, as if each one had an unseen weight to it. Leon looked disappointed, but even as he opened his mouth to say something, the lights came up and the HVAC thunked into sudden life. From outside, I could hear Eric shouting "Come on, people, back inside!" and the doors opening as people trudged back to their desks.

"You really think that?" Leon asked. I nodded. "I don't know if I'm glad to hear it or not."

"Why would you be?" I reached under my desk and rebooted my system. "I mean, I just told you I don't actually like the project we're going to be killing ourselves over for the next year or so."

He scrunched up his face for a minute before answering. "I guess. But it's nice to know you think we had something good going. Even if it was theoretically your idea."

I grinned at him. "Yeah, well, I can't help it if I'm brilliant." The cold—well, cool—air pouring down from the ceiling vent had me feeling much better in record time. "Now get out of here so I can read these things and you can go do whatever the hell it is you do when you're not ignoring the documentation."

"We're going raiding while we wait for some stuff for the closing kit to compile," he answered, already halfway out the door. "Level 40 on the Argentblade server, if you want to come along."

I waved papers at him. "Some of us have work to do, Leon. Have fun storming the castle. I'll catch you later."

He grunted something at me and was halfway out the door before I realized there was one other thing I wanted to talk to him about. "Hey, Leon!"

He stopped and half-twisted back so that his head was in the doorframe. "What?"

I shoved the dysfunctional iPhone across the desk. It slid past the edge, teetered for a moment, and fell. Halfway to the floor, it landed in Leon's hand. He'd reached back to snag it, which was pretty much what I'd expected he'd do. His long fingers wrapped around it, cradling it for a moment before pulling it in and staring at it. A look of confusion crossed his face. "Dude. It's your phone. What's the deal?"

"It shit the bed when I was coming in this morning. You like messing with that stuff, so I figured you might want to take a look at it. If you can get it running, that would be cool. If not, feel free to salvage it for parts."

Leon's face screwed itself into a frown. "You sure about this? I thought Sarah gave you this one."

I shrugged. "I'll by a new one, same model, if it's fried. No need for her to know."

He shot me a look that suggested that I had just placed myself on the endangered species list. "Whatever, man. I'll see what I can do with it."

"Cool, thanks," I said to his retreating back, and settled in to mount another attempt on the ramparts of documentation in front of me. "Eenie, meenie, miny, ah, the hell with it," I muttered and pulled what looked like a preliminary mission design from the middle of the stack. "Here goes nothing."

I read. I drank coffee. I read some more. I took a few notes, took a leak in order to deal with the coffee, and read a few more docs. The shape of the game became clear to me, the features arranging themselves in neat cascades while the storyline and mission progression hung from them like low-hanging fruit.

A loud banging startled me into dropping a dozen sheets of paper. They fanned out, snowing themselves onto the floor.

I looked up to see Shelly standing there, my phone dangling by an earbud cord off the tip of one of her fingers. Behind her, the sunlight creeping down the hallway was shockingly red. I'd apparently been reading the docs for hours. "This is yours, right?" she asked. "I mean, nobody else in the building has quite the same taste in dinosaur rock that you do."

"Looks like it," I said. "I take it you've been listening to it?"

"Just checked the active playlist," she said, stepping far enough into the office to slap it down on my desk. "Leon said it was yours, but I wanted to make sure. I don't think there's anyone else on the planet, Pete Townshend included, who needs that many versions of 'Eminence Front' in one place."

I started in with "Well, actually the alternate guitar line on the studio outtake version," but the sight of her eyes glazing over brought me up short. "What were you doing with it, anyway?" I asked. "Leon was either going to fix it or cannibalize it for parts."

She fixed me with a disdainful glare. "Leon gave it back to me to give to you because he had to take off; and for the record, he said there was nothing wrong with it, other than a few unlabeled tracks that you'll probably want to generate song data for. It's fine, and you're crazy. At least, that's what he told me to tell you." She gave me a tight little smile. "He said I could get creative telling you that, too."

I picked it up gingerly and looked at it. "It wasn't fine in the car this morning."

"Then maybe your car sucks," she said sweetly. "Not my problem anymore."

She cocked her head to one side. "And you should be going home. It's getting on seven."

I blinked. "It is? How the hell did that happen? I was just sitting here reading docs—"

"And you've read about two hundred pages' worth. That's a decent day's work, Ryan. Go home." Without waiting to see if I was going to follow her advice, she left.

Leaving me still at my desk, behind a now-broken wall of papers and looking suspiciously down at piece of hardware that had decided to play it coy. "Let's see what you've got," I told it, and hit play.

From the earbuds, I could hear a tinny, distant rendition of the last good song The Who ever wrote. It played clean, all the way through.

"Huh," I said, and stuck it in my pocket. It was still playing when I turned out the lights and shut the door, and for all I cared, it could play all night long.

Chapter 9

Naked and lovely, Sarah said to me, "I think dinner's gotten cold."

"I am willing to accept those consequences," I said contentedly, and snuggled her against my chest. We'd made only the barest of starts on supper before making our way upstairs, and had wreaked absolute havoc on our bed sheets and the neatly stacked laundry thereupon. Now the tasteful cream-colored carpet was covered in untastefully strewn colors and whites, and the sheets dangled off one corner of the bedframe.

I stroked Sarah's hair a couple of times and was rewarded with a contented purr. Linus sat on the corner of the bed, faced deliberately away from us; I snagged him and tucked him into Sarah's arms. She purred again and snuggled into me. "That was nice," she said. I nodded and kissed the top of her head.

"We should do that more often."

"Start getting home earlier and we just might."

"I'm going to try," I said, not trusting myself not to turn this into another debate. "But I'm here right now."

Sarah yawned. "I know. And it's wonderful." She yawned again, theatrically this time, with a sound like a lioness settling in to watch her cubs. "I hear you nearly threw away one of my presents today."

"I did?" I thought for a minute. "Oh, the phone? I wasn't throwing it away, I was going to let Leon have it if it was broken."

"That's generous of you," She poked me in the ribs. "And when were you going to explain to me that you'd broken something I'd given to you?"

I grinned. "I was going to buy another one just like it and never tell you, that's how. I liked it a lot and didn't want you thinking you'd gotten me something that wasn't good."

"That's sweet," she said, sleep dulling the edge of her words. "I got an email from Leon about it, you know. He didn't want to play with it without asking if I was OK with it. Are all your friends afraid of me?"

"Only the smart ones," I said, chuckling. "Leon, on the other hand..."

"Mmm," Sarah said, and then she was asleep, snoring softly against my chest. My left arm was pinned underneath her, no doubt priming itself for the moment when it would fall asleep, but I'd deal with that when it came. For the moment, I had her, and she had me, and work was far away.

I decided that it, like the dishes, could keep until morning.

* * *

Six chairs around the table in the conference room, two people in them. Eric was at one end, hunched up in the "daddy" seat. His back was to the far wall, framing him against one of the whiteboards. They rarely ever got cleaned, so there was a faint halo of old dry-erase marker squiggles all around him.

"You look like a *Peanuts* character." I said, looking up from my laptop. I was on the near side of the table but not at the end. That would have put my back to the door. Sarah called that sort of thing bad feng shui, and so did I when she was around. The rest of the time, I just hated having my back to the door.

"Pigpen," he answered, filling in the missing name and leaning back. "So who does that make you? Sally? Charlie Brown?"

"BlackStone already yanked the football out from under me," I pointed out. "And I'd go for Snoopy, but Sarah would probably think that was weird."

"Heh." He kicked the underside of the table once, twice, a third time, and rubbed his eyes. "So what's the deal, Ryan? Are you in?"

"In?"

"In." He cracked a couple of knuckles, not the complete set. "I got a call from Sarah this morning, you know."

"Oh did you," I could feel my stomach sinking. "What did she want?"

Eric gave me a weak grin. "She wanted to know if I was going to work you to death on this one, or if she had to go public like EASpouse did a couple of years ago."

I cracked a smile I didn't feel. "She's not shy, is she?"

"No, and she's not stupid, either. She also told me that you're thinking about quitting. Something about writing full time, or at least until you get bored and get ready for a real job."

"That was supposed to stay between me and her," I said softly. "She shouldn't have brought you into it."

"No, she shouldn't have," he agreed. "But now she has. And what are you going to do about it?"

I looked at him, licking my suddenly dry lips. "I've given this a lot of thought," I said. "A lot of thought. I thought about what you said, and about the company. I thought about what I actually want to do. And I decided, God help me, that I'm in."

"Thank you," he said. His arms dropped off the sides of his chairs like all the bones in them had just gone on coffee break, and I suddenly realized how nervous he'd been about the whole thing. "We're going to make this work," he said, as much a prayer as a statement of purpose. "We'll give everyone but the leads a couple more days to shake it out of their systems, but in the meantime, you and I lay the groundwork for hitting the ground running next week. Once people are working again instead of chasing their tails, we'll be just fine."

I nodded. "I don't see what choice we have," I said, and I meant it. Either we moved on this, or we'd die, and I'd just bet...what? My job? My career in gaming? My relationship? I wasn't sure, but I was reasonably certain I'd bet something on this project, and this company.

There was a pile of docs in front of me, the edited highlights of the stuff I'd read yesterday. I tapped it with one finger. "I can give a debrief on what we're dealing with here if you want to get the ball rolling."

He shrugged. "Save it for when we get the leads in here."

A sip of coffee went down with moderate success. "And when might that be?"

Eric made a big show of looking at his watch. "About ten minutes. You might want to go pee or something before this one starts."

I blinked at him. "You scheduled that without knowing if I was walking?"

He shrugged. "I scheduled it. If you'd walked, it would have been to discuss finding a new CD. Instead, you get to tell everyone about Salvador, and what cool and exciting features we're going to get to try to cram into a last-gen box."

More coffee. "Well, that starts with you and the financials. But I can walk them through the design, maybe point out where the trouble spots are."

Eric nodded and stood. "Good. I'll let you handle that, then. I'm going to go start shaking trees to see if I can line us up something for when this particular sleigh ride comes to an end."

I looked at him and shook my head. "That whole tree-sleigh ride thing is way too Ethan Frome for me."

"Ethan Frome?"

"Jesus, Eric, didn't they make you read that in high school? One of the great American classics, by virtue of the fact that it's depressing and it's short."

He pursed his lips. "Sounds like my kind of book. Now what does it have to do with our project? Or is that a crack on the length of the dev cycle we've got to work with."

"Nope. Just that there's a sleigh ride in that one, too."

"What happens?"

"They wrap themselves around a tree, and everyone's crippled for life."

"Heh. Sounds perfect." He grinned, a little bit, and started toward the door. "Just one question," I added. He turned to me.

"Yes?"

"Who are the leads on this one?"

He smiled, or at least the lower half of his face did. "We're rotating. The art and engineering leads on BL were both in my office this morning, telling me they'd rather eat their own testicles than be leads on this one."

"Charming," I grimaced. "Distaste for the project?"

"Burnout. They pretty much said the same thing, which was they'd rather be doing work than schedules and meetings."

"Lucky them." I shrugged. "So you're dropping a couple of new suckers into the barrel. Who are they, and do they know they have to deal with the deadly combination of you as producer and me as lead designer?"

"Leon and Shelly are probably aware of that, yes."

I stared at Eric, my mouth hanging open. "Leon and Shelly?"

"What? You don't think they're qualified?" The bastard was actually smirking at me now, just waiting to see how I could dig myself in deeper.

"No! I mean, of course they're qualified, but the three of us? Me and Michelle? Do you really think that's a good idea?"

"Actually, I kind of do." Eric said. He sagged forward over a chair, elbows and forearms flat on the table. "I figure you need as much of a comfort zone on this one as any of us, maybe more. And since the heavy lifting on this one's been done, I can give it to you. It's not like they're not qualified."

"No," I said, shaking my head. "It's not that. And I'd better not get too much of a comfort zone with Shelly or Sarah's going to kill me."

"No fishing off the company pier, especially with ones you already threw back." He said it with grim humor. "So it's settled, and you can give me a debrief after you talk with your leads. Anything else, or can I go chase the almighty dollar?"

"Chase Euros instead," I told him. "And could you please give me a little more warning about stuff like that next time? Pretty please?"

"Since you asked so nicely, I'll think about it." He moved to the door. "And go sit at the head of the table. You're leading the meeting." A moment later, he was gone.

I purposefully did not watch him go, choosing instead to riffle through the papers for the overview doc I'd written up. I'd intended it for Eric's eyes as a basic assessment as to the geography of the world of hurt we were in for, but it could serve as crib notes for a briefing as well. Where to start? Well, with an overview, I thought, and then a rundown of the features that we were going to have to either cut, gut, or redo in order to cram a next-gen title onto an old-gen box. That's where the real fun was going to come in, a roll call of doomed features that we'd have to ruthlessly execute in order to get the game out on time and on spec. Then there was the stuff the hardware just wouldn't support, stuff we were going to have to rip out and rebuild from scratch—the entire multiplayer interface, for one. Even better, buried deep within the docs had been the hint of some additional feature requests that BlackStone clearly planned to hit us with at the least convenient time possible. Put them all together, line them up and call them out, and I might have a halfway-decent look at what we were looking at going forward on Salvador.

All of which kept me nicely preoccupied from thinking about how I felt over what Sarah had done.

A hard thump on the back of my chair jerked me back into the real world, or at least the board room. I looked up to see that it was Michelle. She'd elbowed my seat on the way toward taking the chair at the head of the table.

"Wait a minute," I said. "I'm supposed to be over there."

"Were," she said sweetly. "You were supposed to be over here. But you aren't. And I am." And with that, she dropped neatly into the seat and put her feet up on the table. I stared at her, and she stared back. "What, is this a penis-only chair?"

I cringed. "Look, Shelly, I know it's a fairly casual work environment and all, but all things considered, I'm not sure it's a great idea for the word 'penis' to come up in any conversation we have."

"Because she's seen yours?" Leon ambled in and took the chair opposite me. "I mean, I knew this was a small project, but—"

I made rimshot noises while miming a cymbal crash. "Can we get started, or is there anything else you want to share with the class?"

"I got nothing," he replied and took a pen out from behind his ear.

"Him too." Shelly slid a notepad across the table to him, saving one for herself and none for me. "Is Eric going to be joining us?"

"Not unless you start throwing things," I told her. "Something about running the studio in the meantime. Don't worry, though. I'll give him the full debrief. That is, if we can actually get this thing off the ground."

Leon started to say something half-witty about my briefs, but Michelle shushed him. "Okay, point made. What do we have?"

And I told them, in agonizing detail. Without a build, it was impossible to be sure, but most likely we were in for a tough, tight development cycle. The entire multiplayer system would have to be redone, including most likely the networking code and the UI. Textures would have to be downsampled. Objects would need their polygon counts slashed, and not in a way that could be done programmatically. The number of enemies onscreen would have to be drastically reduced or else the game would slow to a zoetrope-level frame-rate flicker. And on and on and on it went, with Leon and Shelly asking questions every so often. Most of them I could only answer with "I don't know" or "We'll have to wait for the build." The ones where I had more concrete information didn't make them much happier.

Eventually, I wound down. Leon looked at Michelle, eyebrows raised with an unspoken question. She spoke it. "Is that it?"

I nodded. "Yup. Doable, but a bastard, I think. There's going to have to be some crunch."

She nodded distractedly. "It would be a lot easier if we didn't have to touch every single object."

"But you do. And the schmucks at BlackStone's main studio never document their code, so my guys are going to be flying blind once they get in there." Leon sounded like he was in the process of crapping out a sea urchin, one of the really big ones. He looked up at me. "Any chance of getting a couple of their engineers out here to help us?"

"You'll have to ask Eric." I shrugged. "I'd hope so, but you never know. Don't count on it so you can be pleasantly surprised?"

"Heh." He scooped up his notepad and riffed through it, then stood up. "If that's all, I'm gonna go break the bad news to the engineering team. You kids play nice, you hear me?"

Michelle grabbed a dry-erase marker from the board behind her and whipped it at his head. He ducked, and the marker hit the wall cap-first, sending shards of splintered plastic everywhere. "We lose more markers that way," Leon said in a mock-mournful voice, then ducked out.

Michelle stood as the door swung closed behind Leon. It hit the frame with a solid thump, followed by the click of the latch dropping into place.

Michelle frowned. "That was weird."

"What was?" I found myself looking back and forth between her and the door, and mostly seeing a lot of the space in between. "Leon making a joke? I mean, OK, it was kind of funny, which is unusual for him, but—"

She threw another marker, but more softly. It hit my arm and cartwheeled off to the floor. "Ow," I said. "What was that for?"

"To shut you up," she said. "Not that it's doing any good." She walked around to stand by the doorway, thankfully out of reach of any more felt-tipped ammunition. "Leon didn't close the door."

I rubbed my arm and rolled my eyes, more or less simultaneously. "Is that it? Come on, it was air pressure or something. Someone opens the front door and half the doors in this place slam, the ones that aren't blocked by someone's action-figure collection."

Michelle gave me a long, slow look of the sort that used to mean that I'd forgotten a dinner date and which now meant that she was glad I was someone else's problem. "That's something you're going to have to work on if we're going to make it through this project in one piece."

"What, my understanding of the laws of physics?" I gave her my best smile.

She wasn't impressed. "No. Your having an answer for everything. If we're going to make this work, Ryan, then you're going to have to get better at listening.

I bent down to pick up the fallen marker, as much to hide my annoyance as to buy time to think of a response. It had rolled away, and only the sight of the blue cap sticking out from under my chair gave the slightest hint as to where it was. "It'll be fine, Michelle," I said, in between grunts as I fumbled for it. "Most of the hard decisions will be made for us by the hardware or BS. The real thing I'm worried about is the time this is going to take."

"Idiot," she said, with only a vague hint of affection, and walked around my chair. She knelt down in front of me, grabbed the marker, and placed it in my hand. "You're really worried about all those long nights we're going to be spending in the office and how Sarah's going to take it."

I shook my head, even as my fingers closed around what she'd given me. "Sarah and I have other things to talk about right now."

"Arguing over rings?" she asked, then saw my face. "Oh. Oh, I'm sorry, Ryan. What's wrong."

"Nothing," I muttered. "She's not real thrilled with my decision to stay on."

"Ah." There was a pause, and then, "Is that it?"

"She offered to support me if I wanted to just stay home and write, or carve duck decoys, or whatever." The words came out unaccountably bitter.

"And you said no." Shelly's voice sounded odd now, slightly fuzzy, as if she were congested or sniffling.

I nodded. "Because I wanted to feel like I was pulling my weight. Because I didn't want to let everyone down by quitting. Because…"

"Because you love what you do." There was a ring of finality there, and a ring of truth. "And because you believe in what you did."

"Yeah," I said, and stood. "I guess I do. Or did. Blue Lightning really felt special, like something had reached down and given me just that little bit of inspiration that makes a game magic. Like I'd finally done what I was meant to be doing, what all those years and other projects had led up to. That I'd, I dunno, I'd found my calling."

Abruptly, the ridiculousness of what I'd said hit me, and the air went out of me all at once. "Or whatever. Thanks for listening, Shelly. Though honestly, I have no idea why I'm talking to you, of all people about this. Still, I appreciate it."

I turned my chair around to face her, and to finish thanking her.

She smiled, put her finger to her lips, and walked out the door.

Chapter 10

My first reaction was to call Sarah and ask her what the hell she thought she was doing, trying to leverage Eric like that. The decision, when I made it, was mine, and I had no idea what she thought she'd accomplish by trying to apply pressure. It wasn't going to provoke Eric to fire me, though it might nudge him toward treating me a little "better" and thus make it even less likely that I would walk. None of it made any sense, and Sarah not making sense didn't make any sense.

It added up to "don't call." Instead, I decided to take a walk outside to see if I could work off some steam before I blew up at someone who didn't deserve it.

Slipping out the back door, I stepped into what was jokingly called "the smokers' lounge." Smoking was prohibited inside the building, of course, and Eric strongly discouraged it out front where guests, visitors, prospective hires or anyone else might see it. That left the area outside the back door from the lunchroom, which opened up onto a tiny, vaguely paved chunk of parking lot that only got used for desperation overflow. Small cells of smokers were scattered here and there, some on the sidewalk under the vague overhang that provided a little protection from the elements, some scattered more widely on the asphalt itself.

Everyone looked up when the door opened, sized up who was coming out, and then went back to their conversations. A small knot in one of the parking spaces edged a few steps further back, as if to keep themselves from being overheard. I recognized Terry as one of them.

"Hey, Terry." I wandered over in his direction. He didn't look thrilled to see me, but he didn't turn his back on me entirely, either.

"Hey," he said. The others with him—a couple of artists whose names I couldn't remember, a networking engineer named Larry, and one of the QA temps—kept their heads down or nodded. None of them looked at me or said anything.

There was a moment of awkward silence, and then another one, and a third before Terry shuffled his feet and reached into his pocket for a pack of American Spirits. "You smoking now, Ryan?"

"Naah," I replied. "But the air out here is cleaner than it is in there, if you know what I mean."

That got a chuckle from a couple of them, and Larry started grinning. "Bullshit's too thick for you, man?"

I nodded. "Something like that, yeah. Thick enough to spread like peanut butter." That got another laugh, and a half-smile from Terry. "So what are you guys doing out here?"

Terry waved a half-smoked cigarette. "Smoking. And talking. And waiting."

"For something to compile?"

He shook his head no. "Waiting for a few things and a few people to come around, if you know what I mean."

"I'm not sure I do."

The group started to break up then, people looking at each other and then at me and muttering darkly the whole time. "I told you this was bullshit," Larry said, and one of the artists agreed with him, and then it was just me and Terry. He looked at me, took a drag on his cigarette, and then deliberately spat right between my feet. "She said you'd come around, sooner or later," he said. "Looks like it's later."

"She said? Who said? Sarah? Shelly? Come on, Terry. Work with me for a minute, OK?" But he just looked at me and shook his head, then shuffled off like the smoke had knotted his lips to silence.

I thought about going after him, but by this point half the smokers out there were watching our little tableau, and I didn't want to run the risk of having things escalate in front of a couple of dozen of witnesses, any number of whom were no doubt holding phones with 4+ Megapixel camera capability.

Instead, I squared my shoulders and stomped off around the building widdershins, hoping that anyone I ran into would at least make a little goddamned sense.

Walking was supposed to work off some of my burn, so of course I got the exact opposite effect instead. As I trudged past the just-planted holly bushes and artistically spread mulch that lined the parking lot, I could feel myself getting steadily more steamed. What the hell had Sarah been thinking? What was Michelle pulling with her disappearing act? Why was Terry going all spooky, and why wouldn't any of these people leave me the hell alone to do my job? Speaking of which, why hadn't Eric—

"Hey."

I stopped and looked up. Leon stood there, a little winded, small half-moons of sweat under his pits. He'd had to run to catch up with me, or so it seemed. He was breathing hard, and his hair was a mess.

"Hey Leon," I said, and started walking again. He stood still for a moment, startled, and then scurried to catch up.

"I'm glad I caught you, man. Shelly says she heard you're quitting. WTF?" A car with a handful of junior designers in it zipped past on its way out to something lunch-like, the occupants waving. I waved back.

"Not true," I said and sped up a little. Leon rolled his eyes, and panted a little harder catching up. "Let me guess—Shelly heard it from Sarah?"

He blinked, or maybe that was just a way of getting sweat out of his eyes. "How'd you know?"

"Because Sarah has apparently been telling everyone that I'm quitting, God knows why, and the fact that she's now calling my ex-girlfriends to tell them is really chapping my ass."

"So you're not quitting?" Leon's voice was suddenly hopeful. I stopped, turned, and stared at him.

"I don't know, OK? Maybe I am and maybe I'm not, but right now, all I do know is that my girlfriend informing everyone that I am quitting is making me want to stay more than ever, because I'll be damned if I let her paint me into a corner by telling everyone in the world what I'm supposed to be doing. All right? You happy? You got your answer? I don't goddamned know!"

He took a couple of steps back, and put up his hands like he was trying to talk down a jumper from a high window. "Easy there, Captain Caveman. Just chill out, OK? And maybe once you stop shooting blood out your eyeballs, you can call Sarah and, I dunno, maybe ask her to cut it out? Instead of going apeshit all over me, you know? Geez."

I took a deep breath. "I'm sorry, man. I'm just a little freaked out."

He looked at me for a moment, then shook his head. "It's OK. Just think decaf thoughts for a while or something, you know? I don't need you wigging out on me, and you don't want to be freaking when you talk to Sarah."

Somehow, I found myself staring at my shoes. "You're right. I should call her. She wouldn't do something like this."

"Now you're getting it." He started to shuffle off. "I'll be out front," he said. "Lemme know if you need to talk after, OK?"

"Will do. Thanks, Leon."

"No worries. I just don't want to have to break in a new CD. Took three years just to get you housebroken." We both laughed, then he headed off and I pulled my phone out of my pocket. There was a long moment of staring at the screen before I punched in Sarah's number.

It rang twice before Sarah picked it up. "Ryan?" she said. She didn't sound happy.

"Sarah? What's wrong?"

"I don't know. Why don't you tell me? After all, you're the one who just called to say you and Michelle would have to be working late tonight."

I caught myself gawping and yanked my jaw shut through sheer force of will. "What? That's impossible. I didn't call you. I've been in meetings all day!"

"You called," she insisted. "And if that's what you've got to do, Ryan, fine, I understand, but that's really kind of a crappy thing to pull on me today, and—"

"I didn't call!" It came out louder than I expected, and harsher. "I swear, honey, I didn't. I was actually calling now because Eric said you called him—"

"Eric? Why would I call Eric?" There was shock in her voice now, and suspicion.

Deep breath in, deep breath out. "Eric said that you called him and that the two of you talked about your offer to me. Later on, Shelly told Leon that you'd called her..." I waited for the explosion, and when none came, I continued. "And that you'd told her I was quitting."

"That's ridiculous!" Some more choice invective followed, and I had to pull the phone away from my ear until the volume finally tailed off.

"Look, honey, I'm sorry. I have no idea what happened here. I just wanted to call you to make sure that it hadn't been you. You know, just to be a hundred percent."

There was a sharp intake of breath. "So you're not working late with Michelle?"

"No, honey. We're on the same project, but nobody's working late tonight, I promise."

"Then who called?"

"I don't know. I was hoping you did." I looked up, looked around. There was no one else on that side of the lot. Leon had already vanished back toward the building. It was just me and the phone out in the middle of the asphalt pancake, but even so, I couldn't shake the feeling that this private conversation was somehow on display, that someone was listening in and judging what was said.

But there was no one, and I put the phone back to my ear.

"Maybe we should talk about this when we get home," I offered.

"No, Ryan. I want to know what's going on here, and I want to figure it out before any other mysterious phone calls get made." Sarah's voice was resolute, her tone dropping rapidly from heated anger to frosty suspicion.

I sighed. "I don't know. Eric told me you called him. Leon said Shelly said you called her. Both of them told me you'd said things that, well, that I wasn't too happy about. And—"

"Why would I call either of those two?" There was a muffled thump, and then, more quietly "No, I'm fine. Just some personal stuff. I'll be in the board room in a minute." There was another second's pause, and then she was back, swearing softly under her breath.

"Sarah? Listen, if you've got to go…"

"I've got a meeting in about two minutes, Ryan, but let me make this clear. I did not call Eric, and I most certainly did not call Shelly. He's responsible for your insane work schedule, and she hurt the man I love. I've got no love and little respect for either of them, and I most definitely would not discuss our future with either of them. The fact that you even thought I might do something like that hurts me, Ryan. You know me better than that."

A jolt of pain startled me, along with an unpleasant taste in my mouth, and I realized I'd been biting my lip hard enough to draw blood. There were two things I could do here. I could apologize. Sarah was right; the woman I knew and loved was most certainly not the sort to pull that sort of junior high trick, and to have thought that she might was unworthy.

The other was what I said next. "You're right, honey. And by the same token, don't you think I deserve a little benefit of the doubt here? Why would I call you to tell you I'd be working late tonight or working with Michelle? We're just getting started. You know that. There's no need to stay late."

There was wordless silence on the line, intercut with the sound of too-ragged breathing. "You deserve...some of the benefit of the doubt, Ryan. You've made calls like that too many times before."

"Not this time," I said. "And I don't want to keep making them."

"That's good to hear." She let out a long, shuddery breath. "I'm sorry too, Ryan. It's like that's what I was afraid I was going hear when I picked up the call, and it sounded like you..."

"Maybe an old voicemail stuck in the system. I don't know, honey. And I don't know who could have called, pretending to be you. But I'll find out."

"If you can. If not, well, just go set everyone straight, okay?" She was all the way back now, 100% in control. There was steel in her voice, and a little edge of anger on top of this. "If they're trying to get rid of you, fine. But they don't get to drag my name into this. Not for a second. And they don't get to do this to us."

"I know," I said. "I know." And then, "I love you."

"I love you, too. Have a nice day not quitting." Then she cut the call, and there was silence.

I stared at the phone for a second, then flipped through my "Dialed Calls" menu. And there it was, the evidence in its LCD glory, a record of a five-minute phone call to Sarah's work line. No doubt her phone would have displayed the incoming number; no doubt she would have taken it as evidence the call was genuine. And I had no doubt, now, that Shelly and Eric's phones would show perfectly legit calls from a number that could be traced back to Sarah.

All of which meant that someone had somehow cracked our phones and was spoofing from them, sending calls and attaching our numbers. They'd chosen those calls to make, and they'd known just what to say to set both of us off. I thought back to that sensation of being watched during the phone call and wondered if instead it had been a sense of being listened to.

Either way, I wasn't happy, and I didn't want to deal with something like this again. Pulling my phone from its protective case, I dropped it to the ground. It hit, bounced once, and landed with a plasticky crack. Before I could think better of it, I brought my foot down on it and ground it into the asphalt—left, right, left again—until it was an unrecognizable smear of electronics and glass. It took me a minute to pick the smartchip out of the mess, but I did and tucked it into my pocket.

"Dude!"

I looked up. Leon had come back out into the lot and was gaping at me like my head had turned purple. "What?" I asked, in the most reasonable tone I could manage.

"Why...?" He choked to a stop, waited a minute, and then tried again. "Why did you do that?"

I shrugged. "Someone is playing games."

"Well, duh," he said and fell into line next to me as I started walking again. "I mean, that's what we do, right?"

I shook my head. "Not like this," I said. "Someone's playing games with me."

* * *

It was July before everything shook itself out, or at least felt like it had. The question of whether I would be quitting Horseshoe died a lingering death from attrition, as evidenced by the fact that I kept going to the office. Sarah's new job took more and more of her time and attention, for which I was thankful—it kept the pressure off the fact that I was once again falling into old habits of working late. The game itself was progressing reasonably well, as we lifted assets bodily out of one build and slammed them into another, making the necessary changes, cuts, and adjustments along the way. By the middle of the month, the build was working well enough to playtest, which the team did, dutifully if not always enthusiastically. Michelle and Leon and I formed a solid, efficient working triad, with Leon keeping a lot of the same hours I did.

I noticed after a while that Michelle had started keeping those same hours, too.

The incidents of high strangeness seemed to have faded. A new cell phone was put to work, and it mostly behaved itself. No more spoofed phone calls, but I never was able to figure out who'd made them in the first place, or why they'd stopped. And the Blue Lightning soundtrack cuts stayed off the playlist from that point forward.

"Maybe it's God telling you something," Leon said when I brought it up for the four hundredth time. "You know, like, maybe it's a sign you and Sarah need to work on your communication issues."

"Oh, shit, that reminds me!" And I dug out my new phone and texted Sarah to tell her that'd I'd probably be running late that night, though not with Michelle.

Mysterious brownouts continued to plague the building, resulting in some truly classic shouting matches between our IT maven Dennis and the head of our landlord's maintenance crew over whose fault it was.

Life went on. Work went on. Things continued in the directions they had already been traveling in, and I never felt inclined to change course. There never seemed to be a need.

* * *

There had been almost seven minutes of silence before I realized that I'd had come to the end of the queued-up playlist, and iTunes was patiently waiting for me to select something else. Not wanting to get started on anything that would drag me under for an hour—or to get another lecture from Dennis about sucking up bandwidth by switching over to Spotify—I popped the buds out of my ears instead and stood up. The usual popping noises ensued—knees, lower back, neck, in that order. For the thousandth time, I reminded myself that sooner or later I'd have to take advantage of our wonderful medical benefits to go see a chiropractor. One of these days when I had a little time, I told myself, and then gave it up, because that line of reasoning led nowhere. It had taken me six months to replace my glasses after I lost a pair on a business trip, as Sarah never failed to remind me, simply because I couldn't find (or make) the time to schedule the appointment.

The speaker on my desktop phone buzzed, the red indicator light flashing, and I nearly jumped out of my skin. "Jesus," I said to myself. "Calm down, dumbass." My finger hovered over the phone for a moment as I tried to remember which button turned on the speakerphone, then I pressed my best guess. To my right, I could see my screensaver kick in, the monitor fading to black.

"Ryan here," I said. "What's up?"

"Yo, man," a staticky voice called over the phone's speaker. "We're setting up a server for Happy Fun Time. You in?"

Happy Fun Time was in-office slang for multiplayer testing. Everyone who could spare the time would log in to the latest build for some therapeutic annihilation of their coworkers while simultaneously performing a gut check on the status of the game. QA was all well and good for telling you if there was a hole in level geometry, but Happy Fun Time was where you went when you were looking to see how the game actually played.

"CTF or Deathmatch, Leon," I said to the air in the phone's general vicinity. There was a crackly moment of near silence while I waited for the answer. I could hear Pink Floyd playing faintly in the background. Someone in the Engineering room was always playing Pink Floyd.

"Deathmatch," he said finally. "We've got ten, no, twelve people already in. Some of them might even suck worse than you do." In the background, I could hear a general buzz of laughter. "And we're using yesterday's build. You should have it already, if you're doing your job in that fancy office of yours."

"Yesterday's?"

"Yeah. Dennis said there was some kind of hiccup with the database and the build wouldn't compile today, so we're using yesterday's. Are you cool with that?"

"Cool, but not in," I said to the phone. "Maybe next time."

"Aww, come on. We need the numbers, man. Networking wants to beat on the join-on-the fly stuff for a while, and we need bodies."

"The networking engineers want to see if they can rack up more kills than usual," I told him. "You've got plenty of pigeons without me."

"Pussy," Leon said and broke the connection. The laughter and trash-talk had already started at the back of the building, typical evidence of Happy Fun Time.

"What the hell," I mumbled and headed back to the team room. If I wasn't going to play, I could at least watch. An observer mode that would allow you to watch the action like it was a football game was planned, but not implemented yet, so if I wanted to see any of the on-screen play I needed to do it the old-fashioned way: go stand behind someone's monitor and heckle.

The room was in full swing when I got there, smack talk going back and forth freely. A couple of the guys were using headsets, the rest just yelling a mishmash of positions, expletives, and on-the-fly tactical decisions. Everyone had debug kits on their desks, long controller cords snaking out of them. A lucky few, Leon included, had wireless controllers and guarded them jealously against theft and confiscation.

There were nods as I went past various players, headed for Leon, but nothing more—take your eyes off the screen and you were asking to be sniped. In the complicated calculus of multiplayer bragging rights, a long-distance headshot was worth more than just about anything other than an execution-style kill, and with competent players those were rarer than rubies.

Leon sat at the back, in the corner near a window. It was privilege, proof of seniority and skill. The more time you put in, the more say you had in where you sat, and Leon had put in a lot of time. His desk was angled so that his monitors were arranged away from the rest of the room. You could only see what was on them by standing directly behind him or by going outside and looking through the window. What that said was that management trusted Leon not to screw around and get his work done, a rare and rarified privilege in a team room environment.

"Hey, lamer," he said as I sidled in behind him. "What brings you down here?"

"I wanted to watch you get pwned," I said. "How's it looking?"

He shrugged. "Second pass textures are in, but there's something messed up with the particle emitters. All the explosions are purple."

"It's not a bug, it's a feature," I repeated automatically, and we both chuckled. "Gameplay holding up?"

He made a noise in the back of his throat, and not a happy one. "Enh. This map needs some serious rework. You can camp three of the spawn points, and there are a couple of bottlenecks where the whole thing just turns into a turkey shoot. See?"

He gestured toward the screen. I leaned in over his shoulder and looked.

The space in question was a vaguely futuristic ruined city, appropriate for the near-future sci-fi feel of the game we were putting together. Wrecked cars, empty streets and damaged buildings made up most of the landscape, a scene painted in grey and black and brown. The only flashes of color came from the bursts of weapon fire, mostly green and blue, as players moved back and forth, guns blazing. Here and there were pure white patches, indicators for missing textures that peeled away the illusion of the world and showed the naked geometry beneath.

"What am I supposed to be looking at, Leon?" My glasses slipped a fraction of an inch down my nose, and I shoved them back into place. "Is there a topdown view?"

"Hang on one moment," he twitched the left thumbstick on his controller. The onscreen view spun left, the gun in the middle of the screen barked, and an armored and armed figure about half a virtual block away fell, smoking, to the digital street. At the top of the screen, the system spelled it out in system font: D3XTER has killed muffyfluffy.

"Muffyfluffy?" I asked, incredulous, even as the action continued and new lines of text were drawn. Robz0r has killed Demonyght. Shadoo has blown himself up.

"Jay, over in level design," he replied. "And no capital letters. He insists you pronounce it all lowercase." A raised eyebrow indicated he thought this was as goofy as I did. "Now, let me show you what I was talking about."

He turned his attention to the screen and zig-zagged his way down an alley and up a low-hanging fire escape. In the virtual distance, explosions and the whine of high-tech imaginary weaponry played soft and loud in turn, mixed in with clanks and thuds and the omnipresent chatter.

Onscreen, the fire escape gave way to rooftop and the sound of gravel crunching under Leon's avatar's feet. The rooftop was rimmed by a low brick wall, surmounted with the iron ladder we'd just climbed over. Vents and antennae dotted it strategically, and I winced, thinking of the problems with collision detection those were going to cause. In the center was a small shed with a single door which led, presumably, to a stairwell and down into the building below. That is, if the building actually had an interior, as opposed to merely a shell. That was the trick to virtual construction that most people outside the industry never got. The only things in the world were the ones that someone deliberately made and put there. Don't make a floor? It doesn't exist. Don't make an interior? Then your building is a big empty box. Nothing happened by implication or by extension. It all had to be created with intent and loving labor, or else it never existed.

"Over here," Leon said and sprinted to the corner. A quick drop in vantage point indicated that he'd gone into a crouched stance, the better to hide from snipers on other rooftops, and then he peered out into the fictional night.

"Where's the spawn point?" I asked. "And is that the base for CTF?"

"Down that street there." He launched a glowing purple blob that I was fairly sure was intended to be a plasma grenade. It arced out into the dark, then landed with a boom to emphasize his point. "But you can see that while it looks like there's two ways out, there's all sorts of problems with it."

I nodded. "You can drop grenades on it from here, for one thing. And I'm assuming you can get up on those other buildings?"

"Some of them. Plus, if you look down the secondary access route, you'll see the next problem."

"Oh, yeah." I could see at once what he was talking about. The side alley that led away from the spawn point did so in a long, straight line. At the far end, overturned vehicles and a dumpster had been set up in such a way as to provide superb cover. Anyone coming out of the base and down that alley was going to get taken apart like funnel cake. And, depending on the game settings, they might just spawn right back in there and have to do it again.

"Not fun," he agreed. "Got any suggestions?"

I thought for a minute. "Move the spawn point to a rooftop, say, that one." I pointed at the tallest building on the screen. "Put two fire escapes on it—we've got the objects, right—and maybe build the interior as well, so you have multiple routes in and out."

"Mmm. Maybe not on the last. That building's just a frame—we're talking a lot of polys to make the interior anything more than a staircase and a lot of locked doors."

"It's occluded. It'll be fine."

He grunted. "That's what you creative types always say. Hmm. That building there might work."

I shook my head. "Too short. You can rain down fire on the rooftop from there, there, and there. So maybe no interior, but put a walkway across to another roof or two and spread some occlusion around the base of the building so that there aren't a lot of direct lines on the fire escapes."

Leon nodded his approval. "Though we'll need cover on those fire escapes—it's a long run down, and stairs are always a bitch."

"Details, details," I said. "Shoot me the name of this map so I can write up the proposal and...wait a minute, what's that?"

"What's what?" With business concluded, Leon had gone into zoom mode, looking through a scoped and magnified view for targets. One was in his crosshairs now, a humanoid figure in gleaming armor with a massive helmet and an equally massive gun. As I watched, it belched green fire at an unseen target, accompanied by a faint sound of bacon frying.

"Not the guy. Behind him." I moved around Leon's chair and leaned in close. "Do you see it?"

The figure sprinted off to the left. Where he'd stood, I could see a pulsating blue box, resting on the sidewalk. Crackling fingers of electricity wrapped themselves around it and played down into the gutter. Then there was a purple flash and the sound of an explosion. The image of the box was replaced with a wildly cartwheeling view of sky and building, mixed with a sickening sense of vertigo as Leon's avatar went spiraling toward the ground. It hit with a wet thud, and the screen faded to black. Up top, the letters told us what we already knew: Shadoo killed D3XTER. Across the room, a war-whoop rang out. Shadoo—one of the new guys we'd hired on to make deadline—had finally killed someone besides himself.

"Shit," Leon said, and leaned back in his chair. "And I'm out of respawns, so we can't go back and look at whatever you were trying to show me. At least, not until the next round. What were you looking at, anyway?"

I frowned. "I thought I saw something right past where that guy you were scoping was standing. It was supposed to be an ammo box, I'm pretty sure, but the model was wrong."

Leon grinned. "And that's what you're worked up about? The wrong model? Bug it in the database and move on, my friend. We've got way bigger problems than that."

"It's not the fact that it's the wrong model," I started to say, then trailed off. "Has the replay feature been implemented yet?" I asked instead.

Leon pursed his lips. "I think so. You want me to pull this one to see if I can spot your magic box?"

I nodded. "Yeah. Pull it, save it, and dump it to my In/Out. I want to take a closer look at this thing if I can."

He shrugged again. "You're the boss, more or less. You should have it in twenty minutes."

"Beautiful," I said, and walked off. Behind me, the chaos of battle slowly receded.

Chapter 11

Half an hour later, Leon knocked on my door.

"Come in," I told him. "It's open."

He was already halfway through. "I figured, but I wanted to be polite. The video capture of the replay is in your shared folder. Pull it up. I want to see what you're talking about." He flung himself into the spare chair I kept in the corner, then walked it over benind my desk with his feet.

I'd already found the file by the time he stopped thumping the chair legs against the floor, and clicked on it to open it. "Jesus, that's big."

"It was a long match," he said, unapologetic. "I tried to trim it down for you a bit. That's what took so long."

"No worries. Now let's see what we've got." We both sat there for a moment, waiting for the playback to catch up to the frame I was looking for. Game footage scrolled past, kills and near-misses and explosions galore.

"There." I clicked the pause button. "You see it?"

Leon peered in. "Behind the character model?"

"Yeah." I tapped the screen with a pen. "You can see some of the particle effects over the shoulder here, and there."

He frowned. "Could be. Advance it frame by frame?"

I nodded and started the slow playback. With agonizing deliberateness, the figure onscreen stopped, turned, and then strode away, leaving behind it…

"There!" I shouted. "You see it? There!" I froze the image onscreen.

Leon sat back in his chair. "Son of a bitch, you were right. That's an ammo re-supply box from Blue Lightning."

Almost unconsciously I wiped my forehead. "Shit. I was getting worried that I'd been seeing things."

"Nope, that's definitely an immigrant from the other asset list. Good eye, Cap'n."

He stood up, stretched, and stared suspiciously at the screen. "That's going to have to come out before the next build, I think."

"The real question is, how did it get in there." I frowned, thinking about what I'd seen and what it implied.

"Shit, that's easy." His face showed relief. "Some smartass artist stuck it in as an Easter egg thinking we wouldn't notice. It shouldn't be too hard to figure out who did it, and it'll get pulled out without any hassle."

I looked up at him, not smiling. "I'm not sure that'll take care of things. I don't know if you saw it, but it looked like the object swapped in during the play session."

The wave I got was dismissive. "That's impossible. The engine doesn't support on-the-fly switching. You're dreaming, man. Come on, there's no need to go all Scooby Doo on something like this."

"Fine," I said and spread my hands. "Tell you what—re-run the sequence and tell me when you start to see the SFX. Then tell me if the box was there all along or if it just swapped in after we started looking at it."

"I will," he said. He grabbed the mouse. "Let me just rewind…hey, hang on there…"

Onscreen, the image had frozen. Despite Leon's frantic zig-zagging of mouse against mouse pad, nothing on the monitor was moving.

"Locked up," I said. "I'll reboot." I hit Control-Alt-Delete, waited a moment, and did it again. Nothing happened.

"Need to cold boot," Leon offered, and reached under the desk to hit the power button. There was a brief, spitting, sparking noise, and the screen went black. A familiar whiff of burned peanut butter wafted up, and a thin stream of smoke trickled out of the back of the monitor.

"Oh, man," he said, and stepped back, dismayed. "What the hell is going on here?"

"You owe me a monitor," I told him. "Screw it. I'm getting out of here for the night."

His glance went from the screen to me and back again, his expression worried. "Yeah. Just make sure the fire's out before you go. And, uh, don't let anyone else see the monitor before you trash it."

"Why not?" I asked, but he was already headed for the door. I watched him go, then looked back at the now-broken screen.

Etched into the glass were a series of jagged lines, emanating from a central shape that could have been a box of some sort. If you looked at them long and hard enough, they sort of looked like lightning.

* * *

"You need to stop downloading so much porn." That was Dennis's take on the broken monitor when he ambled in to take a look at it. He spun the broken flat panel around on my desk, cocked his head, looked at it for a moment, then whistled. "Seriously, what did you do to this thing?"

"I played the build," I said. "No, scratch that—I played some captured video footage from the build."

"Huh." He scratched his head.

"New tat there?" I asked. He nodded and grinned like a madman, then shoved a meaty forearm underneath my nose. A stylized whale in dark blue ink stared up at me with a huge, empty eye. The tail curved around past Dennis' elbow and vanished, not that I was terribly eager to see where it went.

"Yeah. Salish Indian design. I saw it online and it sort of spoke to me, you know? Figured it was maybe my totem animal talking. But you don't care about that, you care about what happened to your monitor."

I did my best rueful grin. "Sorry, man. I'd love to talk about the ink, but duty calls."

"Yeah, yeah, I know." The arm, complete with whale, retracted, and he started disconnecting cables from the back of the equipment. "No two ways about it, this thing is totally fried. Good thing you were still under warranty."

"Any idea what happened to it?"

Instead of answering, he ducked under my desk and continued disconnecting the dead flatscreen from my tower system. "I think," and there was a grunt and a pause, "that you maybe got some kind of power surge," another pause, another grunt, "and the thing just ate itself." His head popped up over the desktop. "Man, you'd better hope nobody walks in right now."

Despite myself, I chuckled. "Everyone knows you're irresistible, Dennis. They'd just be surprised it wasn't me under the desk, blowing you to get better gear."

"Hah! Good one!" He disappeared again, only to re-emerge with a clutch of cables in his fist. "Old school CRT, generally you got something like this by switching resolutions a lot. An old monitor just couldn't take it, and you'd end up blowing it out. A lotta games did that, actually—fixed screen resolution for the shell UI, but once you went into gameplay, kablooey. I remember this one game I bought..." His voice trailed off into indecipherable mumbles.

I leaned down in hopes of hearing him better. Dennis was talking under his breath now, fiddling with cables.

"But that was a CRT, right? Antique. And this one was new?"

He cocked his head. "New-ish. Like I said, it's still under warranty. But honestly, this looks like it came from outside. We'd better get you a replacement monitor fast so we can see if your system got fried, too."

I groaned. "Don't even say that. Do you have anything I can use?"

Dennis stuffed the cords into a pocket of his jeans and hefted the dead monitor. "I think so. Just hang in and I'll be back with something teevee-shaped."

"Okay." He turned to go, and a sudden thought struck me. "Do you need to ship that back as part of the warranty?"

He paused. "Eventually, but they're always slow with the shipping labels. Could be a couple of weeks. Why?"

"No reason," I said. "But if you could hold onto it for a while, I'd appreciate it."

"Sure, whatever," he said and ambled into the hall. "Don't go anywhere."

"Not going anywhere, my man," I told him. "Just bring me back something nice."

"Yeah, good luck with that," he called back. A couple of steps and he vanished around a corner, though I could still hear his voice as he held court, explaining to all and sundry that I'd managed to destroy another piece of equipment.

The explanation he offered seemed sensible, and as such, was tempting. We got power surges all the time, the result of operating in an area where thunderstorms and massive construction combined to make brownouts and power surges near-daily occurrences.

Sensible also meant that I could stop poking at this, and get back to my job of delivering a working, fun game to BlackStone instead of chasing phantoms. All in all, it definitely seemed to have some benefits.

My new phone buzzed. I swiveled in my chair to pick it up. "Yello."

"Green," said Sarah, giggling. "Seriously, though, honey, do you really need to answer the phone like that at the office? What if it's someone expecting something a little more…professional."

I closed my eyes and counted to three—slowly, and in Spanish—before answering. "Honey, we have entire company meetings in fake pirate-speak. The guy who's fetching me a new monitor lets the spirits tell him what to draw on his arms, and we had four guys come in last month dressed appropriately for Internet No-Pants Day. I don't think anyone's going to mistake this place for a button-down office any time soon."

"Not now," she said primly, "but someday. Just wait. I'll make a million dollars here, then buy Eric out and fire you so you have to spend all your time at home peeling grapes for me." I opened my mouth to say something, but she'd already moved on. "Are you coming home soon?"

I gave a silent prayer of thanks for getting an easy question this time. "Yes. My monitor just blew up, so we're going to put a replacement on to see if anything got lost. Then I'm coming home."

There was a pause on the other end of the line. I could imagine a different set of mental gears clicking into place before she spoke next. "It's not going to make a difference whether you check now or in the morning, is it?"

"It might," I said gently. "If the system is fried, too, then Dennis can start fixing it tonight."

"Dennis should go home once in a while."

"Dennis sleeps here half the time because he lives out in East Assburger and he gets connectivity at the office for playing Guild

Wars." We'd had this conversation at least a half-dozen times, mostly in private, usually ending with "Poor Dennis. You should invite him over for dinner some time." "Besides, with any luck, everything will be fine, and both he and I can get out of here soon."

I paused and thought about going home on time. "I really want to get home and see you," I added, and meant it.

"Good." There was a wistful note of satisfaction in her voice. "If you get home early enough, maybe we could watch a movie. There's stuff here from NetFlix with dust on it."

"We switched to NetFlix digital two years ago," I said before I could stop myself, then continued. "I'll call you once I get on the road. It shouldn't be long."

"You'd better," she said, but there was no heat in it. "I love you."

"I love you, too," I said, and cut the connection.

Dennis peeked around the corner of my doorway. "Trouble?"

I grinned, or at least made the attempt. "For a change? Naah. Come on in."

"Today's your lucky day, man." He leaned back, out of sight, then emerged, staggering under the load of a massive black CRT monitor. "Twenty-three inches, and it's all yours—at least until I can replace the other one." With a creak of straining plastic, he set it down on the desktop.

I peered at it. So help me, the blank, unpowered screen looked like it was staring back at me. It was huge, deep enough to cover the entire desktop and tall enough to hide behind. At the top of the frame, where the manufacturer's logo should have been, someone had planted a puffy sticker of one of the Powerpuff Girls.

"Does it work?" I asked dubiously. "What's that thing made out of, dinosaur bones?"

He shook his head and grinned expansively. "Naah. It'll do you just fine until we can order you a new one. In the meantime, try not to peel off Buttercup. I know it's tempting, but leave her be."

"If you say so." I nabbed a tissue from the box on my desk and wiped the screen down. Thick dust came away as I cleaned it, giving me vague hope for the picture quality. Meanwhile, Dennis had crawled under the desk with power cord and video cables in his hands. "Let me plug this into your system first. Then I can handle the power cord and get a look at your UPS while I'm down here." He coughed. "Remind me again why you've got a laptop and a desktop?"

"Because the laptop can't play games for shit. At least, not according to you, the last time I asked, and because I can't take the tower on the road with me."

There were thumping sounds, and abruptly the indicator light on the side of the titanic monitor flickered from dead to amber. Another minute, and it flashed green.

"So I'm the asshole," I heard Dennis say. "Serves me right." He stood, a fine coat of white dust on his hands and in his hair. "You're good to go. Just don't blow this one out, too, all right? At least not until I can get your replacement in."

"No worries and no resolution shifts," I told him. "I'm going to live in low-resolution land until you get me my new 36 incher."

He gave a short bark of laughter. "You don't have to go that far, but don't go too crazy. I don't have any more monitors back there except some dinky-ass seventeen inchers than run on coal."

"I'll be good to her," I promised. "Catch you later, man?"

"Sure thing."

I turned on the monitor. Apart from the slightest of greenish tinges to the image onscreen, it looked fine.

"Good enough," I said, and shut everything down. I could see in the hallway that the sunlight spilling through the windows had just started to acquire that syrupy, late-afternoon glow. A look at my watch, it told me it was a little after six, plenty early by my standards. In the distance, the hubbub of the back room was still going strong.

And Michelle was waiting in the hallway, with just a few things she wanted to talk about before I took off.

* * *

Sarah was curled up on the couch when I got home, eating a salad while a Colin Farrell movie played on the television.

"Hi," I said, dropping my bag on the floor and leaning over the back of the couch to kiss her forehead.

"Hi," she said distractedly. "There's more salad in the fridge, if you want it. Otherwise it's leftovers."

"Huh." A quick check of the fridge provided incontrovertible proof that she was lying; there were no leftovers to be had. I cracked open a leaf-filled vat of tupperware and spooned it out into a bowl. It hit the sides with a faint slapping sound, which the addition of croutons didn't do much to dispel.

"I thought you were going to wait for me." I settled on the couch next to Sarah. She tucked her legs up further underneath her and poked at a particularly recalcitrant bit of baby spinach with her fork.

"For the movie? I was. I did." Her fork finally speared the evasive green, and she popped it in her mouth, chewing thoughtfully. "For about an hour. Then I waited a little while longer, and then I decided that if I couldn't get you home on time, I could at least tell Alexander the Great when to start and stop. It felt like a good tradeoff."

I shoved a forkful of salad into my mouth, as much to avoid having to respond for a few seconds as anything else. "I got grabbed on the way out the door," was what I finally offered. "I was headed for the door, and Michelle grabbed me." Too late, I realized how that sounded. "I mean—"

Sarah cut me off. "I know what you mean. There was just one more thing. I know how this goes, Ryan." She jabbed viciously at a cherry tomato, which fairly exploded under the impact of the tines. Tiny jets of tomato guts spattered the inside of her salad bowl. "So I decided to start the movie, because if I'd waited, it would have been too late to see the whole thing by the time you got home."

She looked up at me, and after a second I found myself staring into my leafy greens. "It was work, you know. It's not like I was messing around."

"I know." She put down her fork and grabbed the remote. The volume on Alexander telling someone off went up, abruptly.

"You've been staying late for work, too, lately…"

"Because there's no reason to come home early, now, is there?"

When I looked up, she was aggressively staring at the television, the set of her jaw telling me how deliberately she wasn't looking my way.

"I guess not," I mumbled, and ate my salad.

Chapter 12

After work meant Montague's, and Montague's meant beer. I'd spent the day in meetings, going over the results of the various playtest sessions from the past week and what they meant for our production schedule. By the end of the day, my back felt like a mattress spring, and Leon had suggested going out to unwind a little bit.

"Sarah going to be OK with this?" Leon asked, leaning over the foosball table like the unlamented Varney. He held the ball in his left hand; his right deathgripped the rod attached to his goalie.

"She called to tell me she was working late." I put my hands on the striker and midfielder bars. All of Leon's men had been painstakingly painted in the colors of the Irish national team. All of mine were in the colors of the English team, and most of them had been deprived of their snap-off heads at some point in the two weeks since the table had been installed.

"Fair enough, then. Loser buys?" He dropped the ball.

"Loser buys." I lined up a midfielder and twisted, rifling the ball at his goal. He slid a fullback in the way and easily deflected my shot, sending the ball spinning around to where another one of his men could pick it up. His hands flew from rod to rod as I struggled to keep up. I'd just gotten my fingers around the grip on the goalie bar when he flicked his wrist and rocketed the ball into the corner of my goal with a solid thunk. My goalie slid into position too late.

He grinned. "I'm ordering something expensive." I ignored him, fishing the ball out of my goal and adjusting the score to reflect the fact that I was already behind. Two taps on the side of the table, as per custom, and then it was in play again.

It was four to nothing before either of us spoke. I dropped the ball onto the table and watched it carom away from my line of strikers. Leon caught it with his, then spun it back a line and pinned it in position under one of his midfielders, lining up a shot. "I did some checking on that box for you," he said conversationally, and then flicked the ball at my goal.

I shunted it aside, barely, and spun a couple of fullbacks in vain as the ball rolled by, just out of reach. "What did you find?"

He brought up the ball and passed it to the center of his line, slamming a hard sideways shot that evaded my defenses and cracked against the back wall of the table. "The thing we saw?"

"Yeah?" My goalie brushed against the ball, enough to send it on a slow roll toward midfield.

"Yeah." He skated the ball from man to man, line to line. "I checked the build. It wasn't in there."

"What?"

He took advantage of my surprise to slam another shot home. The ball hit the back of the goal so hard it popped right back out. I gave it a whack with my goalie and somehow sent it skittering down the length of the table, avoiding both my desperate swipes and Leon's more reasonable ones. "If it doesn't stay in, no goal."

"No goal." He turned his attention to corralling the escaped ball. "It wasn't in there. I checked everything. No bad calls, no misnamed objects, no nothing. It's just not in the build." A quick swipe, and the ball was careening toward my goal again. I nearly fell forward trying to get my defenses in place, and managed to deflect it just enough to have it bang off the back wall and spin away.

"Then how did it get in there?" I cranked the spin on one of my defenders, which merely resulted in the ball going backwards into my own goal. This time it stayed there.

Leon shrugged. "I don't know. I don't know a lot of things about this project. For a simple port, it's got more than its share of weird-ass shit going on."

I nodded. "It does seem that way. Did you purge all the Blue Lightning stuff out of the database?"

He stared at the ball pointedly until I picked it up and put it in play again. Seconds later, it was back in my goal. "Blue Lightning was never in there, you know that. All that's over in its own database. I could scrub that easy, but there's no point—it's all self-contained. No crossover possible. Mind you, wiping it would just get it off the network, maybe. It's all backed up offsite, plus whatever crap guys have sitting on their hard drives. But even someone who had the whole project database on their system couldn't have inserted something into the build. It's just not possible."

"We saw it," I reminded him. I rolled the ball onto the table again.

"Once, and then your system shit the bed." He spun his forwards as the ball meandered down the center line. "And something ate the dump off my machine, too."

The ball hit the far side of the table with a gentle click, then bounced off and started rolling back the way it at came. Experimentally, I spun a line of kickers. They whipped up a tiny breeze that didn't affect the ball's trajectory in the slightest. Leon just stood there and watched it, fingers tensing on the grips of his rods.

"You're kidding me, right?"

Leon shook his head. "Nope. No proof. But with all the weird shit going on, you almost kind of expect that. Of course there's not going to be any evidence left for anyone else to see. That would be too easy."

"Weird shit?" I asked, trying to keep my voice level. I knew which weird shit, so to speak, I'd seen.

He ticked them off matter-of-factly, his hands never leaving the foosball rods. "The object in the game, and what came after. Brownouts even when nobody's running their AC. Weird equipment failures all over the back of the building. And that."

He nodded down at the table. I looked.

The ball had stopped, dead center on the green-painted field of play. One of Leon's guys twitched, but didn't come close to batting the ball. I didn't bother.

"Pick it up and do over?" I asked. He shook his head.

"No way, man. You don't stick it in the crazy, and you don't mess with the weird." He relaxed his death grip on the handles and backed away from the table. "Besides, my beer's getting warm."

I followed him back to the booth and slid in on my side. Leon's beer, mostly full, was still there. Mine was gone, the mere couple of inches left in the pint glass having proved irresistible to the waitstaff.

I tried to ignore Leon's beer. "Got anything else on the weird list? Or is that it?"

He looked at me for a long moment before taking a swig of beer. "There's other stuff. And I know you've seen a couple of things, too, not that you ever talk about it. But every so often you do that clench thing with your face that means you don't want to say something."

"Heh. You're not doing a lot to convince me here, Leon."

Another sip of beer, and he shrugged. "I don't have to convince you. But if I tell you nobody saw shit like this before we started working on Salvador, would you believe me?"

I thought about it for a minute. "I don't know. And I don't know if there is anything to see. God knows we're all stressed out enough on this one."

"No," he corrected me. "You're stressed out. The rest of us just see weird little things once in a while. No big deal, really."

"If you say so." I slapped a twenty down on the table. "This ought to cover me, man. I'll catch you later."

Leon's eyebrows went up. "You're not pissed, are you?"

I shook my head. "Nope. Just want to check something else at the office and then go home. Another beer and I won't be able to drive." I stood up, and as I did Shelly walked through the door, shaking an umbrella dry. "Besides," I added, "she's better company than I am."

"She's got a better rack than you do."

I grinned at him. "I won't tell her you said that."

"She's the one who told me."

With a flourish, I turned to go. "If you need her to tell you that, you're in worse shape than I thought. Catch you tomorrow, man."

"Tomorrow." He didn't sound entirely enthusiastic. I nodded to Michelle as I passed her, and she put a hand out to stop me.

"Hey."

"Hey yourself." Gently, I removed her hand from the center of my chest. "I was just taking off."

"I can see that." She cocked her head sideways and grinned. "Sure you won't stay a little while longer? We can pretend it's a leads meeting and charge Horseshoe for it."

Over her shoulder, I could see Leon. He caught me looking and raised his glass in a mock toast. I grinned, then turned back to Shelly. "Would love to, but I can't." Her face fell a little. "It's not you, it's Leon. He stomped me so badly at foosball that if I don't get out of here now, I'll never hear the end of it."

"You're full of shit," she said sweetly, and patted my cheek. "If I call the office in fifteen minutes, are you going to pick up?"

"No," I said. "I'll let it ring and bitch about how it's distracting me from my work."

She laughed at that. "Same old Ryan," she said, shaking her head. "All right, you win. I'll see you in the morning."

"See you then." I walked away. The closer I got to the door, the more I could hear the rain hammering down. It was a real summer cloudburst, each fat drop visible as it pounded the asphalt of the parking lot and exploded into watery shrapnel. Little rivers were already rushing toward the drains, carrying hapless trash along with them.

The bartender caught my eye as I stepped up to the door. "You might want to wait," she said, shaking her head back and forth. "It should be done in a few minutes."

I nodded, then turned to look at Leon. He and Michelle were already deep in conversation. Over in the corner, I could hear the clack of a spinner on foosball, or foosball on wooden tabletop.

"Naah. I won't melt," I said, and ran out into the rain.

* * *

The rain was still coming down four hours later, not that I paid much attention to it. I was sitting in a dark room with only screenglow to keep me company.

There was no one else in the building, of that I was sure. If there had been, they undoubtedly would have come to complain when I settled in with the latest build at the station in the center of the main team room and cranked the volume. There was motion on the screen, but none else anywhere in the building, except perhaps the steady growth of the forest of empty Coke Zero cans next to my chair. The last evidence I'd heard of anyone else had been an hour ago, a door slamming shut.

In front of me was a scene of post-apocalyptic devastation, decorated in late-period dead mutant. The main character, whom marketing had imaginatively code-named "Sal," was in the middle of the frame, doing a short, jerky idle animation loop that was supposed to make him look natural and at ease while he waited for the action to begin. Unfortunately, the loop wasn't long enough to really sell the illusion, instead giving the image of a guy who really needed to get out of his gleaming battle armor fast and find the nearest rest room. Off in the background, individual pixels slowly coalesced into advancing enemies, and the controller buzzed in my hands to simulate the earth's quaking under their warlike tread. Bits of special effects razzmatazz onscreen indicated that sufficient "hyperbattle charge" had built up, enabling me to use powers that would lay waste to both my enemies and the scenery around them.

What really mattered, though, was the small box in the upper left corner that showed a steady series of numbers fluctuating between six and forty-six, the frame rate indicator. Our goal was sixty, but we'd settle for thirty, the refresh rate of the human eye, if we could get it. In a game where one of the sell points was going to be the sheer number of things we'd have to get onscreen at once, keeping the frame rate up was going to be vital, and I'd spent the last four hours since getting back from Montague's watching the numbers creep up and down.

I settled in for what would hopefully be one of the last runs. Next to me was a notepad where I'd been marking highs and lows and other things like how many enemies were on screen, how many special effects were going off, and how many buildings and other bits of interesting terrain were in the vicinity. All of it was important data and all of it was being tracked automatically by tools built into the game, but the numbers had been coming up wonky recently and I wanted to double-check with my own eyes. The trick had been pausing the game in time to write it all down before getting killed.

The controller buzzed again, stronger this time. The rumble of approaching enemies shook the chair I was sitting in and set up a sympathetic buzz in my sternum. I could hear alien battle cries, or at least the placeholder versions we'd stubbed in to see if the sound system worked.

And somewhere in the room, a phone started ringing. I ignored it and gripped the controller, leaning forward in my chair a little bit in anticipation. So far the play had been…decent, even if the frame rate had slowed to a stuttering crawl every time things got interesting.

The ringing stopped for an instant, then fired back up again. "Great," I said out loud, "A persistent one," and turned my attention to the screen. Blasting ensued, explosions exploded, and somewhere in there the phone stopped ringing again. "Good," I said, and returned my attention to darting out between buildings and strafing enemies who, lacking full AI implementation, didn't have the tactical sense God gave a cheeseburger.

As if on cue, the phone jangled once more, somehow louder than the action onscreen. It was enough to get me to look over at it, to make sure it was really the phone making all that noise, and as I did so I got the sudden, sharp jolt from the controller that told me something had blown Salvador's electronic head off.

"Well, shit," I said, and let the controller drop. It hit the thinly carpeted concrete of the floor with a crack that was a little too loud, and I said something else not nice. The impact had yanked the controller cable out of the console, leaving the game frozen. The ringing of the phone filled the sudden silence, painfully loud.

"Fine," I snarled, and grabbed the receiver off the hook. "What?"

"Ryan?" It was Sarah's voice. "Is that you?"

I blinked. "Sarah, honey? How did you know I was back here?"

She snorted. "Well, I knew you were at work, and where else would you be besides your office?"

"That's not right," I said, and meant it. "I'm not in my office. I'm in the back, testing the build."

"Right. Whatever." She sounded unhappy. "I don't know the numbers on any other extensions. Your office number is the only one I know."

"I'm serious," I said. "I'm not at my desk."

"Like it matters. Maybe Eric put in call forwarding or something. And it wouldn't have mattered if you'd answered your cell phone the six or seven times I called."

"I didn't get any calls." I shoved the receiver under my chin so I could dig my cell phone out of my pocket. "It's…oh, crap. The battery is drained."

The exasperation in her voice was palpable. "Of course it is. Tonight, maybe you'll remember to plug it in?"

I took a deep breath. "I plugged it in last night to recharge. This afternoon, when you called to tell me you'd be working late, it still had three bars on the power meter."

"If you say so." She sighed. "Look, I know I said I'd be late, but this is ridiculous. It's eleven thirty, Ryan. There can't be anything that important at the office right now, can there?"

I rubbed my eyes, and was surprised to find that they stung like hell. "That late? Christ. I had no idea. I'm just going to wrap this last test up, and then I'm coming home."

"You promise?"

"Promise." A sudden noise distracted me. I turned to see that the game had reloaded and restarted, even though the controller was unplugged and by all rights it should have been frozen. Multiple explosions detonated onscreen, deafeningly loud and too virtually close for comfort. "Shit, shit, shit!" I dove for the controller to pause things, the phone tumbling out from under my ear to crack against the desktop. Grabbing the controller, I mashed the pause button, only to realize it was still unplugged and that pressing the buttons would have no effect. "Hang on!" I shouted over the onscreen din, reaching out to shut off the television before it blew out my eardrums.

The power switch clicked. Abruptly, there was silence, except for the low grinding of the disk drive in the guts of the debug kit. I'd shut that off in a minute, I decided, and reached for the phone instead.

It dangled off the edge of the desk, the cord sawing back and forth as it did. Gingerly, I picked it up, holding it between two fingers like it might jump out of my hand if I held it too tightly. "Hello? Are you still there?"

"What the hell was that?" Sarah's voice had managed to shed any of the gentleness of a minute ago. "It sounded like a bomb going off in there."

"Technically, it was a series of cluster grenades—" I began, before realizing too late that the question had been, at best, rhetorical.

"Whatever. Come home when you feel like it, once you've finished playing."

"Sarah, I—"

There was a click. The line went dead.

"Crap," I said out loud, then hung up the phone. It didn't feel sufficiently dramatic, so I walked over to the television. "It's your goddamned fault, you know. If you'd just stayed paused, none of this would have happened."

The television didn't say anything, but the debug kit kept making chunking noises, the sign of a hard drive that was thinking hard about ending it all. I turned and glared at it instead. "And you were supposed to stay paused, jackass. What the hell happened?"

Stooping down, I picked up the stray controller and pulled the cable in. Regardless of my personal feelings, it still needed to be connected, if for no other reason than to get it ready for the regular crew in the morning. Walking over to the debug kit, where it sat humming and sassy on the desktop, I reconnected the cable and set the controller next to it. My finger jabbed out at the power button...

...and then stopped. Maybe it would be best to give Sarah some time to cool down. There was no sense rushing home just to walk into a fight. I could wait until she was asleep and then come home. I could even do something nice for when she woke up in the morning.

The more I thought about it, the more I liked that plan. There was a 24-hour Harris Teeter on the way home. I could stop in and get flowers and maybe something for breakfast. And, if I tiptoed in and didn't make any noise, then maybe I could arrange the flowers in a way where she'd see them before she saw me in the morning, and…

Without really thinking about it, I grabbed the controller, then turned the television back on. The game sprang back into life, even as I settled down into my chair. Just a little while longer, I told myself, and as long as I was here, I should at least get a little more done on the frame rate testing.

In front of me, a brand new Salvador materialized onscreen, glistening and ready for battle. I gave him my full attention.

Chapter 13

It wasn't the pounding on the door that woke me up the next morning. It was the pounding on the desk next to my head.

"Whurr?" I said, or at least I think I said, as I began the laborious task of extricating my face from the slightly sticky puddle of drool in which it had become stuck. My eyes opened roughly at the same moment I realized that A) my head was on something much harder than my pillow and B) there was a really loud noise being generated somewhere very close to my poor, tender skull.

Trying again, I came up with "Whaa?" at least until I got my head off the desk and myself sitting vaguely upright. In front of me, I could see Eric, or at least the section from waist to mid-torso. Any more would have meant opening my eyes wider and that wasn't a challenge I was really up to at the moment. "Good morning?" I finally croaked, and rubbed my eyes. "It is morning, right?" I swear, crinkling up my forehead to think about that made an actual sound.

Or maybe it was just my imagination, and anticipation of what I knew was coming.

I managed to pry my eyes open a little wider. It wasn't a win. Eric did not look happy, and since he was looking in my direction, he specifically did not look happy with me. "Yes, it is morning," he said. "And by the…looks of you, you've been here all night. Is that the case?"

Slowly, I nodded. "I think so, yeah. I was doing some frame rate testing, and I got caught up in it, and then before I knew it, it was late, and I was just going to write some emails, and...oh my God."

Eric sighed. "At least you didn't fuck up the coffeemaker this time."

I thought about that for a second. "That's because we switched to the single cup packets."

He snorted. "Yeah, well, that was because you kept on letting the pot boil dry and stinking up the whole building. So I have to ask, what the hell were you doing here?"

"I told you," I began, but got no further. Eric's warning hand was up and that was the end of that.

"No, you gave me an excuse. We're still way early in the project, Ryan. What the hell are you doing pulling crunchtime hours?"

"I just thought—" I tried to interrupt, but he barreled right over me.

"No, you didn't. If you'd thought, you'd have realized that if you're pulling all-nighters, then you're going to burn yourself out before there's a need for you to be doing that. Even better, you're going to get other people thinking that if you're in, they have to be in, and they'll burn out, too. Is that what you want?" He was practically shouting now, and if the veins in his forehead weren't actually throbbing, they were at least stretching and warming up to do so.

"Jesus, Eric. I was just trying to get a little ahead of the curve." I was honestly at little shocked by the vehemence of his tone. Eric was one of the good guys, as far as employers in the industry went, but even he wasn't exactly the sort to complain when guys wanted to put in a little extra work.

"It's still early days," he said, exasperated. "There isn't that much curve to get ahead of, especially with half the team still beat to shit after the hours we were running on Blue Lightning." He grabbed the back of his neck and started rubbing it, eyes fixed and staring at the floor. "Was anyone else in that late?" he asked. "Just tell me. They're not going to get in trouble. I just don't want them doing it until it's called for."

I racked my brain, trying to bludgeon it into looking at its tape backup of the evening before. "The last thing I remember," I said carefully, "was someone leaving around nine thirty, maybe ten, and then the building going quiet." I thought about it for a minute more. "Terry. Terry was the last one out. I remember him saying something about good luck with whatever I was doing, and then hearing the door slam. There wasn't anyone after that, at least not that I heard."

Another noncommittal nod. "Do you know what he was here working on?"

I gave my best "dunno" gesture, hands spread wide. "I couldn't tell you. For all I know he was downloading buckets of hamster porn."

Slumping back in my chair, I started cataloguing my aches and pains. A throbbing between my shoulder blades reminded me that I'd slept awfully funny, and the pounding headache that had just managed to manifest myself was chiming in with the fact that there hadn't really been that much sleep involved. All of a sudden, I was out of one-liners. "If you're that worried, why not ask him what he was doing? As far as I know, he's getting his work done, right?"

Eric coughed, gently, into one fist. "According to Leon, he's not. He's already a week behind."

"A week?" I sat up in a hurry. "We haven't been at it enough weeks for him to be a whole one behind."

The smile Eric gave me was not a pretty thing. "Now you're getting it. Plus, he's been coming in late, calling in sick a lot, and generally acting like he's exhausted. I was wondering if he was following you around, but from what you say, that's not the case. But whatever he actually is working on, here or at home, needs to stop because he's paying too much attention to it and it's going to get him fired."

I rubbed my forehead wearily. "Why are you telling me this?"

"So you don't get any surprises," he said, his voice a little softer. "Go home. Take a shower, take a nap. Come back in after lunch, assuming Sarah hasn't changed the locks."

"Don't joke about that," I warned him, but he was already walking out the door and pretending he couldn't hear. A minute later, he was gone, and I heaved myself out of the chair.

Moving meant air moving around me, which meant getting a whiff of myself, which in turn was a seriously bad idea. Eric was right; home and a shower was definitely on the agenda. I sent a quick email to the team list stating where I was going (home for unspecified reasons), when they could expect me back (after lunch) and how they could reach me in emergency (cell or text or email), then shut everything down and headed out the door. A quick check of the now plugged-in cell phone told me that it was nine thirty. Core work hours didn't start until ten, so the building was still mostly empty, with the occasional slam of car doors outside providing counterpoint to the ping of machines booting up.

I didn't see Terry out in the parking lot as I headed to my car, not that I was expecting to. From what Eric had said, he'd probably be pushing the ten AM buzzer, if not going past it, and waiting around on the off chance I'd run into him before Leon or Eric did struck me as a lousy idea. In theory, we had a mandatory eight-hour work day with core hours between ten and four. Folks could come in when they wanted and leave when they wanted as long as they put in their time and were there during core so other people could find them or schedule meetings as necessary. In reality, it meant that the engineers started coming in around seven and the artists started coming in around nine-thirty, and while most people put in their hours, there were always a few who came in around ten, took an hour lunch, and left before five in hopes that no one else in the building could actually do the math.

Folks like Terry, apparently. Odds were he was still taking the whole Blue Lightning cancellation pretty hard, but sooner or later you just had to snap out of it and move on.

Unless, of course, he wasn't moving on. The thought stuck with me as something to explore when I got back in.

After a nap and a shower, though. Definitely after a nap and a shower. And with that thought, I got in my car and went home.

* * *

Sarah was not at the house, which did not surprise me. That indeed had been my hope and the reason I'd stopped off at a supermarket to pick out what looked to be a reasonably healthy bouquet of roses to set in a vase, half peace offering and half apology. What did surprise me was that there was a small vase on the table in the breakfast nook, which someone had filled with carnations. Next to it was a note from Sarah, faintly perfumed.

Ryan, it read, sorry I snapped last night. I should know better by now that sometimes, things just happen. Let's make it up tonight. Love you—Sarah.

I screwed my eyes shut tight and held onto the note tight enough to feel it crumple under my fingers. She was apologizing to me? It made my head spin. If anyone should be apologizing, it should have been me, on bended knee and—

A sharp pain in my hand told me that the note wasn't all I'd been squeezing. I'd apparently gotten a good grip on the roses as well, and the thorns had punctured my palm and fingers in a half-dozen places.

"Heh. Stigmata," I joked to myself, then put the note down gently on the table so that I might better ponder the problem of the roses. Taking the carnations out of the vase seemed like a poor idea, and putting another vase of flowers next to them seemed worse. Instead, I ended up taking a lemonade pitcher from the cabinet, then trimming the rose stems and setting them in there with a healthy dose of plant food and some Sweet'n'Low. Sarah had told me once that adding the stuff to cut flowers helped them last longer, so I added a packet's worth, and then put the empty paper next to the pitcher on the counter. Its mission was to serve as evidence that on occasion, I did indeed listen.

A cup of coffee, a shower, another cup of coffee, and a quick bowl of cereal later, I felt somewhat closer to human. The clock over the kitchen sink told me it was still a quarter to eleven. The shower and associated ablutions had taken less time than I thought, and I could get back into the office without missing much of a beat.

My feet took a couple of steps toward the door, and then stopped. I realized I didn't need to be back into the office until around one, possibly even later. I could go in, but I'd given them all night. They could spare me for another couple of hours, and the place probably wouldn't explode in the interim.

My head felt oddly clear, as if it were suddenly unfogged with caffeine and sweat and stale air and all the other smells that intrinsically, subconsciously, told me that here was a place of work.

"I could stay home for a little while." Hearing the words aloud, surprised me, so I said them again. "I could stay home for a while." I could smell the perfume from Sarah's note, drifting up from my fingers and across from the table. There were roses in the mix, too, and the faint leftover scent of last night's cooking, and meanwhile sunlight was making golden diamonds on the kitchen floor as it spilled in through the half-drawn blinds.

My cell phone buzzed. I pulled it out and looked at it. One of the level designers was calling, no doubt with a question of supreme importance having to do with box placement or how many exploding barrels to put in. Holding the still-vibrating thing up, I told it, "Sorry,

I'm in the shower," and tossed it on the counter next to the roses. It shook once more, then was silent. After a minute, the message notification came up. I turned the phone over, so I wouldn't have to see it if I came back downstairs, then grabbed a can of Coke and headed for my office.

The fact that the phone had been completely drained of juice twelve hours ago never crossed my mid.

* * *

I'd been telling people about the novel I was writing for about as long as I'd been in games. They'd been nodding and rolling their eyes for almost as long, once it became clear that the odds of my ever finishing anything were worm's-belly low. Still, it was a much-cherished dream, and one that I took out occasionally to see if I could breathe some life into it. There was a large crossover in ambition between writing and game design, or so I'd noticed at various conferences and conventions. Writers always wanted to get their books made into games, and game writers and designers always wanted to write novels. On the designer side, I'd chalked it up to auteur syndrome, the desire to do something creative that didn't require committee meetings and approval stage-gates. For the writers, I mostly figured it was about money. Beyond that, I had never given it much thought, except to sit down occasionally and try to hammer out something of my own.

The Novel Projects folder on my system looked like an untended graveyard when I booted the machine up. Folders marked the graves of a dozen or more projects, lined up neatly to show where they'd fallen. And at the bottom of the list, tagged Active with a splash of red, was the one marked CURRENT PROJEKT. Inside, was a single document file, named CHAPTER ONE.

With a look at the clock—it was now almost eleven—I opened the file, and started writing.

* * *

The front door cracked open at twelve thirty, shocking me out of what had been a pleasant writerly fugue. "Hello?" I called downstairs, and did a hasty save, just in case. "Hello?"

"Ryan?" Sarah's voice floated up the stairs. "Is that you?"

"I hope so," I said, and got up to meet her in the hallway. Her footsteps had already announced she was coming upstairs, the peculiar thump-tap of her footfalls instantly recognizable. "What brings you home for lunch?"

I stepped into the hallway and she was there. Navy skirt, cream-colored blouse, gold necklace—she looked beautiful. I had to look close to see the dark circles under her eyes, and the places where the makeup just barely failed to hide them.

The look on her face told me she didn't think I was looking so wonderful myself. Then her eyes softened, and we just fell into holding each other.

"Hey."

"Hey, you." She looked up to kiss me with dry lips. "I'm sorry I yelled last night. I was just getting worried."

I kissed her again, to stop her apologizing. "Shhh," I said, when we broke the kiss. "You have nothing to apologize for. I should have come straight home from the bar, but I just wanted to check one thing and—"

This time, she stopped me. We came up for air a minute later, both grinning like idiots. "How much time do you have?" I asked her.

"Not enough," she replied primly, "but I hope you have a good reason to come home on time tonight now."

"Oh, yes," I said, and then there were a few more minutes without talking.

"So why were you home?" she finally asked, when we reached a point where we had the choice of stopping or making ourselves very late.

I adjusted my jeans to make them a little more comfortable, and tried hard to think about baseball. "Eric sent me home for a few hours after he found me asleep at my desk. I'm not supposed to come in until after lunch."

"What a coincidence. I came home to check on you and to grab some lunch." She looked at me, and then past me at the door to my office. "Were you...working in there?"

"No." I shook my head, the last few drops of water from my shower flying away as I did so. "I was actually, you know. Writing. On the novel."

Her eyebrows went up fractionally. "You were? Really?"

I nodded. "Really. I think I wrote about fifteen hundred words, give or take." I blinked, and a small but insistent throbbing took up residence behind my left eye. "I think that's all I've got in me today, though."

Sarah looked disappointed. "So I couldn't talk you into calling in sick, and staying home to work on it a little more?"

"Afraid not. I think I'm all out for today. Besides—" My stomach rumbled, loudly, saving me from trying to explain further. "Tell you what. Why don't I go downstairs and make lunch, and if you want, you can read what I've got so far and tell me that it's brilliant. Does that sound good?"

"It sounds great." She gave me a peck on the lips, then slid past me into my office. "Any naughty bits I shouldn't be reading?" she teased from inside.

"None that I put there," I answered, and headed downstairs to make sandwiches.

* * *

Sarah was six or seven bites into her sandwich before she said anything. I hadn't asked, hadn't wanted to seem like I was angling for approval or leaning over her shoulder as she was reading. Instead, I concentrated on my sandwich, and on the low-fat low-sodium chips I'd put out on the plates with them.

"Where did you come up with the idea for the story, Ryan?" she asked, and her voice was low and surprisingly wary.

"Juf sorra mayv unh," I said, then chewed a few more times and swallowed. "I don't know," I clarified. "I just sort of made it up. Why?"

"Interesting," was all I got out of her, and then the sounds of thoughtful chewing.

"Did you like it?" I asked, hating myself for the question.

She stopped, swallowed, and looked thoughtful for a minute. "It's very well written," she finally said, and then took a two-handed death grip on the remnants of her turkey and lettuce on seven-grain bread.

I put my sandwich down and took a sip of soda. "So you didn't like it."

She chewed slowly and deliberately, her brow furrowed as her teeth bought time for a response. "It's not that I don't like it," she said finally. "It's that it feels like I've heard it before, and I don't know where."

"You're not a big science fiction reader," I pointed out, which was true. Our reading tastes generally intersected at places like *The Time Traveler's Wife*, when science fiction or fantasy topics got themselves remade into book-club friendly versions. Her tastes ran more toward Jodi Picoult and Mitch Albom; mine went from Neal Stephenson on out. "I don't know where you would have come across something like this on your own."

Slowly, she nodded. "I know. And I don't think I've seen it in a movie. I mean, it's like a science fiction spy novel, what with the main character jumping into computers and whatnot. Like I said, the writing is good, but you're a little sloppy in a couple of places. You got your pronouns mixed up—you kept switching back and forth between 'he' and 'she' when you were—honey, what's wrong?"

I could feel the blood draining from my face. "Did I really do that?" I asked. She nodded mute agreement. I thought about it for a second. "Were most of the male pronouns up front, and the female ones toward the end of what I'd written?"

She sat back in her chair, the sandwich forgotten and her eyes wide. "Yeah. Why is that important?"

"It means I don't have the goddamned game out of my head yet." I shoved back from the table, about as interested in the rest of lunch as I was in performing elective self-surgery. "Bloody hell."

"It really is good, Ryan," Sarah offered consolingly. "Apart from the pronoun stuff, I liked it."

I smiled at her, or tried to. It came out mostly a failure. "Honey, it's Blue Lightning. I don't know what happened, but somehow, today I started writing the novelization of Blue Lightning." I stood up abruptly enough to send my chair teetering backwards; reaching back to steady it just spun the thing into the kitchen floor that much harder.

Sarah stayed at the table, sitting very still. Her hands were down now, flat against the tabletop, pressed there to keep them from trembling with tension. "I don't see why that's so bad," she said softly. "If you're not doing the game…"

"I wanted this to be something different." I kicked the chair, hard, and it skittered over the floor to crash against the pantry. "If I'm going to write—if I'm going to write at all—I want to write something that's mine. That's not a game, or about a game, or ripped off from a game. That's not another version of what I'm doing at the office. Otherwise, I might as well be doing it at the office. I might as well be at the office. If it's not going to be anything different, I might as well not even try."

She took a deep breath, held it for a minute, let it whistle out between her teeth. "Even if it was a game, Blue Lightning was your idea," she said, each word getting bitten off precisely. "If they're not going to use it, you should. You put so much into it."

"And now I just want to leave it alone." I ran my fingers through my hair. "Oh, Sarah, I'm sorry. It's just that I didn't even realize what I was writing, or how thoroughly that crap was knotted up in me, or, or anything." I sat down on the floor, heavily. "God, I'm a screwup."

"You work too hard. And you're too hard on yourself." I looked up. She was still sitting at the table, looking down at me. "And this is what happens. Promise me you'll take some time off soon, Ryan."

"I—"

"I don't care if you go anywhere. I don't care if you spend it with me, or by yourself, or hop in the car and drive and don't come back until you're feeling better. But I don't want to watch you blow up every time you make a mistake, and I don't want to watch you tear your own guts out every time you realize you blew up for no reason."

"Sarah, I—"

"I love you, Ryan, and I'll see you tonight. You should get to work." Smoothly, she stood and carried her dishes over to the sink. With perfect economy of motion, she scraped half the sandwich into the garbage disposal, then ran it for precisely five seconds. The dishes clattered in the sink as she set them down and turned to go.

"The roses are lovely, Ryan," she said. "Thank you." And with that, she was gone, her footsteps in the hall and the sound of the door shutting behind her blending into a cacophonous goodbye.

"Great," I said, and sat there for a moment. "Why don't I go to the office?"

Chapter 14

Shelly was conveniently near the front doors when I walked through, and she fell into step with me before I'd gotten a yard inside.

"You look like shit," she said cheerfully. "Not a good nap?"

"Not now, Michelle," I warned her. I fumbled for my office keys. They fell out of my fingers and bounced once. "God dammit!" I dropped to my knees to look for them, then looked up at Michelle. "Would you mind? You're blocking the light."

"So sorry." She took a step back and to the left. The sickly glow from the hall lamp fanned through her hair, giving me just enough light to spot my keys right in front of me.

"Thank you." I grabbed them, dusted myself off, and stood. "And whatever it is, can it wait five minutes?"

She made a great show of looking at her watch, a Hello Kitty number I'd gotten her about six watchbands ago. "Eight. Then you're due in the small meeting room."

"Great. What's this one about?" I jammed the key into the door, missing the lock twice before finally nailing it, and shoved it open. It banged against the wall and slammed into my shoulder, leaving me wincing even as I turned on the light.

"Terry," she said. "You might want to block off the rest of the afternoon."

"Wonderful." I dropped my keys and my bag on my desk, in that order, and did a quick email check. There was the meeting invite from Leon to discuss Terry, and it looked like Terry was invited. That felt like bad news; we weren't going to have enough time to figure out what we were going say before it was showtime. I checked the time on my monitor just as a reminder window popped up—five minutes. Maybe I could get down there and grab Leon for a couple of minutes beforehand. Grabbing a pad and a thoroughly chewed-on pen, I hurried down the hall.

* * *

To my surprise, Leon hadn't taken the chair at the end of the table in the meeting room. Instead, he was seated along the side, his shoes off and a pen twirling between his fingers. He looked up as I stalked in, and the pen stopped moving. "Who pissed in your cornflakes, man?"

"I did it myself. I like the taste." I slammed the pad down onto the table and dropped into a chair. "What have we got, Leon?"

He shrugged. "Informational meeting, that's all. I just have to let Terry know that we're concerned about his feature, and if he needs to talk about the spec..." His voice trailed off as he made a grand gesture in my direction.

"You could have just pulled systems design in here. Or given me some warning."

"I did. You didn't pick up." He leaned forward. "And before he gets here, let's just walk through it fast. I'll do the talking, you're here for backup in case he wants to talk about the intention, or if he comes over the table and I need you to restrain him. Got it, man?"

"I don't think you have to worry about Terry coming over the table at you," I said. "Whatever. I'll be here."

"Thanks." There was a knock. "Just don't jump in and jump down his throat, OK? I got this one."

"Right." I made a big show of biting my tongue for Leon. He flipped me off, then shouted "Come in" at the door.

Terry didn't walk in. He just sort of shuffled, like he was perpetually falling forward and insisted on making the smallest movements possible of his feet to avert catastrophe. "Hey," he said, his eyes flicking back and forth nervously between us. "Where do you want me to sit?"

"Wherever," Leon said magnanimously. Terry nodded, and shuffled over to the Daddy Chair. Leon looked mildly surprised. Inwardly, I groaned. We were five seconds in and it already felt like things were going off the rails.

"So, uh, what's up, guys?" Terry's voice was uneven. He tapped his fingers on the tabletop like he was doing piano scales, and hunched over them like he didn't want us to see. "Is something up?"

Leon smiled. "I just wanted to make sure that everything was cool with the implementation on your feature, and that you didn't have any trouble with the concept. I know Ryan's kind of a pain to get hold of sometimes," I opened my mouth to say something, and Leon kicked me under the table. Even without shoes, he kicked hard. "So if you had any questions, or there was something holding you up, I figured we could just talk it out." He threw a glance my way. "Right, Ryan?"

I nodded dumbly, watching Terry out of the corner of my eye. His head was practically down to the table, his gaze focused on the spot just in front of his hands. "It's fine," he mumbled. "The docs are good."

"That's cool, man." Leon scooted his chair over a little closer. I stayed where I was. "But if it's all good, I have to ask, as your lead, if something else is wrong? Cause I'm looking at the Engineering schedule and we're not meeting it. That means I've got to explain to Eric what's up, and I want to be able to tell him not to worry. So..."

Terry stared at him, eyes wide. "So?"

"So what's up?" His face was maybe a foot from Terry's now, his arms crossed in front of him. "Is it something I can help with?"

"No, no, everything's fine." Terry turned, hunched over, and stared at a wall. "I'll catch up, don't worry. It's just something else has been taking my attention a little bit lately, and I haven't been getting a lot of sleep, and I promise I'll be back on schedule real soon now." For some inexplicable reason, he shot me a look that was one part desperation, two parts loathing. "Really. Nothing to worry about."

"Don't turn your back on me, Terry," Leon said in the deceptively soft voice that meant that he was getting seriously pissed off. "In case you didn't hear me, I'm your lead, and I asked you a question. I invited you in here so we could have a nice friendly chat before I had to get Eric involved. But if you're not going to be straight with me, we might as well all go home." There was a moment of silence, broken only by Terry's shuddering breathing and the faint tick of the clock on the wall. "Terry?"

"I'll get the goddamned work done, okay? Just leave me the hell alone, or fire me, I don't care which!" He spun around, eyes bulging, lips pulled back in what could only be called a snarl. "You don't know shit about what I'm doing or how important it is, and at the end of the day, I'll have everything done I need to. In the meantime, you can take that schedule of yours and shove it up your ass!"

"Wait a minute, Terry." Leon warned him. "You should maybe think about what you're saying here."

"Think? You've got no goddamned idea how much thinking I've been doing. This Salvador horseshit doesn't take any thinking at all. I've got other stuff to think about." He pulled himself up out of his chair and stomped past me. As he did, I turned.

"Take it easy, Terry," I said. "Leon's just trying to help."

He stopped and looked daggers in my direction. "Yeah. He's trying to help. I don't know what the hell she sees in you." He hocked up a wad of spit and looked me up and down before thinking better of it. Instead, he settled for lurching out and slamming the door behind him.

"You know," I said idly, "That door gets slammed a lot."

"Heh. Funny." Leon rubbed his forehead like it was causing him pain. "Wow. I don't know who that was, but it wasn't Terry."

I was still looking at the door. "He's hiding something, that's for sure. Is the feature he's working on really that much of a bear?"

Leon shook his head. "It's cake. I gave it to him because he was really deep into the guts of the matchmaking stuff on Blue Lightning, and I wanted him to have something relatively easy to work on while he, you know, got over it. Give him an easy win and all that."

"That worked out well." I turned to face Leon, who looked grim as death. "So what now?"

He made a sour face. "Now that I've officially had a meeting with him, HR says I can go on to the next step and dig into his network access history. And since we had this nice talk, he can't say shit about how I should have talked to him first."

"Very clever. But what are you expecting to find?"

"If he's been accessing something naughty from work, I'll find it, or Dennis will. Maybe he's working on his own thing, maybe he's doing the BitTorrent thing with movies, maybe he's just getting a shitload of porn. It doesn't matter."

"What if he's doing a black project?"

"Hmm." Leon drummed his fingernails on the tabletop, little tiny clacking sounds accentuating his thought process. "You mean a blue project, don't you?"

"Same thing." I thought for a minute. "He had a little knot of guys he was huddling with out in the smoker's quad a while back, and they all had that 'we're doing something we shouldn't' look when I came over to talk."

"Heh. You're practically management. No wonder they look guilty." He stood up. "Eric warned Terry about doing anything else on Blue Lighting. Called him into his office for a little 'come to Jesus' talk. If he's still digging into it, we'll get the access records from the Blue Lightning database. I might even have to ask Dennis to call in the tape backups from offsite, just to see what he was touching."

"Hopefully, not himself." Leon shot me a look, and I raised my hands to show I was sorry. "My bad," I said. "What happens if you catch him still working on Blue Lightning?"

Leon made a face. "I tell him to cut it out. And if he doesn't, then I take some steps." He strode toward the door. "You think I'm handling this right? I mean, that was pretty batshit, what he did just now."

"You're doing fine, man. And I'd try and get more info on what he's doing before talking to HR or Eric again. Otherwise they'll just nibble you to death with questions and it'll take twice as long," I said. "It could be that all you need to do is tell him that you're not going to get him fired, and he'll calm down. Seriously, he's wound tighter than a spring up a snail's butt."

"Eww... Tell you what. I've got a few ideas to try to figure out what's going on with Terry, man. If things go a certain way, I may need your help with some of it."

"Sure," I said, puzzled. "But what else is there to do besides looking at his records, unless you're going to plant someone in his room to watch him?"

Leon showed me a shark's grin. "Don't need people, man. I gots me some cameras."

* * *

"Do you have any idea what the hell Leon means when he says he has cameras?"

Michelle turned her attention from the vending machine to stare me down. "Just that they'd better not be in his bedroom. Why do you ask?"

I grimaced. "Because he mentioned them in connection with Terry, but after that comment I think I need a few rounds on the brain lathe."

She smirked. "Oh really? I didn't think you were such a prude."

"I'm not. But I really don't need to think about Leon's skinny ass flapping in the breeze, at least not during work hours." There was a general cloud of snickering from the other folks getting their coffee or microwaving their lunches. "OK, maybe I should rephrase that, but can we talk about this for a minute?"

"Hang on, let's take this somewhere private." She turned back to the machine and studied the selection of crap junk food—candy bars that had half-melted in the truck on the way over, salty snacks that were more sodium than anything else, overcooked cookies—as if her selection really mattered. I watched her study them. She was wearing some sort of lightweight black blouse, unbuttoned over a sullen pink tank top held up by spaghetti straps. The ensemble made her look like the manager of a particularly stylish roller derby team, and the thought made me grin.

She caught my reflection in the glass front of the machine. "What are you smiling at?"

"Nothing," I said, and turned away. "I'll meet you in my office, OK?"

In return, I heard the beeping of buttons, and then the solid thwack of a candy bar falling too far, too fast, and hitting the merciless steel of the bottom of the machine. "Hang on," Shelly said, and reached in to snag her Butterfinger. The top half of it sagged at an odd angle; the fall had clearly broken it.

"You want another one?" I reached into my pocket for change.

She shook her head. "It tastes the same, and this way, there's more crumbs for you to clean up. You said your office?" Without waiting for an answer, she walked out of the break room and down the hall.

I hurried to keep up. "So about these cameras…"

Shelly shrugged and took a bite of the candy bar. After a few seconds' thoughtful crunching, she said something that might have been "Why don't you ask him?"

"I tried. He just smirked at me."

"Ah." We turned a corner, Shelly taking the inside. "If I had to make a guess, I'd say he's going to set up cameras. Was that helpful?"

I stopped. After a second, she did, too. "No. Not really. Come on, Shelly. I can smell the wacky hijinks a mile away."

"You sure it's not shenanigans?" The joke fell flat. She was gnawing on her lip as she thought about it. "I'll tell you what. If you're so worried, I'll talk to him. Maybe he's just messing with you."

"Maybe..." To my own ears, I didn't sound convinced, or convincing. "If you could do that..."

"If it'll shut you up, I'll do it." She looked down at the crumbling Butterfinger, then made a face. "God, why do I eat this crap?"

"It's a manifestation of your deep-seated self-loathing. Duh." For a minute I thought she was going to throw it at me, but instead she folded the wrapper over the remaining bits and stalked off. "I'll let you know," she called out over her shoulder.

"Thanks." If she heard me, she didn't show any evidence of it. I waited until she disappeared back around the corner, then turned to go back to my office. Eric was standing there, arms crossed over his chest, looking bemused.

"Do you want to tell me what that was about?" he asked, planting himself across the hallway so that there really wasn't any graceful way to get around him.

"Meh. We had a little talk with Terry today, and this is just due diligence on the followup." I peered at him. "Can I get to my office now, or is this suddenly a pass-rushing drill?"

One of Eric's eyebrows went up half an inch. "I had no idea you knew what a football was." He stepped aside, pivoting like a door swinging on its hinge, and made a gesture that looked like it was stolen from an old ZZ Top video. "By all means. Don't let me keep you."

"Thank you," I grumped, and walked past.

"Let me know how it goes," he called out as I turned in to my office.

"It already went," I muttered, too low for him to hear. The instant message alert was blinking on my monitor as I settled in at my desk, and I clicked on it to see who it was from.

No surprise, it was Shelly. I opened the chat window and read, LEON SAYS EVERYTHINGS COOL. NEEDS A COUPLE OF NIGHTS TO SET UP.

I typed back, NEEDS TO SET UP WHAT? WHATS TERRY DOING???

There was a pause, and then the reply came back, WTF IM NOT UR SECRETARY. AND HE SAYS TERRYS BEEN IN THE BL CODE BASE.

"Crap," I said out loud, and then repeated it with my fingers. CRAP. I sent it, then added SO WHATS WITH THE CAMERAS?

TURN OFF YOUR CAPS LOCK was the answer I got, followed by LEON SAYS THERE'S SOMETHING WEIRD. HE'S PUTTING A SNIFFER ON TERRY'S MACHINE & SETTING UP WEBCAMS TO TRY TO GET A LOOK AT THE SCREEN. Another pause, then THURSDAY NIGHT IS SHOWTIME. 2100 HOURS.

I said "Yes ma'am," and tapped the caps lock key. Jesus, I typed. Can't we just tell terry to quit it? This cannot end well.

There was a long, long break before the alert popped back up. LEON SAYS IT BEATS HAVING 2 FIRE HIS ASS.

I thought about it. If Terry was doing something dumb with the Blue Lightning code base, it behooved us to get him to quit it before it ruptured him permanently. On the other hand, throwing spyware on his machine and setting up cameras to watch him was, if not technically against the rules, at least the sort of thing that was going to cause all sorts of employee relations issues down the road. As soon as word got out that we were spying on someone, even if it was for the best of reasons, people would think they were next and start running for the exits.

Tell him to kill the sniffer, I finally typed back. Terry will find it and then we're boned.

OK, came back after a minute, followed by, ALL THE NETWORK STUFFS LOGGED ANYWAY.

Principle of the thing. Are we done?

YOU HAVE NO IDEA.

I laughed, and shut the window. There were other things I had to attend to. Lots of other things.

* * *

The sugar ants crawling over the tablecloth we'd brought along as a picnic blanket didn't much care about video games. They snuck up over the edges, scurried for cover behind the squeeze bottle of mustard and empty soda cans, and launched a full-on commando raid toward the open bag of veggie chips we'd left unguarded.

"Shoo," Sarah said, picking up the bag.

"I don't think they speak English," I told her as I reached into the bag for another handful of munchies. The debris of dinner was all around—crumbs, dirty paper plates shoved into a plastic Food Lion bag, a small foldable cooler bag with its top unzipped and a Horseshoe logo on the side—and we sat under a tree, holding hands and watching it all.

I'd put the picnic together on a whim, a spark of inspiration that came from actually having beaten Sarah home from work for once. While Leon was pottering around with his Terry project he wasn't much available to collaborate with me, and Shelly was enjoying being mysterious, so I packed up and headed home. Then the muse struck, and when Sarah came through the door I turned her around and bundled her right back out of it.

"What are you doing?" she asked. "Ryan, I've had a long day."

"Which is why we're doing this," I told her, shutting the door. "Now get in my car."

"I still don't..." She saw the cooler on the floor in the front seat. "Ryan, you didn't."

I grinned at her. "I did. And now we're going to. Or something like that. Come on. Bond Park is still open for a couple of hours, plenty of time for a picnic."

She was grinning when she got into the car.

She was grinning now, too. "So you're saying I need to start teaching English as a Second Species to ants?"

I shook my head and popped a chip in my mouth. "No, I think we just shake out the table cloth and let them have whatever crumbs fall out. Inter-species cooperation. It's a goal worth striving for."

Sarah nodded. "Like sharks and those fish that clean them off?"

"Or secretary birds and crocodiles."

"The *Finding Nemo* fish and sea anemones."

"Right. And beautiful women and gamer geeks."

Sarah snorted with laughter at that one, and took my hand. "Well, are you sure that's a different species?"

I nodded solemnly. "Absolutely. If we ever have kids, they're going to have treat us like Spock's parents on *Star Trek*. All sorts of shots from Dr. McCoy and everything."

"Spock was older than McCoy," she said, and when my jaw dropped open, she grinned wickedly. "I've been teaching myself a foreign language. Geek. Which reminds me, why is my favorite geek not at his office? Not that I'm complaining."

"Leon's got some sort of super sneaky thing he's working on because of a problem with one of his people, and I didn't have a lot to do, so…" I shrugged. "I thought it would be nice to be together for a night."

Sarah squeezed my hand. "Eww. Grease. You need a napkin. And whatever Leon's working on, it sounds serious."

"It is. He's trying to keep one of his guys from getting fired. I might need to help him out later in the week, but…that's later."

"It certainly is." She snuggled closer. "And we've got an hour until they chase us out of the park there, and it seems a shame to let the ants have the whole blanket to themselves, don't you think?"

"I don't think," I said truthfully, and kissed her.

Chapter 15

I pulled up at Leon's place at quarter of nine. It was raining, so it was a relief to edge up to the curb and kill the engine before another sweep of the windshield wipers creaked its way across my nerve endings. The sky was purple, clouds hanging low and lit up in the near distance by the lights of Raleigh. There was no sign of lightning, though, rare for summer but a good sign for us. The last thing we needed was a blackout or Terry sensibly shutting down and going home for fear of having his system fried.

I hopped out of the car and walked up the driveway. The house stood well back from the street, a white-painted example of the cookie-cutter house farms that were springing up all over the area. His car was in the driveway, which wasn't a surprise—he'd long since turned the two-car garage into a workshop/arcade, picking up old game cabinets at auctions and on eBay. All of them got refurbished and wired so that quarters were no longer necessary to enjoy their old-school charms. This made parties at Leon's very popular, especially with the older members of the staff.

It also meant that there was no room for anything else in the garage, like, say, his car. Tonight, as with every other night, it stood in the driveway, its dark red paint washed mostly clean. Next to it, however, was another car, one I recognized. Michelle's Acura had been there long enough for new raindrops to have erased any sign of wiper action on the windshield, and the hood was cold when I put my hand on it.

That was a surprise. I'd invited Michelle to the evening's observation, mainly because I wanted someone there with a low bullshit tolerance as a witness. I hadn't expected her to show, to be honest. I certainly hadn't expected her to show early, not to Leon's.

Interesting.

I could hear his voice as I came up on the front door. "It's open. Come in." Sure enough, it was cracked enough that I could just push my way inside.

There were two sets of shoes next to the mat by the door, Leon's ratty old Reebies and a pair of woman's flats. I shucked my own sneakers and looked around. There was no telling where Leon might have set up, though I could see that the living room was deserted. Framed comic book covers dominated the walls; wicker furniture did the same for the carpet. Prominently positioned against the far wall was a mini-bar, with a half-dozen bottles of imported rum displayed atop its counter. "Where are you, man?" I asked.

"Den," came the answer, and an echoing chuckle that had to come from Michelle. "Don't touch the rum. We've got beer in here."

"Wouldn't dream of it," I said, reversing my step and instead walking straight past the stairs into Leon's kitchen. It was a semi-open floor plan, which meant that the rumpus room and kitchen were open to each other. This had its benefits—it made it easy to get another beer during one of the marathon Xbox sessions at Leon's house—but it also meant that you had to brave the kitchen to get to the room with all the electronic toys. And while the kitchen was nice enough, or had been before Leon got his hands on it, it was always a crapshoot as to how recently he'd done dishes or taken out the trash.

I sniffed experimentally. "No funk," I reported. "What's gotten into you?" A quick look showed no dishes on the counter or in the sink, no half-empty beer bottles on available flat surfaces, and no crumpled paper towels or Hot Pocket wrappers.

"I cleaned up for company." Leon was leaning over the back of his overstuffed sofa, a blue monstrosity that looked like it had been made from skinned Muppets. There was a low table in front of it, covered with various pieces of consumer electronics—game controllers, a projection TV, remote controls, and a laptop—and no other furniture in the room except for a couple of orange beanbag chairs. The far wall had been painted white for use as a projection screen, and at the moment it was showing a screensaver.

Michelle sat on the couch next to Leon, holding a bottle of Sam Adams Summer Ale with both hands and looking straight ahead.

"Pull up a beanbag," Leon invited as I walked over to the den. "Beer's next to the table, and the show can start any time you're ready."

"We've just been waiting for you," Michelle added, and took a swig of her beer. She was wearing a black blouse, button-down—very fetching, in my unprofessional opinion—and jeans. No socks, and her hair was loose and down. There was space between her and Leon on the couch. She saw my eyes measuring and scooted over to the left an infinitesimal bit. Leon looked at her, looked at me, and did the same to the right. I had to bite my lip to keep from smiling.

"So," I said, and snagged a beer as I came around the couch, "is it working? Do we have signal on your little camera thingie?"

Leon nodded as I dropped myself into one of the beanbags.

"Camera array," he said proudly, even as he leaned forward to adjust the video input. "And it's running like sweet, sweet honey. I tested it earlier, while we were killing time waiting for you."

"Sorry," I mumbled, twisting the cap off the beer. "Sarah wasn't really excited about my coming here tonight. It took a while to convince her that I was just heading out for some gaming, and not for, well, I have no idea what else she thought I'd be doing."

"Did you tell her I was coming?" Michelle again. "I'm sure she's probably not real thrilled about that."

I took a sip of beer. "I don't think she's worried about me having a hot threesome with you and Leon, Michelle. More like she thought I was going back into the office for another couple of hours."

Leon poked at the top of the projector one last time. A box in the upper left read "Video 2"; the screen was now pure black. "Man, she's sort of right. I mean, we are checking in on work here, right?"

"We're checking in on Terry," I said, shaking my head. "Work's the least of it."

Michelle suddenly uncoiled herself from the couch and stared down at me. "You should have brought her along."

I blinked. "Why?"

Her face curled into a look of disgust, one with which I'd once grown intimately familiar. "Because it beats the hell out of lying to her about what you're doing. Assuming, of course, you actually want to keep her as your S.O. If not, keep it up. You're doing just great."

My eyes must have rolled involuntarily, because Michelle's face went from "disdain" to "fury" in a heartbeat.

"Come on, Shelly," I said. "What am I going to tell her? 'I think one of the guys at the office is trying to get himself fired by working on a nonexistent video game, and I'm going to go spy on him to see what he's typing in the middle of the night in case I have to go save him from himself?' Yeah, having her think I'm crazy is so much better than having her thinking I'm a workaholic."

Her tone softened, even if her face didn't. "You believe this is important. Maybe she would, too."

"Kids, kids, now's not the time to discuss this." Leon was all bullshit bonhomie. "We've got a friend to spy on, remember? We can argue over why Ryan is lousy boyfriend material later."

Michelle looked unhappy but sat back down. I opened my mouth, found I had nothing to say, and drank more beer to keep from accidentally saying something anyway.

Leon nodded and smiled benevolently at each of us. "That's better. Now, let me explain what we have here. I've rigged a series of webcams all over the team room, targeting Terry's desktop. With a little focus, we can see what he's doing onscreen. We can switch between them with this," he lifted the laptop, "which will give us a good view, no matter how he bobs his shaggy little head. The whole thing is dumped to a password-locked external site, which we're about to log into, and I bought Dennis lunch and got him to promise not to look too closely at the bandwidth usage tonight. So, any time you two are ready, we can do what we came here to."

I looked at Michelle. She looked away. "I still don't feel right about spying on Terry."

Leon shrugged. "We're not spying, we're looking out for him. If he's doing something really stupid, we can see it and set him straight before we have to take it to Eric, and Eric blows him out the door. Seriously, how many all-nighters do you think he can pull on a black project before he starts screwing up the day job beyond repair?"

"He's already screwing it up," I added, looking back and forth between the two of them.

"It still doesn't feel right," she finally said. "But what do I know? I'm just the girl."

"Michelle..."

Leon waved me off. "Sooner we start, sooner we finish and can start flagellating ourselves about being terrible friends to Terry." He hit a key on the laptop, and the image of the team room resolved onscreen. "Or the sooner we save his ass."

"Same thing, really," I said quietly. "Let's get this over with."

"Right you are, chief," said Leon, and flipped open the laptop. He hit a few keys, and a Godzilla shriek cut through the room at deafening volume. Michelle jumped and I winced.

"Sorry, folks. Startup sound. I forgot the volume was up that high."

"No harm done." Michelle crowded in next to him. "Now let's see this."

Leon glanced up at me, one eyebrow raised. I had two options—crowd in on the couch next to him and Michelle, or lurk behind them. I picked number two and settled in behind them.

"What are we looking at?" Michelle asked.

"Just a minute, just a minute." Leon fiddled a bit more, and a series of windows popped up onscreen. On all of them was Terry, or some portion thereof. The picture quality was grainy as all hell, but it was unmistakably him. There was a small palisade of Monster energy drink cans next to his keyboard and a double monitor setup behind them. To his right was a dev kit, a circle of green light shining out from its power indicator and fuzzing up the picture.

"Kill the ones from the left side," I said. "The image is crappy, and the light's messing up the picture. All we're getting is the silhouette." Leon nodded, and two of the windows went away. The refresh rate went up as he did so, treating us to a slightly more realistic vision of Terry typing, leaning forward, then typing some more.

"Let me scan the room," he said softly. "Make sure there's no one else in there."

"Can you do that?" Michelle asked.

He nodded. "Camera four is on a swivel. It's got 270 degree coverage." Slowly, the window at the top right treated us to a view of empty desks covered with equipment and empty soda cans, game cases and action figures, and the occasional candy jar. No people, though. No computers that showed anything onscreen, no other sign of life or work or light, only Terry and his machine.

"We're clear," Leon announced with some relief. "Nobody but Terry in there. Which is good, because I'd hate to be doing this and catch someone watching porn or something and beating off at his desk."

I punched him lightly on the shoulder. "You've never done that."

He turned and looked at me, his face a mask of indignation. "The hell I haven't. There was this one guy we called Dr. Spankenstein, back when I was working at—"

"Guys, can we focus here?" Shamefaced, we turned back to the laptop. Michelle's expression was half smirk, half disgust. "The important thing is that if he's the only one there and nobody's running any processes overnight, then we know that whatever we see is his."

"Exactly." Leon gave her a grin. "But I still think it's a good thing we don't have sound. Just in case."

Michelle let that one go without comment. Instead, she tapped the screen with one finger, clicking her nail against it to avoid leaving a smudge. "That one," she said. "It's from directly behind him. All we're getting is his back and his hair."

"And his back hair," Leon quipped.

Michelle ignored him. "Can we kill that one?"

"Not yet," I said, the beginnings of an idea coming to me. "Leon, can you zoom in enough to show us what's on his screens?"

"I can try," he replied, and hit a few controls. The images in half the windows grew larger and blurrier in roughly equal proportions.

"No good." Michelle frowned. "The only angles you've got are side ones. It's too distorted. Maybe we could get a better feed if you killed the back cam?"

"No," I said, "And here's why. We want to see what he's looking at, right?" They both nodded. "OK, put that one on max zoom and get ready to do some screen captures."

"What are you going to do?" Michelle asked, but I was already whipping out my cell phone.

"He's in the way? We'll get him out of the way." I dialed in the number for the work switchboard and hit an extension at more or less random, then let it ring. A second later, Terry's head jerked up and to the left, presumably in the direction of the now-ringing phone.

"What are you doing, Ryan?" Michelle turned, puzzled. I couldn't help noticing that she was pressed up awfully close against Leon as she did so. "He's not going to answer someone else's phone."

"He will if it keeps ringing." I hit redial. Onscreen, Terry put his head down in an obvious attempt to concentrate.

I hit redial again. "And ringing." Terry looked left, looked straight ahead, then looked left again, longer this time.

"And ringing." Another press of the button. A jerk of the head, definitely annoyed, and he leaned forward to crank the speakers on his system.

"Now I'm really glad we don't have sound," Michelle said. "He's probably cranking some old Floyd B-side they recorded in a cave while tripping on acid,"

"And grooving with a Pict," Leon finished. "But I still don't get what you're trying to do."

"I do," Michelle said, and flipped open her phone. "Two phones are harder to drown out than one." She dialed, hung up, redialed. I grinned and redialed.

And just like that, he stood up, glanced left and right, and stomped off-camera. "Now, Leon!" I shouted as I killed the phone connection. I could see Michelle doing the same as we zoomed in on the center screen.

"Maximize it, you idiot," Michelle said. It jumped to fill the entire screen. "Are you getting screen caps?"

"Screw that," Leon replied, intent on the laptop. "I'm capturing the feed. We can look at this later to see what he's working on. Though I can tell you right now, that looks an awful lot like the detection algorithm from Blue Lightning."

"The code's got to be commented," I said. "Can you read any of it?"

He peered forward. "Yeah, good call. That's what it is. He's running with Shawn's stuff and—oh, crap."

Terry's shape filled the screen as he hastily adjusted the volume on his speakers. I looked over to see Michelle's thumb poised over her phone. "Don't," I said. "We got what we need."

"Aww," she said but put the phone away. "That was pretty sneaky of you."

I kept my poker face on. "I don't like doing this any more than you do. I figured the faster we got it over with, the faster we could stop. The phone thing was just a way to speed things along."

Leon half-turned around. "But now that we have the evidence, what do we do? I mean, we could go over there right now and tell him to cut it out."

"How's that going to help?" Michelle asked. "He'd be angry at us for spying, or he'd hear us coming and hide what he was doing. Short of scrubbing his machine while he sat there and then disconnecting it from the network, how exactly could we stop him from telling us to get screwed and getting right back to it?"

I raised my hand. "We don't need to do anything tonight. Tomorrow, I'll talk to the appropriate folks and we'll sit down and have another little chat with Terry. Nothing serious, nothing that's going to make him think he's about to get fired because he's not, just a friendly request to ease up on the hours on the black project. Or else."

Leon snorted. "Horseshit. He's hiding this for a reason. We say one word to him about it and he's going to freak out. And when he freaks out, he'll go back to doing exactly what he's doing, just even more so, because he'll think he's running out of time."

I sighed. "Look, Leon—"

Michelle interrupted me. "Guys."

Leon waved her off. "Don't 'Look Leon' me. I know Terry, and—"

"Guys."

"Michelle, we're trying to have a discussion here, and—"

"Guys!"

We stopped, mouths opened, and turned to look at her. She was pointing at the screen. "I think this is important," she said.

I looked at the screen. The image of Terry's back was still maximized, but now it was silhouetted, framed in a brilliant white glow. Streamers of light fanned out around him, like the sun's corona during an eclipse.

"You still have the side views open?" I asked softly. Leon nodded. "Good. Minimize this one."

He did so. And we stared.

The angle that showed it best was the window in the lower right, and Leon quickly maximized it. On it, we could see Terry in profile. He sat there, hunched forward, hands still on the keyboard. In front of him was his work setup, speakers pushed well back, monitors positioned to ergonomic perfection.

And leaning out of the monitor was the shape of a woman.

Not all of her, at least, not all that we could see. What I could see was a face and perhaps as far down as halfway to her waist. Her features, what I could see of them, had a faintly Asian cast to them, while her figure was slender and her breasts small. She wore no clothes that I could see, and her hands gently stroked Terry's hair and face.

That's what I think I saw, anyway, because she was made of fierce blue-white light. Shot through with static, flickering toward darkness for milliseconds before blazing more intensely than ever, she leaned forward. Her eyes, pure black and empty, closed as her mouth half-opened.

Terry pulled his hands off the keyboard. One flew up to clasp hers as she stroked his cheek. The other drew her closer, pulling her into a kiss. Or perhaps she did the pulling, white fingers laced with sparks tangled in his hair.

Their lips met, and for an instant, I could have sworn the light was in Terry, too.

"Oh my God," Michelle breathed. "This isn't happening. We can't be seeing this."

Onscreen, the woman had emerged further from the monitor. I could see the beginning of the curve of her hips, even as she drew Terry's face down to bury it between her breasts. His hands moved over her back, tentative at first, then more and more confident. One slid around to her belly and down, reaching to the edge of the monitor where woman-shape met cold glass.

"Turn it off."

I tore my eyes away and looked at Michelle. Her face was flushed, her eyes wide with horror.

"I said turn it off," she said. "I can't watch this. I don't want to watch this!"

Leon shuddered and shoved the laptop away as I saw the tips of Terry's fingers start to ripple into nothingness. A low moan, the tinny quality of the laptop's speakers doing nothing to disguise the raw need in it, the sexual power, filled the room.

"We don't have sound," I said. "Leon, you said we don't have sound."

"We don't!" He turned from me to Michelle to the screen. "I swear, I didn't hook up any mikes!"

Terry's hand sank into the screen, fingers splayed as it trailed down into the imagined shape of womanhood. Her head was thrown back, eyes closed, mouth open, and the groans of desire we were hearing were coming from her lips.

"I said stop it!" Michelle lunged for the laptop. Her fingers hit the keys, disabling the connection.

And the woman onscreen opened her eyes.

Turned.

Stared straight into the camera.

And smiled.

"No!" Leon snatched the computer away. The image of the woman stared out at us, her moans still echoing in the corners of the room. For a long instant the picture hung there, and then suddenly, abruptly, the machine powered down.

The screen went black, and I found I could breathe again.

"We've gotta go," Leon said. "I don't know what the hell we just saw, but we have to stop it. Get your coat. I'll drive." He stood, visibly shaking, and the laptop fell out of his fingers to the table. There was a sharp crack, and he stared at it. "Goddamn," he said reflectively, then more emphatically. "Jesus goddamn fucking hell shit!"

I was already heading for the door. "No. I'll go to the office and make sure nothing happened to Terry. You stay here and see if you got any video capture of that…thing. Michelle, stay with him and make sure he doesn't do anything stupid."

She opened her mouth to argue, but saw the look on my face and nodded instead. "Call if you need help."

"I will," I said, and went out into the night.

Chapter 16

The parking lot was empty when I got there. Terry's car, a gunmetal-gray Chevy Impala with some rust along the sides, was gone. The only lights I saw were the red of emergency exit lights and the dim yellow of the hallway fixtures. There was no dancing light to give away the presence of someone playing a console game on a television, no monitor glow leaking out the windows. There was just silence, and darkness, and a feeling of desolation.

I sat there in my car, a feeling of dread seeping into my bones. I knew I had to go inside to check on Terry. I knew I had to see, to make sure he was all right. But the thought of doing so, of walking in on more of what I'd seen, terrified me.

My phone buzzed. I grabbed it, thankful for the interruption. "Yeah?"

Michelle's voice crackled over a bad connection. "Well?"

"Well, what? I just got here. I can tell you that his car is gone, though." I found myself snapping and not caring that I was doing it. "I'll go inside as soon as I finish doing a circuit around the building."

"Uh-huh." The doubt in her voice was plain. "In this of all things, Ryan, don't be chickenshit."

"I'm going, I'm going," I groused. I cut the connection before she could say anything else hurtful and true. Killing the engine, I stepped out into the night.

"You did a shitty parking job," I told myself as I marched to the front door. Somehow, I dug the keycard out of my wallet and waved it in front of the sensor. There was a moment's hesitation, then the loud thunk of the lock disengaging. The door swung open a half an inch. I grabbed it before it could re-engage, or before I could change my mind, and went inside.

* * *

The building was empty.

There's a certain feeling an uninhabited office has, a sort of echoing purposelessness that bounces off the walls and can only be assuaged by the return of the workforce in the morning. Only then does the building acquire its proper hum and vibe, the right level of chatter and argument bouncing through the halls. Until then, the office sits and waits and feels sorry for itself.

There was none of that when I went inside. Instead, there was a nervous energy that didn't belong, a feeling of something that had been interrupted, unhappily.

I had a feeling I knew what that was.

The lights were dim, providing enough glow to see but not enough to do anything useful. It gave the hall a sinister air, yellow light on dead-orange carpet and taupe walls. Termites would feel right at home, I thought, and headed for Terry's team room.

It was dark, but it was always dark. The shades had been drawn to make sure no stray light—whether from street lamps, stars, or that old devil sun—ever made it inside. This room was made for huddling over your work and getting it done, plain and simple, and night did not improve its character or sociability one bit. Green and amber lights shone off monitors and dev kits, making scattered constellations here and there.

"Terry?"

I didn't expect an answer. He was gone, and frankly I wasn't exactly sure what I'd say to him in any case. "Getting any from your monitor lately?" didn't seem like a good start to a potential conversation, and the other openers I had were worse.

"Hello?"

I stepped inside. The room smelled odd, with the sharp crackle of ozone layered over the usual aroma of stale bodies and snack food. I'd been half expecting the place to smell like sex, but there was no hint of that at all. There was just the sharp tang of electricity, as if there'd been a spring thunderstorm, one of fearful intensity but short duration.

"Terry? If you're here, pal, let me know." His desk was halfway down the room and on the left-hand side. I passed other desks slowly, hesitantly. It may have been my duty to try to find Terry, after all, but that didn't mean I wanted to run into whatever he'd been communing with.

Another step forward, and something gave a hesitant crunch under my foot. Pulling out my phone for light, I eased back a step and took a look at what it might have been before I'd bigfooted it.

That part was easy. It was a webcam, one of Leon's. A length of wire jutted out of the back, maybe six inches' worth, before it had been melted clean through. I held up the phone and looked around. Other black shapes lay on the floor, little tails of wire sticking out behind them.

The phone buzzed, and I nearly dropped it. Another chirp, and I felt sufficiently recovered to answer. "What?"

"What yourself?" It was Michelle. "Where are you now?"

"The team room. He's gone, all right."

She didn't sound satisfied with that answer. "What about the other…thing? Is it there?"

I glanced around the room. No electronic enchantresses met my gaze, and from where I stood, the monitors on Terry's desk looked deeply unerotic. "Not that I've noticed. Though you may want to tell Leon he's going to need some new webcams."

She chuckled nervously. "He'll be thrilled to hear that." In the background, I could hear Leon moaning, his anguished voice asking after the fate of his equipment. Michelle shushed him, then turned her attention back to the phone. "Have you checked his desk yet? There might be something there."

I opened my mouth and swallowed back a double shot of annoyance. "Gawrsh, I never thought of that, Michelle. I was on my way there when I had to stop and answer my phone. Maybe when I'm done talking, I'll be able to get back to it."

"Uh-huh." She sounded unconvinced. "It's been twenty minutes since I called you in the parking lot, Ryan. How long does it take you to go down a hallway?"

I blinked. "That long? No way. I just got in here."

"Whatever. Tell it to your girlfriend. She's gotten used to your interesting time sense, I hear. In the meantime, how about you walk over to that desk and use your camera app to take some pictures and send them back here. I'd like to see what the hell happened."

"Then you should have come yourself, or were you too busy comforting Leon over his poor widdle webcams?" My bitterness surprised me. I hadn't thought I'd cared what she did with herself these days, or who she did with herself, for that matter.

It didn't surprise Michelle, though. "We can argue about our personal lives later, thanks. Just see if there's anything weird at Terry's desk, then go home, all right? I'll be happy to have a screaming fight at work tomorrow."

"Can't. Too many meetings scheduled. Can we have the screaming fight on Thursday?" That was a joke, a weak peace offering. Silence told me she was considering it.

"Just go look at his desk, and don't tell me if there's anything sticky there, OK?"

Offering accepted, sort of. I didn't say anything further, not wishing to push my luck, and instead pocketed the dead webcam before walking to Terry's desk. Michelle kept quiet, too, though I could hear faint echoes of Leon providing worthless suggestions and advice.

Something had happened there, I saw when I reached it. Terry's chair was flipped over, backwards, on the floor. It looked like he'd left in a hurry. His desk was a mess as well, speakers on their sides and monitors turned at angles that would have been damn near impossible to use for work.

"Ryan?" Michelle's voice, hesitant.

"Not now," I answered. "Hold on one minute." Slowly, I leaned forward to examine the new angle the monitors made. Something about it triggered a thought…there. A look over the top of one confirmed it.

I was staring at a desk that had a length of cable dangling off of it. That cable, I was quite certain, had previously been attached to a webcam. He'd moved the monitors for privacy, which meant that he'd found the webcams.

A memory struck me, the woman-shape Terry had been caressing staring directly into the camera and smiling. No, Terry hadn't found the camera. Terry had been in no shape to notice anything. She'd done it. Maybe he'd moved the monitors, but that was all.

And now he was gone.

"All right," I breathed into the phone. "He was here, he's gone, and he left in a hurry. I've also got circumstantial evidence that he and Miss Zinger, or whatever that thing was, did something after our connection shorted out. What, I'm not daring to speculate."

"Ewwww."

"Your guess is as good as mine on that," I told her. "But he's gone. Do you still want pictures?"

She thought for a minute. "Yeah, not that they'll do any good. But give it a shot."

"OK," I told her, and started snapping away. Monitors, chairs, speakers, dead webcams, you name it. A thought struck me, and I put the phone to my ear. "Hold on a minute," I told Michelle. "I want to try something."

"Nothing stupid," she said, but I was already putting it down on the table.

Terry's system was off, unlike most of the others in the room. It had most certainly been on earlier, and I was curious to see whether it would still boot up or if it had been fried by his encounter. The case was under his desk, placed there to save desktop footprint, so I dropped to my knees and hit the power switch.

Nothing.

I pressed it again, and held it. Still nothing. Faintly, I could hear Michelle demanding to be told what the hell I was doing. I ignored her, and pressed the button. Third time was the charm, or so the story went, and I pressed and held it for a full ten seconds.

There was a shriek of static from my phone, and Michelle's voice halfway through calling my name before it was abruptly cut off. White light flooded the room over my head, and I debated for an instant whether it was worth it to look and see what was making it.

Brave man, that's me all the way. The light grew brighter. I peeked up over the edge of the desk.

I didn't see a woman, at least, and that was a plus. No face, no anomalous features, no static shaping itself into something I'd rather not see. Instead, there was just light pouring out of the monitor, light so intense that it could only be described as pure.

One by one, the other monitors in the room started showing it as well. Beams of brilliance shot out, one to the next, and the brightness was a sudden knife to my eyes. My fingers jabbed at the power switch on Terry's system, but it didn't do any good. More and more light poured out while the whine of the fan inside his CPU case reached an agonizing pitch. All across the room, the process repeated until it sounded like the computers were screaming, howling in agony at what they were being forced to do.

I couldn't see any more. There was too much light, too much brilliance. Everywhere I looked was white. I shut my eyes, but it did no good. The webwork of veins in my eyelids stood out, bloody pink against the brilliance behind them. Part of me wondered if this was going on all over the building; the rest just wanted to know how much of it I could take before I went blind.

My hand slipped off the power button and I let it. Instead, I reached along the case. I could feel it shuddering, bucking under my hand. Inside, the grinding of the hard drive provided an ominous counterpoint for the scream of the fan. I got a faint whiff of the burnt peanut butter smell that always accompanies a computer flame out, and that spurred me on to panic. Blinded, in a room full of burning computers? No thank you.

The back of the system was unpainted metal, not plastic or enameled aluminum, and it was hot to the touch. I jerked my fingers away, burned, but quickly shoved them back, my hand splayed against the machine as I looked for what I needed.

It was there, right where it was supposed to be: the power cord. "When in doubt," I whispered, "pull the goddamned plug."

I pulled. It came out easily, the half-melted plastic painfully hot under my fingers. I let it drop to the floor, somehow heard it hit, and realized that I'd been able to hear it because everything else had stopped.

Cautiously, I opened my eyes. Black spots the size of dinner plates swam in front of them, masking the deeper darkness that I hoped was just the usual gloom of the room. It was silent, silent and dark, and there I was on the floor under Terry's desk.

"Well, goddamn." A little later, I added, "What the hell?" and made a game effort to stand up.

And promptly banged my head on the underside of the desk, causing me to drop to the floor like I'd been shot. I lay there for a moment, breathing in plasticky fumes and laughing because I was still alive.

It took me a solid three minutes before the last snickers were out of my system. With my unburned hand, I grabbed my phone, which had fallen as I'd fallen down. I made my standard, reflexive check for messages, or tried to. Once again, all the power was gone.

"All the pictures, too, I'll bet," I told myself with a groan, and rolled left before heaving myself to my feet. Dead phone meant a couple of things, but the most immediate was that whoever might be calling me—like, say, the woman who'd heard an agonized shriek from my phone just before it cut off—would be getting the sort of voicemail message that said "dead phone." And since dead phone was in this case equivalent to suddenly dead phone, I figured I could expect either Michelle and Leon riding to the rescue or the cops, and I really wasn't up to either.

My eyes still smarting from the beating they'd taken, I stumbled over to one of the nearby desks and picked up one of the room's few desktop phones. I thought about calling Michelle to tell her not to worry, but for one thing, I wasn't sure that she shouldn't. For another, I could no longer remember her number without the cell phone there to provide it for me.

Instead, I called home. The phone rang six times before the answering machine picked up. "Hi, this is Ryan and Sarah," I heard my voice saying as the recording kicked in. "We can't come to the phone right now, but if you leave something pertinent at the tone, we'll try to get back to you as soon as we can."

I racked my brain for a moment to try to come up with something amusing to say, or at least pertinent, but nothing came to mind besides the realization of how painfully cheesy the greeting was. It would have to be changed, I decided, as recognition came that the recording had beeped and was waiting for my message.

"Hey honey, I'm fine. I'm at the office. I'll be home soon." There was nothing else to say, really, so I hung up. My cell phone was still dead, so I stuck it in my pocket and made my way out of the building and onto the front steps. The concrete was colder than I expected, but I sat and waited anyway. Sitting in the car would have provided too much temptation to drive away and go home.

It took fifteen minutes for the headlights of Michelle's car to appear, followed shortly by the rest of it. That was five more than I'd anticipated, five fewer than driving anywhere near the legal speed limit would have allowed. She parked, skewed across three spaces, and hopped out before the glare from the headlights had died completely.

"What the hell happened?" she demanded as she stomped over to where I sat. "One minute we're talking, and the next—"

"I know," I interrupted her. "I was there. Where's Leon?"

"In the car. You still haven't answered my question." And lo and behold, there was Leon shifting himself out of the passenger door, moving a good deal slower than Michelle had.

I glanced over in his direction, and he threw me a gesture that could only be interpreted as "What?" I threw him a wave, and then turned my attention back to Shelly. "What happened? I don't know. Hell, your guess is as good as mine."

For that, I got a grim little smile. "Funny, here I was thinking that the only way my guess would be as good as yours would be if I had been there when everything went nuts, which I wasn't. You, however, were, which means that not only is your guess better than mine, but you can probably actually tell me some of the details, which I would dearly love to know. Now, are you going to tell me, or should I just beat them out of you?"

"She'll do it, too, man," Leon added, having ambled over close enough to catch the back end of Michelle's explosion. "Besides, I want to know what happened to my cameras. Those things were not cheap."

"Here," I said, and pulled the one I'd salvaged out of my pocket. I tossed it to him, and he caught it reflexively.

"Oh, man!" His face papered itself over with dismay. "No way I can salvage this. There's no way!"

"Take a look at the cord." I could sense Michelle getting ready to erupt at being ignored and briefly enjoyed the sensation before looking at her. "As for what happened, you know most of it."

Her stance relaxed a bit but not the look on her face. "Try me."

"I turned Terry's machine on. When it finally booted, it went nuts, and the monitor shot out white light like a searchlight. Every other system in the room went just as crazy until I pulled the plug on Terry's."

"And then they all stopped?" Leon didn't sound convinced. "There's no way that unplugging one should have affected the others."

"That's your issue with this?" I asked, my voice on the ragged edge of incredulity. "There's no way any of this should have happened. Honest to God, I'm not sure how much of it actually did happen, and how much was just me breathing in weird plastic fumes. But you know what? Right now, I don't care. I just want to go home"—I looked at Michelle—"to Sarah and forget about this until morning. And no, I'm not going to check email or do a damn other thing online until then."

I stood and took a step toward my car. Michelle moved to block me. "What about Terry?" she asked. "Shouldn't we make sure that he's all right?"

"His car's not here, and neither is he," I said irritably. "If you want to go by his place to make sure he's still alive, you can do it. But my money says he went home. Which is what I'm going to do."

"Are you sure you're OK to drive?" Michelle asked, a hint of concern getting lost and accidentally wandering into her voice. "I mean, what you described sounds pretty screwed up."

"I'm fine." A pause. "Thank you." She stepped aside.

"Come on, man," Leon said. "You can't just leave it here."

I thought about what we'd seen over the webcam. About the melted cables and that pure white light. I thought about what I'd seen, and what possible explanations there could be for it, and what might happen if I kept poking. Then, I turned to Leon. "Tonight," I said, "I can," and walked past him.

"You're chickening out," he called after me. "This is too screwed up to let go."

"Maybe it's too screwed up to keep poking at tonight," I called back without turning around. "Look, you guys do what you want. Me, I've seen enough for one night. Whatever it is in there, I'm leaving it alone until morning because," and I stopped, and I turned back to face them. "Because I am afraid. Maybe I could have died in there. Maybe I could have gone blind. Maybe whatever we think we saw Terry getting close to could have popped out of his machine again and eaten my brain. It doesn't matter. I'm not going back in there, and I'm not going anywhere near Terry or a computer until I've had a chance to think about this crap logically and tamp down the heebie-jeebies to a dull roar. Do you understand?"

"Yes," said Michelle. "Get some sleep. We'll talk tomorrow." Another pause. "Say hi to Sarah for me."

"Yeah," Leon added awkwardly. "Come see me when you get in, OK? We'll figure something out."

"I'll try," I said softly, and got into my car. The two of them watched me drive off. Neither of them said anything else, and I was reasonably certain they weren't holding hands.

The drive home took exactly as long as it should have. I didn't speed, nor did I drive unnecessarily slowly to baby my still-recovering eyes. Sarah had left the outside light on for me, but the interior was dark. I left it that way, shrugging out of my clothes and into bed. Sarah was there, of course, already asleep.

"Mmm?" she asked as I curled up next to her.

"Shh," I said, and kissed the back of her neck. "Go back to sleep."

She yawned. "You're shaking. Are you cold?"

I put an arm around her. She pulled it close. "Parts of me are," I told her. "Parts of me. That's all."

Chapter 17

"Hey."

I was fairly sure that was Sarah's voice, but until I was sure, I didn't want to commit to anything as permanent as opening my eyes. Instead, I made a noise that probably came out as "manurmble," turned over, and tried to bury my face in my pillow.

"Ryan. Hey there. Wake up."

It was definitely Sarah. It was also definitely too early in the morning for her to be trying to wake me up, according to my never-yet-proven-wrong internal clock. I simultaneously pulled the blanket up over the top of my head and tried to stay as motionless as I imagined a sleeping body would, muttering "Lemme 'lone" as I did so.

Sarah seemed unimpressed and pinched my foot through the comforter as evidence. "Come on, Ryan. It's time to get up." She sounded mildly irritated, which could go one of two ways. Either she'd get more agitated the longer it took me to get out of bed, in which case it behooved me to get up now and answer her, or she'd get more agitated the longer it took me to get out of bed, in which case I should just stay under the covers until her annoyance reached a sufficient level for her to give up and wander off.

While I thought of that, she pinched me again. Hard.

"Ow." Clearly, strategy number two had outlived its usefulness. I threw off the covers and sat more or less up, tucking my feet up under me as I did so. "Good morning. What was that for?"

"I don't know," Sarah said. "Why don't you tell me?" She was, I saw as I rubbed the sleep out of my eyes, standing fully dressed at the foot of our bed. One corner of her mouth was turned down in what could only be called a practice frown.

A yawn made a mad dash for freedom from my innards. I fought its escape for a minute, then gave up, treating Sarah to what had to be an unpleasant view of my unbrushed teeth and tonsils in all their glory. "You're not going to believe me, honey," I said when I had control of my facial muscles back, "but I didn't do anything." Last night's memories came flooding back, and I shook my head to clear it. "Nothing bad, anyway."

Something of the sheer strangeness of the evening's encounters must have made its way into my voice, because instead of debating with me, Sarah sat down on the bed. "What happened? You didn't come home until late." A pause. "Really late." Another pause. "You were at the office, right? I mean, you never said, but I assumed…"

And there it was, the real question. The problem was, I had no idea what I could tell her without sounding like I was either lying or completely insane.

I thought about it for a minute and picked insane.

"I was at the office for a little while," I said, doing my best to keep my voice level. "Mostly, though, I was at Leon's. We were, ah, hell, are you sure you want to hear this?"

She settled in, smoothing the comforter next to where she sat. "Yeah. I think I do, because you sound a little freaked out right now. Let me hear it, and then I'll decide whether to be mad at you for staying so late or worried that you and Leon did something stupid, all right?"

"I'm more worried about you thinking I should be committed," I told her quietly. "Let me think of how to say this, because you're not going to believe a word of it."

"Start with 'I was thinking of my beautiful girlfriend,' and I'll believe that much."

I chuckled. "Believe it or not, I was, and not just because Michelle looked like she was snuggling up to Leon."

Sarah straightened up like she'd been shocked. "What? Those two? What the hell is he thinking?"

"That his wrist is hurting? I have no idea." I shrugged, trying for casual. "As long as she's looking at someone else, I'm happy."

That brought Sarah back down in a hurry. "I guess. I'm still not crazy about you spending all night with her over at Leon's."

"With Leon," I pointed out. "Trust me, honey. There's nothing to worry about there. And all this is beside the point. We were at Leon's because of that thing I'd mentioned the other day. He'd rigged up cameras at the office. We…I thought…" I tried to figure out how to explain what came next without sounding like a paranoid dickweed.

"You thought what?" Sarah was no longer patting the bed next to her in invitation, I noticed.

I let it out all at once. "You remember Terry? Skinny guy, bad hair, no social skills?" She nodded minimally. "Terry's been acting weird, and we thought that if we figured out why he was acting strange, we could help him out." She started to tell me this was a dumb idea, and I held up my hand to forestall it.

"I know, I know. But hear me out. So Leon rigged some cameras at his desk so we could see if he was staying up all night at the office working on Blue Lightning on his own and if anyone was working with him. And before you say anything, he's behind and he's screwing up badly at work, and I was honestly thinking that if we had proof he was doing the black project thing, we could use it to convince him to cut it out before he got his stupid ass fired. Which he still might." Sarah looked unimpressed, so I continued. "It was supposed to be just me and Leon, but Michelle was there when I got there, and she'd apparently been there for a while, and then we watched."

"Watched what?"

"Watched Terry get it on with a ghost."

To her credit, Sarah did not scream. Nor did she immediately stomp out of the room calling me a liar, nor did she throw anything heavy or sharp-edged in my general direction. Instead, she just looked at me. "You did what?"

"I think," I said, pronouncing every word slowly and carefully, "that we saw Terry getting it on with a ghost. Or at least most of one. I couldn't really see below the waist, as Terry had his—"

"I don't think I want to hear any more." She stood, not looking at me. "I'm not going to say I don't believe you, but what you're saying, well, it's kind of hard to believe." I scooted halfway down the bed toward her. She didn't back away, but she looked like she was thinking about it. "I'm not even sure whether I want to believe you or not," she added.

I shrugged. "I don't know if I want you to believe me. Maybe it would be better for both of us if you told me I was out of my mind, and then I could start trying to forget what I saw last night. Tell me often enough and I just might be able to do it."

Sarah shook her head. "Now I definitely don't believe you. You want me to believe you, or you wouldn't have told me at all. If you really didn't want me to know what happened, you would have come up with some sort of idiot lie, and I would have called you on it..."

"...Because I can't lie to you for shit," I interrupted, "and then we would have had a huge fight and then really awesome makeup sex. So, honestly, considering how amazing the makeup sex usually is, I would have been much better off doing a crappy job of lying to you in hopes of getting laid. Am I right?"

I thought I had her with me then. I really did. And then, the alarm went off, bleeping like someone was backing up a dump truck under the bed.

"I've got it," we both said simultaneously, but she just stood there as I dove across the bed, reaching down to hit the snooze button on the clock we always kept within arm's reach on the floor. The first tap didn't do anything, as was often the case, and neither did the second. The third worked, but by then Sarah had her game face on, and when I looked back up at her, there wasn't any laughter there.

"Hi," I said, acutely aware of the fact that I was hanging half over the edge of the bed and looking up at her sideways.

"Hi, yourself," she said back, but with her mind somewhere else. "Pull yourself back up before you fall onto the alarm clock. I don't think I can lift you if you get yourself knocked out."

"Wouldn't dream of asking," I said as I hauled myself back into the bed. "Look, Sarah, about last night—"

"Here's what we're going to do," she said briskly, stepping toward the door. She stopped and looked at me over her shoulder. "You're going to pretend that you didn't tell me what you told me. I'm going to pretend that you were just working late, like you always do. We both can pretend that I've already nagged you about spending too much time at the office, and that will be the end of it. Because, honestly, a little more suspicion and resentment is going to do this relationship a lot less harm than you asking me to believe you saw one of your friends screwing a ghost." She blew me a kiss. "Don't forget to pay the Time Warner bill, OK?"

And then she was gone.

"He's not a friend," I said and collapsed back into bed. From downstairs I heard the sound of the front door opening and then closing, then the more distant sound of a car engine rumbling to life. For my part, I lay there for a few minutes until the magical effects of the snooze button wore off, and then I kept laying there some more as the alarm beeped its most frantic beeps in my direction.

Eventually I got tired of the noise and killed the alarm. The clock read eight fifteen. It meant that Sarah had left for work at least half an hour earlier than usual, for which I couldn't blame her. There was no sense staying for breakfast when her boyfriend was toting a full load of crazy.

I shoved myself into my slippers and out of bed. The morning rituals—shower, cup of crappy coffee as I logged in and scanned my Twitter feed—seemed to take longer than usual, or maybe I just wanted them to. Every time I thought about going into the office for the morning, my mind just slid off the idea. Seeing Michelle and Leon would mean talking about what we'd seen. It wasn't a conversation I was looking forward to.

There was also the little matter of talking to Terry.

I had no idea what to say after seeing something like that. "So, Terry, what exactly were you getting it on with last night? The camera images were a little fuzzy toward the end there." I mean, I couldn't even express concern for the guy without admitting we'd been spying on him, and as for the other stuff we'd seen, well, that was way out of bounds. Even starting that conversation would be impossible. So would facing him.

At the same time, he was part of the team, and he was clearly in what Leon would call "some serious shit." Walking away from that didn't seem like such a hot idea, either.

I took another sip of coffee and read down the feed. Most were the usual—my life sucks, here's the stupid thing politicians did yesterday, here's another pointless meme—but one Tweet caught my eye.

It was a link to an article titled "Great Games We'll Never See" from a gaming blog called Yar's Vengeance that I visited only when there was work I really, really didn't want to do. There wasn't anything wrong with it—for one thing, it was generally written in complete sentences, which I regarded as a plus—but there wasn't anything that particularly compelling about the content, either.

Today, though, there was, because the hashtags for the link included #BlueLightning.

"You've got to be kidding me." I clicked over and skimmed the intro. It was the standard bullcrap about how great games are always getting cancelled despite the fact that they were going to be really, really awesome, and how it sucked for everyone involved.

Which it generally did, but not for the reasons they imagined. Of the games that usually ended up in articles like this, half were never anything more than marketing vaporware, and another two thirds had all the fun quotient of sticking your hand in a blender.

On the other hand, Blue Lightning had never made it to the lists before. They were always full of big-name titles, or experimental projects from big-name developers, and I'd always assumed that we were too far under the radar for BL to grab any mindshare for something like this.

But there she was, sitting at number seven. I blinked a couple of times and read what they said about my dead project.

"A hot-looking shooter from well-regarded indie studio Horseshoe Games, Blue Lightning promised a combination of heady gunplay with an innovative movement system that was, literally, fast as lightning. While the shooter action would have been enough to hold our interest, particularly considering Horseshoe's solid track record, the mechanisms of the teleportation system—players could lay down cable that they could zap themselves into, only to re-emerge somewhere else on the map's "grid"—would have made for a real break from the traditional rail shooter we've all gotten way too used to. Don't even get us started on what multiplayer would have been like. From the footage we've seen, it would have shaped up as serious challenger in the shooter arena. And keep those cards and letters coming, kids—rumor has it that the project may be resurrected."

"Bullshit," I told the computer, and then, since I didn't sound angry enough for my own taste, I shouted it. "Bullshit!"

To add insult to injury, there, next to the paragraph, was an image, clearly a screenshot from one of our test multiplayer sessions. The graphics were nothing better than OK, the placeholder textures were clearly visible, and the gamertags could just about be read. It was all very real, in the sense that it was 100 percent, no bullshit, absolutely authentic. That was a screen capture from Blue Lightning.

And this, too, was a problem, because we'd never released anything like that, officially or unofficially. Which meant that somehow, someone had leaked it, probably as part of a half-assed effort to get the fan community to try to pressure us to start the project back up again. That wasn't going to happen, not in a million years, but in the meantime we'd have one more hassle to deal with, and after last night, I was all full up.

"You," I said to the author of the piece, an anonymous type whose byline read EvilJohn, "are a pain in my ass. Thank you so much for adding to all the crap I was dealing with." Then, feeling somewhat better for having flung virtual poo in the man's direction, I composed a "Hey, you'd better look at this" email to Eric, complete with link to the article. "Your problem now," I told the computer as I hit Send, then headed back to the bedroom to put on some pants.

Pants were a necessary part of going in to work, after all, and as much as I might have wanted to dodge any and all of the unpleasant scenarios I'd come up with, there was really no way of getting around it.

And if I was going to do it, I might as well get it over with.

Chapter 18

Michelle texted me on the way in with, "R U GOING N?" I checked the light I was sitting at—still red—and texted, "DUH. WORK 2 DO." The light changed, I sent the message and hit the gas. She didn't text back.

The parking lot was mostly empty as I pulled in, which didn't surprise me. It was still early. Eric's car was there, though, parked in its usual spot a couple of spaces down from the door. He got in earlier than anyone most days but refrained from taking the closest spot as a matter of principle. I'd asked him about it once, and he said that it felt like a reproach to everyone else when he parked there, like he was showing off how he'd gotten in earlier than they had and was therefore working harder than they were.

This was one of the reasons most people at Horseshoe liked working for Eric. The ones who didn't tended not to stick around too long.

There was no sign of Michelle's car, which didn't surprise me, nor did I see Leon's. As for Terry, he usually parked around back, and I wasn't about to drive past his usual parking spot in the quest for mine.

I parked a couple of spaces past where Eric had and headed inside with a mix of dread and adrenaline riffing through my veins. Email from Eric was waiting for me when I got there, a response to the one I'd sent him earlier. "See me," it said, with a couple of exclamation points for emphasis. I figured that trumped more coffee, so I went down the hall into the lion's den.

"Ryan," he said as I walked in, but didn't look up. His attention was focused on his laptop screen. From where I stood I couldn't see what he was looking at. Even the reflection in his glasses didn't provide much of a clue. "How'd you find this little bombshell?"

"Twitter feed. It found me," I said truthfully. I dropped into a chair. "We didn't release that screenshot, did we?"

"No," he said, and gave himself up to a minute of furious typing. "We didn't release any screenshots because BlackStone marketing was in charge of all that, and near as I can tell, they never did much more than tell people it was coming at some point. Third party doesn't get the marketing love." He looked up at me, his expression pained. "Damn. I thought I'd let this go."

"Nobody has," I said, shrugging. Choosing my words carefully, I added, "I wouldn't be surprised if some people were running a black project to finish it after hours, to be honest. Even if they'd been warned against it." I thought about saying more but something stopped me. I'd already convinced my girlfriend I was crazy; I didn't want to add my boss to the list. Instead, I finished with a lame "That's just speculation, of course."

Eric looked down his glasses at me for a long minute. "Uh-huh. Look, if anyone does have any half-assed ideas about resurrecting the project before we can find someone to pay for it, I know that there's no hope in hell you'll sign on with them, because Sarah will skin you alive if you do." I started to say something, but he held up his hand. "Don't. If there were a black project, and I'm not saying there is, and I didn't know about it, which we both know would be damn near impossible, and if you were approached to help out, which I'm not saying you were, I know you'd have a hard time saying no. But because Sarah is a lot smarter than you are and likes to see you occasionally, and because you don't want to lose your girlfriend and your house by staying at work even more than you do, you wouldn't do anything that stupid. Which means this entire discussion is moot, except for one thing."

"What's that?" My voice was suspicious and low. "You don't think I leaked this stuff?"

He shook his head. "You're smarter than that. Besides, I blew up the screenshot." He spun the laptop around so I could see the screen. There, in the upper right hand corner of the image was a clear shot of me—or at least my avatar—eating a grenade to the face.

"Nice ragdoll," I said. "This one shows off the physics engine really well."

"Don't change the subject. What it also shows is you demonstrating your usual skill level, which is to say that you couldn't have taken it because you were too busy getting fragged."

"Yeah, all of mine looked like an incoming RPG." I turned the machine around. "So you've cleared me of the leak. What next?"

He smiled, but it wasn't a happy smile. "What's next is that you get to find out where this came from."

"Whoah, whoah, whoah," I said. "I've got deliverables. Somebody, I'm not saying who but I think his name is Eric, tasked me with trying to figure out a leaderboard system that a nine-year old can't cheese."

"You've got another deliverable now," he said. "Come on, you want to know as badly as I do."

I thought about some of the weird stuff that had been happening and paused a moment before answering. "I'm not sure about that," I said. The flatness of my tone gave Eric pause. "But if you really want me to, I'll give it a shot."

"I do," he said. "Now go get some coffee. You look like you got ridden hard and put away wet last night." He turned his face to the laptop. "I hope it was a good time, at least," he added noncommittally, by way of a dismissal.

"For somebody," I answered, and walked out.

One part of the conversation with Eric seemed like a good idea, and that was coffee. If I was going to get through the day, I would need bean juice.

The break room was quiet when I got there, the usual morning buzz of conversation subdued. There were only a couple of guys, clustered in the middle of the room and shooting occasional, expectant glances at the microwave and coffee machine. The smell of warm oatmeal had overpowered the usual stink of overstuffed trashcans and leftovers, mainly because the packets of oatmeal that the vending machine in the corner spat out were so over-seasoned with cinnamon that they'd make a Keebler elf cry.

"Hey, Ryan." One of the guys staring vulture-like at the coffee maker gave me a nod. Thomas was one of the engineers who worked on the physics engine; he often joked that his job description was "things fall down go boom." What he was technically responsible for was making sure that bodies acted like bodies and objects acted like objects, which was a lot harder than it looked. He was one of the smartest guys in the company and usually one of the quietest. Most of my conversations with him consisted of curt nods. But today, he felt like talking, even when nobody else did.

I nodded back and went over to the dish rack to see if my mug was still sitting there after yesterday's half-hearted attempt at a wash. "Hey, Thomas. How's it going?"

"Doing all right. Did you see the piece on Yar's this morning? Pretty cool, huh?"

"Yeah." The mug was there, much to my surprise, so I grabbed it and joined the orbiting cloud of coffee-seekers. "I was kind of surprised to see BL show up."

He grinned. "I don't care how it got there. It's nice to see some love. Maybe it'll help us get the project back someday."

"Yeah," I said, hoping to avoid getting too deep into this particular conversation. "Nice to see someone saying nice things about the studio." I edged into line a bit behind Thomas and the others. They'd been there before me, after all; they had dibs on the machine.

The guy at the front of the line pulled a packet of coffee concentrate, then put it back, then pulled another one. "Anyone know which is better?" he asked, starting a debate among a couple of the other folks up close. "So do you know who took the screenshot that ran with it? It looked pretty decent."

Thomas stirred off-white powder into his coffee until it turned the color of melted milk chocolate. "I dunno. I just figured it was some marketing goober playing with the build. Why do you care?"

I tried to grin. "Honestly? Because it's a great shot of me getting fragged, and I wanted to give whoever took it some shit for making me look bad."

He looked at me and shook his head. "Ryan, if your years in the industry should have taught you one thing, it's that you don't need any help with that." He took a look at the still-lengthy line for the fountain of life, did some complicated calculations, and decided that it was clearly too long a wait. "Screw it, I've got some Monsters in the minifridge. Catch you later."

One by one the other pilgrims at the caffeine shrine either took their offerings or wandered off as well, finally leaving me face to face with the key to my future productivity. "Which one, which one," I asked myself, digging into the drawers of single-cup pods. They had different names—Jamaican Blue, Colombian Morning, Kona Aroma—but near as any of us could tell, they all tasted exactly the same. I grabbed one at random, dumped it into the machine, and waited.

"You're supposed to press the 'brew' button, genius," I heard Michelle say from behind me.

"Just testing you." I pressed the button, which I'd completely forgotten about.

"Uh huh." There was a pause. I waited for the inevitable, and counted to three in my head before it arrived. "Ryan, we have to talk."

I turned to look at her. She looked, by any estimation, like hell. It was the standard "sleepless night" package—bags under bloodshot eyes, messy hair, sallow skin, and mismatched clothes. She stood there, shoulders slumped, eyes on the floor, and waited for me to say something. She was wearing one earring, I noticed. She never wore just one earring.

"About last night?" I gave her a week grin. "Come on, if we phrase it like that, people will think we're sleeping together again."

"Cut it out!" Her head snapped up and she glared at me. "You joke, and you joke, and you joke, and this isn't funny. Last night? Not funny. The other thing you mentioned? Not funny, either. So for the love of God, can you be serious, just once?" Her hands were balled into fists at her side. White knuckles, too, the sort you see on people who are about to go for an axe.

"I'm sorry," I said. "Look, Michelle, this is not a break room conversation, OK? You're right, I should be taking it more seriously. I just don't want to get too freaked out about it and screw up any chance we have of figuring this thing out. And I'm sorry I made the joke. I shouldn't have."

"No, you shouldn't," she said, but her hands unclenched and she took a long, shuddering breath. "What do you want to do?"

"Right now?" I pointed at the coffeemaker, which had started dribbling thin brown fluid through its innards and out its nozzle. "I want to wait until the coffee finishes brewing. Then I want to finish up the bullshit assignment that Eric just gave me, and maybe by the time that's done, I'll have figured out what I want to say about what happened. That's all I've got."

Michelle stared at me. "You're kidding me."

"No." The coffee machine belched and burbled; we both ignored it. "The last thing I want to do is charge into this half-assed. So let me get this other stuff done and get my head right, and then we can tackle it with our full attention."

"Fine. Call me when you're ready." She stomped past me, out the door.

"OK," I told her retreating back, but softly. Too softly for her to hear, or at least that was the intention. First things first, though, and that meant trying to track down the source of the screenshot.

* * *

Dennis was mostly at his desk when I poked my head into his office; the rest of him was on it. He was leaning back in his chair, feet up and planted next to his titanic flatscreen monitor, his keyboard in his lap as his onscreen avatar hacked and slashed his way through what looked like another fantasy MMO. I didn't go any further in; there wasn't really room, not with the guts and cases of a dozen machines spread out across the floor. Behind him, more equipment sat jammed onto wire racks, boxes of cables and mice with their cords hanging down, speakers in twos and fried motherboards stacked like kindling.

"Hey, what's up, man?" He flashed me a grin, then turned his attention back to the screen. "Sorry, got some aggro to deal with. Gimme a sec."

"No worries." Onscreen, bright green and purple carnage erupted as Dennis tapped away at his keyboard. Strange, gargling howls emerged from the speakers, muted out of courtesy to the rest of the building.

I scanned the rest of the room, wondering how Dennis ever actually made it to his desk in the morning. It looked like a jumping puzzle from an old-school platformer—step here to avoid that empty tower case, then hop this way to avoid the steel lockbox for the offsite backups, then dodge the stack of still-boxed video cards to keep them from toppling over onto the invoices for Microsoft Office upgrades, and…

"So what can I do for you?"

Whatever Dennis' homicidal dwarf character had been doing, he'd finished doing it, since he stood on top of the fading corpse of something half-dragon, half wild boar. Bright lights chased one another off in the distance, other players doing unspeakable things to each other's characters or the local virtual ecology.

"I've got a challenge for you," I said. "Eric asked me to track down a leak, and I figure you're the man to talk to."

He stretched his arms out and cracked his knuckles melodramatically. "No sweat. What am I looking for?"

I thought for a minute. "Mail logs, to start. Did someone send anything with attachments to Yar's Vengeance?"

Nodding, he minimized the game window and pulled up a connection to the mail server. "Dunno, but I can check. Anything else you can tell me about it?"

"Start looking after Blue Lightning got cancelled. No one would have had reason to leak anything until then, right?" He nodded. "And you can probably rule out any of the artists. The screenshots aren't good enough. They would have done touchup before they let them out of the building."

"What a sad state the world is in when people can't let the games speak for themselves." Dennis shook his head, even as his fingers were flying. "What happened to honesty in marketing, man?"

"Didn't know there ever was any," I said, and we both laughed. "Anyway, if you come up with anything, let me know."

"You know it's a longshot, right? They could have just dropped the images onto a USB drive and mailed them from home, or posted them somewhere the Yar's guy grabbed them, or, well, there's a lot of ways they could have gotten out there."

I grimaced. "I know. But it's worth checking, at least."

He swung his feet down onto the floor and leaned forward. "It is. I'll let you know if I get anything. You'll be at your desk?"

"Unless Michelle kills me in the meantime, yeah."

Dennis gave a short bark of laughter. "She ain't going to kill you. She still likes you a leeetle too much, bro."

I shook my head. "She and Leon hooked up. I'm just hoping they let the kids call me Unca Ryan."

He blinked. "Leon and Michelle? No way!"

"Yup." I looked back out into the hallway for a second. No one was there. "Keep it under your hat, OK? Eric's not real fond of people fishing off the company pier."

"That's 'cause Eric don't get laid." He gave another bellow of laughter. "Well, goddamn. Tell you what—let me get on this for you, and I'll have something by the end of the day. You think of anything else, let me know, all right?"

"All right." I pulled myself back out into the hall. Behind me, I could hear him still chortling to himself. "Shelly and Leon? And fucking Leon?"

I shook my head and kept going.

* * *

Talking with Dennis had given me an idea. If it was going to be tough to track down how the images got out, I could at least start by figuring out how they might have been made. Screenshots were, after all, just that—a snapshot someone took with a screen capture utility while playing or pulled from recorded footage of gameplay. And the stuff on Yar's Vengeance had looked genuine, like it had been pulled from someone's personal play log and not a carefully choreographed play session designed to show off the game's best assets.

Back at my desk, I pulled down the last build of Blue Lightning off the network and installed it on my debug kit. I'd had one on there, but like a good soldier I'd wiped it when we switched to Salvador. Now I needed it again.

While it was downloading, I sent a quick email to Sarah asking if she wanted to go out for dinner, then dealt with a few other issues that all seemed terribly important to somebody.

At last, a ping let me know the build was installed. I picked up the controller and fired the game up.

The screen flickered for a moment, and then the familiar shell appeared. I felt myself grinning at the sight of it and at the memory of what the game was going to be. That faded quickly as I thumbsticked my way through the menus to the Quick Play option, then started scrolling through the maps looking for the one that had so prominently featured my electronic demise.

There were twelve maps in the list, plus a test space that we'd used for testing out features. I scrolled down quickly, past a post-industrial wasteland and a battle-ravaged space station, past a mile-high tower and a burning oil refinery and a nuclear power plant perpetually about to go critical.

And then, there it was—Urbanscape. It was one of my favorite maps, one we'd done strictly for multiplayer. It didn't quite fit the game's story, but we didn't care because it was so much damn fun, a war-ravaged downtown with hunks of architecture liberally appropriated from New York, Chicago, Paris, London, and Poughkeepsie. The central premise, as Michelle had described it, was "blow the crap out of your favorite buildings," and really, it had been all about the collateral damage.

I selected it, and the game began cycling through load screens. On my laptop, I pulled up the most egregiously offending screenshot and zoomed in for comparison. Finding where the screen capture had been taken might give me a clue to who had taken it.

The loading screen vanished, and in its place was the imaginary cityscape I remembered. I put the game on PAUSE, then inputted a series of cheat codes. One would render me invulnerable to enemy fire, another would let my character run at ten times normal speed, and a third would allow me to fly as needed. All of these had been immensely useful in building and testing the space, letting us get to particular spots on the map to examine them without having to play through again and again. Now, though, they were just helping me get to where I needed to be.

There were enough landmarks in the screenshot to allow me to find the general location easily. I could see a chunk of modified-just-enough-to-not-get-us-sued Sears Tower, which immediately placed the site in the southwest corner of the map. Also visible was a row of brick-fronted shops I'd insisted on, relics of the six years I'd spent growing up in Connecticut. From the relative angle, the shooter on the image had been almost due south of the spot and elevated about thirty meters.

I went hunting. My avatar—faceless as a default, as I hadn't bothered to go through the customization screens—sprinted through the streets. Generic enemies spawned in and took potshots at her, but they mostly missed, rockets and blasters taking chunks out of the level geometry as I sped past. The few rounds that hit bounced off, leaving explosions hanging in mid-air as my Blue Lightning maneuvered past them, ignoring them.

Within seconds, I'd reached the spot where my avatar had died so spectacularly. I checked the screenshot to double-check, and there it was. Same sidewalk, same steaming manhole in the middle of the street, same storefront with glass as yet unbroken by hostile fire, and same dirty snow-grey sky overhead. All that was missing was my virtual corpse.

With the spot established, I turned to the source of the screenshot. I oriented myself south, guesstimated the angle, and flew along the best-guess vector. After a second, I turned myself around so I could try to match the onscreen image with the screenshot for distance.

And I promptly flew out of the world. One second I was staring at the streetcorner in question, the next I was looking at the untextured back side of one of the buildings that marked the map boundary. The map, in its entirety, sat there floating in space, a titanic playset cast adrift from any context. This was perfectly normal, the standard effect of moving outside of the playable space on a map. After all, the levels really had more in common with Hollywood sets than anything else. They were elaborate fronts and showpieces, but there was no context to them. They just floated in virtual space, until someone found a bad bit of level geometry and fell out of the world.

Like I said, it was normal, except for one thing. The shot on Yar's Vengeance looked like it had been taken from roughly this distance, far outside the level's playable boundaries.

"What the hell?" I stopped, then zoomed forward until I was back in playable space. The second I was back in, I checked the image for reference. It was no good; it was too close. A thumbnail guess on the image gave it a range of fifty meters scoped; I was maybe thirty and running up against the map boundary. Maybe unscoped would work, but the image had shown the tell-tale signs of the sniper scope user interface effects around the edges. That meant, in simplest terms, that the screen capture had been taken from outside the map and through a building. It could have been taken from an earlier version of the space, when that building hadn't been there, except that I knew for a fact that the outside boundary had been one of the first things the level artist had built.

So that, then, was impossible.

Another possibility was that the internal landscape had been re-arranged and that the corner in question had been moved closer to the edge. I shot off an IM to the artist in question, and ten seconds later I got my response. NO CHANGES TO SW CORNER OF THAT MAP—IT PLAYED GR8. Y U ASK?

Just curious, I wrote back, and OKTHX. If the distance didn't work, maybe I had the angle wrong. If I went up, maybe I'd get the distance I needed to make and take the shot.

I guided my avatar straight up, looking for a spot where the shot might have been taken. There had to be a ledge, a fire escape, something that the shooter could have stood on.

There was nothing. I stopped and thought about it for a minute. If there was nowhere to stand, then they had to be using a cheat code, except that by the time the distance was right, the angle was way off.

In other words, the screen shot was impossible. It couldn't have been taken, not without a massive rework of the level that had never happened.

Below me, on the street, enemies were gathering, taking potshots into the air where my avatar hovered. As more and more showed up, the game's frame rate slowed. Missiles crept through the air, their smoke trails burgeoning behind them. Individual bullets whined and nicked off the architecture while more and more AI took up firing positions on the street below.

Impossible. I sat there and thought about it. The explosions and bullet ricochets got more and more infrequent until finally the game locked up, a full sixty or so hostiles frozen in the act of firing. I let it sit there, then turned and tapped out a message to Dennis. Got anything???

There was a long wait, then his response popped up. YEAH U WONT BLEIVE THIS 1.

I sent him back a quick, ??? When that didn't get a response, I added, won't believe what?

SOMEONE HACKED THE MAIL SERVER CREATED AN ACCOUNT SENT PIX DELETED IT.

Can you do that? I asked.

U CANT, came back, followed by, DON'T KNOW WHO COULD NO LOGIN ATTACHD 2 HAX

I hesitated for a minute, and then typed leon? terry?

Another window popped open. It was Eric, and he wanted to know how things were going with the hunt for the leak. Just fine, I typed in. Onto something, give me a minute.

His message flashed back an OK, just as a third window, this one from Sarah, winked into existence. I'd rather stay in tonight, if that's OK with you. Maybe we can order something.

Sure that's great, I typed back, then bounced over to Dennis' window, which was now blinking for attention. PARANOID MUCH?

It's because of who I work with, I dashed off, and went back to Sarah's window, which was now blinking again.

What do you want? Chinese? Pizza? I could go for Thai. She added a smiley-face emoticon at the end, which told me that she really wanted Thai and she really wanted to talk about it to make sure I did, too, which was exactly what I didn't have time for with chat windows blowing up all over my screen.

I answered her with, I'm good with whatever you decide, then went back to Dennis just as Eric's window flared open with a request for details and a new one from Leon took up a chunk of increasingly crowded screen real estate. D00d. Got a minute?

Not right now, I typed back at him, then went back to Dennis, who'd announced, DON'T THINK THEY COULD BUT I COULD BE WRONG.

No, no, I wrote back to him. That's good to know. Then it was I'm working on it to Eric, a quick look at Sarah's Is everything OK that required either a thousand word answer or no answer at all, and then can you give me five minutes to Leon.

It's just a quick thing, he wrote back. OMW.

"No!" I found myself shouting, as the message tag attached to Leon's window went into AFK mode.

With only a moment's hesitation, I jumped back to Sarah's window. Everythings fine, I wrote. Just a little busy.

If you don't want Thai we don't have to have it, she wrote back instantly, leading me to believe she'd already typed it in and had just been waiting for a sign of life from me before sending it. In the meantime I'd hopped to Dennis' window and thanked him, then over to Eric's to respond to his query about all the busted equipment that had been found on various engineers' desks. Personal equipment, I wrote back. Leon's. Trying an experiment with realtime picture-in-picture that we didn't want to present before we had an idea if it was worth trying. It was a lie, but as the entire point of the exercise had been to shield Terry from Eric, I didn't want to rat him out at this juncture.

How did it fly? he wrote back, and I cringed. Rather than answer, I jumped back to Sarah's window, just as Leon walked into my office.

"Hey, man," he said, and shut the door.

I looked at the chat windows, then at him, then at the windows, then at the door, then back at him. "What's up?"

Instead of responding, he dropped into a chair. "You got five minutes?"

"If I say no, you're going to sit there and keep asking me until I do, right?" With an unspoken groan, I pushed back from the desk and folded my hands in front of me. "What's up?"

"It, uh, it's about last night," he said, looking around nervously.

"The equipment? I'll help you replace the cameras, if you want. Even if it was your idea to put them in there."

"No, no." He waved his hands like he was calling for an incomplete pass. "Though if you want to chip in, that's cool. It's something else."

"Leon, I don't have time for twenty questions. Does it have something to do with the glowing female we saw last night? Just maybe?"

He stood up and started pacing. "That's a whole other discussion. But I wanted to talk to you about Shelly."

I blinked. "Michelle? What about her?"

He didn't look at me, just kept pacing back and forth in the tight space between my desk and the door. "I just wanted to make sure that we were still cool even though Shelly and I have kinda hooked up, with us being buds and all." The words were a rushed mumble, barely distinguishable from one another as he stumbled to get them out. Only when he was finished did he turn to look at me.

I laughed. "Jesus, Leon, is that what you're worried about? She's my ex-girlfriend. EX. Eee-eks. Whatever happens with you two is between you two, OK? Me, I'm going to spend a little more time trying to figure out who's taking impossible screenshots to leak to a fan site and where the naked women crawling out of the monitors are coming from, if that's all right with you."

Leon's face collapsed into an expression of hurt. "Are you sure, man. 'Cause I don't want there to be any problems if there's anything, you know, lingering."

My eyes rolled. "There's no lingering. Period. If you want me to get upset, I'll try, but I really don't have time right now. Come back around four o'clock and I'll see what I can do then."

"If you're not going to take it seriously," he grumbled, and took a couple of shuffling steps toward the door. "Wait a minute. What did you say about impossible screen shots?"

I turned the laptop around so he could see. "The only way to take this shot was from outside the playable space and behind a piece of level geometry. Which makes it impossible."

Leon thought about that for second and scratched his chin for emphasis. "If it's impossible, there's only one person I can think of who could take it."

I leaned forward. "Yeah? Who? Terry?"

"You gotta lay off this Terry thing. He's good, but he's not that good. No, I'm thinking it was the blue lady."

"Aw, come on!" I threw myself back into my chair, which bounced itself and the back of my head off the wall. "That's the stupidest thing I've heard in…OK, in minutes."

"Why is it so stupid?" he asked. "If you ask me, she's impossible. Besides, if she lives inside the network, she can probably do things in there that we can't."

I shook my head slowly. "But why would she be sending out screenshots?"

"Maybe she liked the game?"

"Heh." I thought about it for a second. Inside the game, inside the network—the pieces fit, if I was willing to believe the first one. "I have to admit, I'm still having a hard time trying to believe that we actually saw her. And I'm having a harder time thinking of how we could explain this to Eric if she is the one who did it."

"Yeah, I can see that. It's just a thought." He put his hand on the doorknob and half-turned it. "I'm not sure I believe it."

"Me neither. Which is how I'm getting through the day."

He stepped out into the hall, hand on the doorknob. "Good call, man. Open or shut?"

"Better leave it open," I told him, but my eyes were already on the screen. Hastily, I pulled up Sarah's chat window.

If you don't want Thai, you just have to say so. Chinese is fine. I'll see you tonight. This was followed by a smaller, system message informing me that Sarah had logged off of the chat. It was time-stamped five minutes ago, right after Leon had first come into my office.

"No! No no no no no no!" I frantically typed in a message to the now-grey messaging window. Thai is fine! I love Thai! Leon came into the office and I couldn't shut him up! I sent it, on the off chance that she'd log back in later in the day and see the message waiting for her. Then, when it didn't immediately cause her to log back in, I grabbed the phone and dialed her cell number. Two rings, and her voice mail picked up. "Hi, you've reached Sarah Bogdan. Leave a message at the tone and I'll probably get back to you."

My throat was abruptly dry, my voice scratchy. "Hey, Sarah. It's me. I'm sorry I didn't answer the IM, but Leon came into my office and wouldn't shut up and I couldn't get him out of here, and look, Thai sounds great. Do you want to pick it up, or do you want me to, or…just call me, okay? I love you, and I'll see you around six thirty at the latest. The absolute, utter latest. Bye."

"Problems at home?"

I looked up to see Eric sticking his head through the gap in the doorway that Leon had left. He looked faintly bemused, as if he'd had the same conversation a few dozen times himself.

"Nothing important," I told him, devoutly hoping I was right on that one. "Just missed a chat window while Leon was in here talking about—"

"I know what Leon was talking about," Eric interrupted. "Most of it, anyway. Is there going to be a problem?"

"With me and him over Shelly? No. With me and Shelly? Naah. With Leon and Shelly if they break up? God only knows." I ticked them off on my fingers, one by one. "Worst comes to worst, I get Leon drunk and we can commiserate about what a ballbreaker she is, then I apologize to her profusely and tell her that Leon's kind of a dickweed and she did the right thing."

"And when they get back together and compare notes, they'll both hate you."

I nodded. "Which is the way it should be, really. Everybody hates the creative director."

He gave a short bark of laughter. "I'm so glad you've got the proper perspective on this. Now," and he let himself the rest of the way into my office, "let's talk about this leaked screenshot."

So I told him what I felt comfortable telling him, about the deleted email address and the fact that I was trying to track down how the shot had been taken by going back into the build. I did not mention anything about anyone glowing blue, climbing out of monitors, or interfacing with Terry, nor did I mention anything else from the previous night's misadventure. From there, we moved on to following up on the screenshot, and a discussion of scheduling for the documentation on the revamped multiplayer features.

It was another hour before we were done, at which point I needed to go to a meeting with the level designers to talk about some recurring sightline issues, and then after that there was a sitdown with the AI engineers to discuss the list of enemy behaviors I was asking for and how many of them they could deliver in a reasonable timeframe. By that point, it was almost five, and I finally had enough time to start on some of the work I'd set out for myself as the day's labors, some of which had to be done if I wasn't going to bottleneck some of the feature implementation that had to start tomorrow.

And when I looked up, it was dark.

Chapter 19

Sarah was waiting for me under the porch light when I got home, sitting there on the stoop with her hair tied back and her eyes on the sidewalk. She was wearing her favorite red blouse, that and jeans and a look of utter weariness. Her feet were bare, and I wondered how long she'd been sitting there.

She didn't look up when I pulled in, nor when I cut the engine and got out in the driveway. I walked around to the passenger side of the car and grabbed my laptop from the shotgun seat and got nothing as a response. She just stared at the sidewalk, stared at the ground, stared at anything but me.

"Hi," I said softly as I made my way up the walk to where she sat. The door was open behind her, golden light spilling through it and around her, but I didn't go past. I didn't dare.

"Hi back," she said, not looking up. "How was work?"

"Long," I said before I could think better of it. "Tiring," I added after a minute. "How was yours?"

She shrugged. "The same. I got home around six. What time is it now?"

I fished out my cell phone and looked at it. "Nine thirty," I said, and knew that she already knew the answer. "I'm sorry I wasn't home sooner."

"No you aren't," she said, softly. "This is what you do." I started to protest, but she held up her hand to stop me. "No. Don't. It's very simple. If there is work, you do work. When the work is done, you come home. If there is no work, half the time you invent work. Tell me I'm wrong."

I sat down, heavily, on the cement in front of her. Her eyes flicked to my face for a moment, and then back down to the ground. "I can't," I said after a long while. "I don't know why."

"I do," she said, but without heat. "I know you. You let the job define you so you don't have to, and I'm just here to fill the space around the edges."

"That's stupid," I protested, and her head shot up, eyes staring.

"Is it now?" she asked. "I'm not the one doing it. Let me tell you something about yourself, Ryan. There are certain people in this world who, no matter how talented or clever or smart they are, inevitably end up getting shoved into the gears of the machine for the sake of everyone else. Maybe they do it because they're afraid to stand up for themselves. Maybe they do it because they worry too much about everything but themselves. And maybe they do it because they're selfish, and don't think they deserve any better, no matter what anyone around them thinks. You're one of those people, Ryan Colter. You always have been and you always will be."

"Am I now?" I whispered.

Her eyes were bright, wet with tears she wasn't going to let herself shed. "Yeah. You are. There's not a grenade out there you won't throw yourself on just to be the one who does it, and you know what? I'm stuck with you. I get to watch you blow yourself to bits again and again and again, and there's nothing I can do about it because that's just what you are."

"Sarah…"

She shook her head violently. "Don't say anything, Ryan. Please, don't say anything. If I don't get this out now, I never will, and if I don't say this once it's going to kill me. There are two things that happen to people like you, the people who like throwing themselves into the gears."

My hand reached out for hers. She brushed it away. "What two things," I asked.

"Either you get chewed up and disappear forever or you get used to it. Get to like it—having yourself be chewed up, that is. You get addicted to the agony of the fresh calamity every time you get tossed on the fire."

I drew back, felt my arms crossing themselves across my chest involuntarily. "Which am I?" I finally asked after a moment of silence.

Sarah stared at me. "It doesn't matter. Either way, you end up in the same place—nothing left, and the machine goes looking for a new victim. The only question is how far I'll let myself be dragged along with you."

Abruptly, she unwound herself and stood up. "I love you, Ryan. Your pad thai is in the fridge. It got cold waiting for you. Oh, and the DVR is cued up for your usual. I'll be upstairs if you need me."

"Sarah—"

But she had already gone inside. After a moment, the porch light winked out and left me sitting there in the faint, golden light from the lamp in the front hall. The door was left open, an invitation or a challenge or a warning.

I sat there, for how long I don't know. There was some noise from upstairs at first, then nothing but the comfortable quiet creaks of a well-worn house settling in on itself for the night. And I sat there, watching gnats and moths swarm around the top of the screen door and the azaleas move in what passed for a breeze, and didn't move. Couldn't, really. Couldn't force myself to get up, to go inside, to take that cold dinner and that television routine and then inevitably flip open the laptop and see if there were any late emails that needed attention.

Couldn't. Not tonight. Not with Sarah's words hanging in the air, daring me.

Like an old, old man, I got to my feet. One step, two steps, and then up onto the porch, and I swung the screen door open. The wave of cool air inside hit me like a physical blow, the differential between home and the world outside almost enough to twist my gut through its last unknotted half-inch. Another step and I'd be all the way inside, wrapped in the cold comfort. From there, it would be easy to take another step into routine, and another, and another, all the while pretending nothing had been said. Nothing was wrong, nothing had changed, nothing mattered—that's what I could pretend if I kept walking.

Instead, I slipped the laptop bag off my arm and gently set it down by the door. I was supposed to have it with me everywhere I went but, well, the hell with it. Who was going to report me? Myself? Screw that.

I shut the door behind me as I went back out, shaking my head and rolling my shoulders in hopes of unraveling the knot that had taken up residence between my shoulder blades. A mouse knot, we usually called it at work, but this one was the size of King Rat. For a moment I stood there and waited for a sound from inside the house, feet coming down the stairs or a voice calling my name and asking where I was going.

There was nothing. She probably thought I was going back to work, I realized bitterly. Why wouldn't she?

I thought about the laptop for a moment. It was fine right where it was, on the other side of the door from me. That's where it would be staying. My feet took me back down the walk and to the car. Normally I locked it, but not this time. It was an omen, perhaps, or just an indicator as to which way escape lay.

I got in and slammed the door behind me, jammed the key into the ignition, and got the hell out of there. A light might have gone on upstairs as I was leaving. Might have. I don't know. I didn't look to see.

I'd left the house determined just to go, to be alone with my thoughts without Sarah's presence as a reminder or the lure of the keyboard.

To just be, whatever that meant. I threw the car into gear and headed away from home, away from work, away from any place I might see anyone or anything I knew.

And ten minutes later, I found myself turning into the office parking lot, not surprised by it all.

* * *

There were four cars in the lot when I pulled in. One was Terry's. It was near the door, the sure sign of a late-night dinner carpool. The other three were scattered around the lot, unrecognizable and anonymous.

Pulling in next to Terryis car, I killed the engine before killing the radio or the lights. The beams illuminated the front of the office and a stretch down the hall, brighter cutting through the glass than the interior lights were. I could imagine blind salamanders and white-eyed cave fish scuttling for cover somewhere in the vicinity of the supply closet, then shut everything down and headed inside.

* * *

The building was quiet. That was the first thing I noticed when I got inside. Normally when folks were working late, it was an excuse to take off the headphones and crank the volume, especially if there wasn't anyone else around. Instead, what I heard was funereal silence. Even the chunking, thunking noises of the HVAC were oddly muted, hushed by the weight of the dim light.

I didn't bother turning on the overhead lighting on the hallway leading down to my office. I didn't bother turning on the lights in my office, either. Instead, I just slung myself into my chair and fired up my computer. The bluish-white glow from the screen filled the room, washing out all of the color that might have been there at the same time. Even the faint green glow from the debug kit, the tell-tale indicator that it was still running in spite of itself, looked weakened.

Seeing it reminded me that I'd left it on all afternoon, ever since the poking around I'd done in the Urbanscape level. The screen itself had long since gone dark, a power-saving measure built into the monitor to rescue it from people like me, but the steady, low whirr coming from the debug kit told me that something was still going on in there.

I grabbed the controller from where it sat on my desk and pressed a few buttons to wake the monitor up. It flashed white, then black, then white again before slowly drawing in the familiar scene I'd been stymied by earlier.

Except that it wasn't the same. When I'd left it, the scene was frozen, the simulation overwhelmed by the sheer number of entities onscreen. Now it showed a clean street, my avatar hovering over it like an avenging angel inspecting her handiwork. The dozens of enemies were gone. A quick check of the radar subscreen showed me that they weren't anywhere on the level, either. They were gone. Wiped out. All of which was eminently possible if someone very good had snuck into my office and played the game exceptionally well, but not so possible if the game was frozen.

I shook my head. Leon was right. The weird little things were adding up in conjunction with the big ones, and they almost scared me more. I ended the mission, then set the log to dump to my system. Looking at the record of all of the AI decisions on the level would tell me who had done what to whom and when. While that was going, I dove back into the level design documentation for Urbanscape.

Something about the freeze was nagging at me, and I wanted to double check what I thought I remembered.

After a minute of digging, I found the level design and opened it up. At the end of the doc were notes from the QA lab, the testers whose job it was to push things to the limit to see if, how, and when they'd break. Usually, they'd put something in there about the maximum number of enemies a level could support while still maintaining frame rate.

I scrolled through the doc. The space had been designed for 60 enemies at a time in hunter-killer game modes, with more respawning in to replace the ones the players had killed until the timer ran out or the desired number of kills had been reached. A decent frame rate was thirty frames per second, thirty redraws of the onscreen image. Officially, we had been gunning for sixty, but as Leon had said, he could give us sixty if the game involved sitting in a white room with no furniture and fighting invisible rocks.

Toward the back of the doc, I found what I was looking for. Written in the notes section by one of the testers—all that was there were the initials C.M.—was a small entry noting that frame rate dropped below acceptable levels with 74 enemies on screen and 16 players. This was dated three days before the project was shut down, and there was no note of any change to the geometry that would wreck the frame rate in those three days. There was barely any record of it being touched at all. And yet, somehow it had sprung a memory leak that choked it at two-thirds of its expected performance.

Or, and I felt a chill go down my spine, there was something else in there that was chewing up processing power.

I was saved from following that train of thought by a window popping up to inform me that the game log was ready to be read. I wasn't sure exactly what I was looking for in there—notes on the kills, I guessed—but it was information, and it might help me figure out what exactly had been happening.

In the hallway, something moved. I heard the sound just as I clicked to open the log file, the unmistakable shuffle of sneakered feet on office-park carpet.

"Hello?" I called. "Anyone out there?"

There was no response, just the sound of a couple more steps fading into the dark, and what might have been some asthmatic breathing. "Hello?" I called again and moved from behind my desk.

"Look, if you want something, you just have to ask, okay? Okay?" By the time I finished, I was halfway into the hall myself, staring down the better-lit sections of the building and hearing the sound of someone beating a hasty retreat.

Whatever, I told myself. Probably someone who heard noise up at the front and wanted to see what was going on. Either that, or someone who'd been downloading porn and thought he might get caught in the act. Either way, I didn't consider it my problem and retreated to my desk.

The log file was open when I got back, a sprawling scroll of raw, steaming data. I could read it well enough to pick out the basics—where routines had been triggered, what loops had come into play when, where and when casualties had occurred—but it was dense stuff, and slow going. The fact that the mission had been running for something like ten hours, generating data the entire time, didn't help to speed the process up much, either.

Looking down at the bottom of the screen, I saw that the logfile ran to somewhere near two hundred pages. Line-by-lining it could take the rest of the night and then some. Doing a quick skim instead, and trying to pinpoint the exact moment when the stuck had become un-stuck and the live and hostile had become dead and nonexistent, seemed like the best way to tackle it with any reasonable hope of completion.

Maybe a quarter of the way in, I stopped. Not because I'd found what I was looking for, but because I'd found something else. In the middle of the log, there were six empty lines, followed by two words, and then six more blanks.

HELLO RYAN, the logfile said.

I gawped. Sat there for a moment, trying to comprehend what it was I was looking at. And then, very slowly and very carefully, I started scrolling down again.

Fifty lines further down was another message: I HOPE YOU DON'T MIND.

There was another noise out in the hallway. Spooked, I looked up. This time, I caught a silhouette, a tall, skinny silhouette.

"Damnit, Terry, have you been screwing around on my system?" I hurried into the hallway. Terry was mostly gone; I saw bits of him disappearing around the corner, flying feet and waving hands as he ran for it.

"Stupid bastard!" I shouted after him. "You've got to come up with something better than commenting a log to screw my head!" I listened for an answer, but there wasn't one.

"Idiot." I shook my head. "Tomorrow, I'm definitely talking to Leon." Outside in the parking lot, a car door slammed. Someone taking off, most likely. Someone who didn't want to play tag with Terry.

When I got back to my desk, there was another comment in the log, a new one right under the last one I'd found. TERRY'S NOT DOING THIS, it read. I AM.

And then, as I watched, the letters formed themselves on the screen, inserting themselves into the document one at a time with deliberate, careful slowness. I REALLY THINK WE SHOULD TALK.

My first instinct was to run, to head for the door, drive home, and tell Sarah I was quitting effective immediately.

PLEASE?

Please. Whoever it was had said please. "Jesus." My fingers found their way to the keyboard. I could see them shaking, each at its own frequency. I took a deep breath and tried to steady them, then typed, WHO ARE YOU?

There was a pause, then the words, I'M YOURS, inched their way into being.

SARAH? I typed back. WHAT ARE YOU DOING HERE? HOW ARE YOU DOING THIS?

The answer, when it came, was swift and furious. The lights went out, not dramatically and in sequence, but rather darkness came down, and came down hard. Every light in the building went, snuffed out in an instant. The emergency lights flared on for an instant, then they, too, faded away. The HVAC wheezed to a stop, and the air thickened as it ceased circulation.

Somehow, my laptop stayed on. NOT THE BITCH, appeared almost instantly. NEVER CONFUSE ME WITH THE BITCH.

I'M SORRY, I wrote, hurriedly and with enough typos to require retyping it and then retyping it again. WHO ARE YOU? SHELLY?

CLOSER, came back, followed by, YOU KNOW ME. YOU JUST DON'T KNOW HOW WELL.

My heart rabbited along in my chest, beating a little faster with each exchange. Crazy stalker? Crazy stalker with mad hacking skills? Crazy stalker with mad hacking skills who was in the building and had cut the power? In the hallway a couple of voices rose, people saying they were getting the hell out, then the front door closing and opening and closing again.

Common sense told me to get out, too. No sense being trapped in the building with whoever was on the other end of the surreal conversation I was having.

Common sense told me to get out. Curiosity told me to figure out who it was, which might make any possible defense—or restraining order—that much more effective.

But there was no sense taking too many unnecessary chances. I got up to shut my door and lock it and shoved a chair in front of it, just in case.

And when I had finished, I turned around to sit back down, and she was there.

She was sitting in my chair, arms folded demurely over her breasts. She was naked, her legs crossed in front of her and the chair spun halfway around. She looked at me over her shoulder, and as she saw that I saw her, she smiled.

It was her smile that scared me the most. Because the face that looked at me and smiled, a dazzling, seductive, beautiful smile, was not the same face that I'd seen on the webcam the night before. The figure was the same, but the face had changed, metamorphosed into something equally, heart-stoppingly attractive, but different.

There was Shelly's chin and cheekbones. There were Sarah's eyes, the curl of the hair that fell down across her forehead. There was the small, sensual mouth of a woman I'd known and lusted after for four years of college but had never spoken to. There were pencil-thin and razor-sharp movie star eyebrows, there was the button nose that my junior prom date had hated but that I'd found irresistible, all blended together to make one stunning whole.

"Like I said," she said, "I think it's time we talked."

No intelligent sounds came out of my mouth. I sagged against the whiteboard instead, blinking furiously. For she was bright, and with every breath, getting brighter. The blue-white light from her swallowed the output from the laptop's screen, ate up the monitor's empty cityscape, washed away the indicator light on the debug kit.

"Who are you?" I finally stammered. "Why are you here?"

She laughed, the sort of laugh you only hear during lovemaking when you've done something spectacularly right. "Ryan, don't be silly. I'm here because of you. By you. For you. With you. Isn't that enough?"

"It's a little too much," I said, and put my hand up to shield my eyes. "Could you…put something on, at least? Something dimmer?"

Again, the delighted laugh, and it suddenly got very hard to concentrate. She spun the chair back around, uncrossed her arms, spread her legs. As she did so, the light dimmed, and she sat there in what looked to be a high-necked unitard, a deeper shade of blue than her skin, form-fitting and marked here and there with patterns that looked like circuitry or language or both. "Is this better," she asked. "I didn't think you'd want the armor."

"The…armor?"

"The combat armor, silly. It's not very comfortable the way it was designed, and I don't think it would have been very good for your chair." She shook her head. "Anyway, I just wanted to say hello. We got off to such a bad start last night, and I've been trying so hard to talk to you."

I gulped. "Talk to…me?"

She nodded. "Of course, you. We should thank Terry. He's the one who figured it out, of course. He's been working on it all along." She looked up at me, pouting. "I had to thank him somehow, you know, and he loves me so much, but it doesn't change the way I feel about you."

Slowly, I edged toward the door. "The only thing that Terry's been working on has been..."

She smiled. "Exactly." Unwinding herself from the chair, she stood up. "Don't worry. We'll be seeing more of each other. There should be some…benefits for working so late, don't you think?"

And as I stood there, paralyzed by her words and their implications, she kissed me.

Not on the lips, just a soft, gentle peck on the forehead. Where her lips touched me, I felt fire.

My eyes closed. When I opened them again, she was gone.

There was a sudden, sharp noise out in hall, the meaty thwack of a fist hitting drywall. Then, footsteps trailing off into the dark.

Terry, I thought wearily. Good goddamn, and staggered back to my desk in the dark.

Chapter 20

For a long time I sat there, hands gripping the desk for the sheer, blessed solidity of it. Onscreen, the Windows logo bounced back and forth on a black background, utterly placid and utterly unaware of what it was replacing. My skin felt tight and hot, as if it had been sunburned, on my forehead where it—she—had kissed me. The lights had not come back on, nor had the ones in the hallway.

Eventually the screen saver timed out, clicking over to sleep mode and fading to black. I let it, closing my eyes and leaning back and wondering what the hell had just happened. I'd seen…something.

No. I'd seen the same thing that Terry had seen, that Terry had made some kind of contact with. I'd seen the thing that had tried to fry my eyeballs in the team room that night.

I'd talked to it. Touched it. Listened to it. Learned what it was.

The knowledge left me shaking. The thought that we—that I had created that, dropped the bottom out of my gut. It...she was Blue Lightning. Of that, there was no doubt. She'd as much as confessed to it, and the fact that she looked like the game's main character, even wore the face I imagined on that character, told me all I needed to know.

When she'd been doing improbable things with Terry, that had been bad enough. But I'd attracted her attention now, and she wanted mine.

She wanted me. And that terrified me.

"Hey. What did you do to the lights?"

Michelle's voice cut the darkness from the other side of the door. I opened my eyes and called out "Wait a minute," clearing the chair away from the door and opening it for her.

She didn't step inside. Instead, she chose to hang on the doorframe, leaning with her head peeking into my office.

"What are you doing here?" I asked. "I thought everyone else had gone home."

"You didn't answer my question. I don't have to answer until you do." She gave the ghost of a grin in the dim light.

I walked back to my desk. "I didn't do anything to the lights. They got shut down."

"Say what?" Shelly let herself off the doorframe and walked in. Experimentally, she waggled the light switch a few times, up and down. The light itself didn't change, nor did we get the tell-tale hum of a fluorescent powering on. "Huh. Blown fuse?"

I pointed to the computer. "That's still running, and not off the UPS."

"Then how…" She stopped and thought for a second. "Oh. Oh, no."

"Yeah." Suddenly, my neck hurt like hell. I reached back to massage it. "She was here. She wanted to talk to me."

"She?" Shelly stepped over to my desk. "Since when was it a she?"

"Since the art department gave the model hi-poly count boobs?" I shook my head and grimaced. "I'm sorry, that was unfair. But it's definitely a she. And I think I know what she is."

Michelle cocked her head to one side and looked at me. "You look like crap," she said. "And I don't like where you're going with this, and right now the office is creeping me the hell out. Do you want to get out of here? Maybe go over to Montague's and have a beer?"

I rubbed my eyes. "Deal. I'll drive." A sudden thought struck me. "And I answered your question, now you answer mine. What are you doing here tonight?"

Shelly made a face, the corners of her mouth turned down and her brow wrinkled up in disgust. "There was a huge mess with the check-in on about a thousand objects. I had to go back and correct it manually."

"Ow." I caught myself wincing. "So who dies tomorrow?"

"Nobody. Innocent mistake. It happens." She stepped out of the office and into the hallway, where the lights were slowly coming back on. "So, shall we?"

"We shall." I followed her into the hall, and turned to shut the door behind me. "But you'll have to tell me who you are and what you've done with Michelle." Not quite arm in arm, not quite lockstep, we headed for the door.

"This is really tired Michelle, Ryan. And are you sure you're OK to drive? You look shaken up."

I got to the door a half-second before she did and buzzed us out. "I'm fine. I think. And yeah, I'd rather drive. It'll take my mind off of things."

"Things." Shelly followed me, making sure the door was shut behind us. More than once, it had failed to latch and the alarm had gone off at ungodly hours as a result. Eric was the only one who could shut it off at times like that, and he was never much fun the day after.

"Things," she repeated, as we headed for my car. I dug out my keys and opened the door on her side first. "It's still naked, right?"

Walking around to my side of the car saved me from having to answer. By the time I got there, Shelly had reached across the seat and unlocked my door. I swung it open and got in, reflexively plugging my phone into the aux cable as I did so.

"Montague's it is, unless you've got a better suggestion?" I threw the car into gear and peeled out.

"Montague's has beer," Shelly answered, her hands fiddling with the phone. "Mind if we get some music."

"Go ahead," I told her, "but I'm warning you, all it seems to want to play these days is the sample tracks from the Blue Lightning soundtrack."

She gave me a smile of such frightening plasticity that I nearly rear-ended the car in front of us. "Really. And why would that be, do you think?"

I didn't smile back at her. "I think I'm starting to get an idea."

Michelle hit play. Music flooded the interior of the car, cranked too loud and with the bass mixed way too high. "Jesus, Ryan, what the hell do you do in here?"

"Sorry, sorry." I adjusted the settings and turned the volume down. The thrumming caterwauls resolved themselves into something off an old Todd Rundgren album, and I rolled down the windows to keep the sound from bouncing around inside quite so much. "I hadn't realized they were up so high."

"Don't worry about it." She leaned out the window and let the wind catch her hair. It had cooled off considerably. There was a fat, full moon in the sky, and enough stars to be noticeable. No clouds, and there was a faint cool snap in the air.

We didn't speak the rest of the way to the bar. I concentrated on the road, keeping to some of the less busy, less well-lit routes so we'd stay more in the moonlight. The music did all the talking necessary, which wasn't much, track after track touching on angry or mad or sad or alone or some combination in between.

Shelly skipped one song, once, that I'd put on a mix for her back in the day. I didn't say anything, just let it go.

The parking lot was just on the wrong side of half-empty when we got there. I picked a spot near the dumpster and pulled in. Shelly wrinkled her nose as she rolled up the window. "Jesus, Ryan. You always take me to the nicest places."

"It's the last place anyone else parks," I said as I got out. "Less likely to get my door dinged."

"If you say so." She sounded unconvinced, and her expression didn't help sell it, either. We headed inside.

The bartender gave us a nod, then went back to racking glasses as they came out of the dishwasher. Only one of the televisions was on, a small cluster of middle-aged men sitting underneath it in silence as it showed a rebroadcast of a rugby match from halfway around the world.

"Bar?" I asked. Shelly shook her head and headed for one of the back booths. After a second, I followed her, a glimpse of the game having proved insufficient distraction. Behind me, there was cursing and cheering in equal measures. Someone must have scored.

Shelly was seated when I caught up to her. She'd taken the inside, her back resting against the high dark wood of the booth and her eyes looking out past me toward the door. I slid in opposite. Behind her, the tops of the bathroom doors were visible. I kept my eyes on Shelly instead.

The table was made of the same dark wood as the benches, pitted and scratched and scarred from untold patrons who'd been unkind or ungraceful. Against the wall was a napkin holder flanked by an honor guard of condiments, a beer menu tucked in behind them. The wall held a framed reproduction copy of *The Irish Times* from 1924, next to a print of a black and white photo of the Dublin GPO. Neither of them looked particularly authentic, and the frames were mismatched.

"You think there's a company out there that sells this crap?" Shelly asked as the waitress set down glasses of water on coasters stamped with the Guinness logo. I looked up at her. "Two Harps?"

The waitress, a woman with a brunette pageboy cut and a figure like the Venus of Willendorf, nodded. "Sure thing, hon. Anything else?"

"Bushmill's," Shelly interjected. "Two. For starters."

The waitress looked back and forth between us for a second. "Those for you, honey, or one for each?"

"One for each, thanks." She dipped her fingers in her water glass and started sketching on the tabletop, even as the server turned her back on us and ambled off.

"Bushmill's?" I asked.

Shelly didn't look up from the table, where the lines she was sketching joined the dents and dings and cuts the tabletop had suffered. Something was taking shape there as she raced to build it, even as the water beaded up and flowed away where she drew. "You look like you need it. I figured I'd be sociable and join you."

I chuckled, but my heart wasn't in it. "Can't argue with that logic."

"You never could," she answered, and kept sketching. The level in her water glass had already dropped a good inch and a half. I pushed my water glass over toward her, careful not to disrupt any of what she'd already done. "Here. Take mine."

"You want my fingers in your glass?" she snorted, but the next time she needed to reload, she dipped into my glass. Then she flicked the cold water at me, and I ducked reflexively. "Pointillism," she said, and laughed, and pointed at the flecks of water on the table.

That time, my grin was real.

The waitress chose that moment to return with the tray of drinks, setting the whisky down first and then the beer. Both came down at the end of the table, far from the water sketch. She served Shelly first. "What are you doing?" she asked.

"It'll be finished by the next round. I'll show you then. Deal?"

"Deal," said the waitress, and then "Is there anything else you need? Food? A menu?"

I wrapped my fingers around the glass of whiskey. "We're fine for now, thanks."

I got an "Okay" in a voice like she didn't believe me, and she melted back behind the bar. The rugby fans were yelling about something. I caught hints of a call that had gone the wrong way, or maybe a misinterpretation of a rule. It made no sense to me, so I did my best to ignore it.

Shelly picked up her whiskey and held it there, looking at me through the amber light of the glass. "Do we need a toast?" she asked. "Or do you just need a shot?"

"Yes," I said, and clinked my glass against hers. "To getting the hell out of there tonight before something serious happened." I threw it back, and slammed the glass down on the table. Shelly's eyes widened, but she did the same, and then reached for the beer.

"Now that you've got a drink in you, can you tell me what happened?" She took a sip. A pencil-thin foam mustache formed on her lip, sitting there until she wiped it away with the back of her hand. "Or were you and Terry and the thing having a threesome?"

I shuddered. "Don't joke about that." To cover up the shakes, I took a swig of beer, which turned into draining half a pint glass before I knew it. "Jesus," I said. "The way I'm going, you'd better finish that sketch in a hurry."

"Uh-huh." She tapped a finger on the table impatiently. "So. Story."

"Story." I took another drink, and got halfway through what was left. "The short version? I was at my desk, the lights went out, and she showed up."

"What were you working on?"

Rather than meeting her eyes, I looked past her. One of the rugby fans stumbled into the bathroom, missing the door twice before finally finding the handle. "I was looking at some of the old Blue Lightning docs."

Shelly said, "Interesting," in a voice that indicated it was anything but. "Did she materialize, or beam in like *Star Trek*, or what?"

"You called her 'she' just now, you know?" I finished my beer. "Are you going to finish yours?"

"Order another," she shot back, and took a healthy swig. "And call the waitress over. Someone needs a refill."

"Someone needs to get laid," I shot back, then turned to scan the room for the waitress. I caught her eye as she was offloading a tray of empties at the bar, and she nodded. "She just showed up in the monitor."

"Your monitor's not that big," Shelly said. "There's no room for her in there."

"That's what you're worried about in all this?" I shook my head in disbelief. "Look, she talked to me, OK? She told me that I needed to help her. She told me..." I couldn't repeat the rest of it. "She told me a lot of things," I added lamely. "And she talked about Terry."

"That must have been skeevy as all hell." Shelly looked like she was about to say something more, but the waitress chose that moment to appear.

"What else can I get you?"

"Two more of the same," Shelly announced. "And we'll start a tab. Ryan, give the nice woman your credit card."

I dug out my wallet and tossed the MasterCard to the server. "What's your name," I asked.

"Leah," she answered, checking the back of the card for a signature. "You got a picture ID to go with this?"

I flashed my driver's license at her. She looked at it, nodded. "Good enough. Two more Harps and two more Bushmills?"

"Just the Harps, I think," I said, as Shelly looked daggers at me. "For now," I amended.

"Got it." Leah leaned over the table. "Is it done?"

"It's done," Shelly answered, and leaned back. "What do you think?"

Leah looked at the table, then looked at me, and then flicked her glance back and forth a few more times before saying anything. "It's good. It's really good. I don't know how you did it, but…" She looked at me again. "Yeah."

"Thanks," Shelly said. I looked from her to the waitress and back again, and then down to the table. By then, though, Shelly had already run her arm across the tabletop and wiped the sketch away.

"What was it?" I asked. Shelly and Leah looked at each other, sharing a wordless moment of disgust at the male of the species, and then one went off to fetch our drinks while the other stayed to keep badgering me.

"Now, what did she say to you?" The emphasis Shelly put on the word made it clear she wasn't comfortable with it, didn't actually believe it, or at least didn't want to.

"Personal stuff," I answered, shifting uncomfortably. "Look, is this really necessary?"

She looked me in the eye, and gradually I stopped fidgeting. "I'd say so," she finally said. "Come on, Ryan, talk it out. I can see you're still shaken up. Just tell me and maybe we can figure out what to do next. After all, I've seen that…thing, too."

I shook my head. "She's not a thing. She's Blue Lightning."

"How can you be sure?"

I started ticking off the evidence I'd come up with on my fingers. "One, she looks like the main character."

"The main character has no face," Sarah interrupted. "This chick's clearly got one, at least if you believe that video feed we got off Terry."

"Her face changes depending on the person she's talking to." I thought for a minute, struggling to find the best way to explain it. "It's their idea of what she should look like."

Shelly looked unconvinced, so I plowed on. "She only started showing up after the project got cancelled. All the weird stuff that's happening, like my phone freaking out, it's Blue Lightning-related. She got into a log file as I was looking at it. She's the only explanation for the screenshots and the leaks. And most importantly," I'd saved the best for last, "she told me. Not in so many words, but...she told me."

There was silence, then. Shelly stared at me. I stared down at the table and wondered what she'd drawn. "That's not possible, you know," she finally said.

"I know."

"It's just a video game. It's not a person. It's not alive. It doesn't have...superpowers, or whatever this thing can do."

"I know."

"It shouldn't be real. It can't be real!"

"I know. But it is."

As Leah dropped off the new round of beers, Michelle settled into a sulky silence. "I don't understand," was all she said, and then attacked the beer fiercely.

I took it a little more slowly. "I agree it should be impossible. But it is. I know it. You know it. Terry sure as hell knows it."

"Screw Terry," she said, and drank more beer. "Screw all of this. I should quit."

"Don't run out on me, Shelly," I said. I was surprised to find that I meant it. "There's got to be some logic to this thing."

"Logic? You want logic? How's this, then? The game gets cancelled, but because everyone's put so much into it, it gets a little boost of love or belief or whatever, and that's enough to bring it to life. And now it wants to say thank you by giving everyone a big, sloppy kiss? Sorry, I don't swing that way." She spat the words out like they tasted bad and washed her mouth clean with beer after each sentence.

"Fine," I said. "I'll play along. So everyone sweated so much and loved the game so much that it woke up. And then, what, the guys on the black project kept it alive?"

"It did show up to Terry first, right?" She finished her beer and signaled to Leah for another one.

"That we know of, yeah." I thought about it. "Though maybe not. You remember the Powerpoint?"

She nodded. "The one where neither of us made the changes, and—oh God, I'd almost forgotten about that. You think it was—"

"Yeah. I think it was. And—bear with me here, because this is going to sound shitty—maybe she's more solid to me because, I don't know, there's more of me in her?"

"That's gross, Ryan." Michelle frowned.

"For God's sake, Michelle." She had the good grace to look slightly embarrassed, and I went on. "Seriously, my job is to hold the vision of the game, right? The dream of it. Everyone else kicks in, but everyone else has, I dunno, a specific part of it that's theirs. Levels and features and objects. But the way they all come together? Eric keeps telling me, that's mine."

Shelly pursed her lips to one side. "Jesus, you're an egotistical bastard. But you might be right. Ah, hell. Where's the next beer?"

"Coming," I said, as I saw Leah cresting through the sea of rugby fans, now mostly wobbly in their chairs or standing under the television.

"Good." She grabbed my pint glass and took a drink. "You should finish yours."

"I'm driving," I reminded her. "Besides, it's got your germs on it now."

She missed the joke, or maybe she dodged it. "Never bothered you before."

I said nothing, just looked away, embarrassed.

"Oh, come on, Ryan. I'm just messing with you."

"Yeah." I grabbed one of the menus and changed the subject. "Do you want anything to eat? I hate drinking on an empty stomach."

"God, yes." Leah arrived at our table with more beer. "Water for my next round," I told her, and she made a note of it. "And an order of the potato skins to split, and I'll have the chicken sandwich, and my friend usually gets the shepherd's pie."

"Coming up." She turned on her heel, vanishing into the crowd, half of which was now doing an unintelligible chant for one team or another.

"They're having fun," Shelly said softly. She put the menu down. I nodded. "Are you still having fun? With what we do, I mean. Is it fun for you?"

"The stuff with the weird blue glowing woman or the bit where we make games?"

"Either. Both. Is one enough to put up with the other. If it is, what the hell is wrong with us? This isn't funny, Ryan. "

I thought about it for a second. "What brought that on?" I finally found myself asking. "I mean, we're in the fun business. We make games."

Shelly finished my beer, maybe a little faster than I would have expected. "That's not the same thing. We make things for other people to have fun with, sure. But do you actually have fun doing this?" The empty glass hit the table with a clank, turned upside down for emphasis.

I looked at her, at the open question on her face, then looked down at my drink. There was still some head on the beer, so I poked at it with my index finger and drew a little smiley face in the foam. "See?" I said. "You're not the only artist here."

Shelly snorted but didn't back down. "You're not answering the question."

"You're right," I said. "It's not an easy question to answer."

"Best shot?"

I nodded. "Best shot. No, it's not fun." I saw Shelly lean forward, but I held up a hand to stop her. "It's not fun, and it was never about fun for me. I mean, there are bits of it that are a lot of fun, that I really enjoy, but those are chrome. They're not the heart of it for me."

"Then what is?" She cocked her head sideways and rested it on her palm.

"Creating something," I said, after a long minute of looking for the right words. "Dreaming something up, and getting everyone else to buy into that dream and share it and make it better, and then making it happen. And there's more, there's always more. Maybe what we do is going to be something no one has ever seen before. Maybe some kid sitting in his living room is going to see what we made and go "Whoah!" and tell his friends "You gotta see this!" and have that little bit of magic happen to him from what I—what we—dreamed up and worked so damn hard on."

I was half up out of my seat now, pointing and waving my arms and thumping my hand on the table for emphasis, before I noticed her looking at me. There was a question in her eyes, but a different one than she'd been about to ask a minute ago. "Shelly?" I said.

"Thank you, Ryan." She took a long, deep, shuddering breath and turned her face to the wall. "Thank you for telling me that."

"It's just the truth," I told her, and dropped back into my seat. "That's really all I've got to keep me going in this."

"It's all you've got," she answered. She waited a long time before continuing. "Not everyone has that. There are people in there who really do think this is fun, and God bless them for it. And there are people in there who are convinced that they could never, ever do anything else in a million years. So they're stuck doing this if they don't want to be working the deep fryer at a McDonalds, and they'll never get out until they're pushed, and they hate every minute of it because they're supposed to be having fun, cause it's games, right? And there are people who got in and got settled and then figured out that it's not what they want, but they're caught, because the money's just good enough that they can't walk away and start over."

"And what about you," I asked her, leaning across the table to put my hand on her arm for comfort. "None of those sound like you."

Michelle turned to me, her eyes wide open and serious. "I'm one of the ones who doesn't know what else to do, Ryan," she said quietly. "I'm one of the ones who knows I'm really good at this but doesn't know why. And then every so often, someone like you comes along, someone who really believes in this stuff and who makes it sing, and that's enough to pick me up and carry me along for a year or two. That's enough to give me a reason to keep coming back for more. And when that dream isn't there, then…" She shrugged, and to cover her embarrassment she noisily tossed down the rest of her beer.

I pulled my hand away. For a moment, I thought she was going to grab it and hold it in place, but her fingers only twitched and didn't move, didn't reach for mine.

"It's okay," I said, not knowing what else there was to say.

"It's not okay." She shook her head. "I hate it. I hate not being able to find whatever it is that I need to drive me on my own. I hate having to latch on to something else. It's why I hate you. Because you don't have to."

"You hate me?" I sat back, and pulled my hands off the table entirely. "I thought we were, well, friends, or something."

I got a wan smile in return. "Just a little bit," she said. "God, watching you get hyped up about Blue Lightning, about all the cool stuff that was going in there…you really picked up the room and carried it, you know? It was like falling in love. You loved it, so we loved it. We all believed in that game, Ryan. I believed in it."

"Terry still believes in it," I said softly. "And I'm starting to."

"Well, I don't," Shelly leaned forward across the table. "I believe in you. Even when I hated you, you made me fall in love with an idea. No wonder it's sticking around. If I were a ghost of something you'd dreamed up, I'd stick around, too."

"Shelly, I…" I sat for a moment, with her almost looking up at me in the way she used to, once upon a time, when I loved her. "I don't know what to say."

"Don't say anything." She smiled. "Just do me a favor. If you can find a way to believe, just a little bit, in this new crap thing we're working on, I'd like that. I'd really like that a lot."

"I'll try," I heard myself say. "No promises."

Her words came out almost a choke, almost as a sob. "Your promises were never worth much anyway." She slid out of the booth. "I'll be back in a minute. Don't eat all the skins when they show up, all right?" Without another word, she headed for the restrooms.

I watched her go, at least as far as dignity would allow, then just stared at the wall thinking about what she'd said.

The clank of a plate landing on table yanked me back to reality. Leah set down silverware and a giant offering of what I presumed were potato skins, a bubbling volcanic mass of day-glow cheese product and bacon and chives with a thundercloud of sour cream in the center. "Your meals will be out in a couple of minutes," she said. "Eat fast."

"I'll wait for her to get back," I said. "Thanks."

She didn't leave. Instead, she looked at the door to the restrooms, then down at me, then away again. "That's nice," she said. "You're waiting for your girlfriend to start. Most guys wouldn't do that."

"She's not my girlfriend," I corrected her. "Friend, coworker…ex… whatever."

"Uh-huh." Leah's eyes narrowed. "Does she know that?"

"She'd better. She threw a full can of Sprite at my head when we broke up. I had to clean up the mess when it hit the wall."

"Proves nothing," she said, picking up the empties. "Another round?"

"Sure," I said. "And honestly, we're not together. We're both with other people now. We just had a rough day at work and wanted a beer."

"That must be why she drew your face on the table," she said, then walked away.

By the time Shelly came back, the bubbling cheese had stopped bubbling, the singing rugby fans had stifled their noise, and I'd mostly managed to snap my jaw shut. "Hey," I said as she sat down. Her face was wet, like she'd been splashing cold water on it. I said nothing about it.

"Hey. Works every time, doesn't it? I go to the bathroom and the food shows up."

"Like magic. I waited for you."

"I can see that. You didn't have to."

I shrugged. "There's a lot of 'didn't have to' out there. It just seemed like the right thing to do."

"You're sweet," she said around a mouthful of grease and starch.

"When I forget I'm a bastard. And I think I'm good, Shelly. Thank you for suggesting we get out of there for a while. I needed that."

"We both needed it," she said, and patted my hand with greasy fingers. I didn't pull away. After a minute, she rested hers on top of mine. "And I'm glad we talked."

"About that thing at work?"

"About everything." Her fingers tightened around mine. Mine did the same around hers, as if by reflex.

I looked around for Leah, but she was nowhere to be found. Words, I told myself. Get the conversation on something else. "So about Blue Lightning…"

Shelly sighed and brushed the hair back from her eyes. "God, you are obsessed with work."

"Yeah, well, I'm more worried about work getting obsessed with me."

"Very funny. So what do you want to do about it. Her. Whatever."

"Even if she is what we think she is, she's just a ghost. I don't think she can show up in the daytime or she would have done it already. So tomorrow, I'll tell Eric all about the black project and get it shut down, she'll go away, and everyone will be happy."

Shelly sighed, shifting her hand on mine. "Almost everyone," she said. She leaned forward to kiss me.

After a moment, I said, "Shelly, we shouldn't…"

She put her finger on my lips. "We saw a ghost. I don't know about you, but right now I want to do something that makes me feel alive."

"You're drunk," I told her but didn't pull away. "In the morning…"

"I'm not drunk. I'm tipsy. And you're driving." She kissed me again.

It was a good kiss, the pressure of her lips firm against mine, the taste of her mouth overwhelming everything else. I could feel Michelle's tongue tracing the line of my mouth and then gently moving against mine, and I gave myself up to the feeling. I'd missed this, I realized, without even knowing I'd missed it. For all that I loved Sarah, for all that our lovemaking was sweet and gentle and caring, this had always been lacking from it, the feeling of challenge met and shared and passed back and forth to heighten the pleasure.

"Sarah..." I gasped when we broke for breath. "I can't—"

"She gets you back tomorrow," Shelly whispered. "Not tonight."

We kissed again.

"The ghost—"

"—Isn't here," she finished for me. "And we shouldn't be, either."

And when I looked up, Leah was standing at the foot of the table with my card, our bill, and a look on her face that said "I told you so."

Not knowing the going rate for silence, I left her a large tip. Then Shelly and I went back out into the night, her leaning on me just a little more than she needed to, and me letting her.

Chapter 21

I woke up staring at a familiar ceiling, my head on a familiar pillow.

"Oh, Jesus." The words came out like a prayer, a prayer that I wasn't where I thought I was, wasn't with who I had to be.

I lay there for a moment, feeling the warmth of a body cuddled up to mine. The regular, gentle pattern of her breathing told me she was still asleep, which I took as a small blessing. The moment I moved, though, she'd be up. I knew this from experience. After all, Michelle had always been a light sleeper.

So I stayed there on my back and looked up at the night sky she'd painted on the ceiling; deep blue sky and yellow stars that were supposed to glow in the dark and sometimes did. I'd spent a lot of nights looking up at those constellations, ones Michelle had done with painstaking precision. I knew this; I'd helped her. Here and there, darker spots on the ceiling showed where I'd misplaced Zeta Reticuli or Aldebaran, and she'd had to paint over my handiwork.

I'd thought that after all this time, they would have faded.

Instead, it looked like she'd been touching them up.

She'd re-painted the walls. The last time I'd been here, they'd been a stark and unforgiving white. Now, they'd been done in a gentler tone, the warmer color of a late summer afternoon, and all around she'd done silhouettes of Chinese bamboo, black brushstrokes standing out stark against the background. There was nothing else there, no sun or sky or lone panda munching his way through the scenery, just those long black stalks reaching up and out.

In lesser hands, they would have looked like prison bars. In Shelly's, they looked like someplace you could lose yourself, someplace to hide.

"Mmm?" I felt Shelly as much as I heard her, her body snuggling up next to mine. Risking a glance over at her face, I could see that she was smiling. There was a hard set to her jaw at work these days, but here and now it was gone. She was relaxed, calm, even innocent. She was happy.

Frost crawled all over my insides at the thought of it. I could feel her skin against mine, smooth and soft and decidedly unclothed. We were naked, in her bed, and in her sleep she looked happy.

When she woke up, I was certain that would change.

Change how, though, I didn't know. For her, for me, for Sarah—for Leon, whom I thought of belatedly—some kind of genie had been let out of the bottle.

"Hmmm." Shelly purred a bit, rolling onto her side. Her back pressed up against me, an unconscious expression of trust. I felt like a heel.

Getting back together with Shelly was out of the question. For one thing, I loved Sarah. I thought about that, tested and probed the idea, and every answer came back true. For all the sparring that we'd done over my work habits (and the memory of last night was strong and sour), for all that she wanted me to get the hell out of gaming and get a respectable job, for all that she was The Real World personified in a blonde and impeccably dressed package, I loved her. The thought of leaving her was a physical wrench, a tug on my insides that threatened to tear me in half if I gave it too much play.

And yet, here I was in Shelly's bed. I liked Shelly, had grown to like her more as a friend after we'd had our final detonation at work. I'd learned to respect her more as well, her professional competence on constant display in everything we did at the office. And, I admitted, I still wanted her on occasion in a way that I never felt for Sarah.

I'd just never expected to act on it ever again. Even when I'd caught myself looking, I'd smacked the daydream down ruthlessly. I shouldn't. It was wrong. It would mess things up with Sarah. Shelly wouldn't want to. It would mess things up at work.

Work…that was going to be a nightmare now, no matter what. How the hell could I sit across from Shelly in a team meeting? How could we work together? How could I look at her?

From somewhere off in the wilds of the living room, something yowled. It was Marley, most likely, Shelly's cat. It sounded like he wanted his breakfast. I gave it three minutes before he wandered in and started jumping up and down on the bed, not to mention whoever was still in it. Marley was that sort of cat, a tuxedoed drama queen.

I missed the little bugger.

Something brushed my thigh. I rolled over and saw Michelle, her hand groping at the air over the sheets. It looked like she wanted something to hold.

I kept my hands by my sides, my body rigid. It would be bad enough when she woke up. Why make it worse?

Why not give her a little comfort, a voice in my head asked. Why not take a little for yourself?

Because, I decided, I'd taken too much for myself already.

Besides, I needed to pee.

I eased myself out of the bed and padded across the floor to the bathroom. Behind me I could hear Michelle spreading out into the space I'd vacated, taking up the warmth I'd left.

Marley greeted me in the hallway. "Hello, you little bastard," I greeted him.

"Mwraor?" was his response, along with a rub up against my ankles, so I detoured into the kitchen. Gambling that Shelly still kept the cat food in the same place, I rummaged through the cabinets as quietly as possible. A short stack of Nine Lives in the cupboard over the sink told me I was right. The can opener was in the same drawer next to the dishwasher. Marley, for his part, jumped up on the counter and paced back and forth excitedly, meowing all the while.

"Hush. You're going to wake her up." I opened the tin and plopped half the contents into a bowl, then put some plastic wrap around the can and shoved it into the fridge. Marley followed me down the counter until I put his food on the floor, at which point he purred ferociously and jumped down. I got one last rub, and then he dug in, the metal of his tag making tiny clanking sounds against the rim of the bowl as he chowed down.

I watched him, bemused, then headed back on my original mission. Everything in the bathroom was lavender—the walls, the towels, the scented candles doing their best to hold off the stink of Marley's litter box—but I tried to ignore it and take care of the business at hand. The toilet gargled loudly as I flushed, cringing at the sound. I put the seat, down when I finished. It seemed like the polite thing to do.

I washed my hands as quietly as I could and dried them on one of the lavender hand towels. I avoided looking into the mirror. This was not the time for long, deep introspective moments or trying to find character in a face that clearly lacked it. With luck, I could sneak into the bedroom before Shelly woke up. Then, it was decision time—climb into bed and wait for what was coming, or try to get dressed and sneak off, delaying the inevitable. I still hadn't made up my mind by the time I reached the bed. Both courses of action seemed to have their merits, but both depended on Michelle still being asleep.

Which, of course, she wasn't.

"Was it as good for you," she said, and rolled over lazily so that she could lean on one arm and look at me, "as it was for me?"

"Honestly," I said, cupping my hands in front of my groin, "I don't remember."

"Ah. Lucky for you, I do." She yawned. "And you really don't need to do that. I know what it looks like."

"It makes me feel better." I did my best to look graceful while doing the junk-in-hand shuffle.

She shrugged. "If you say so."

"Marley's fed," I told her, not looking at her, but rather casting about for where exactly my underpants had ended up. They weren't immediately visible among the other garments on the floor, most of which were hers.

Shelly nodded. I snuck a glance over at her. Her face still had that calm it had possessed while she was sleeping. She was just watching me, a little amused, a little…something. It wasn't love. Affection, perhaps, or nostalgia. Or something. "I know," she said. "I heard you." There was a long pause. "Thank you."

"You were up?"

She smiled. "I've been up for a while. I was just enjoying the moment."

"Oh," I said, and turned my attention back to the floor. Most of it.

"Oh, you're no fun," she announced, but there wasn't anything behind it. Instead, she turned herself sideways to face me, propping her chin up on both hands like a sphinx. The bedsheet slid halfway down her back as she did so, not that she seemed to notice or mind. "So what are we going to do now?"

"I don't know." I spotted my underwear on the floor at the foot of the bed, and reached down to grab them. "This is…this is a big deal."

"Yeah. Yeah, it is." Her glance flicked around the room. "I think your pants are over there," she added, pointing in the direction of the rocking chair. Sunbeams peeked through the Venetians blinds and illuminated it in stripes, as well as revealing my jeans wrapped around one of the runners. How they'd gotten there was a mystery.

I shrugged myself into my boxers and walked across the room to rescue my pants. The socks I figured for a lost cause; maybe Michelle could use them for paint rags or something. I disentangled the jeans in silence, thankful that Marley had chosen that particular moment for his entrance.

"Hey there, kitty," I said, and turned to scratch the critter behind his ears. He yowled a hello, then jumped onto the bed.

Shelly ignored him for the moment, causing him to march across the bed and present himself for affection. I obliged as best I could while trying to slip into my pants; from the angle of the sun, it was well past seven and heading toward eight in a hurry. Marley, however, didn't seem to care. He unleashed a full-throated purr that threatened to shake my fingernails loose, and twisted his head this way and that to afford the best angle to suit his whim.

"You used to do this all the time, you know." Michelle interrupted our communal reverie. I looked over at her, while Marley let out a small yowl and jumped off the bed near my feet.

"Do what?" I finished tugging my pants on. The belt was still threaded through the loops, so I thanked God I wouldn't have to go hunting for it and buckled it instead.

Michelle sat up, one arm holding the sheet loosely over her breasts. She watched Marley as he sauntered away, then looked back at me. "Use the cat as a distraction. Every time we had a serious fight or I brought up a topic you didn't want to talk about, you'd start fussing over Marley."

"That's not true," I snorted. I pulled my shirt up from the floor. It was crosshatched with cat hair, the black and white fuzz indicating that Marley had taken ownership of it during the night. I sniffed it experimentally for the tell-tale scent of pee that would indicate he really liked it, but there wasn't any. "And now is not the time to be bringing that stuff up, is it?"

"Oh, please." She swung her legs out and planted her feet on the floor, then stood with the sheet wrapped around her like a toga. "Ryan do you want to get married? Oooh, look at the kitty. Ryan, I think we need to talk. Listen to the purring. Ryan, I don't think I love you anymore. Sorry, I was looking at the cat." Suddenly, she was very close to me, angry. "You and Sarah don't have a cat. What are you going to do when she asks you where you were last night?"

"I told you, I don't know!" I spun away and stalked over to the window with my t-shirt still bundled up in my fist. "It's not like I had a plan for what to tell my girlfriend when I cheated on her, you know?"

"First time, huh?" Shelly kept staring at me. I turned around to slip the shirt on. I could feel her eyes boring into my back. "Then again, you were never the run-around type."

"No, and I never thought I would be." I finished pulling the shirt on and tried to dust some cat hair off. All that did was move it into different patterns. "I never thought—"

"You'd come back here?" She let the sheet drop.

"Yeah." I looked down at the floor, at the walls, anywhere but at her. "I never thought I'd come back to you."

"You haven't," she said conversationally. "We just screwed. Now take a good look, if you want. I think it's probably the last one you'll ever get."

"I've heard that before," I muttered, my eyes still on the floor. "Look, Shelly, I'm serious. I never meant for anything like this to happen—"

"I know."

"—And I don't know what I'm going to do next." Automatically, I ran my hands through my pockets. Wallet, check. Keys, check. phone, check and buzzing like crazy to let me know I had unheard messages. Probably Sarah.

Definitely Sarah.

"I know what you're not going to do," she said, her jaw tightening into the lines I knew from work. "You are not going to use this as a lever to pry yourself out of whatever you've got with Sarah. You are not going to go to her and make a lame-ass tearful confession. And you are not going to 'accidentally' let Sarah find out so she gets to leave you because you don't want to deal with what she wants from you. If you decide this was a mistake, then fine, it was a mistake. I had a great time, you had a great time, and apart from some laundry, that's the end of it. But I want you to ask yourself, Ryan, why you're here. Why you're really here."

"I told you," I said as my anger rose to match hers, "I don't know."

"Then figure it out, and we'll talk." She turned away from me. "The door will lock behind you. But you knew that." And with that, she walked off toward the bathroom, completely nude and unashamed, disdain for me dripping off her with every step she took.

That, I watched.

The bathroom door slammed. I heard the sound of a shower starting, and over it, Shelly's voice saying "You can leave any time now."

My sneakers were by the door. I scratched Marley one last time as I went out, but only once.

* * *

Home or work, work or home. Both lay in roughly the same direction from Michelle's place, which let me put off the decision for a little bit. The clock on the dash on my car read 7:56, which meant that if I delayed a little longer, Sarah would be gone for work before I got back to the house, and I could delay facing her for a while. If I went straight to work, I could maybe steal one of the promotional t-shirts that seemed to breed like mushrooms in the dark corners of the storage closet and hope no one noticed I was wearing the same jeans as yesterday.

My cell phone buzzed. I checked it and saw that it was just a reminder that I had messages, not a new call. "Might as well listen," I mumbled to myself and pulled up voicemail.

"First message. Yesterday. Six. Twenty-two. P.M. From," The voice changed here, to Sarah's pre-recorded mailbox reading of her name, "Sarah Bogdan." There was a pause and a click and then Sarah's voice again. "Hi, honey, it's me. I know you're busy. I just wanted to know if you were going to make it home for dinner. Call me if you get this message, okay?" There were a few seconds of dead time, then she hung up. I pressed seven to delete the message, slamming the button down hard, and cued up the next one.

"Eight. Fourteen. P.M. From." Again, Sarah. They were all Sarah. I knew this already. "Ryan? It's quarter after eight. When are you coming home?"

Click. Beep.

"Nine. Forty-six. P.M." "Ryan, if you haven't been taken hostage at the office, I'm going to be really upset with you. Come home already."

Click. Beep.

"Eleven. Oh. Nine. P.M." "Ryan, where are you? You don't have to come back home. I just don't know where you are, and I'm getting worried. I don't care if you went back to the office. Just let me know, all right? Please? I love you."

Click. Beep. Hearing the strain in her voice rise, hearing it go from amusement to anger to real worry, that was agony. Knowing I'd caused her that kind of worry while I was doing what I'd done with Shelly was torture, self-inflicted and heartily deserved, a fractional penance for what I'd inflicted on Sarah.

"Today. Twelve. Twenty. A.M." The click of a hang-up was all that was there this time.

Click. Beep.

"Two. Oh. Seven. A.M." Sarah's voice was thick with sleep and worry. "Ryan, I'm going to bed now. Just come home when you hear this, all right? Please."

Click. Beep.

"All messages have been erased. First saved message."

I shut the phone and threw it into the passenger foot-well. It bleeped once, then nothing. For another hour, I drove around in circles, listening to clips from the Blue Lightning soundtrack interspersed with random chunks of Coheed and Cambria and Old Crow Medicine Show and Mastodon. With the windows rolled up, I blasted them, one and all, until I could hear the plastic of the molding rattle and feel the glass of the windows shake. The music pushed against my ears, loud enough to be physically painful, almost loud enough to drown out the memory of "Two. Oh. Seven. A.M."

And when that didn't work, I shut it all off and avoided Sarah's route into her office, just in case. Not until the clock hit nine did I feel brave enough to head home, and even then, I drove past the house once to see if Sarah's car was, by some miracle, in the driveway. The phone buzzed once during that time. I left it where it was.

* * *

Sarah had indeed gone into work by the time I got home, something that surprised me slightly. For all my shenanigans to avoid a confrontation, I'd been half-expecting her to be waiting on the front step, red-eyed and equal parts worried and furious. That was romantic fantasy, though, not the reality of Sarah. She'd wait until she had to get to work, and then off she'd go. There would be plenty of time to talk later, or so her thinking would go. I knew it well.

I ran inside, stripping off my t-shirt as soon as I got in the door. Upstairs I went, heading for the master bathroom, my shirt balled up in my fist. I ran through the bedroom, not bothering to shut the door behind me. If Sarah came home now, a locked bathroom door wasn't going to make any difference. Besides, the key to my salvation was in the bathroom, hidden away and waiting.

I rummaged through the drawers under the double sink until I found what I wanted, tucked in with the unused whitening strips and dental floss: a lint brush. I'd carried the damn thing with me for years, from move to move and apartment to apartment, and this was maybe the third time I'd ever used it. It seemed simple enough, though—lay the shirt out flat, then run the brush over it until all of the incriminating cat hair was gone.

The shirt took a minute to unravel on the floor, and I knelt on two corners to keep it from rolling up as I brushed it. Mute evidence of Marley's passage was all over, but slowly and steadily the brush did its magic. Cat hair transferred itself off the shirt, though I had to scrape it from the brush and dump the resultant hairball into the toilet. When one side was done, I flipped the shirt and did the other, then turned it inside out and did that as well.

At last, satisfied with my work, I tossed the shirt into the hamper. It was maybe a third full, which gave me the better part of a week to bury it under an avalanche of other laundry. Hide the evidence, bury the body, and when the hamper was sufficiently full, do the laundry myself and Sarah would never know.

Feeling sufficiently confident in that plan, I stripped down and threw my other clothes in after the shirt, then mixed up the stuff in the hamper so as to cover the evidence a little more thoroughly. A fast shower, a quick change, and I could head to work with no one the wiser.

* * *

It wasn't until I was halfway there that I remembered that I'd driven us to Montague's from work, and to her place from the bar. Her car was still at the office. Michelle was going to need a lift from someone, and that someone was going to ask questions, and the scenario unwound itself merrily from there.

At the next stop light, I reached down and grabbed the phone from where it had managed to slide under the seat and texted Shelly. sorry forgot your car was at office need a ride?

She won't answer, I told myself. She doesn't want to hear from you, she doesn't care, she's mad—

The answer came back immediately. IN THE OFFICE. LEON PICKED ME UP 45 MINS AGO. Then, a second later, BUT THX FOR ASKING.

My innards wadded themselves up like a used paper towel and jumped into my throat. Breath wouldn't move, in or out, up or down. I swallowed, and it was like there was a knife tucked in there, sharp on both sides. Flicking looks back and forth from phone to road, I sent NICE OF HIM.

There was a pause this time before she answered. DIDNT TELL HIM. YOU WONT EITHER.

thank you...

DIDNT DO IT FOR U. DID IT FOR HIM.

"Ah, hell," I said. I dropped the phone onto the seat next to me. I'd call Sarah when I got to the office. Calling now would just look suspicious, and with the state I was in, I needed all my concentration for the road.

The music rattled the windows all the way to work. Somehow, iTunes had gotten stuck on repeat, spitting out the "Level Complete" music from the game soundtrack in an endless loop. I didn't bother to change it. Instead, I turned up the volume to painful levels and let it batter me over and over, until by the time I got to the office, I was numb to the sound.

The parking spaces near the office were full when I got there. I cruised around the building twice, looking for something close to the entrance and finding exactly nothing. Eventually, cursing under my breath, I drove over to the next building and parked in one of their numerous empty spaces. The sign over their door said "Houghton Point Industries," which told me precisely nothing about what they did, but they only had a half-dozen cars parked in the spaces allotted to them. That made the rest fair game, and I took one.

The walk to the front door of our building took me past Michelle's car. It was parked where it had been the night before. I read the bumper stickers on it as I walked by, those that weather hadn't already stripped to illegibility. There were a couple of political ones from long dead campaigns, and few more for bands like the Pietasters and Operation Ivy. On the end was what looked like a fresh one, blue writing on a white background. It read "Stop Continental Drift!"

"Good luck with that," I told the empty air and went inside.

Chapter 22

There was work waiting for me when I got to my office. Work, and that was all, and for that I was deeply grateful.

I opened the door cautiously, peeking inside before cracking it wide enough to walk through in case there was a naked blue female figure waiting for me. There wasn't, so I shoved the door open hard enough for it to bang off the wall and went in.

As my office went, it looked normal enough. The piles of paper were stacked where I'd piled them, and there was still an empty coffee mug on one side of the desk. I could see nothing out of the ordinary, nothing that looked like it had been displaced by ghostly hands, no evidence that anyone other than me had been in there. A quick look at the trash can confirmed this—the cleaning crew had given it a pass the night before—but even so, I did a nervous triple-check around before allowing myself to sit down.

Right, I told myself. Check email. Get to work. Whatever happened in here last night, it was last night.

She's gone now.

I took a deep breath, in and out, and got to work.

* * *

At four-thirty, I gave up. The entire day, not including a seven-minute trip to the vending machines in the break room for lunch, consisted of three lines of introduction on the revised multiplayer document and sixteen emails answered in monosyllables. By half past four, I was tired, cranky, and frustrated. No one had been to see me all day, no questions to be answered or fires to put out. The email traffic had been light, the usual mailing-list pissing matches had been the equivalent of light drizzles, and the questions all easily answerable. Any other time, a day like this would have been a godsend.

Instead, it drove me nuts.

"The hell with this," I announced, and killed the power to my system without doing a proper shutdown.

Hah. Living dangerously, are we?

I told myself to shut up and grabbed my bag. Eric looked up at me as I stepped out into the hall. "Leaving?"

My office door slammed shut. I'd barely touched it. "Yeah," I heard myself saying. "Not getting anything done, and last night was a long night."

Eric nodded, and looked sagely down at the papers on his desk. "So I heard," he said, assuming the look of intense concentration that meant he was ignoring me. I shrugged, turned my back on him, and tried not to ponder what he meant by that as I headed out to the car.

Shelly was in front smoking a cigarette when I came out. She looked at me once, then down at the ground, and turned her back on me.

"I thought you stopped smoking," I said. There was no answer. I stood there a moment and scuffed the sidewalk with my shoe. She stood stock-still, the lazy curl of tobacco smoke winding up into the air giving her the faint look of an incense burner long left to its own devices.

That, and the hard set of her shoulders.

I stood there for another moment, mumbled an "Umm, yeah. See you tomorrow," and walked down the steps toward the parking lot and my car. Out of the corner of my eye, I saw Michelle changing her angle in increments, always making sure I got nothing but her back squared to where she thought I might be.

The office was out of sight in my rearview before I worked up the nerve to kill the music and pick up my phone. It was four forty-seven, thirteen minutes before official quitting time for Sarah. She'd be on the road by five ten, home by five thirty, and wondering when the hell I'd be coming home by six. Calling her now wouldn't make any sense. She'd be on her way soon enough, and I'd see her at home before too much longer. Besides, our next conversation wasn't likely to be pretty. That was exactly the sort of distraction I didn't need while driving.

Only then did I realize that I hadn't called her during the day, either. No email, no phone message...it had just slipped my mind.

Jesus. She must have been worried sick.

I activated the phone app. "Name-dial, Sarah," I barked at it. It bleeped once, then announced in Siri's soothing tones that the request didn't match any names in memory. "For God's sake, name-dial, Sarah. Sah-rah. Sarah!"

The phone thought to itself for a moment, then told me once again it had no idea who the hell I was talking about. I thought seriously about throwing it out the window, looking up just in time to realize I was barreling toward a red light. Forgetting about the phone for a moment, I stood on the brake and screeched to a halt just short of the intersection. The car shuddered as the brakes grabbed, and the phone tumbled off the seat onto the floor.

It bounced once and started dialing.

"Shit shit shit shit shit!" I reached down for it, hand fumbling in the foot-well as it started ringing. Once, twice, a third time, and my hand closed on it.

Someone answered.

"Hello?" It was Sarah's voice. "Ryan? Is that you?"

"Yes!" I shouted, face to face with the air conditioning panel, one hand gripping the wheel and the other squeezing the phone hard enough that I could feel the plastic groaning under my fingers. "Sarah! It's me!"

"Oh my God, are you OK? Is everything all right? You sound like you're underwater. What's going on?" Two parts panic to three parts relief, all hidden unless you knew her—that's what Sarah sounded like. I took a minute, took a deep breath, then hauled myself and the phone up. The light flicked to green, and I nudged the car forward as I brought the headset to my ear.

"Hey," I said, and let about two years' worth of tension out with that one syllable. "It's me. I'm OK. I…went back to the office last night, and got caught up, and ended up sleeping...."

The words "at the office" caught in my throat. On top of what I'd done, a lie was just a small betrayal, a molehill on top of a mountain. But it was a lie, a deliberate hunk of falsehood tossed into the still waters of the relationship. Last night couldn't be excused, but it could maybe be explained in the sense that it had, well, just happened. That one thing had led to another, and another, and there I was in Shelly's bed in the morning.

Lying, on the other hand, felt premeditated, like a deliberate backstab of whatever Sarah and I had. It was an intentional devaluation of the relationship, of whatever open and honest communication we might have left. It—

"Ryan? Are you there?" The relief was fading, the anger growing. Now that she knew I was all right, she could unload on me for all the worry I'd caused her. In a way, it was a relief.

"I'm here," I said, and swallowed, trying to moisten my traitorously dry throat. "The phone just cut out for a minute there." My voice cracked a little on the last word, but I pushed through it and got the traitorous syllable out.

There. A little lie. That wasn't so hard. I could do it.

"Where are you?" I could hear papers rustling in the background, computer keys clicking loudly. Those were the sounds of Sarah shutting down for the day. She'd be on the road soon.

Up ahead, the traffic light flashed yellow. I thought about gunning it and trying to beat the red but thought better of it and coasted to a stop. "Briarwood and Francis, I think," I told her. "I should be home in a couple of minutes."

"Home?" There was frank disbelief in her voice. "At five o'clock? What happened? Did you get fired?" Somewhere, a pinging noise announced that Windows was shutting itself down.

"No, nothing like that. I just got caught up at work, like I said, and—"

I paused, swallowed, stared into the red light like I wished it were the eye of an angry god who could strike me down before I could speak falsehood. "I ended up crashing at the office."

The words were tumbling out now, the lies and explanations all tripping over one another. "I came home when I woke up, but you were already gone, so I just did a quick shower and change, but I really wasn't getting anything done at work, so I decided to just come home a little early for a change because God knows they got enough time out of me last night." I stopped and felt myself squeezing the phone so hard the plastic bent under my fingers. "And I missed you."

Behind me, someone honked. I blinked. The light had gone green. Foot on gas, hands on wheel, I rolled forward. It was six blocks to home, three turns included. A faint beep told me someone had felt the need for last licks on their traffic dissatisfaction. I flipped a genial behind-the-head bird in their rough direction and shoved the incident out of my mind.

From Sarah's end of the line, there was silence. Then, "Ryan? Are you feeling all right?"

I licked my lips nervously. "Yeah, sure, why?"

There was another pause. "You're coming home early. You sound, I don't know, feverish. Is something wrong?"

"Just tired, honey," I said. "Just tired. And I can't wait to see you."

"That's sweet," she said. "I'll be home soon."

* * *

Dinner was takeout Mexican from the new place on Maynard, which Sarah picked up on the way home. We ate it sitting on the couch, catching up on back episodes of *The Following* and not talking except when she occasionally would say things like "Eww" and "Why do we watch this while we're eating?" whenever various bodily fluids appeared on screen. Once in a while she sneezed, putting it down to an oncoming cold. I cleared away the plates when we finished, and then we both just sat there for a minute until the episode wound itself down.

"So," she said finally, resting her head fractionally on my shoulder.

"So?"

"So I think we need to talk." I stiffened. She put her hand on my arm to keep me from pulling away. "Not like that. Just…talk."

I turned to look at her, her feet curled up on the couch, shoes kicked off under the coffee table. She looked comfortable and vulnerable all at once. I wondered how I looked to her, but she was staring at the floor.

"Look," I said, forcing the words past the catch in my throat. "I…I haven't been a very good boyfriend. A very good partner, at least not lately. And I think…I want that to change."

She didn't move, just kept her hand where it was and said softly, "Do you mean that?"

I nodded and knew she could feel rather than see it. "I do. I don't think I'm going to be terribly good at it, at least not at first, but if you're willing...I mean, if you're still willing to put up with me while I do it, I'd like to try."

For a few minutes, she didn't say anything, just letting the credits scroll by. "What does that mean?" she finally asked, softly, as if she weren't sure she wanted to hear the answer.

"I don't know." I thought for a minute. "Figuring out what my life is outside the office, I guess, and paying more attention to it. To you." A hesitation. "And maybe to stop making some bad choices that I've made." The thought of confessing hovered at the back of my mind, but I shoved it firmly away. If this misadventure with Shelly was the kick in the ass I needed to get my life in order, then melodramatic confession struck me as a particularly stupid idea. Better to let it encourage me to do right by Sarah—by everyone, really—from now on than to have that one moment of catharsis and the resultant train wreck of consequences.

And besides, that meant not having to tell her.

"I guess..." she said. "I guess I haven't been entirely understanding about what you do or why you do it, either. Maybe we both have to bend a little, recognize that there are places where we're just not going to overlap." She shifted, and suddenly her head was in my lap and she was looking up at me. "I'd like to stay with you, Ryan. I'd like to make a life together with you. I think you're worth it. I think what we have is worth it. If you don't think so, now is the time to go."

"I think so," I said, and leaned down to kiss her.

Sarah blinked, once. "Is that all?"

"And I'm sorry."

I kissed her again. Eventually, we went to bed. She never asked me what I was sorry for.

* * *

Sarah rarely snored, but she was snoring tonight. Light, soft, little lady-like snores; they escaped at regular, reassuring intervals. After a while, I started counting them; after I got to two hundred, I propped myself up on my elbow to watch her. She lay on her back, right arm flung dramatically above her head, left arm holding the covers in place instinctively over her breasts. Her hair was fanned out behind her, and her mouth was slightly open.

Sleep had visited briefly after Sarah and I had consummated our renewed commitment to what we had together. I'd almost dropped off, the warmth of her next to me helping me to drift along, and then the next minute, my eyes snapped wide open. I was as wide awake as I'd been all day, a full three-cup-of-coffee buzz.

I lay there for an hour or so, doing my best not to move, to let myself waft back asleep. That had the opposite effect of the one intended, as the strain of not daring to move lest I wake Sarah proved to be more of an agitator than anything else.

When watching her failed to soothe me, either, I decided enough was enough. Slowly, carefully, I hoisted myself out of bed. Shuffling steps took me across the bedroom and down the hall to my office. I shut the door and disconnected the speakers before I booted the system up, then sat down to check work email.

Maybe, I decided, it would put me to sleep. And even if it didn't, there was work to be done.

* * *

"You look tired," Sarah said over breakfast. I nodded and buttered my freezer bagel. "Couldn't sleep?"

"Nope," I said. "Watched you sleep for a while, though," I added around a mouthful of inauthentic bagel-shaped bread.

She smiled at me. "That's sweet, in a stalkerish kind of way." With professional precision, she pulled the bag out of her teacup at precisely five minutes, then drained it and set it on the side of her plate. Two sips, and she looked at me again. "I had some weird dreams last night. Did you?"

I shook my head. "I don't even remember when I fell asleep." There was an expectant pause, and I realized I was supposed to ask her what she'd dreamed about. "What were your dreams like?"

"I don't know," she said pensively, fiddling with her cup without drinking anything. "I guess that story you told me about that thing you thought you saw the other night. You know, with Terry,"—she parsed the words precisely, making sure she didn't add any credence to what I'd said or seen—"got in my head a little bit. I dreamed about your ghost."

"You did?" I felt myself shifting, sitting more upright. "What was the dream like?"

She shook her head, as if she were trying to shake the memory loose, or out. "There was just this woman…ghost…thing. I was in bed, and you weren't there, but there was a dent in the blanket where you were supposed to be. She was sitting at the foot of the bed, and we just…talked."

"Talked?" I felt a dozen questions rise up in my throat and choked them all down. "That's way up there on the weird-meter."

"I guess." Another sip of tea, and she made a face before dumping a spoonful of Splenda in it. "She seemed very, I don't know, serious. And possessive. About you." Abruptly, she reached across the table and grabbed my hand. "But it was just a dream, and I shouldn't worry about it."

I detached my hand long enough to put the half-eaten bagel on the plate, then wove my fingers through hers. It was entirely sensible, after all, for her to dream about things we'd talked about. Blue Lightning had shown no real ability to do anything like appear outside the office, to manifest in dreams, to do anything other than sashay around the office and muck about with the electronics.

No. It was just a dream. "Just a dream," I repeated out loud, as much for my benefit as for Sarah's. "I wouldn't worry about it."

Sarah smiled at me. "I know. I'm not worried. It was just strange to dream about that."

"I can imagine." I gripped her fingers tighter, and she squeezed back. Then, hating myself, I asked, "Do you remember anything you talked about with her?"

She scrunched her face up cutely and thought about it for a second. "All I remember," she finally said, "was one sentence. I think she said, 'We're not finished with each other.'"

"Weird," I said, and nodded, and didn't say anything else for the rest of breakfast.

* * *

I checked my appointment calendar before heading to work. The morning was clear of meetings; the first one wasn't up until one. I'd be meeting with Michelle and some of the level artists to talk about concepts for original multiplayer maps that we'd potentially be adding. BlackStone had politely sent a request to Eric that we investigate producing content unique to the versions of the game we were doing. This polite request was being treated as the strict marching order everyone knew it was. The meeting, then, was to allow us to walk through the proposed content to see which maps could be done within time, budget, manpower constraints, and the vagaries of good gameplay.

Until then, my time was my own to try to catch up on stuff that had started to slide yesterday. There were a dozen docs to update, a presentation to BlackStone to start working on, and a massive spreadsheet of proposed text strings for the game that I needed to double check to make sure they were in actual English. I decided to start with the spreadsheet when I got in and to work from there. It seemed the best use of my time.

At quarter oftwelve, I was still staring at the spreadsheet. I'd looked at maybe thirty rows of text, changed two of them, and spent the rest of the time brooding over whether I'd infected Sarah with a particularly vicious strain of hallucination. When someone knocked on my door, it was a relief. I nearly knocked my coffee mug off my desk in my eagerness to get up.

"Come in," I called out, steadying the teetering mug with one hand.

Leon shoved the door open, looked around, and stood there. "You sure? I thought I heard something banging around in here."

"Just me being a lamer," I said. "You know, you're the first person down to see me today?"

"Really." He gave a low whistle, impressed. "Normally you gotta beat 'em off with a stick to get anything done."

"I know." I shrugged. "Maybe it's just my lucky day."

"Beats me, man. All I know is that every time one of my guys talks about coming down here or shooting you an email, they end up talking themselves out of it. It's like you got bad vibes or something."

"Or something," I agreed. "You want to get some lunch?"

"It's why I came to see you," He looked back and forth, as if to check if anyone else were on the hallway and might overhear him. "Besides, you kinda look like you need to talk to somebody."

I'd already grabbed my keys. "Or to get talked to?"

Leon looked down at his shoes. "Maybe that too, yeah." A second later, he looked back at me and his face brightened. "Burgers at Jonesy's?"

I had to laugh. "Burgers at Jonesy's," I said, and followed him out.

Chapter 23

"How's Sarah?" Leon asked across the table. He didn't look up as he asked, instead choosing to fiddle with his multiply-layered, cheese drenched, bacon-warded, BBQ-sauce-doused burger. As I watched, he somehow managed to lard it up with two layers of cross-hatched French fries. A spiral of ketchup from a squeeze bottle finished it to his satisfaction, and he slammed the bun back down. "Ah, perfection."

"That's kind of gross," I told him, picking absently at my chicken tenders. They'd been left in the deep fryer too long and had acquired a distinctly chewy, leathery consistency. Jonesy's was one of the office defaults for lunch, but that was due more to proximity and price than the quality of the cuisine. At other tables, I could see coworkers digging in with various degrees of gusto. Terry and his little cabal were hunched over in one corner. They'd scowled when I waved at them, which was all the encouragement I needed to pretend they weren't there at all.

"Naah, it's great." As if to lend weight to his words, he tucked in with a serious two-fisted chomp. Bits of fry dangled from his mouth as he put the garnished burger back down on his plate. "Mrrrfmm yrrrfummm dddrrrr nnnn."

I ripped off a strip of chicken with my teeth and winced. "I beg your pardon?"

Leon wiped his mouth with the back of his hand, then wiped the back of his hand with his napkin. "I said, it's European style. They like fries on their actual burgers. In a pita, even."

"Remind me of that fascinating fact the next time I get the yen for a burger in Paris." I took another bite of chicken. "And Sarah's fine, but I think she's fighting off a cold. She was sniffling and sneezing this morning."

Leon nodded sagely. "Everyone's getting sick. By this time next week, the team rooms are gonna be ghost towns. Either that, or someone's gonna be puking in every single one of them."

I threw a fry at him, which he ducked. "Nobody's ever thrown up in the office."

He picked up the fry and ate it, grinning. "What about Hector back in April? He puked pretty good."

Shaking my head in disbelief, I raised another French fry menacingly but thought better of it before launch. "Hector," I pointed out, "had been mixing energy drinks, chocolate cake, and whisky all night. Any two of those combined would be enough to make most humans vomit, let alone all three."

"Hex isn't human. He's a network engineer."

"Good point," I said, and tapped my forehead with a couple of fingers in a salute. "But I still blame the booze."

Leon tried to look indignant and failed. There was too much of a smile behind his shocked expression for it to hold. "You're just saying that because you made it outside before you unloaded."

I pushed my plate away. "Well, I'm enjoying this lunch. How about you?"

"Sorry, man," he mumbled, taking another bite of burger. "Oh. That reminds me. When's our next leads meeting?"

Arm's length was the right distance away for my food, I decided, and I made no effort to close the gap. Instead, I sipped my Diet Coke and put on my best thoughtful face. "I don't know, Leon. I keep on scheduling them and Michelle keeps on opting out because she's got something else to do."

"Yeah. It's weird." Another two bites of burger disappeared, messily. Strings of cheese dripped out of the bun and pooled on his plate. "Ddddumm gummmm hrrrmmm annnummm fummm?"

"What?" I asked, exasperated. "Oh, wait, I know. Mumm fumm yumm lumm dumm."

He swallowed, his Adam's apple bobbing up and down furiously. I was reminded of nature shows where a snake caught something a little too big for it but wouldn't give up the meal without a fight.

"Ha ha, very funny." He stared at the burger remnants in his hand but thought better of digging in again. "What I said was, did you guys have another fight."

"Oh." I sipped at my drink, which was already at the "mostly empty" stage. Crackling noises echoed up my straw. "Why do you ask?"

"I dunno." He set his lunch down. The bun was no longer structurally sound. Half-eaten French fries spilled out in all directions. "You guys haven't talked today, you don't IM, and every time someone mentions your name she looks like she's gonna be sick. Other than that, I got nothing."

I looked at my empty glass, then reluctantly moved it to the edge of the table. "OK, you've got me," I sighed. "Yeah, we had a little fight. Hopefully it won't hurt the project too much."

"Oh, yeah, that's great. The creative director and the art lead aren't talking, and that's not going to hurt the project? Whatever you did, man, you gotta apologize."

For an instant, I thought about saying something like, "Yeah, you're right, I never should have screwed her," just to see the look on his face. Then the moment passed, and the well-intentioned badgering didn't rankle quite as much. I reached for the chicken to buy time to think of what to say.

"So, have you seen it again?" Leon asked when I was mid-chew.

I gulped, then reflexively said, "Her."

"Her?" He gave me a look of frank disbelief. "I mean, it's got boobs, but that don't make it a her."

"It's a her," I said. "I've talked to her. It's the game."

"It ain't Salvador. She don't got a moustache." He jabbed the air with a grease-soggy French fry to make his point.

"Not Salvador," I said irritably. "Blue Lighting. It's Blue Lightning."

"Huh." He popped the fry in his mouth and chewed it contemplatively. "No shit?"

"No shit."

"OK, then. What's she want?"

I looked at him as he pulled a few more fries up from the plate and stuffed them into his mouth. "You're really taking this awfully well, you know."

"Like you said, man, what else are we gonna do? It's a situation. We find a solution. Ain't no different from trying to figure out that pathing issue we had last week."

"I guess you're right." I tried to force down another bite of chicken strip and couldn't. "So. To answer your question, yes, I've seen her. More than once. She talked to me, once, when there was no one else around."

"Ah." He thought about it for a minute. "I've seen something that might be it…her. I think. It's hard to say."

"I think she's focusing on me these days." As the waitress swung by, I waved for the check. She nodded and swirled back into the distance.

Leon smirked. "Terry can't be happy about that."

"I could give three shits what makes Terry happy. Is he getting his ass back on track?"

"Honestly?" There was some introspective chewing. "Not so much. But I live in hope."

"Someone has to, I guess." I checked the time on my phone. "We'd better start thinking about getting back."

Leon didn't bother to stop eating. "Clock on the wall says you've got twenty minutes before the map concept review meeting. What's your rush?"

Because it's really uncomfortable sitting across the table from the friend whose girlfriend I just nailed, I thought but didn't say. "I just want to make sure I've got all my notes ready," I told him instead.

"You don't bring notes to a meeting like that. You take notes." He chuckled to himself, then polished off the rest of the burger in two bites. There was a tricky moment when it looked like he'd have to unhinge his lower jaw to get the meal down, but it passed, and after a moment he patted his gut. "Ah. Cheeburger, cheeburger, man. Nothing like it to fuel a man for a day of meetings."

"Heh."

Our waitress, who looked like she was about fourteen, dropped the check off at roughly the midpoint of the table. I grabbed it, a half-second before Leon's hand hit the table with a meaty smack. "I've got this one, man," I told him. "You got last time."

"No, you got last time," he corrected. "And the two times before that, now that I think on it. Not that I'm complaining. But it's cool, Ryan. You don't have to get it every time."

"Let me grab it today, and you can get it next time," I said, feeling deeply uncomfortable about the whole thing. "I promise."

He gave me a look that was mostly unreadable. "OK, man. But ease off on the intensity pills. You're starting to freak me out a little."

"Sorry," I said, reaching for a credit card. I stuck it with the check and waved it in what looked like the waitress' general direction. "It's just…"

"Just what?" He blinked. "You're not quitting, are you? Don't tell me you're quitting, and buying me lunch is your way of saying goodbye, 'cause you know you won't be around for me to get the next one. Oh, you are such an asshole!"

"I'm not quitting," I said wearily. The waitress swooped by and grabbed the check and my card, warbling "I'll be back with this in a minute!" I revised my estimate of her age upwards to maybe seventeen and precocious and watched her fade off into the crowd. "It's just…there's something about Shelly you should know, OK?"

I was surprised to hear the words coming out of my mouth. I had no intention of confession, of messing up my friendship and working relationship in one blow. Nor was the guilt I felt over the whole thing an unbearable, obsessive thing. Instead, it scuttled around the edges of my thoughts, there when I talked to Sarah or tried to talk to Shelly, but mostly shoved into the dark corners of my mind with the excuse that there was nothing I could do about it.

"Shelly?" Leon's eyes narrowed. "I thought we were cool with all that. We are cool, right? Right?"

I opened my mouth to tell him that no, things were profoundly uncool, and no words came out.

"You okay, man? You look like you're choking or something."

I realized I couldn't do it. I couldn't go forward and confess, couldn't go back and pretend I hadn't started this conversation. I was stuck, balanced in the middle before taking the plunge into an even deeper professional and personal nightmare than the one I was already in.

"Come on, Ryan, what's the deal?" Leon was half out of his seat now, busily trying to determine whether he needed to beat the crap out of me or save my life. I waved him back down, even as my throat squeezed any words I might have said into voiceless rubble.

"Here's your check, gentlemen. Have a terrific day!" Salvation came in the form of the waitress. She put the credit card slip and my card down on the table and slid both across to me. "Come back and see us again!"

"We will," I finally croaked, and took the check. Leaving her a large tip, I signed, flipped it over, and tucked my card back into my wallet. Experimentally, I swallowed a couple of times to see if my throat was letting air through for a change. It was, or at least swallowing only felt like I'd sucked down a pocketknife instead of a Bowie.

Leon was still looking at me, eyes narrowed. "You were saying, man?"

I stood. "Look," I said, and it came out a dry rasp, "I just wanted to…I don't know how to say it. Just be careful with Shelly, OK? She gets really passionate about stuff, and sometimes you get caught up in it, and the next thing you know you're hurting, bad. OK?"

"Oh-kay." He looked puzzled. "You don't need to warn me, bro. I can take care of myself. And passionate"—he licked his lips in cartoon lasciviousness—"is just fine by me."

With a sinking feeling, I nodded. I'd tried to tell him, I told myself. If he'd been thinking about what I said, he'd have known.

Whatever.

And as I stood there with a sick smile on my face, Leon pointed to the neon-faced clock on the wall. "Let's get going, man. Like you said, gotta get the notes in order."

"Yeah," I followed him out. "Got to get everything in order."

Terry and his crew were already in the parking lot when Leon and I left. They watched us pull out without making a move toward Terry's car, and they were still watching us when we went around the corner and away.

Chapter 24

At five of one, I made my way to the conference room. A few of the level artists and designers were already in there, setting up to show off their sketches and rough map proposals for how they were going to translate Salvador over. I nodded, said a few hellos which might or might not have been answered, and then took the seat to the left of the head of the table. This was Shelly's meeting, I reasoned. Might as well let her have the big chair.

More artists filed in. The clock hit one, then five after, then ten after. I looked around. No Shelly. Her absence didn't seem to be slowing down the other artists, who were engaged in an animated conversation about some Eastern European tactical shooter they'd picked up pirated copies of. It hadn't been released in the States yet and was, from what I could gather, "the shit."

Experimentally, I cleared my throat. A couple of heads swiveled in my direction. "Uh, guys, isn't Michelle supposed to be in on this meeting?"

One of the indistinct figures around the table—I recognized him by voice as Sean, the lead level designer—shook his head. He was seated at the end of the table, "driving" the presentation material, and his dreads caught the edge of the projector beam. "She said she wasn't coming."

"Wasn't coming? She's got to be here," I said. "This is her meeting."

Sean shook his head again, more slowly. "She said that she didn't think she needed to be here because, and I quote, that prick Ryan is just going to pick whatever maps get him hard, anyway." He paused for a minute. "Sorry, man. Should have told you sooner."

Competing thoughts tied my tongue in knots as laughter raced around the table. She couldn't just walk out on the meeting—she had a responsibility to the project, and to the team. If she had personal problems with me, it wasn't right for her to drag the team into it. And the line about getting me hard was dangerously close to pulling Blue Lightning out into the open, which I didn't think any of us wanted to do.

And, to my surprise, I wanted her there.

In the end, I waited for the laughter to stop and pulled out my phone. "Whatcha doing?" asked the guy sitting a few seats down. It was, I realized, one of the guys Terry had been talking with out in the smokers' lounge the time we'd had that odd conversation. His name, I remembered now, was Lucas; he was beefy, heavyset, and unshaven. He wore an old Blue Lightning team t-shirt, and his unbrushed hair stood out like the silhouette of a palisade against the projector's light.

"My job," I said, and called Michelle. Without a word, I put the phone on speaker and slapped it down on the table. It rang seven or eight times without her picking up. Around the room, I could see the artists' eyes, Michelle's people's eyes, watching me. The whites reflected the glow from the projected screen at the front of the room, the lurid colors of the Salvador project logo. It made them look oddly demonic, gave them the impression of being inhuman creatures waiting for some unspoken signal to pounce on the poor unsuspecting fool who'd walked into their lair.

Michelle didn't answer. I tapped the phone to disconnect, then redialed It rang twice, loud and tinny, and someone picked up.

"Michelle?"

No one answered.

"Come on, Michelle. We need you down here for the multiplayer level concept review. We can't wait for you forever."

There was another pause, then Michelle answered. "You're not really good with that word 'need,' Ryan. Go have your little meeting. Let me know how it comes out."

Someone whistled. Sean muttered a single, drawled, "Daaaamn." I felt my face flushing and fought the urge to hang up there and then.

"Come on, Michelle. This is an art meeting. Whatever we come up with here needs your signoff."

"I'm sure whatever you come up with will be fine, Ryan dear." Her tone was all sugary poison. "After all, you always make the best decisions."

"This is not the time or the place–" I began, but didn't get any further. Michelle's voice, cutting, cut me off.

"You do whatever you want, Ryan. I'll sit back here and make sure we make it," and there was a pause then, a cold one, "pretty."

Then she hung up.

I was left in the light from the screen, the phone dangling limply from my hand, the cord coiling back and forth while the rest of the room watched and giggled and said nothing. There was nothing they needed to say.

Shutting my eyes, I took one deep breath, then set the phone down carefully. Sean coughed, once, and said, "You think maybe we should reschedule?"

I shook my head. "No. You heard her. Sean, if you could leave the presentation with the top downs open, I'd appreciate it. I'll send notes back after I've had a chance to look at everything."

He wrapped his arms around the computer possessively. "But we really should—"

"You heard her," I said. We locked eyes for a moment, and then he looked away.

"Yeah, OK." The other artists were already shuffling out of the room, golden rectangles of light spilling in to the darkness where the boardroom doors had been opened.

Lucas was the last one out. He stopped in the doorway, just a blocky silhouette, and turned to look at me.

"She isn't going to like this," he said.

"At this point, I don't care what she likes," I said, colder and meaner than I needed to. He shook his head and walked off, shutting the door behind him.

I waited a minute to make sure that the last of them were gone, then moved down to Sean's chair and started skimming through the proposed level concepts. Most were excellent—a processing plant of some sort, an underground defense bunker, a desert missile base—and I resolutely gave them my full attention.

I did this even when the light in the room changed to include a harsh, blue glow. I ignored it for a while, until the light was bright enough to interfere with the images on the screen, and the sense of eyes burning into the back of my neck was too much to ignore. Then and only then did I turn around.

When I did, the light was gone, and I was alone.

* * *

The first timid knock on the door came an hour later, well after the next meeting the room was booked for was supposed to have started. I didn't say anything, and after a moment, someone cracked the door and stuck their head in. It was Dennis, with a sheepish expression on his face. "Look, man, I don't mean to rush you," he said, "but we sorta got to get the room now, if that's OK."

"It's fine," I said, cutting him off. I disconnected Sean's laptop from the projector and set it into its cool-down cycle before standing up. "Sorry I took so long."

"It's cool, man," he said, still hanging on the door and layering each word with a heavy slather of calculated inoffensiveness. "If you need anything else—"

"I take it the whole building knows about my little chat with Michelle?"

He paused for a minute, mouth agape, and scratched his head. "I don't think the QA guys have heard yet. At least, not most of them. Everyone else?" He shrugged as eloquently as he could with only one shoulder visible.

"Yeah." I headed for the other door. "Could you make sure Sean knows I shut everything down? I know he's got some tight deadlines, and I don't want to disturb him."

"Whatever, man," Dennis said, and then I was out of the board room and into the light. Head down, I bulled my way back into my office. First things first: write up the notes and send them to the art team and around to the leads. Second things second: check the calendar to see if there were any more meetings with Michelle scheduled for the day and, if so, cancel them with prejudice. Third—

"Ryan. My office. Now."

I didn't need to look up to know who was speaking; I barely needed to check to see if my door was open. It was Eric's voice, Eric's commanding tone, Eric's caustic disappointment I was hearing.

"Can it wait until I get these notes done?"

"I don't know. Can it?"

I sighed. "Probably not."

"Good call." He came into my office and shut the door behind him. "Want to explain to me what the hell happened to turn a simple level concept review into a soap opera today?"

I didn't stand up. He paced back and forth, turning his face to me every third or fourth word to see what effect they were having.

Keeping my tone even, I said, "I think Michelle is mad at me."

Eric sputtered. "In other news, water remains wet. What the hell did you do to get her pissed off enough to pull that stunt?"

I coughed gently into my hand. "With all due respect, she's the one responsible for the stunt-pulling. Shouldn't you be calling her on the carpet instead of me?"

He stopped and stared at me. "Do you really want me asking her the hard questions?" he asked. "Do you think you're going to like the answers I'm going to get out of her? That's why you've got this chance to give me a plausible excuse so I can pretend we're having business as usual and not a full lead-level implosion that could take the project down with it."

With difficulty, I swallowed. "Got it. What do you want to hear?"

He looked at me like I was an idiot child playing with power tools. "Whatever the hell I can take back there and get Michelle willing to be in a room with you so the business of this company can go on, and so that my CD isn't laughed at for being a thumb-dick every time he walks into a team room."

"Right." I thought about it for a minute. "Tell her I said she's right," I finally said. "And that the issue in question won't be a bother anymore."

Eric shook his head. "I thought you knew better than to stick it in the crazy."

"I didn't. Maybe she did."

"Ah." He stood there for a moment, hands clasped behind his back. "I'll start this ball rolling, but it's up to you to get it where it needs to go. Or something like that."

I looked up at him. "I will eat crow, dirt, shit, or whatever, Eric, to get this project done. Whatever happened, whatever you think happened, I am not going to let it endanger either my work here or my relationship with Sarah. You can take that to the bank, and beyond that, I really don't care." I pulled up the pad I'd taken my notes on and started transcribing them.

"I see," he said, and then he was gone. He shut the door behind him.

I concentrated on the notes, managing to extract some sort of coherent feedback from them over the space of the next hour. Pouring over the various map concepts I'd seen, I ranked them in order, made suggestions about changes to geometry that might jibe a little better with Salvador's idiosyncratic AI and combat model, and otherwise made it clear that I'd looked at each one very carefully and professionally.

"You shouldn't be the one who has to apologize," a voice in my office said. I hadn't heard the door open, but then again I hadn't expected to.

"He's right," I said without turning around. Reflexively, I reformatted the notes to fit our standard format, an automatic process that somehow lent comfort and continuity. "I should apologize."

"But why?" The room's illumination grew brighter, acquiring tinges of bluish-white. "Not that I mind anything that slows down your other project."

I attached the file to an email and addressed it to Sean, to Michelle, to Leon and Eric and a couple of other folks I thought would appreciate the contents. "It's the company's project," I said tonelessly. "The sooner it gets done, the sooner the company gets paid, and the sooner we can move on to something else."

"Something old?" There was a dreadful eagerness in her voice, and desperate longing, too. "You could go back to something you'd been working on, couldn't you?"

I shook my head. "I don't think BlackStone will let us." A brief message went with the document, an explanation of what I was sending along amidst a raft of compliments for the level team on their work and ideas. "They want us working on their stuff, and I'm not sure when we'll ever be able to break away."

"Oh." There was silence, crinkled at the edges by faint sounds of static and popping electricity. The hair on my arms stood up. "Ryan? Why won't you look at me?"

I hit SEND. The email leaped away, into the system. A soft ping told me it was safely gone. "Because I don't want to see you."

She laughed. "Don't be silly. Of course you want to see me. You want to see all of me."

"No, no I don't." I locked my eyes on the monitor, on the long list of emails demanding immediate answers. "If I see you now, I have to believe in you. If I see you in broad daylight, during working hours, then I have to admit you're real." A thought came to me. "You can't walk into dreams, can you? Sarah—my girlfriend—said she dreamed about you."

"You can tell the bitch she's just dreaming."

"That doesn't answer my question."

With a kick, she spun my chair around so that I was looking up at her. She stood, far too close, lithe and graceful, balanced on the balls of her feet as if she were about to turn my office into her own personal parkour workout. "It's not supposed to," she said. "Besides, don't you know that women hate to share?"

"This isn't happening." I screwed my eyes shut. "This isn't happening, this isn't happening, this isn't happening!"

"Tsk tsk tsk." Her fingers traced a cold line down my cheek, one that somehow let warmth linger behind her fingers. "It is happening," she said, her lips very close to my ear. "It's just happening a bit slower than it might happen otherwise, because you're not very good at admitting to yourself what you really want. Soon enough, everything will be where it needs to be." The word "needs" was drawn out, a painful parody of Michelle's scorn in the board room.

Someone knocked on the door. "Come in," Blue Lightning said, even as I was shouting "Don't!"

The door swung open. Shelly stood there, face grim, a sheaf of printouts in her hand. In an instant, her eyes took it all in: Blue Lightning leaning into me, my hands clutching the armrests of my chair, the twin charges oozing through the air of my office.

The printouts fell to the floor. "Ryan..." Michelle said, even as my visitor turned and smiled and blew her a kiss. Then, without another word, she vanished.

"Shelly," I said faintly, and then: "Help."

She left the papers where they'd fallen, and ran.

* * *

Shelly's response to the notes I'd sent was polite, precise, professional, and brief. She suggested one change in the prioritized map list I'd sent around, and then Okayed it.

I read it from home.

For about ten minutes after Michelle had run from my office door, I'd just sat there, paralyzed. I was afraid she'd come back, afraid Blue Lightning would come back, afraid Eric would come back, afraid any move I made would result in disaster or chaos or another step into the abyss I could feel myself sliding into with each interaction.

Eventually, gingerly, I found it in me to scoop up Shelly's papers. They were a printout of my notes with her comments on them, I saw. Maybe she'd wanted to go over them, or perhaps just leave them there. A peace offering? I didn't know. But I did know that I didn't want to sit in that office any longer.

I sent a "Not feeling well—going home" email around the company. Some of them would no doubt laugh, thinking Shelly had kicked my ass. Let them, I decided. I'd work on getting their respect back another day. Today, there were bigger things I needed distance from. I took another minute to put some key docs on my flash drive, then thought a minute and added what I had of the Blue Lightning files as well. There was enough room, although barely, with the hundreds of megs of sketches and screenshots that were included, and maybe by studying what there was of Blue Lightning I could figure out what she wanted, or how to stop her.

A ping, a disconnect, and I was ready to go. Eric brushed by me in the hallway, opened his mouth as if to say something, and then just shook his head. "Feel better," he finally called out as I headed for the door.

There were no further incidents as I went home. The iPod didn't misbehave, no mysterious female figures appeared in my rearview, and the weirdest thing that happened was that I hit a run of four green lights in a row.

It didn't reassure me.

I left Sarah a message on her voicemail, telling her I'd come home early and that I'd be making dinner. I didn't tell her about the fight with Michelle, or about lunch with Leon, or about the visitations I'd had in my office, natural or otherwise. Then I pulled something roughly steak-shaped out of the freezer to defrost, threw it on the counter, and went upstairs to pretend to work.

By the time I'd finished with emails, Michelle's included, I was bored. All of the questions I had to deal with seemed to have obvious answers—yes, we wanted to keep the weapons selection scroll horizontal, the same as all the other menus in the game; no, we didn't want to incorporate a matchmaking feature that bracketed potential players by age group. With each email I felt myself getting increasingly exasperated, with the senders and with myself for my impatience. After all, these were questions that needed to be asked, decisions to be confirmed, details that needed to be ironed out with all parties lest someone interpret a conversation the wrong way and end up pouring weeks of effort into work that would have to be thrown out. Answering those emails was part of the daily routine and far from the most onerous aspect of it. The problem, really, was me.

"Bored now," I told the computer as I hit Send on the last answer. In response, it gave me the ping of an incoming message.

"Great. One more," I muttered, and clicked it open. It was, I saw with some interest, from Terry. Reflexively, I looked for oddly-named attachments, knowing even as I did so that suspecting Terry of sending along viruses was just plain silly. Besides, if he did send one along, there would be no way I'd spot it.

The email itself was brief and to the point. It read: ARE YOU IN? 4 HER, NOT ME.

I stared at it for a while, then typed a response but didn't send it. Instead, I popped my USB key into the computer and opened up the folder of Blue Lightning documents I'd taken home. For a moment, I hesitated. Technically, I was still working. It was not something I needed to be spending time on.

More than that, though, opening them felt like opening a door. It was an acknowledgement, somehow, that I had been talking to Blue Lightning, and that I was responding to her presence.

To her need.

"Stupid, stupid, stupid," I muttered, and scrolled down the list. They sat there, innocent and harmless like a line of rattlesnakes looking the other way. Weapons systems. Simulation. AI. Narrative. Everything that had gone into the concept of Blue Lightning. And in those files, I knew, were gaps, places that were marked "TBD" or "Finish later" or just left achingly, gapingly blank.

She wanted me to fill those places in. She wanted Terry and whoever else he might be working with to realize them. She wanted to live.

I checked the dates on the file. All were April or earlier, all predated the project's cancellation, if only by a single day. They were fossils, insects stuck in amber, a look back at something that had died.

I clicked the first one open. It was the narrative doc, a simple one to look at first. The story of the game was here, along with the character histories and motivations, what there was of the world bible, and so forth. It was as resolutely non-technical as anything in the bunch, and I'd selected it precisely for that reason. Looking at this was just getting reacquainted with the game, not making a promise. Besides, I knew everything in it already, knew it by heart and memory.

Paragraphs skipped by. I read a few, cringed at clunky prose or stuff that should have been updated, and hit PageDn to keep rolling. But the spirit of the game was there, clean and strong and vibrant. I could feel where the good ideas connected, where they got together and sang, and where the stuff that didn't quite ring true waited patiently to be replaced with words that were more inexpressibly Blue Lightning.

Almost unconsciously, I found myself correcting mistakes, tightening grammar and fixing spelling errors, arranging the document in its funeral best. From there, it was a small step to adding phrases, filling in small gaps, making connections that were obvious upon a fresh read-through, deleting passages that had outstayed their welcome. It was a light edit, a toe dipped back in waters I'd abandoned.

And at the very end of it were two words I hadn't typed.

THANK YOU.

Shuddering, I closed the doc and re-opened my email to Terry. Other messages had come in, other questions needing to be answered, but I ignored them.

We need to talk, I wrote back to Terry, and sent it. Then I shut the computer down, turned off the power strip, and pulled the plug out of the wall for good measure.

* * *

Sarah found me sitting on the couch when she got home, fast-forwarding through a month's worth of DVRed episodes of MythBusters. "Hi." She leaned over the back of the couch to kiss me.

"Hi," I said back. "I'll make dinner if you want."

She didn't move, resting on the couch back to keep her face near mine. "That's it? I'll make dinner? What about hello, what about how was your day, what about glad you're home, now let's have passionate sex on the coffee table, huh?" It was said with a smile I could hear, laced with pleasure at finding me home.

I reached back to touch her face with my fingertips and turned away from the TV. "Sorry, honey. Just a weird day, that's all." I dug up a decent attempt at a smile and let it crawl onto my face. "I'm really glad you're home."

"I can tell," she said, tousling my hair. "What happened?"

"More of the same," I said, feeling oddly unwilling to share the details. "I'm probably taking it more seriously than I need to."

Her finger tickled my ear as her other hand slid across my chest. "You're right. You need to stop worrying about that stuff, and about ghost women who don't really exist, and instead you need to start worrying about the real live woman you've got right next to you." Her breath was warm in my ear, promising a serious threat to the furniture's structural integrity and more.

"I love you," I said. I covered her hand with my own. "And you're right. I shouldn't be thinking about this."

Sarah bounced back up like she was on springs. "But right now, you're distracted. 'sokay." She leaned down to kiss the top of my head. "Make dinner. I'll go upstairs and change out of my work clothes, and we can discuss this again," she paused dramatically, "later."

Without waiting for me to answer, she bounced off. There were footsteps on the stairs as she headed up, and that encouraged me to hoist myself off the couch and toward the kitchen.

My head was still in the fridge when she came back down, anxiously scanning the crisper drawer for something that could conceivably be added to the steak to provide a vague nutritional benefit.

"The hamper's getting full," she announced, and sneezed once. The sound startled me into an abrupt collision with one of the refrigerator shelves. Bottles clanked and teetered, and I reeled back rubbing the back of my head and mumbling "Ow."

"Oh, honey, I'm sorry." Sarah stepped back out of my way, a look of concern on her face. I waved her off.

"No big deal," I said, and backhanded the refrigerator door shut. "The steak isn't defrosting fast enough. How do you feel about pizza?"

"Ethiopian?" she countered hopefully. I nodded as I stood up. "Good, then. And I'll do laundry tomorrow, unless you're out of socks or something."

"I just don't want to lose any more fights with our appliances," I told her, and kissed her forehead, and then led her out the door.

* * *

The last thing Sarah said to me before heading to work in the morning was that I was suddenly racking up serious boyfriend points.

"Bachelor party coming up," I told her. "We're going to Diamond Girls, and I need to have enough boyfriend points that you'll let me go."

She'd laughed at that, and then left. I watched her go and shivered. The air conditioning was turned up just a touch too much, enough to raise goosebumps on my arms, and I adjusted the thermostat down in preparation for leaving. The temperature seemed to change almost immediately, as if it were glad to adjust itself to what I wanted. I stared at the thermometer on the wall for a long moment to be sure that nothing actually had changed and got the mute evidence of numbers to tell me I was imagining things. Still, there was a sense of tension loosening, of something tight in the house easing away from snapping once I'd closed the door behind Sarah.

Then again, the most likely suspect for that was me and my own guilty conscience. Best, then, to get to work, to a space I wasn't tainting with lies, and to focus on something I actually could do.

Like, for example, talk to Terry.

He wasn't in my office when I arrived, but it didn't take him long to send me a chat message once I logged on to the network. It read, LUNCH.

I answered in the affirmative, then settled in to try to work. The unanswered questions from yesterday were still there, with a plus-sized batch of fresh ones. There were three meetings on the schedule, two before lunch and one after, and a progress report for BlackStone that I needed to get moving on as well. All in all, it was a perfectly normal workload for a perfectly normal day, which didn't keep the minutes from dragging past. A couple of times, emails came back requesting clarification on my clarifications, and then clarifications on those. Eventually, I stopped answering.

It wasn't until nearly one that Terry appeared outside my door. "Are you ready?" he rasped as I looked up from the meeting notes I'd been trying to compile for nearly an hour.

"Yeah," I told him, and then noticed the shadows behind him. "What are they doing here?"

He turned and looked. I could see faces now, Lucas and the others he'd been hanging with in their little cloud of suspicious smoke. "They're all in this. They're all part of this. They should be there."

I caught myself frowning. "I wanted to talk to you, not the entire Cub Scout troop."

Terry just stared at me for a minute. "Maybe they have something to say. Or maybe they deserve to hear what you'll say. It's not all about you, Ryan."

"No, it's about her," I answered, and got nods and murmurs in return. "Tell you what, then. Let's go grab a conference room or something and do this."

"I don't want to meet here," Terry said, the lines on his face pulled down in a clown-painting frown. "It's not the sort of thing Eric should be walking in on."

"Then you probably shouldn't have everyone hanging out in the hall in front of his office," I pointed out. Terry turned around in a panic, and I hauled myself up out of my chair. "Fine. Have it your way. Let's go grab McDonalds or something. I'll even buy everyone a Happy Meal." I marched out past him, and, as if by reflex, Lucas and a couple of the others followed.

Terry didn't. He just said, "You don't have to be a dick about it," and then stalked along, careful to keep his distance.

* * *

In the end there were six of us. Terry, another engineer, Lucas, two other artists, and me. There was no one from QA, no level design or project management. It was just a bunch of guys who, for all intents and purposes, could be hanging out for any reason at all.

"Is this the whole black project?" I asked. They flicked looks back and forth while silently deciding how to answer that one.

"Yeah," Terry said finally, which earned him a disgusted look from Lucas' wingman. "So far, anyway."

I waved a French fry around like a pointer. "How long have you been working on it?"

"Pretty much right from when she got cancelled," he admitted.

Lucas jumped in to clarify things. "It was just Terry at first. The rest of us were looking to, I don't know, keep her alive, I guess. Not lose what we'd done."

"So you started working black. And when did she start talking to you?"

Terry's food sat in front of him, untouched. I could see it slouching visibly toward room temperature. He ignored it and practically snarled at me. "Hasn't she been talking to you all along? Didn't you see her in your head from the beginning? Didn't you hear her?"

"Not like that," I said softly. "And I never touched her."

"You will," he said bitterly. "Oh, you will."

"Dammit, I don't want to! I just want to know if it's worth my time and my sanity to work with you guys on this, because honestly right now I'm not sure if I'm going nuts or not."

"You're not," Lucas reassured me. "We've all seen her. We've all talked to her." He paused. "She talks to Terry more. But she talks about you."

"Great." I wiped my forehead with a napkin. "I think I'm flattered. But you're really not helping the whole 'not nuts' thing right now."

Terry stared down at the table, not meeting my eyes. "It all seems crazy. I know. I remember the first time I saw her. I was working late trying something with her code, and she...reached out. Reached right out of the monitor. Offered me her hand. And I took it, and I was hers. I understood."

"Understood what?"

It was Lucas who answered. "What she was. What she needed. Why we needed to be the ones to finish her, and what that would mean."

"Would it mean that I'd stop having a freaky naked blue chick appear in my—" I nearly said "girlfriend's dreams" or "document files" or a dozen other things. Instead, I ended lamely on "work," and dared anyone to tell me I'd thought of saying anything different.

Terry sighed. "Why does it always have to be a joke? You're smarter than that. We all know it, and we all know you believed in her, back when she was our project. Why don't you admit it—you want to finish her as much as we do."

"Maybe," I said hesitantly. "So, if I were hypothetically to help you out, what would you want from me?"

He looked at the others before answering. "It's not what I want. It's what she wants. And she wants you." Each word was ground out bitterly, the verbal equivalent of someone turning big rocks into small ones with a tiny, tiny hammer.

"Because?" I let the word hang there. Terry's face got red; Lucas rushed in to fill the gap.

"Because she wants you to finish her. There are parts of her that are missing, and she needs to know what they are."

I shook my head. "Why don't you guys just fill it in, then? Ignore the documentation like you always do, and there you go. There she goes."

"It doesn't work like that," Terry said, after swallowing a few times to get himself able to speak. "We could make stuff up, yeah, but that wouldn't be the original vision. That wouldn't be the missing parts of her. It just wouldn't fit, and she'd be hurt because of it. In pain. Crippled."

Lucas nodded. "She needs the stuff you never wrote down that belongs to her. Until she gets it, she's incomplete."

I thought about that for a moment. "And then what?"

Terry blinked. "Then what what?"

"Then what happens? I finish the design, and you guys," I waved in their rough direction, "implement it, and then what happens? Does she go away? Transmit herself to the Sony plant and get discs pressed of herself? What does she do?"

"It doesn't matter. She'll be free." Terry's voice was dreamy. "After that, it's all details."

"Free." I stood up. "Free," I repeated, walking to the door. "Will that be a good thing?"

"It's better than being broken. Or forgotten," Terry said, softly. "Our dreams shouldn't be forgotten."

"Not unless they're nightmares," I said, and walked out.

When I got back to the office, I sent Terry an email. It read, I'll think about it. I didn't sign it, but I did bcc it to my home account, and then I started prepping for another meeting.

* * *

It ran for nearly two hours, which was about an hour longer than I thought it needed to. What was clear from the beginning was what we had time to do; what took forever was figuring out what we had to leave on the chopping block in order to get there. In the end, nobody was exactly happy with the decisions we'd made, which meant that everyone's ox got gored a little bit and that we'd probably made a mistake somewhere. In my experience, it was usually safer to hack out one system rather than snip out bits and pieces of a lot of them—the game tended to end up with a lot of not-quite-satisfying elements that way—but no one was willing to either throw their favorite on the pile or mandate that someone else's go, so we ended up with lots of little trims everywhere.

Afterwards, I retreated to my office. The message light on my phone was blinking when I got there, an insistent little red eye winking at me way too fast. I thought about ignoring it, or, better yet, deleting whatever message was on there, but duty won out.

A closer check indicated that there were six messages waiting, which was odd. Normally I didn't get six messages in a month, let alone in the course of a long lunch and a single meeting. Thinking it might have been an emergency, I checked my cell phone to see if someone—Sarah, I confessed to myself—had been trying to reach me that way, but there were no new messages, no missed calls, and no evidence I'd even needed to bring the phone along with me.

Curious now, I punched in my code and let the voicemail playback begin. The first one was blank, probably a wrong number, and there was the tell-tale click of the fumbling hang-up five or six seconds in. I deleted it and kept going. The second one was an automated voice mail message informing me that certain messages I'd stored in the system for ninety days were about to be deleted, and that I should do something about it if I wanted to keep them. I ignored that one, too, and skipped to the third.

Breathing.

That's all it was, the sound of somebody breathing. Not heavy, not obscene, just the faint whisper of breath in and out on the other end of the line. No voices, no words, just slow, steady breathing. I caught myself on the verge of saying "Hello?" into the receiver, then let it play out to the end.

That one, I saved.

The fourth message was like the third, but longer. The fifth one, though, had words.

At first, it sounded like the others—wordless, voiceless, just the in-and-out of air on the other end. I almost punched in the code to save it and moved on to number six. But then the voice started, so soft at first I wasn't sure I heard it, but rising in volume with every syllable.

"Ryan?" it said. "Ryan? You should pick up. You should talk to me. We have so much to talk about." A pause. "I miss you. Do you miss me? I think you do."

I knew the voice. After all, I'd written the notes for it, heard it in my imagination, gotten as close to it as we could have in the voice casting and placeholder dialogue recording sessions.

And of course, I'd heard it in my office, the night the last bits of my life had started to go to hell.

I let the message play out. There was more space after the last words, more sounds of sibilant breathing left so I'd know whom the other calls were from.

I thought about it, then deleted the message. She'd made her point. When I was done listening to the sixth voicemail, I'd go back and wipe out the other ones, too.

The sixth one was from Sarah. It said that she figured it was easier to reach me on my work number than on my cell phone, and that she was going to make lasagna for dinner. She hoped that was all right.

I thought I was going to cry.

Chapter 25

Quarter of six, and I headed back to the break room to get what I hoped would be my last cup of coffee of the day. For some reason the coffee service we used always resupplied fresh coffee on Friday, which meant that by Wednesday afternoon everything that wasn't decaf was gone. I picked the best of a bad lot, shoved it in the machine, and waited.

There was a click and a thunk beside me, the sound of one of the cabinets opening and then closing. I looked over and there was Michelle, a styrofoam coffee cup in her hand, eyes resolutely straight ahead. If she noticed me watching her, she didn't give any sign. She didn't move any closer, nor did she step further away.

Two can play at that game, I thought, turning back to the coffee maker. It gurgled and hissed, pissing brown bean juice into my mug. Steam leaked out the side, evidence of a broken seal somewhere. One of the QA wonks wandered in, saw the two of us standing there, and backpedaled right out.

The machine finished. I looked at Michelle, who was still resolutely not looking at me, and fought the urge to just walk out and leave her the coffee. Sooner or later we were going to have to talk to each other, after all.

For a moment, neither of us moved. Then I grabbed my cup as she reached for a coffee packet, and our hands nearly touched.

"Ryan..." she said, and stepped back.

"Michelle." I grabbed my mug and pulled it away. "I think there's still some of the imitation Blue Mountain in the back. I, uh, kind of hid a couple of the packets back there."

"Yeah. Thanks." She rummaged a bit, then pulled out one of the stashed packages. I stepped back and let her brew her cup, then handed her the creamer that I knew she'd drown the coffee in once it finished brewing.

"What's with the styrofoam cup?" I asked as she poured. "I thought you wanted us to get rid of them because they're mean to the planet."

"Do you always have to be such a dick about everything," she asked. Her voice was weary. "I mean, come on. Can't you even make a simple cup of coffee without turning this into some kind of mind game? Besides, I gave you mine, and you never gave it back."

"I was just trying to make conversation," I said, surprised at her tone.

Michelle shook her head as she reached for the box of sugar packets on the counter. "No, you weren't. I didn't jump down your throat, so you had to push to see how far I'd let you go. You can go wherever you want, Ryan. I'm just not going there with you any more, okay."

I took a swig of coffee. It was scalding hot and burned going down. "Oww. Jesus. What the hell?" I made a face and tested the inside of my mouth experimentally with my tongue. Michelle stirred in her sugar, unimpressed, and dumped in a second batch of creamer on top of the first. "Look, Michelle. I'm sorry. I'm not really myself these days."

"Oh really? I'd say you're being yourself more than ever."

Another swig of coffee, another burn going down. "No, look, it's her, OK? I don't know what she's doing or how she's doing it, but everything in my life is going insane right now, and I'm just sort of flailing around because of it."

"But that's just it," she said. "It's not just your life. It's my life. It's Sarah's life. It's the lives of everyone you're working with."

"And it's her life," I added. "I don't know what I should do."

"What do you want me to tell you, Ryan?" She picked the cup up, the coffee inside the color of melted chocolate, and held it in front of her like a ward against evil. "That I forgive you because you're in kind of a weird place? Well, I don't. That you should do something about...her? I don't know if or what you should do. I'm just here to make a stupid port of a stupid game and collect my paycheck, not make you feel better because you've got your sensitive artist panties in a wad."

"Michelle," I said, hating myself for saying it, "I don't know what to do."

"Good," she replied, turning away. "Maybe that'll encourage you to think things through. You know, take some responsibility for what you're doing instead of just blundering from crisis to crisis."

"Terry wants me to help him," I said as she started walking away. She stopped.

"Are you going to?" she asked in a small, scared voice.

"Do you think I should?"

"No!" The word tore out of her like a shriek as she whipped around to stare at me. "Jesus, Ryan, that thing they're working on isn't human!"

"Does that make her evil?"

"It tried to kill you!" Her eyes were wide, her face flushed, her mouth open in disbelief that I'd even entertain the idea. "And now, because it let you see its tits, you're going to be its best friend forever? Whatever it is. Whatever made it, it's not normal. It's not right. And nothing good's going to come of it being here."

I took a step forward, hands held out wide in a gesture of surrender, the pose of an unarmed cop approaching a hostage-taker. "I don't know what brought her here, either, but she's here now. She's alive now. And I don't know if letting her go on like this is the kindest or the cruelest thing to do."

"Deleting her would be the right thing to do!" Michelle's voice rose as she stalked toward me, her anger rising. "Don't you get it, Ryan? Whatever's going on now is just the beginning. You're on the edges, but you're going to get sucked in. Whatever she needs now, she'll need more, and more, until she's taking everything." Suddenly, she threw back her head and laughed, a scary, unhinged sound. "You know what? I just got it. Just now, I finally got it."

"Got what?"

"Her." Michelle's head snapped back down and she fixed me with a bemused predator's stare. "She's the job, Ryan. She's the goddamned job, and she's the other woman, and she always has been."

"She's just a game," I sputtered, barely believing the words as I said them.

"I know exactly what she is and what she means, even if you don't."

The words escaped before I could stop them, before I could think about them, before I'd even realized I'd formed them. "You're just jealous, you know that? You're jealous that she wants me!"

Silence. Michelle staring at me, eyes impossibly round, face impossibly pale. Her cup fell to the floor, the coffee spilling out like the blood of a murder victim in a wide, savage arc.

"Oh, God. Oh, Shelly. I'm sorry. I shouldn't have said that. I didn't mean that."

"I only got to be the other woman once," she said, quietly, then turned and walked away.

"Michelle!"

She didn't turn, didn't even slow down. I said something under my breath that would have gotten me fired if HR had heard it and started after her.

My foot hit coffee instead and skidded from under me. I felt myself going over, felt the mug of scalding hot coffee slipping out of my hand. It arced up and over even as I slipped backwards, glistening past as I went down. Somehow it spattered on the tile before I hit, the hot spray splashing across the back of my head as if in anticipation. Scalp wounds are supposed to be bloody, I thought, and then my head hit the floor with a rifle shot crack and everything went white. I felt the impact of the mug on the ground, felt the air whoosh out of me as my back hit, felt something sharp tear into my hand and realized it was part of the now-broken mug spinning off from its demolition.

Then there was silence, except for the ringing white noise in my ears, and the pounding of my heart, and the wheezing of my breath as I tried to figure out how my lungs worked again.

That, and the sound of clapping, slow and steady, low and sarcastic. Someone had seen. Someone had heard. Someone was there.

"Who," I croaked, and then "help me up."

"You're pathetic," replied Leon.

And then, as an afterthought, "Cocksucker," as he turned and walked away.

* * *

For the longest time, Eric just sat in his chair, looking at me, not saying anything. I sat in the chair opposite, an icepack on the back of my head, and looked at the floor. Coffee had soaked the back of my shirt and pants, leaving a ferocious itch as it dried off my skin. In the far distance we could hear explosions; tests of sound files and triggers that rattled the walls at irregular intervals.

Finally, he spoke. "What am I going to do with you, Ryan?" he asked. "You were one of the few people in this building I thought I could trust absolutely. I thought you could be professional. I thought you could do your job without letting any personal issues get in the way. Instead, you wind up flat on your ass in a puddle of coffee. How's the hand, by the way?"

I looked at it. The bleeding had stopped, but I had a fancy new two-inch cut just below the wrist. "It's fine. Flesh wound and all that."

"Good." He coughed into his fist, then picked up where he'd left off. "Right. Flat on your ass in the break room. I ask you to lead the team, and now neither the Engineering nor the Art lead want to be in the same room with you. I ask you to work on a simple port, and instead we end up behind pretty much as soon as we start. Do you have any kind of explanation for this, or should I just advise you to go take a few weeks' vacation?"

"Vacation?" I croaked. "Why vacation?"

"So you don't do anything else stupid that would force me to fire you." He looked at me again, and the anger swapped itself out for pity. "Come on, Ryan, what is it? You're not a screw up, not like this. Is there something else that's going on? This isn't like you."

I opened my mouth to say something inoffensive, like a promise to straighten up, and instead, I started laughing. My head throbbed with each cackle, but I just couldn't stop myself. Bent over, howling, I just shook my head and laughed. "Oh, Jesus, Eric. If you knew. If you only knew."

"Easy there." He was out from around the desk, my head in his hands and cradling me to look up into the ceiling light. "You sound like you might be concussed. Let me get a look at your eyes to see if you're dilated."

"I'm not dilated, I'm screwed," I protested, and suddenly that was even funnier, and I laughed until I couldn't breathe.

"Drink this," Eric said about a lifetime later, forcing a cup of water between my hands. I took a gulp, chortled, and coughed as half of it came out my nose. "Oh, man, man, what did you have to do that for?"

Eric held the cup in my hands until he was sure I wasn't going to drop it, then leaned back, squatting on his haunches. "To keep you from passing out, mostly." He stared at me intently. "Do I need to take you to the urgent care? Do I need to call Sarah and let her do it for me?"

I blinked twice, and suddenly nothing was funny anymore. "God, no. I'm all right, Eric. I just tried to apologize to Shelly and it didn't work and she spilled her coffee, and then I slipped and…" My head was throbbing now, and my hand throbbing with it, and then I thought about Leon. "Oh, God. What a mess."

"You are," he said matter-of-factly. "And I still think I should take you to the emergency room."

"It's just a bump," I protested. "And to answer your question, yeah, there's something going on. I guess I should have told you about it a while ago."

He stood, then turned to face the window. "If it's about canceling Blue Lightning…"

"It is. Sort of." I gathered myself to tell him everything, then stopped. What could I tell him? That our cancelled project was walking around the building, naked, demanding overtime and a hell of a lot more? That would get me sent to a whole different kind of hospital and get Sarah brought in, and sooner or later she'd talk to Leon and Shelly, and…

No. Wasn't going to happen, couldn't happen, couldn't be allowed to happen. In an instant the alternative made itself crystal clear. There was a way out of this, a way to move forward and buy enough time to make penance for my sins later. There was a way to save the project and, if I was lucky, at least put Blue Lightning on hold for long enough for me to figure out what to do about her.

"Yes?" Eric was waiting, and not patiently. He was angry and just wanted me to give him an appropriate target. And if I didn't, I was quite certain, then it would be me.

"There's a black project running for Blue Lightning," I said. Eric nodded but didn't say anything, and after a minute, I continued. "Terry's leading it. There are at least four other people involved.

They've been working on it instead of Salvador, and they asked me to get involved."

"Instead of Salvador?" he finally asked. "Not on top of it?"

"It's gotten kind of intense," I said, and hoped that my voice didn't give away anything more than it ought. "At least, that's what they told me."

"And?"

I took a deep breath before continuing. "And I've been trying to figure out what to do about it for weeks now, because I didn't want to rat them out, but at the same time—"

"At the same time you didn't want to screw the project or the company." He turned around and shot me a look fraught with meaning. "And that's what's been bugging you?" There was a hint of emphasis on the word "that," a suggestion that he knew a little more than I'd told him and he wanted to see if I'd come clean.

Screw it. What was he going to do, I asked myself. Ask Michelle and Leon? They wouldn't give him the straight dope either, not if they wanted to avoid a little psychiatric leave of their own.

"That's it," I said, and then forced myself into a coughing fit so I wouldn't have to say anything else.

"Ah," Eric said. "I see." He walked over to his desk and punched up an extension on his phone. "Marie?" he asked into the speaker.

There was a pause, then the voice of our HR maven came back, crackling over the line. "Yes? Hello?"

"I'm going to need your help. We've got," and he looked up at me, "four termination notices I need you to prepare, and one letter of discipline to go into a file. Ryan will be down shortly to give you the names."

"Four?" she asked, clearly surprised. "Do we have cause?"

"I think so," he said calmly. "Ryan will explain when he gets there." He cut the connection and looked down at me. "That is, if you're sticking by your story."

"It's the truth," I said, and shivered. "But I don't think you need to—"

"Your thinking hasn't been working so well lately, Ryan," Eric said, his voice deceptively mild. "Now go down and talk to the nice lady in HR about how these people have been working on a project they weren't supposed to on company time."

"It's going to be a huge morale hit," I warned him.

"I'll take that chance. It's better than missing a milestone because people are too busy working on side projects to get their shit done."

"But you don't have to fire them," I pleaded. "Yell at them, suspend them, embarrass them, whatever, but all they're doing is caring a little too much about what we worked on."

"The only thing getting them fired right now"—and he pointed a long finger straight down at me—"is your word. So if you really don't want this to happen, just tell me you're concussed or something similar, and I'll call Sarah and she'll come in and take you to the hospital. On the other hand, you might want to think about whether it's best for all concerned if they go. Really, this one's all on you."

I sat there for a moment, staring at my shoes. My head throbbed, the pulsing of the blood in my temples nearly deafening.

"Four?" I finally croaked. "Why just four?"

"We need Terry," Eric said, his voice eminently reasonable. "Now, do you need help, or can you make it to HR on your own?"

* * *

The building was mostly empty by the time I left Marie's office. She'd been very calm and professional about the whole thing, taking my statement and making me verify each element before attaching them to the appropriate termination notices.

It felt a lot like I was being given another chance to back down, to back off and take my chances. Though every word I gave Marie was true, it felt worse than the lying I'd done, and while none of it was lies, it wasn't all of the truth, not by a long shot.

Then again, I was painfully aware that telling the whole truth wasn't going to help my campaign to avoid having Sarah step into the building and risk an encounter with Leon or Shelly. Or, for that matter, with someone who'd talked to them, or who'd heard about what had happened, or who'd talked to someone who'd heard, or…the list went on, and the risk went up, and by the time I was done running it down I'd convinced myself that it was for the best that those four guys would be getting out of the studio and away from Blue Lightning. It would be safer for them, certainly.

The thought that it would be less competition for me, I mostly stopped before it started. Mostly.

Nobody said anything as I made my way back to my office, nobody stopped me or waved or asked me any questions. Folks going out the door kept on going, occasionally looking in my direction but not saying anything. It confirmed my suspicions that the story of my little tete-a-tete with Michelle had already gone viral, and I wouldn't be surprised if some version of it didn't pop up on gamer gossip blogs before suppertime.

Wearily, I sat down behind my desk and tried to catch up. Thankfully, most of the email that had come in required no response. The vast majority were "new in build" announcements, communiqués sent to let everyone know that Something Had Changed. A few were forwarded humor posts. One was an internet meme image, a Sarcastic Wonka with the caption, TELL ME AGAIN HOW YOU DRINK YOUR COFFEE WITH YOUR ASS. Not a one was a question about the game.

The only email directed my way exclusively was from Dennis, who wanted to know how the new monitor was working out for me and to assure me that the new one was coming within a couple of days. Possibly. If everything went right with the requisitions.

I started to answer him, then thought better of it. Instead, I picked myself up and headed over to his warren.

He was neck-deep in a system when I got there. The box was on his desk and open, with various bits of its electronic guts sprawled out around it. I recognized a couple of hard drives, a high-end video card, and something that could have been a heat sink, but the sheer volume of components was overwhelming. There was no way any sane man could cram that much hardware into one case. For Dennis, it would be tough.

"Just a minute." His voice echoed from the vents at the back of the case. "Gotta do a little soldering here, and I'll be right with you." The smell of hot lead drifted then past me as I waited. There was nowhere to sit; every flat surface was covered in bits of hardware awaiting either reconnection or recycling.

Finally, the sounds of banging inside faded, and Dennis stuck his head out. "Hey, Ryan! What's up? I hear you were playing skull hockey in the break room, man."

"More like a gravity check," I told him, and tried to smile. "Nothing too serious, except for some scrambled brains."

"Ahh, you can't scramble what you ain't got," he said, grinning to take the sting out of it. "Now, what can I do for you?"

Gingerly, I stepped to his desk. Nothing crunched underfoot as I did so. "It's about the monitor…"

"Oh, geez. Don't tell me that one crapped the bed, too."

"No, I—"

"Cause if it did, we can maybe use one of the seventeen-inchers until your new one comes in."

"Really, it—"

"And I guess I'll just have to put a rush on the new one I ordered for you, though Eric's not gonna like what that costs."

"Seriously, Dennis, I—"

He scratched his chin. "Maybe we could just go down to Best Buy and get one, and cancel the order. Or I could repurpose that one, and—"

"Dennis!"

He looked up, shocked, and blinked at me twice. "What, man? I'm thinking here."

"You don't need to worry." Almost without realizing it, I placed my hands on the desk and let them take my weary weight. "The monitor you got me is fine. It's just fine, and right now I don't think it would be good for morale if I got a shiny new expensive toy."

That got me another blink. "You're saying you don't want the new monitor?"

"That's exactly what I'm saying."

"Huh." Dennis cocked his head and squinted at me. "You sure? I think maybe you hit your head harder than you thought."

"I'm sure," I said. "If it's too late to cancel it, give it to someone else. One of the artists will appreciate it, maybe. But I've got all I need."

He threw up his hands. "If you say so, man. But that's gotta be the first time anyone's ever turned down an equipment upgrade that I can remember."

"Brett Lewis turned down a widescreen monitor about a year back," I reminded him.

"Yeah, but that dude was looking at porn all the time and calling it 'visual reference,' and he didn't want no one to see that freaky shit he was into."

"Look, when a man and a camel really love each other, it's a beautiful thing. It's not Brett's fault the rest of us couldn't understand that."

Dennis stared at me for a moment, then collapsed into laughter. "Damn, man. I thought I was the only one who remembered that stuff. Okay, you win. I'll find someplace else for the monitor, but I won't tell anyone. You've got until it arrives to change your mind, you hear?"

I gave him a wry smile, the best I could manage. "And the sad thing was, we never even put the camel in the game."

"Stop it, man, just stop it." Still laughing, he waved me out. I turned to go and nearly broke my toe as I did so, kicking a long metal lockbox. Instantly, Dennis stopped his giggles.

"Dude! Watch it!"

I stepped carefully over the box, which, on first examination, seemed to be in perfect repair. It was gunmetal gray and maybe two feet long, with a fold-off top held in place with a tiny Yale lock. Below that was a label with the Horseshoe logo on it and a series of dates. "Offsite backups?" I asked.

He nodded. "About four months' worth. Enough to basically bork the whole thing, if we lost 'em. Eric asked to see 'em. He wanted to check some usage patterns or something over the last couple of months on the Blue Lightning project. I told him he coulda got those from the network log files, but no." Dennis' hands went up in a grand Goth gesture of being put upon. "So I had to call up our offsite provider and jump through nine kinds of hoops just to get the shit back in the building."

I looked down at the box, then at Dennis. "Wait a minute. Those are our offsite backups? Did they make backups of the backups or something before sending them here?"

"That, my friend, would cost extra. And don't even get me started on putting this shit in the cloud." Dennis gave a wicked little chuckle, then extended his hand. "Gimme the box, would you?"

I bent down to pick it up. The metal felt unaccountably warm in my hands. "So if there was a fire or something, we'd be totally screwed for backups? It would all go poof?"

Dennis reached out to take the lockbox. I handed it to him. "Mostly," he said. "After the other ones he made me order get here, then we'll really be up shit's creek if something goes wrong. But," and he placed the container on a sliver of clear space on his desktop, "the odds of that are a couple of zillion to one. What's going to burn in this place? We even got fireproof carpets." He dug a toe into the dried puke-brown stuff at his feet for emphasis.

"People?" I asked.

"No," he corrected me. "People burn out. They don't burn up."

"Maybe someone will get creative," I told him, and then headed for the door. "Thanks again on the monitor thing, Dennis."

"Don't mention it," he said. By the time I was back in the hall, he was back inside the guts of the machine he'd been working on when I came in, crooning sweet nothings to its electronic innards.

"At least it isn't camels," I said to myself, and walked away.

* * *

The trick, I decided as I walked from Dennis' cave to my own, was to get out of the building before Blue Lightning showed up and told me what she thought about getting her other minions canned. Marie wasn't going to call them in until the morning, but if Blue Lightning could get into our email system, she could get anywhere on the internal network, and that included human resources.

I discounted the possibility of Terry and company waiting for me in the parking lot with a tire iron as tomorrow's disaster.

Eric, I saw as I headed down the hall, had already taken off. Indeed, that entire end of the building had already emptied, unusual for a Thursday afternoon. Normally that was the work-late night, the desperate push to get everything done so everyone could feel justified in getting out at a decent hour on Friday.

Today, however, it was just me, and I intended to rectify that as quickly as I could. A quick email check showed nothing new worth mentioning. Saving the documents I had open and checking them back in to the database took another minute; shutting down the other apps not much time beyond that. I put the desktop into standby mode, packed up the laptop, and shoved it into its bag, then looked around. There was no sign of anything untoward, no sign of life other than my own movements. All there was to do was let Sarah know I was coming home, kill the lights, and get out.

I pulled out my cell phone and thumbed in the quick-dial for home. It rang twice, then Sarah picked up. "Hello?"

"Hi."

"Ryan? Don't tell me you have to stay late tonight." Her voice was worried, not angry. "The lasagna's in the oven already."

"No, no, no," I said, doing my best to be reassuring. "It's the exact opposite. I'm coming home now."

There was a pause, then a burst of static. Individual words came through, "can't" and "what" and "call back." Then it faded, letting me hear Sarah's voice. "Ryan? Are you there? Ryan? This isn't funny. Just let me know if you're coming home tonight, okay?"

"Sarah?" I said, and got that flat, dead tone that's an absence of the phone's mike picking up your voice, a sure sign that it wasn't getting through. "Look, Sarah, if you can hear me—"

"She can't hear you," Blue Lightning said, and then the connection dissolved into howling static.

Deliberately, I put the phone in my pocket before turning to face her. It was a small thing, maybe, a way of demonstrating that I wasn't entirely at her beck and call.

If it worked, she didn't show it.

She was perched on one arm of the guest chair, balanced perfectly on something that should have supported neither her weight nor her pose. One foot in front of the other, crouched down like a hunting cat ready to leap upon its prey, she looked at me with wide eyes. "I could have done more than block your call, you know," she said. "I can imitate your voice. I could call her and have her think it's you. I could say terrible, terrible things to her and have her think you said them."

"Why didn't you," I said warily, and thought of "Sarah" supposedly calling Eric. "And why would you want to?"

"Silly." She leaped off the chair without so much as a millimeter's disturbance in where it sat. "I wouldn't do something like that. It's not nice. Besides, I don't need to do anything like that. You're mine already. You just need a little more time to figure it out."

I shook my head. "I'm not anybody's. And whether or not I…finish my work on you has nothing to do with Sarah."

She put a cool finger to my lips. A tiny spark jumped from her fingertip to the tip of my tongue, making me taste ozone and smoke. "It's got everything to do with her. And here. And what you do from now on." Her finger slid along the side of my mouth, catching the faintest hint of moisture between my lips, and trailed along my jawline. I found myself holding still, hardly breathing. She stepped closer to me, and I became aware of how intensely female this thing I'd created was, how much sexuality I'd hidden in her creation and my imagination. Her every move was a hint at what else that body might be capable of, in love or war or both. The sleekness of her skin, the play of muscle underneath it and the smooth curves of her flesh, all said "sex" even though she'd been designed to deal death.

"Please," I said. "I need to get home."

"Do you?" She stepped even closer, pressing her body against mine. I could feel the heat of her now, warm in all the right places to let me know she wanted me, and without wanting to I felt myself responding. "Maybe you should work late tonight. You've got so much to do."

One step back was all I had, and then my back was against the wall. I took it, and she closed with me. "I'm going home," I told her, "And I'm doing it right now. We can talk tomorrow. We'll talk tomorrow." I gulped down air through a throat that felt like it had been twisted shut. "But not tonight. Not now."

"If you say so." She laughed, and her finger tickled my ear before she pulled it away. "But I think you want to stay."

"Not tonight," I said, trying to put a little more finality in my voice, and turned away from her. "That's all I can say right now."

"Oh, all right." Her voice dropped to a pouty whisper. "By the way, it was very selfish of you to get those other boys fired. You didn't need to be jealous, though. You're the one I really want. The one I really need."

"Is that true?" I asked, but she was already gone.

Chapter 26

"Good night," I told Sarah, and kissed her on the back of her head.

She sneezed. "Bless you," I told her, and kissed her again.

"It's not funny." She sniffled once, experimentally. "I've been sneezing all week when I come home."

"Not at the office?"

"No." She sniffled again. "And I have no idea why. It's worst when I'm in here."

"Maybe you're allergic to me," I said, spooning up behind her. "Any minute now you're going to break out with gigantic purple spots."

"Stop it," she said, making feeble batting motions in my direction. "I think I need to go see an allergist."

"OK." I held her for a minute. "I think I got some people fired today at work," I said finally.

"I was wondering." She rolled over to face me. "You were acting so strange during dinner. Not that I wasn't glad to have you home, but still."

"Weird day," I admitted, "and a rough one. I got into some arguments at work, and I slipped in the break room, and then Eric called me on the carpet and I had to come clean about some stuff that I'd been sort of covering up for the guys."

"Oh, babe, I'm sorry." She reached out to stroke my face gently, her fingers tracing up and down where a few hours ago, Blue Lightning had run one finger across.

I tried not to think about that.

"Are you all right? Do we need to get you to a doctor?" I caught her hand in mine and wound our fingers together, held her tight, hand to hand and arm to arm.

"I'm fine," I said. "I just need a good night's sleep."

Sarah said nothing, but her look was one I'd seen before, the one she'd always used to let me know that I wasn't getting away with anything when I tried to be brave.

"Seriously," I told her, "I'm all right. A lot of things have gone wrong, and there's a long way to go, but," and I gathered myself to say it, "I think I'm finally headed in the right direction. With work, with us, with dealing with some old stuff, all of it."

"Uh huh," she said, and sneezed. "Any more ghost sightings?"

"No. Not that it would have made a difference today."

"If they got fired, sweetheart, it's because of something they did. They can't blame you for not protecting them forever when they were doing something stupid."

"Yes, but..." The words ran dry. "I wish there had been another way," I finished lamely.

"It's their fault, not yours," Sarah said firmly. "Now stop worrying about it, and get some sleep."

"You sure you want to sleep?" My fingers left hers and traced a line down her arm. "I'm not too tired."

"What exactly are you suggesting?" She caught my hand with hers and brought it to her mouth and kissed each fingertip. "Don't tell me you're in the mood all of a sudden, now that you've made your grand confession."

"Maybe." I moved a little closer to her. "And maybe you just made me realize how lucky I am to be with someone like you." The back of my fingers brushed her cheek, then she turned away.

"I'm sorry, babe," she said. "I'm just really tired. And some of us don't have flextime." She curled up around her pillow. Half the blankets went with her.

"It's OK," I heard myself saying. "I love you."

"I love you, too." A minute later, she was snoring gently. I curled up around her, my left arm draped over her for protection or comfort, my hand carefully placed not to cup one of her breasts. The rhythm of her breathing soothed, and I closed my eyes and wondered why the single line Blue Lightning had drawn across my cheek still burned.

* * *

Sarah was gone by the time I got downstairs in the morning. She'd left a note on the kitchen table, a yellow Post-it stuck to the side of the sugar bowl. "Friday Night Movie Night? Your pick. —Love, Sarah."

I pulled the note off the bowl, folded it carefully, and tucked it in my pocket. Friday Night Movie Night had been a staple of the early part of our relationship, right up until about the time we moved in together. One of us would pick a movie, and then we'd just cuddle up on the couch and watch it together. We'd get to the end maybe half the time before finding each other much more interesting.

The rest of the Post-its were upstairs, so I sent her a text instead: FNMN sounds good. Will pick something you hate so we can start making out early. Love you.

I hit send, shoved the phone back in my pocket. The last bagel in the bag had definite blotches of mold on it, so I decided to skip breakfast and just head in. With luck, I'd be safely ensconced in my office before either HR or Lucas and his crew got in, saving me from the possibility of bumping into any of them in the hallway and any unpleasant scenes that might ensue.

Halfway to work, I realized I'd forgotten to make coffee. That meant either braving the corridors at work, or doing without.

I compromised by pulling in at a gas station and getting a cup of something dubiously labeled espresso there, the non-dairy creamer distinctly identifiable as non-organic. I bought the stuff, paid cash, and headed back to the car after a couple of tentative sips scalded my tongue.

When I got in, music was playing. I hadn't turned the phone on when I'd started driving; I hadn't plugged it in to the jack in the car when I got in earlier. But it was thundering away, loud enough that I could hear it through the windshield as I walked up.

It wasn't playing Blue Lightning music, which was a mild surprise. Instead, it was playing "Such Great Heights" by Iron and Wine, a song that Sarah had played for me when we first started dating. "It's not quite our song," she had told me, "but it'll do for now."

We'd never gotten around to having an "our song," but "Such Great Heights" still put a smile on her face when she heard it.

And now it was playing by itself. I froze, my hand on the door handle, listening. As if it had been waiting for proof I was in earshot, the volume swelled. The sound distorted, rattling the windows in a way I didn't think the song was capable of. As I listened, it changed. Notes started getting skipped, long jagged tears in the fabric of the song. The singer's voice distorted, warped, choked. The sound was horrific, as if someone were playing a record that was melting on the turntable. All the while, the volume got louder and louder, the distortion greater and greater until I thought the speakers would blow out, or the windows.

"This isn't helping," I shouted, and opened the door. The sound hit me like a two-handed shove to the face, driving me back with the sheer pressure of the noise. I stumbled back, caught my footing, and staggered forward. One hand caught the phone up and pulled it loose, slamming it down on the ground. Abruptly, the music dimmed.

"Like I said, you're not helping yourself here!" Little sparks of blue danced around the cracks in the phone's case, and I was seized with a cold fury. It had been a gift from Sarah, or its predecessor had, and twice now it had been touched by Blue Lightning's hands.

The steaming cup of coffee was still in my left hand, so I dumped it out on the iPhone. It gave a fierce, impossibly loud screech, then lay silent. Tiny popping sounds, the evidence of liquid hitting current, bubbled up for a minute, then subsided into silence.

I nodded, mostly satisfied, then I got in my car and drove over it five or six times. When I was finished, I parked, picked up the pieces, and threw them in four different trash bins. Some of the other customers stared at me; none of them said a word.

"We'll talk later," I said into the last trash can, the one that got the remains of the earbuds and a piece of screen. "Later."

Then I went in to get another cup of coffee. The time on the receipt said "9:24." It didn't look as if I would be beating anyone in after all.

* * *

Lucas was putting boxes into his car as I pulled up. I pretended not to see him as I got out and headed inside, but I could feel his eyes on my back with every step. Eric was at the front desk and nodded fractionally as I passed.

"Morning," he said.

"Morning. It's done?"

He jerked a thumb toward HR. "The last one's in there now. Everyone should be packed up and gone by lunch. Oh, and Terry was looking for you."

"Of course he was," I answered. "Tell him I'll be waiting for him at my desk."

"I should do that, should I?" Eric said, his voice incredulous, but he said it to my back, as I was already gone.

* * *

It wasn't five minutes later before Terry was knocking at my door. I didn't have time to tell him to come in before he'd already shoved it open, his face red, his hands shaking.

"You prick!" he shouted. "You absolute prick! You sold us out!"

"No," I corrected him, gesturing to the empty chair. "I sold Lucas and the other guys out. You still have a job, and there never was an us."

He crossed to the chair and kicked it. It bounced against the wall, hit the underside of my whiteboard and then slammed backed down, rocking crazily on the carpet. "That's bullshit and you know it! You were supposed to keep her secret so we could finish her. And now Lucas is gone, and it's just you and me left, and I don't think I want to work with you."

"That's fine," I said. "I don't want to work with you, either, but we've got a project to finish, and Salvador's on a tight deadline."

Terry actually sputtered at that, and I swear little flecks of foam bubbled at the corners of his mouth. "Salvador? Salvador! What the fuck are you talking about Salvador for? There's one thing we're working on that's worth talking about. One! And that's Blue Lightning!"

"Yeah. And that's the problem." I stood up. "Let's take this outside."

Terry gaped like a fish. "Are you trying to fight me?" he finally choked out.

"No," I said, squinting in anticipation of the headache that I was certain the conversation would bring on. "I just want to talk in private, and we're a lot more likely to get that if we're out of the building."

"Your office door is shut," he said stubbornly. "We can talk fine right here, unless you're trying to avoid me."

"Not you," I said. "Her." I let that sink in for a minute, while suspicion and anger chased each other around Terry's face. "Now, do you want to talk, or do you want to just stand here and yell at me? If that's the case, let me go get some Advil and you can do it all day long. But if you actually want to talk about what's going on and what I did, then we're taking a walk."

I could see his hands clenching and unclenching as he thought about it. "Nothing funny?" he asked.

"There's nothing funny about this at all," I said, and walked past him to the door. "Come on."

Terry followed me at a safe distance, hunched over and with enough steps between us to let any observers know he was just coincidentally going in the same direction I was. Once we got outside, I waited for him. He stopped and lit a cigarette with nervous fingers. One puff, and then another, and then he finally sauntered up to where I stood.

"You're not supposed to smoke out front," I reminded him.

He gave a snort of laughter. "Or what? I'll get fired?"

"Point taken." I turned and started walking. After a second, Terry scuffled after me. "You wanted to talk. So talk."

"That was a shitty thing you did," he said, ever so slightly out of breath. "You didn't have to get them fired. She's not going to be happy with you."

"Funny," I said, "She said it didn't really matter as long as I was still around." I let that sink in for a moment as we rounded the corner of the building and caught the first faint whiff of stale tobacco from the smokers' lounge.

"She…told you that?" he said after a minute. "That can't be right. She told me that she needed all of us."

"Uh-huh." I shot a glance at him. He looked genuinely upset. "You think maybe she was just telling you that?"

"No! And that's not the point. You didn't have to get them fired. Hell, I know things about you that would get you shitcanned, right now. Or maybe I call your house and tell your girlfriend what went down at the coffee machine. You ever think about that?"

I shook my head. "You're not going to get me fired, because she clearly wants me around, and that would piss her off. And besides, from the way Eric handled things yesterday, I'd say you and I are both bulletproof right now." Stopping, I turned to look at him. He nearly ran into my sternum before he realized I wasn't moving any more. "And sure, you can call Sarah if you want, and tell her what you think happened, but if my home life goes in the crapper because of you, I'm going to make your life a living hell through the end of Salvador."

"I could quit," he sputtered. "After all, you got the only people I actually liked here blown out the door."

"As long as she's here, you're not going anywhere," I said. "So let's call off the pissing contest, all right? Yeah, I did a crappy thing, and I did it to save my ass, but they're better off out of here anyway. I don't know what she wants, but I don't think it's going to be about any of us in the end."

"She said she wanted to be with me."

"She told me that, too." I could feel the pressure building behind my eyes, the headache coming on full throttle. "Look, Terry, there's only one way to put this: she's a project. And what do we know about projects?"

He thought about that for a minute, then answered warily. "That they feel good when they're done?"

"Jesus, man, what happened to you? You've been in this business nine years. You've shipped four games. You should know this by now. The project always takes, man. It takes your evenings, and it takes your weekends, and it takes your energy, and it's all in the name of pushing to the end for the good of the project and the good of the company and if you're lucky, the good of the guy in the cube next to you. It's about the project, but we all think it's going to be magic at the end, and that's why we keep on signing up to have the shit kicked out of us. Every. Single. Time!" I was shouting, and I realized it, and I didn't care. "She's a project, Terry. She's going to take everything she needs from us, and a little more, and we're going to be grateful for the chance to work ourselves to the bone for her. She's going to flash her tits at us and tell us she loves us until we believe her, and when it's done, she'll move on and what happened to us to get her there won't matter. Do you understand?"

He looked at me with heavy, sad eyes, and shook his head slowly. "I think you don't want her to leave you," he said, drawing each word out like he was tasting as he said it. "And I think you're worried you're not that good at your job, and that she's not going to be as cool as you thought she was, and that someone else might actually contribute something worthwhile to her." He paused, and thought for a second. "Here's the deal, Ryan. I'll keep my mouth shut about all of your bullshit, because she needs you. But when this is over, and she makes her call, then all bets are off. You understand me."

"No," I said truthfully. "But it doesn't matter. I'll see you at the meeting at three, right."

"Yeah." He spat on the asphalt, then rubbed the wet spot with his sneaker. "I have to ask you one question, though."

"Why am I fighting her?"

He shook his head. "No. If she's really as dangerous as you think she is, why are you still here? After all, if it's safer for Lucas and those guys to be gone, it's gotta be that much safer for you, right?"

"I don't think there's anywhere I could go," I said. "I'll see you inside."

"Maybe," he said, and loped off.

I sat down on the curb and watched him go. Time passed. Maybe it was five minutes, maybe it was half an hour. People drove by, pulled up, went in. A couple pulled out, never to return.

And eventually, a shadow fell across me. I looked up. "Hi, Michelle."

"You need to stop shouting crap like that in the parking lot on a day when people have windows open," she said. "They talk."

"What are they saying? That I'm crazy, or that I'm an asshole?"

"Both." She sat down next to me. "Me, I'd like to call you crazy, but I know better."

"You know that I'm an asshole?"

She nodded. "Yes. You are. And I wish to God I could just hate you, like you seem to want me to."

I picked up a pebble from the parking lot and flicked it away. "You don't?"

"Not entirely. But yesterday I got real close. Now, Leon, on the other hand…"

"Yeah. Leon." We sat there in silence for a few more minutes. I tossed more pebbles into the lot. Michelle picked a blade of grass from a crack in the asphalt and started knotting it.

"Are you going to do it?" She asked the question looking straight ahead, not at me. I shook my head.

"I don't think so. It's getting scary, Michelle."

"Scary? How?"

"She wants things," I said. "She wants them, and she's not going to stop until she gets them. And she's starting to figure out that there are things in the way of what she wants, and I'm thinking she might want to get those things out of the way."

"Those things?" She turned to face me. "You mean Sarah."

"And maybe you, too." I dropped the pebbles and then dropped my face into my hands. "So I'm going to stop it. I've gotten most of the guys on the black project fired, which isn't even the first shitty thing I did this week, but it's going to take away from her getting stronger. At least, I think it is. I'm trying to make Terry jealous enough to quit. And then I'll take a few more steps."

"Idiot." An elbow caught me in the ribs. "Why aren't you asking for help with this?"

I spread my fingers enough that I could see her and she could see my eyes. "Who's going to help, Shelly? The friend I screwed around with, or the friend I screwed around on? Or maybe my girlfriend, whom I cheated on? I screwed up, and that means I need to do this and take whatever hit I have to in order to make things right. Maybe Sarah never learns that I had to do some horrible stuff to protect her from Blue Lightning. That's fine, if she never learns that I did something horrible to whatever we have together. And I'll carry that as long as I have to, because she hasn't done anything wrong."

"And you have." Michelle stood, shaking her head. "You ever think that you wouldn't have fallen back into bed with me if there hadn't been something there you weren't getting at home? It's not all you, Ryan. It never has been, and it shouldn't be now. Most good leads learn that pretty early."

She reached down, hand extended in my direction. After a second, I took it, and she helped pull me up.

"I'll finish Salvador," she said. "But no long nights, at least not working with you. And after this, I think maybe one or both of us should think about working somewhere else, Ryan."

I took a good look at her shoes. They were black Converse hi-tops with electric pink trim, long laces triple knotted and still trailing floppy on the ground behind her. They were perfect; they were Michelle. "I think you're probably right," I said, still keeping my eyes low. "Maybe I should have left after the cancellation."

"Yeah, well, we'll cover that in the post-mortem. I'll see you inside."

"See you," I mumbled after her. After a while, I followed.

* * *

I ran into Dennis on the way back to my office. He was toting a couple of external drives by their cables, looking like a deep-sea fisherman taking his wares to market. "Hey, man. How's the head?"

"Attached," I said. "How's by you?"

"Weird." He shook his head. "You know all those backup tapes Eric had me order?" I nodded. "Well, now he wants me to send 'em back. Only it's too late for pickup today, so they've got to sit in the lockbox on the floor in front of reception all weekend, where some jackass can use 'em for a stepladder."

"Isn't the lockbox supposed to be proof against that sort of thing?"

"Yeah, but you never know. There's always gonna be some numbnuts who accidentally uses a blowtorch to get the candy jar open, and the next thing you know all the backups are crispy fritters."

"Well, good luck," I told him. "I promise—no blowtorches out of me."

He gave me the sort of look he usually reserved for the newbs who didn't realize that you actually had to plug in a network cable on both ends. "No, you'd come up with something interesting."

"Heh. Take care of yourself, Dennis." I waved and headed back toward my office.

"Have a good weekend, man."

I stuck up my hand to do a sort of backwards wave and vanished into my office.

Four guys had gotten fired that morning. Four guys had gotten fired because of me. They were gone now, out of the building, with most traces they'd worked there already gone. I looked around at my office walls and wondered how long it would take me to be gone, to be scrubbed out of this place. A couple of posters, a couple of papers…I decided it wouldn't take very long at all. I could be ready to quit in an hour, if I wanted to leave an orderly legacy for whoever came after me. If I wanted to be a dick about it, half that.

And if I got myself fired, it wouldn't take more than a couple of boxes under Marie's watchful eye, or maybe Eric's, to crate up my time here and haul it away. Everything that had been mine would be gone.

How long could it take, then, to get a project's DNA out of this place? Would it be enough to scrub some of it? Would any trace linger? There were still guys in the back talking about games they worked on ten years prior. "You weren't here for Liberation: First Defiance," they'd say. "Now that was a death march." Ten years gone, and they were still bitching about it. It was as if as much of the game had gone into them as they'd put into the game, the project having seeped into the soul of the place. Maybe wiping out some files wouldn't be enough to wipe out Blue Lightning, if it came to that. Maybe she'd be here as long as anyone who'd worked on her was, a ghost lingering in the memories of those who put something of themselves into her. And even then, we'd probably carry her with us.

If that was the case, I decided, then I was already screwed and might as well get some work in on Salvador while I waited for the axe to fall. The meeting schedule was full right up until five—nobody was looking to get out early, not today. Whatever Blue Lightning was up to, in the light of day it was poor, unloved Salvador that needed my attention.

* * *

There was still plenty of daylight at six, when the last of the meetings wrapped up. It was another level meeting, one that Shelly had decided to attend, and it had gone well enough that we'd just kept rolling after the putative back end had been reached.

She'd caught my arm as the meeting was wrapping up and the rest of the folks were filing out of the room. "You need to talk to Sarah."

I pulled my arm away, but not violently. "One disaster at a time, OK?"

"It's all the same one, Ryan," she said, and walked away.

I was still thinking about that when I got back to my desk. Eric was on his way out, and he gave me a curt little nod as he headed for the door. Dennis was long gone, the lockbox of backups parked prominently in front of reception with a Post-it note warning everyone from staff to the cleaning crew not to touch it on pain of cannibalism. There was laughter from the back of the building, no doubt some serious multiplayer action or other, but otherwise people were drifting out the doors in ones and twos, ready to start the weekend.

A chat window popped up onscreen.

"Are you coming home?" It was Sarah, flinging smileys with abandon. "I thought we had a date, mister."

"Coming home soon i swear i just got out of a meeting" I did a frantic email scan. "Got to answer a couple of emails, wrap a couple of things up, and then i'll head home "

"What are we seeing?"

"Dunno. that's about half of what's keeping me here."

More smileys. "Well, don't let it keep you too long, or I may have to start without you."

"Reaaaallly," I responded, doing my best to type lasciviously, but by then she'd already logged off. I stared at the screen for a minute, then bent to the keyboard. "Damn."

Email was taken care of quickly enough, and I started thumbing through Netflix's streaming catalog to come up with something suitable for the evening's entertainment. It needed to be something that Sarah wouldn't mind missing, but wouldn't object to initially, something that wouldn't gross her out or grab her attention too much. *Mama* was right out—too gross and too nerdy, even with arthouse director cred. The latest *Batman* flick? No, Christian Bale was a little too good-looking. Maybe a giant monster movie…

There was a knock on the door. I looked up, surprised to see Terry there.

"Ryan? Can I talk to you for a minute?"

"Sure."

"Thanks." He slipped inside and shut the door. In his hand was a piece of paper with some tiny writing on it. It looked hand-scribbled, too small for me to read. "Don't want to be overheard," he offered by way of explanation, "especially considering what we talked about this morning."

"Ah yes, that. Been thinking about it."

He nodded. "I have. And I wrote down what I was thinking. I'd, uh, like it if you'd take a look at it. Maybe it would help both of us get a better understanding of what's going on here." He clutched the paper tighter. Wrinkles appeared around his fingers.

"Is that it?"

He nodded and put it down on the far side of my desk. "Would you read it for me?"

"Sure," I said. "Slide it over."

"OK."

I looked down. The paper was not, as I had initially thought, handwritten. Instead, it had been printed out in a handwriting font, shrunk down to eight point and crammed together to be virtually illegible. The words it contained were Latinate nonsense, the standard space-filler used for printer tests. Lorem ipsum dolor, sit amet, consectetur adipisicing elit, and for a brief instant I realized I was in a lot of trouble. Then something bright exploded at the back of my head where I'd hit it the day before, and the light—not blue light, I noticed—washed away everything else.

Chapter 27

It was dark outside when I woke up, but not in my office. That was lit by a warm, soft blue glow, one that seeped through my eyelids and prodded me awake.

"Oh, God," I moaned and rubbed the back of my head. It was sore, but whatever blood Terry had drawn had long since dried. The door to my office, I saw, was shut, and from the looks of things, Terry had locked it before heading out. He hadn't wanted anyone—not a coworker, not the cleaning staff—finding me.

And then there was the glow. I looked around for the source, expecting to find Blue Lightning there, seated improbably on a piece of furniture not designed for it. Instead, there was just light.

"Hello?" I called out. No one answered, and I could hear no other hubbub in the building. I tried to check the time on my monitor, but the system had crashed, and only blank, dead pixels looked back at me. I checked the desk phone, but it was dead, too. There was no way of telling how long I'd been out, only that it was probably long enough for everyone else to clear out.

Which left me alone with her.

"Blue Lightning?" I called out, and opened my office door. "Are you there?"

"I love it when you say my name."

I turned, and there she was, sprawled out on Eric's desk, a pinup for the digital age. She was wearing clothes, she had to be, but I'd be damned if I could tell where they started or ended, or exactly how much of her they covered. Her eyes were bright, white-hot against the electric shade of her face, and her lips were the cool blue of frost.

"Hi," I said, and stepped out into the hallway. "Did you really need to have Terry do that?"

She thought about it for a second. "No, but it worked, didn't it? And it made him feel good."

"I thought I was the one you needed," I said, edging backward a cautious couple of steps.

She swung herself upright, legs crossed and dangling. I tried to keep my eyes on her face. "You are. But he's worked so hard, and I hate to disappoint him."

"If he hits me again, he's going to be more than disappointed," I said with a bravado I didn't quite feel. The back of my head throbbed, and the light from her flared and dimmed with her words in patterns that made me see shapes in the shadows.

"Where are you going?" she suddenly asked and bounced to her feet. In three quick steps she was standing in front of me. "I finally get you alone, and you're trying to run away."

"I'm supposed to be seeing a movie with someone," I said. I felt myself start to sweat. Maybe Terry had hit me too hard. Maybe this was a hallucination. Maybe—

"With who?" she asked, and stepped closer. There was an inch at most between us, a small space filled with the smaller lightning that danced across her skin and then leaped to mine. I felt the hairs on my arms standing up and the ones on the back of my neck, too.

"Sarah," I said, with as much conviction as I could muster. "My girlfriend."

"Is she now?" There was a flash of light and then she was behind me, her breasts pressed against my back, her voice in my ear. "She's waited before. She can wait now." One of her hands slid along my chest and down my belly.

I took a lurching step forward, out of her embrace. "You don't understand. I have to go home."

"Why?" she asked, and it sounded like the most reasonable question in the world. "You spend more time here. You like it here more. This is where you're important, where what you say matters. Why do you want to go home to her, to be nothing, to be nobody." She smiled. The tip of her tongue traced her lips. "Were you thinking about me last night, Ryan? About where my finger touched your flesh? About where you'd like me to touch you, and where she didn't."

"There's a lot more to a relationship, to a life, than just sex." It sounded lame even in my own ears.

"Oh, I know, I know." She advanced on me, a Siamese cat stalking a hypnotized mouse. "But the sex is so much fun. Just ask

Terry. And then you and I would have so much more to talk about once we were…" She paused, inches from me, and leaned forward until her lips were against mine. "Sated."

Her kiss was cool and warm and electric, all at the same time. I leaned into it, and then her tongue was in my mouth and I could feel my knees buckling with the sheer pleasure of it.

"No!" I said, and tore myself away. "I told you, I have to go home!"

"Isn't this home?" she asked, all wide-eyed innocence. "Or have all those long nights been a tease?"

"Look," I said, my voice ragged with desperation. "I'll finish the docs, okay? I'll finish you. But you have to leave me alone. You have to leave everyone I know alone. You have to leave."

"Poor Ryan," she said, and tsk-tsked at me with lips I was aching to kiss again. "It doesn't work that way. If you're going to complete me, you have to…complete me."

"I can't do that," I told her, even as she stepped in close and brushed her fingers along my groin. I felt myself stiffening under her touch, felt the same fire from the kiss but a hundred times more pleasurable, and only the wall kept me from collapsing. "I can't."

"You will," she whispered in my ear. "You want to."

"But I won't," I said, and ran. Stumbled, really, staggered past her and down the hall, lurching pell-mell toward the door. "Ryan!" I heard her call out behind me, but I ignored her. The door wasn't far, and once I was through it, I knew she'd be weaker. After all, I'd taken out the possessed iPhone, hadn't I? Outside of Horseshoe, she could be beaten.

Something hit the back of my legs, sending searing agony along every nerve below my waist. I screamed and went over, just self-aware enough to break my fall and roll, and then she was on top of me. The cool tiles of the reception area pressed against my back as she straddled me. Just out of reach, I could make out the corner of Dennis' box. It wouldn't do me any good now.

"Let me go," I said. "Please. I'll come back after she's asleep. I'll work on the docs. Anything."

"You don't want to go," she said, wriggling against me. "I can feel how much you want to stay." She leaned down closer to me. "Besides, silly man, there's nowhere you can run from me. I'm with you. I'm with you everywhere you go, now. You carry me with you."

I started to say "Then maybe we need some space to work on our relationship," but the words died in my throat. Instead, I could hear a phone ringing

My phone. In my office.

I looked up at Blue Lightning. She was above me, her hands on my chest, her body bent low to bring her face close to mine.

"You'd better get that," she said, grinning impishly. And vanished.

The ringing continued, long after it should have dumped to voice mail. I fumbled toward my office, rolling to my side and trying to hoist myself up at the same time. None of those efforts were entirely successful, but by the time I got to my feet I was halfway to the door.

The phone kept ringing. Twelve rings. Sixteen. Twenty.

Weary, defeated, I stumbled over to it and picked up the receiver.

"Yes?" I said without checking to see who had called.

"You bastard. You utter bastard." Sarah's voice was a knife of white-hot fury.

"Honey? What are you talking about? What's wrong?"

"You know exactly what I'm talking about, you, you, you lying sack of shit."

I blinked, even as a ball of ice formed in my gut and started growing. "Sarah, you're going to have to—"

"I don't have to do anything," she hissed. "Do you know what happened when I got home? I thought, it'll be nice if I do some laundry. I can get that started before the movie. That'll be nice for when Ryan comes home. And you know what happened then?"

She paused, clearly waiting for an answer. I gave her the only one I could. "What?"

"I went to the hamper, and I started sneezing? And do you know why? Because down at the bottom, wadded up all nice and neat, were your clothes with cat hair all over them." There was another pause, one I dared not interrupt. "We don't have a cat, Ryan. As a matter of fact, there's only one person we know who has one. And that would be Michelle." Her breathing was a jagged rasp, a sound like each word was getting sawed out of a block of ice. "Now why, I ask, would my boyfriend's clothes have his ex-girlfriend's cat hair on them? Could it be because he spent a lot of time with her at work?

Sure, it could be, except that didn't explain why there was plenty on his goddamned boxers."

"Sarah, I—"

"No." She cut me off. "You come home. You come home right now, and you explain to my face what happened. And then maybe, maybe, if you get down on your goddamned knees and beg my forgiveness hard enough, I won't walk out on you."

The call ended, brutally, and I found myself holding the receiver in two hands, well out away from my body as if to protect myself from it.

"Shit," I said, and hauled myself up, the better to stumble out, and home, and wherever there was to go beyond that.

* * *

Sarah was not waiting in the driveway, nor was she in the front hall. The door was unlocked, but I shut and locked it behind me before going deeper in to the house. There was no sense, I thought, in giving myself an easy line of retreat.

"Sarah?" I called out. "Honey?"

There was no answer. Upstairs, the darkened hollow at the top of the staircase beckoned, but downstairs was where there were lights blazing, where it seemed more likely that I would find Sarah.

"Sarah?" I poked my head into the kitchen, and there she was, sitting at the table, not quite sobbing. She didn't answer me, just hunched over her hands with her elbows on the table. She'd changed since she'd gotten home. Instead of her usual work clothes, she was wearing a red t-shirt and jeans, her favorite movie-watching combo. Her feet were bare, the better for tucking under her as we cuddled on the couch. Her hair was loose and wild and fell over the sides of her face. She was hidden from me, with only the soft sounds of her breathing and the shaking of her shoulders to let me know she was even alive.

Outside, the light was dying.

"Sarah?" I crossed to her, my sneakers doing an odd whisper-squeak on the floor. She didn't move, didn't look up, didn't react to my presence.

"Sarah?" Gingerly, hating myself for doing it, I reached out and gently placed my hand on her shoulder.

"Don't you touch me!"

Her hand came across my face with a stinging crack. "I hate you! I hate you!" I fell back, hands up in front of my face to defend myself as she swung at me, jabbed at my gut, bulled me and pushed me back. "I hate you! Why, Ryan? Why did you have to do it? Why?"

"Sarah—" I gasped as she landed one on my solar plexus that knocked the wind out of me. "Please. We have to talk."

"Talk? Talk?" Her voice went up a half-octave with each word, the shrill cry of an avenging fury. "What the hell do we have left to talk about?"

"I'm sorry," I said, still gasping. "I'm so sorry."

"You're sorry?" She took a step back, hands held high. "That's all you've got to say? You're sorry? Every fucking night you're sorry, but you know what? I don't think you ever are!"

"Where else do I start, Sarah? I messed up, OK? I know I messed up. I got scared, and then I got drunk, and then I messed up."

"Yeah, you did." An accusing finger came down, the nail jagged and bitten into a serrated knife edge. "Why, Ryan? Why did you lie to me? All week, you've been the perfect boyfriend, and I was thinking 'maybe he figured it out' or 'maybe he's decided I'm important' or 'maybe he just kind of grew up.' But no, you were lying, and you were feeling guilty, and none of it meant anything."

"No! It's like I told you. I woke up that morning, and I knew I screwed up, and that's when I figured it out. That what we had was what was important. That killing myself for work wasn't worth it. That I didn't want to lose more time with you."

"You had a funny way of showing it," she said. Her hand curled into a fist. "I mean, I guess I should have suspected something when you didn't come home or call that night, but hey, you always stayed out late. It was work, you said. It was always work. Well, tell me Ryan, was it always work? How many times did you sneak off with Michelle behind my back and tell me it was because you were working so very, very hard? Twice? Ten times? Every goddamned time? And I believed you!"

"Just this once," I said softly. "And if I hadn't seen her—"

"You saw her every day!"

I coughed. "Not Michelle. Blue Lightning."

"Blue Lightning? Your game? That's what you're calling your ghost?" Sarah's fury blazed to new heights. "You're telling me that you broke my trust, that you lied to me, that you had sex with your ex-girlfriend and smiled to my face about it, and it was because of your made-up ghost?" She laughed bitterly, the sound of broken glass being crushed underfoot. "Oh, that's too good, Ryan. That's just the cherry on top of this whole crap sundae you've made for us. Is there anything else you'd like to add?"

I took a deep breath and closed my eyes. "Yes," I said softly. "I'm sorry. I lied to you. I shouldn't have. I slept with Shelly. I shouldn't have. But there have been things going on that I've tried to tell you about, that you didn't want to hear." I could hear my voice getting louder, feel the anger seeping into it. "What's been going on at work? It's real. What I've seen? It's real, and I've been trying to fight it while keeping any of it from touching you."

I took a step forward, and she took a step back. "But you know what? Even before then, you didn't want to hear it. You didn't care about my job, you didn't understand why I cared about it or worked so hard on it, and all I ever heard was 'when you get a real job' and 'when you're done making games.' Maybe I don't want to be done making games. Maybe I like what I do, and I'm good at it, and I was hoping that one of these days you'd actually, I don't know, appreciate what I do? How hard I work?"

Sarah looked at me, her eyes narrowed. "Don't you dare," she said, her voice shaking. "Don't you dare make this about me and what I did wrong. One of us went outside this relationship and had himself a nice little screw. One of us betrayed the other. Not both of us. Not me. One of us did, and you do not get to pin any of this on me."

"You know what?" I took a step back and pressed my hand against the wall. It didn't drain much of my anger, but what I really wanted to do was punch it, and that would have taken the conversation someplace I didn't want to go. "You're right. It's all my fault. And you know what else? I'm through fighting. I won't fight this thing at work, I won't fight you, and I won't fight anything else that comes along. I'm sorry, Sarah. I really am. But if you're not going to listen to me, that's all I can say."

"Me? Not listen to you?" She stomped past me, everything held rigid until she was halfway up the stairs. "You know, Ryan, when I reached into that hamper, it was like I got a physical shock. It hurt, Ryan. It hurt to think you'd do that to me. To us. It's like you wanted to throw it in my face, and you were laughing at me the whole time I was sneezing and miserable and couldn't figure out why. Did you really have to do that? Did you?"

I stood there, my mouth hanging open. For a second, I thought about telling her about how hard I'd worked to get rid of the evidence because she was allergic. Of how I'd thought if that had been it, I would have done the laundry myself, ten times over. About how if there was a shock, I had only one horrible suspicion as to where it might have come from, or whether static electricity, carefully applied, might be enough to draw all the cat hair together. And then I shut my mouth, and hung my head. "No," I said. "I didn't."

Sarah burst into tears, and fled the rest of the way up the stairs and into darkness. I stayed behind, and below.

Chapter 28

From down the hall, I could hear the bedroom door slam. It wasn't an angry slam, a hinge-rattler that said whoever had done the slamming was getting something out of their system. This was something different, the click of a mausoleum door shutting with someone you loved on the inside. It spoke with finality, and I just stood there, staring into the darkness that led to the door, to the bedroom, and to Sarah.

I waited there a while, hardly thinking, hardly breathing. There was no sound in the house that was not of the house, the creaking of air vents and the hiss of unquiet plumbing, and that was all.

Sarah didn't come down. I strained to listen, but heard nothing of her—not the creak of floorboards, not the thump of drawers being flung open as she packed a bag, nothing. She'd talked of being alone in the house even when I was there, of the palpable silence spreading out from my office. Now I knew what she meant.

There were lights blazing all through the first floor. Slowly, I flicked them off in turn. I turned off the chandelier in the dining room, where the light showed off the cut glass that Sarah had tried so hard to get me interested in, and the blue of the wallpaper set off the arcs of color that the sunlight sometimes cut through the crystal. I turned off the living room light, three bulbs working out of four in a fan that was set too high off the ground to ever do anything but make the ceiling cool. From there, it was off to the kitchen, plates in the sink and on the counter and a half dozen cabinet doors open like a dust devil had gone through in a hurry. There were two lights to turn off in there, and I did each in turn like I was blowing out candles, a ritual or funeral for what had been before. One by one the outside lights went to black; back porch, garage and front in that order, shrouding the house in darkness. No one looking at it from the outside would see shapes silhouetted against the blinds; they'd see nothing moving at all.

Then and only then, with all light in my home extinguished, did I do what I'd known I was going to do all along. Up the stairs I went, guided by the memory of a thousand other trips in the dark. I'd done this before, done it on so many late nights where I'd told myself that a light would be selfish, would wake up Sarah, would…

…Would give me away.

Up the steps, then, while I thought about what I'd done. Third step, go to the left—the right side creaked. Fifth step, up and over. Eighth, avoid the middle; it made a sound like an old man groaning whenever you put any weight on it. I'd talked about getting the stairs fixed a couple of times. Each time, Sarah had said that she liked the nightingale floor effect, that it would tell her if anyone was in the house.

Anyone like me.

My fingers itched. I clenched them into fists, cracked my knuckles, bent each one back in turn and felt the burn all the way up to my elbows. Ahead of me, the upstairs hall was dark. No light shone out from under the bedroom door. Sarah had either blocked it, or kept to the dark herself.

Maybe she was waiting in there for me. Maybe she was waiting for me to come in, to apologize, to ask for forgiveness for what I'd done. Maybe she was hoping that this would be the moment that would open my eyes to how destructive my career was and how much damage it had caused, that I'd have my Saul of Tarsus moment over having screwed my ex-girlfriend and be ready to start a new life on her terms.

I took slow steps down the hall now, my feet landing lightly, my ears pricked for any sound. What was I listening for? Crying? Curses? A sign that she was still there? I didn't know. In front of me was the door, closed and seemingly a deeper black than everything around it. It had a lock on it. That much I knew, though I'd never used it myself. All the interior locks in our place were crap, the sort of thing that you could get through with a MasterCard and ten seconds of reasonably good aim. With that in mind, I'd never seen the point. Maybe Sarah had, though. After all, locks were good for saying "You're not wanted here," too.

I'd never know. The doorway to my office was to my right, a rectangle of emptiness against the mere shadows of the hallway. With a single last look at the bedroom, I went in and shut the office door behind me.

There was no need for light in here, either. I knew where everything was, and the amber indicator on the monitor told me where I was going. My system was waiting on standby, a faithful companion ready for its master's return. I'd known I'd be coming up here tonight, had known it even before Sarah had forced the confrontation and revelation, and had left things prepared for my arrival.

"Still got some docs to look at," I mumbled to myself, a rationale as good as any, and waggled the mouse. The red light underneath it flared and the CPU woke up with an eager whirr. The computer, at least, seemed happy to see me.

"Better check email while I'm at it." Hand still on the mouse, I dropped down into my office chair. The light on the monitor went from amber to a blinking, eager green, then settled in as the hard drive hummed into life.

"And maybe see if there's a new build." The monitor screen flickered to life, the gray popup in the middle asking for the magic words CTRL-ALT-DEL. I hit them, tapped the "mute" button so the Windows startup noise wouldn't play, and input my password into the dialogue box that made its tardy appearance. The light from the screen washed over me, cool and blue and calming. My fingers settled onto the keyboard, curved into QWERTY-seizing claws, the itching gone. This was where I felt at home. This was where I felt like I ought to be.

First order of business should have been to check email, but instead I pulled the USB key out of my pocket and slid it into one of the ports on the side of the monitor. The cursor changed into "I'm thinking" mode, and then a list of files popped up—everything I'd taken home from work in order to fill my evenings and weekends. Design files, mission thumbnails, dialogue spreadsheets, the works—they were all there, sitting and waiting patiently for me to pay them a visit.

I stared at the list for a minute, scrolling down to remind myself of exactly what I had and what I needed to do. There was a meeting with the level builders planned for tomorrow, but that wasn't until three and I didn't need to look at those docs before lunch. Dialogue? The sound engineers were making noise about wanting to do a reorg on the data structure on that stuff, so maybe that was the best choice. Multiplayer game type proposals? Better to wait until morning and see if there was bandwidth to do some prototyping…the scrolling line of docs went on and on. I watched it go, ticked off every item there and what I should be doing with it, and mentally shuffled them like a kid trying to get his Yu-Gi-Oh deck just right.

And there, down at the bottom, was the archive folder I'd pulled out and stuck on the drive for no good reason whatsoever. Zipped up, compressed to hell and gone, company property that wasn't ever supposed to leave the building, it was there. There was no executable with it, nothing that could do anything other than sit and wait to be read, but I'd wanted it anyway, wanted to take it home and look at it one last time at my own pace before doing what had to be done.

Before erasing everything.

Before killing the version control database, before wiping the backups, before setting the entire goddamned thing on fire if I had to.

A chat window popped up in the corner of the screen. It was Michelle, of course, probably the last person I wanted to chat with at this moment, with the possible exception of myself.

HI, the IM read. It pulsed there for a minute, then another line added itself: UOK???

No, I typed back, as much to get rid of the alert flash as anything else.

…FIGURED U WOULD TELL HER. It came back quickly, as if she'd already written it before my response and just waited to send out of courtesy.

Yeah, well, she found out all on her own. My fingers stabbed the keys. Is there something you wanted to say, or were just keeping score?

There was a pause. SCREW YOU, finally popped up. I JUST WANTED TO SEE HOW YOU WERE DOING AFTER…YOU KNOW.

After I messed everything up. Yeah. My fingers sat on the keys for a minute. I have no idea how I'm doing, Shelly. So I thought I'd just get some work done while Sarah figures out if she's going to leave me.

I'M KINDA SORRY.

Sorry. It was an interesting word, and a heavy one. You shouldn't be, My fault. I screwed up, I should say sorry to you. I paused. And to Leon, and to the guys who were working with Terry, and....

YES, YOU SHOULD. & U SHOULD GET OFFLINE&START FIXING UR LIFE.

I felt my lips curve into a weak smile. At that moment, being online was all I had to keep me from doing something truly stupid, though I had no idea what form that stupidity might take. Best that I was sitting there, then. Best that I was chatting with the woman with whom I'd done the stupid thing that had put me in the position to do something stupid that—

I took a deep breath and got a hold of myself. Find a joke, hide behind it—that seemed safest. And still, it came out dangerous for the moment, and wrong. Afraid I'm going to start typing naughty words at you?

U ALWAYS SUCKED AT THAT ANYWAY, she wrote back. AND I DON'T WANT TO GO THERE AGAIN EITHER. IM SORRY RYAN. WE SHOULDN'T HAVE DONE IT. I SHOULDN'T HAVE. BUT ITS DONE AND NOW WE PICK UP PIECES&MOVE ON.

Easy to say, I thought, instead of typing, I'm trying. I've got a lot of sorrys 2 say.

The window blinked. YEAH U DO.

I stared at it for a moment then closed the chat window.

"Yeah," I said to myself. "I do." With a couple more mouse clicks, I changed the settings on the chat to make sure that Shelly couldn't interrupt me, and then turned to the matter at hand.

Or, rather, the matter that had gotten completely out of hand.

But still, one last look at the docs I'd written wouldn't hurt. There might be something in there that I'd missed, something that could be picked up and integrated into Salvador. That way, I told myself, Blue Lightning would live on. Maybe the game and I were the only ones who would know it, but it wouldn't matter. I'd have saved a piece of her. I'd have made the smallest part of her immortal.

And blown the rest away without prejudice or mercy, because frankly, it scared the shit out of me. Whatever it was, whatever it might have been, I needed it not to be anywhere near me anymore. And if that meant eliminating it altogether, then I'd happily stick a twenty-inch magnet up my ass and rub it all over every server we owned before I'd willingly deal with whatever it was that had crawled up out of the electronic depths and called itself Blue Lightning.

So. One last look, and then into the virtual trash. Empty the trash, do a defrag as follow up, and then get back to work on Salvador. It was that simple.

With a reflexive glance at the corner of the screen where Michelle's chat window lurked, I clicked on the folder of Blue Lightning docs. It opened up like an imitation manila flower, the subfolders inside the petals of this particularly tricky blossom. And within each of them were the docs, arrayed patiently in long virtual rows, waiting to be read again.

I picked a subfolder at random. "Combat Model." Perfect. Boring stuff, lots of numbers, not much likely to arouse fond nostalgia for the game.

The doc opened, a wasteland of charts and algorithms. Long lines of modifiers marched down the page. Distance, weapon type, armor type, stance—all of them lined up in endless tables and percentages. Each of those numbers had been guessed at, argued over, and tweaked and re-tweaked as playtesting revealed the inevitable flaws in our best-guess assumptions. Point enough multipliers in the same direction and things could get out of control pretty quickly. Reduce the number of modifiers or make them too small, and there was no palpable difference between weapons and game states—and lack of difference was deadly. There had been one session, I remembered, where Terry had been cleaning up, armed with just a pair of pistols because the distance modifiers had been too screwed up, and—

In the hallway, something moved. A single creak, the sound of a footfall on a floor that really deserved better treatment than I was giving it.

I stopped. Sat up. Listened for a moment. Footsteps in the hallway meant Sarah. Footsteps stopping in the hallway meant Sarah was standing outside my office door. A clever man would realize this and make use of the information, would call out something like "Sweetheart, is that you?" or even just her name. That would show that I was paying attention, that I cared that she was lurking just outside the space that we'd long ago reserved for me.

I waited another minute. There was a second, smaller creak, the sound of weight shifting on that long-suffering floor, and then nothing more.

My fingers found the mouse again and started scrolling back through the document.

I ran the numbers again. Range factors, too high. Armor values, too low until nearly the very end, demonstrated by single pistol shots knocking avatars off of rooftops and ten feet back and beyond. Trajectories that were too steep, then too flat, then somehow off the charts and going every which way but loose. If I closed my eyes I could see each of those sessions in turn, switching back and forth between controller and notepad as I wrote down everything that went wrong and the occasional thing that went right.

The memory was a good one. One playtest session in particular leapt to mind, a full-on six-hour fragfest that just kept going. I'd set it up to test weapons balancing; it had only been supposed to go for an hour. After all, we were still a long way from done, the game wasn't polished, and everyone had other things to do. Except, that day, they didn't. We hit the hour mark and nobody dropped out, so I reset the map rotation on the server and we just kept going. Hour after hour, we kept going, with me getting my head handed to me every which way but not giving the slightest little damn because there was something there, something exciting and ineffably cool that made playing that game the best thing in the world to be doing at that moment. We didn't wrap up until near midnight, and nobody cared. We'd found the "unknown fun," that special indefinable something that made a game sing, and from that moment forward, we knew, knew that the game was going to be something special.

And then BlackStone had pulled the plug, and it was all for nothing.

My gut knotted up like a balloon with all the air sucked out of it double-quick. They'd killed it. And now I was going to kill it all over again.

There was more creaking out in the hallway, the sound of someone waiting to be told they could come in. The pain in my belly unraveled and sorted itself out as anger. I didn't need that passive-aggressive crap, not tonight. I'd messed up and I'd admitted it. If Sarah wanted to stay and work on things, I'd make it up to her. If she wanted to go, then she should go—I wouldn't deny that she more than had the right. But to stand out there making just enough noise for me to hear, to make me have to invite her in—that was pushing it.

The anger felt good, so I went with it. Hell, I realized, that was the same button that she was always pushing, or one of them. I'd said I was sorry, and I'd meant it. But she always had to get me to give a little bit more, to somehow win by wringing out just one little extra twist of apology so that the tally ended up on her side of the ledger. And this time, I was having none of it. She wanted to stand out in the hall? Fine. Let her stand out in the hall. Let her wait. Let her twist in the wind a little bit instead of getting what she wanted.

I was working, dammit. And my work was important, no matter how many times she might have said otherwise. It was what I did. And what I did mattered to me, to the team, to the people relying on my work, and to the people out there who were going to put down their hard-earned cash and play the game that I'd worked on. My name, hell, our studio name was going onto that box, and it wasn't like I could tell some 5'3" physics major who called himself BAD455 that his game sucked because I'd been too busy making nice-nice to my girlfriend instead of making sure I'd gotten the spawn point locations placed correctly.

The door wasn't locked. It was her choice. Like I said, I had work to do.

With shoulders squared, I opened another doc. It was a statement of the principles of level design we were going to have to follow, banged out at great length in conjunction with artists, engineers, and a wild-eyed QA analyst who swore that what we came up with was going to kill him and his crew.

Well, we'd never know now, would we? It didn't matter anyway; the level artists had broken every rule we'd come up with and a couple we hadn't, and the engineers had actually bought an ice cream cake to "celebrate" the day they finally nailed the last one of the lot. A couple of the guys had been offended, until one of the art leads—I think it was Shelly—had pointed out that they weren't going to get cake for screwing up anywhere else.

In the end, we even invited the QA guys in to have some.

There was a tap on the door. Soft, hesitant, but definitely a tap.

I ignored it, and pulled up a map thumbnail. We'd done these to lay out the flow through the space and give the testers—and us—some idea of what was supposed to happen. But documentation never survived contact with the enemy, which was to say playtesting, and we'd modified things so much that the original docs were essentially useless. We hadn't had time to keep them up, after all. There had been more important stuff to do.

Another knock, this one louder. "What?" I answered, a little more harshly than I intended. Then again, maybe not. "I'm working!"

Nothing. No creak of a door opening, no sound of footsteps going away and down the hall, not even the muted whine of the doorknob's hesitant turning. "Fine," I muttered, and then "fuck," and went back to the documents.

Typical Sarah, I told myself. Jesus, didn't she understand that I was working? Didn't she know what was important? What really mattered to me? The righteousness of my anger welled up and over me, leaving the taste of bitter copper in my mouth. If Sarah wasn't going to respect what I needed to do to make my stuff live—and she'd never respected it, never respected me, I told myself—then the hell with her. The hell with Sarah and the hell with her fucking normal life and normal job and taking me away from the thing I loved doing more than anything else in the world.

Something seemed off when I looked at the screen, and it took me a minute to realize what it was. The documents looked washed out, largely because the brightness setting on the monitor had apparently just crapped the bed. Now everything was too bright, too bland—all white with a faint bluish tinge to it that told me if I didn't fix it fast, the monitor was going to fry itself.

"Just great," I said out loud, half-hopeful Sarah-in-the-hallway heard me. "That's all I need. A blown monitor so I can't get anything done. Got to get things done." Without waiting to listen for a response—if there was one to be listened for—I started mucking with the monitor settings. Playing with the gamma worked a little, but not much. It felt like every time I adjusted something, the monitor adjusted something right back. I made a mental note to send a nasty email to the vendor I'd gotten it from, and another one to leave bad feedback at the equipment's listing, and a third to remind myself to look at the other two.

The knock came a little louder this time, slightly more authoritative but still asking, not demanding entrance. I could feel the muscles in my back and neck tighten with annoyance at that tap-tap-tap. Without thinking I spun my office chair around. "What?" I said, more of a demand than a question. "I told you, I'm working!" I meant to say that if she wanted to come in, she should, but somehow all that came out next was "Leave me—and my work—alone!"

There was no answer, just a short, sharp hiss of breath getting sucked up way too fast. The doorknob rattled for a moment; the sound of someone letting go. Then I could hear the quick steps leading away, the creak and slam of the bedroom door. Open, shut, it was done and I was alone.

"Good," I growled. Now I could get back to work, to the things that I should be doing. A little voice in the back of my head was screeching now, telling me that this wasn't quite right, that I couldn't possibly be this angry, that it all felt a little too familiar...

The monitor, I now saw, had switched back to its normal brightness. That meant, of course, that I had to undo everything I'd just done. With a mumbled curse, I looked up at the ceiling, as if I were going to find answers there as to why my equipment was suddenly acting like a coked-up toddle. None were forthcoming, just off-white popcorn with a hint of water damage in the corners, so I set about laboriously undoing the litany of changes I'd just made, bitching about the time wasted when there was still so much to do.

The sound of another door, opening and closing, came though the wall as much as the doorway. Bathroom, I figured, and the sound of water running into the bathtub told me I was right. I sniffed in what was presumably righteous disdain. For an independent woman, Sarah was so goddamned girly sometimes. Yeah, we'd had a fight. Now she was off to take a bubble bath to make her feel better. Calgon, take her away. Hell, Calgon could take her away at this point and I probably wouldn't notice or care.

The last thought surprised me, even as it flashed across my consciousness. It seemed like everything that annoyed me about Sarah, every tic and trait and habit that was less than absolutely fulfilling to me was taking up residence in the lizard part of my brain, stomping around and pissing me off. Yes, we'd fought, but even at our worst, with both of us flat-footed and screaming at each other from two feet away, I'd never felt anything like this, never felt this bone-deep hate for Sarah and everything she did, never dived this deep into defensive rage. Something ugly was flopping around in my head, covering my mental image of Sarah with acid and slime. Sarah, who'd started a life with me…who'd seen something more in me than what I was now…who'd tried to stop me from working so much, or so long, or so hard…who'd tried to get me to do something else…who'd tried to come between me and my work…

From the bathroom came a loud crash, followed by a second one. I knew that sound. That was something heavy hitting a mirror, and a body hitting the floor.

…Tried to come between me and my work…

"Oh, Jesus," I whispered and shoved myself out of the chair so fast it toppled over. On the monitor screen behind me, jaggies danced up and down, crawling out of the spaces between the letters on the doc I'd left behind. Most of them were white. A few were blue.

I took that in somehow without looking back. The chair hit the carpeted floor with a thud and a bounce, but by the time it hit the second time I was out the door and sprinting for the bedroom.

The door was closed. I slammed into it full force, hard enough to hear wood around the hinges splintering. My hand found the knob and rattled it. No luck; it was locked.

Inside, there was another crash, and a sound that might have been Sarah shrieking. I could smell ozone now, sharp and vicious and an utterly wrong thing to be smelling here and now and inside. A couple of steps back, and I threw myself into the door again, leading with my shoulder and praying it would be enough.

It was. The door exploded inward, thc wood around the lock disintegrating as the bolt gave way and spun through the air. The shock of the impact staggered me and I stumbled, but somehow stayed on my feet. In front of me, the bathroom door was locked. The ozone smell was stronger now, tearing at my throat and burning in my lungs. From beneath the door I could see flickers of light, impossibly bright and terrifyingly cold.

"Sarah! Hang on, Sarah, I'm coming!" Inside, there was a moan, a sob, some sort of hiss. I didn't want to think about what was making the last of those sounds.

The door to the bathroom opened out, not in. I tried the knob, just in case, and wasn't disappointed to be disappointed. With the lock engaged, I wasn't going to be able to rush my way through. That left two other options. One was violent, one wasn't.

I picked the violent one.

With studied rage, I lifted up my foot and slammed it into the door as hard as I could. "Don't" slam "You" slam "Goddamned" slam "Touch" slam "Her."

Wood shuddered under each kick. I could feel it splitting, cracking, giving way. I could see steam curling from under the door and that drove me to work faster, to kick harder. Palpable heat was rolling out with the steam, now, a pressure that was trying to push me back and away. And all the time, the voice in my head was still shrieking Screw her! Leave her! She's not worth it!

"Yes, she is," I muttered, and kicked again. Paint cracked and shattered, falling to the floor in long broken daggers. Another few kicks and I'd have made a hole big enough to stick my hand through and open the door from the inside. A tiny part of me hoped that none of the neighbors had heard anything, because if the cops showed up now, it would look a lot like I was trying to kill my girlfriend. A lot.

Then I was through, my foot punching through shreds of pressboard, and I pulled it back out before whatever was in there with Sarah could grab it.

Through the hole I'd made, I could see her. Them. Whatever—pronouns were the least of my worries. There was blood everywhere—blood on the floor, blood dripping down the counters, blood on the broken fragments of mirror that were scattered in every direction. Sarah lay on the floor in the middle of the destruction, rivulets of red running out from beneath her. Jagged slashes marked her arms, her legs, everything I could see. Her face was turned away from me, and for that, irrationally, I was thankful. And on her arms, mixed in with the still-bleeding wounds, were strange marks, ones with an oddly familiar shape.

Handprints. Burned into her flesh.

And next to her was a familiar figure, shimmering blue-white and giving off the stink of bad weather come to town. I could see a slender leg, an arm reaching down to grab Sarah by the wrist, and not much more, but the hissing, electric crackle that accompanied every move told me who was there.

"No!" I shouted, fumbling through the gap in the door to reach the doorknob. "Leave her alone!"

"Leave her alone?" The game's voice was surprisingly cool. Not cold, just professional and precise, each word pronounced like she was biting the end off of it. But that made sense, after all; that was the tone the game was supposed to take, all cool detachment and grace under pressure. And if she sounded just the slightest bit crazy underneath, well, that just would have made the whole thing cooler, wouldn't it?

It didn't seem so cool at the moment.

"You're the one that's going to leave her! Alone!"

I screamed. The pain that seized my arm didn't stop there, white-hot agony running up the nerves like ants carrying razorblades. My fingers spasmed and slipped away, trailing down the inside of the door. The muscles of my face twitched uncontrollably.

"Hang on, Sarah," I tried to call, but what came out was gibberish. My heart pounded to the point where I could feel each beat shaking me. A burned meat smell mixed with the steam, going past "well-done" and straight to "amateur at the grill." Still, I scrabbled for the doorknob. I could feel it dimly, though numbed fingertips. The smooth metal of the plate, the cold brass of the knob…

And she slipped her fingers into mine.

Instantly, the agony vanished, replaced by something far sweeter. Was this what Terry had felt? It didn't matter. We could all share in her, after all. We'd all given to her, we'd all made her. She was ours.

"And you are mine," she whispered through the door. "We belong together. Without you, I never would have been. And you've given yourself to me. The long nights, the dreams of what I'd be—you spent them with me. Not with her. With me. I'm everything you wanted me to be, and you? You're mine."

I felt my eyes slipping closed. She was right, wasn't she? I'd chosen her so many times—every night I stayed late, every excuse I made to get back to work, every extra hour spent at the office or thinking over a nagging issue, all of these were decisions made to be with Blue Lightning, not with Sarah.

On the floor of the bathroom, something moved. A faint stirring sound, the scrabbling of fingers on tile, nothing more.

Sarah.

"No!"

I'm not sure if I said it or she did, but the next moment I was flying backwards through the air, smoke from where her fingers had seared my flesh trailing behind me in thin streams. There was a crunch as my back slammed into a nightstand, a lamp teetering backwards for a moment before falling off and smashing against the carpet. The furniture's legs snapped under my weight, one slicing a line through my shirt and across my back as I fell to the floor. There was glass everywhere, glass and splinters of wood, and as I propped myself up on my hands I could see that the left one looked like overdone meat.

The view into the bathroom was almost completely obscured by steam now. I could hear the bubble of water boiling, could see occasional flashes of that horrible blue-white light and nothing more.

Clearly, the direct approach wasn't going to work. If I tried to reach through the door again, I'd get myself roasted until the flesh fell off my fingers. But if I didn't get through and do…something, then Sarah would get parboiled. Hell, even if I did get through it might happen. I had no idea how to stop this thing, and the old horror-movie standby for electrical-type monsters—water—clearly wasn't going to get the job done.

Knives? Probably not. Guns? Didn't own any. Fire extinguisher? God only knew, and besides, none of it mattered if I didn't get in there. Just on the other side of that door, Sarah needed me. Just on the other side of that flimsy, crappy, cheap-ass door—

I hauled myself to my feet and rummaged in my pocket for my wallet. Sarah had always joked that the locks in the house wouldn't keep out a determined fourth grader and had delighted in opening them with credit cards and straightened paper clips. I didn't have any paper clips on me, didn't have the time or grip to straighten them out if I did. But I did have a wallet full of credit cards.

The wallet and its contents tumbled to the floor as I scrabbled for one. It was a Target store-card, I thought numbly as I staggered forward. Perfect. Just what I was about to make myself anyway.

Blue Lightning was singing to herself as I fell to my knees in front of the door. It was wordless, just her sweet, clear voice echoing the music that was supposed to have been hers. I could hear things in the music now that I hadn't from the demo tracks, a sense of sadness and regret, and underneath them a steely purpose. The game was supposed to have had those, I remembered, to be more than just another shooter. It was supposed to be a little more meaningful, a little more real.

So much for that idea.

I slid the card into the crack between the door and the frame. It went in easily, catching on the inside of the bolt and sticking there for an instant that lasted way too long.

"Ryan?" It was Blue Lightning talking. She sounded unconcerned. "Stop whatever you're doing. I'll just be a minute longer, OK? I'm sorry I had to hurt you, but you made me so angry, I just sort of lost my temper. You know how it goes." She hummed a few more notes of the song, which blended with the sound of fingers trailing in water and the increasingly intense bubbling. "Don't worry about this, by the way. It's going to look like an accident. An electrical accident in the tub. Otherwise, I would have just snapped her neck."

I sawed the card back and forth over the bolt, trying to slip it in behind. Dammit, when Sarah had done this it had seemed so easy. It had taken her five seconds, ten max, to get a door open. I'd always laughed and given her crap about it. When was jimmying a lock with a credit card going to be useful in the suburbs? I guess I knew now.

"Ryan?" I couldn't hear fingers in the water any more, just that sinister bubbling, and below it, a crackling hiss. "You can answer me. I'm not going to hurt you anymore. I just don't want to share you."

If I said anything, she'd know I was at the door. If I didn't say anything, she'd hear the card rubbing up against metal, or maybe the click of the lock as it opened, assuming I got that far. I froze, shuddering, taking shallow breaths through my mouth and praying she didn't come closer before I figured out what to do.

No such luck. I could hear her on the other side of the door now. "I hope you're not hurt. I didn't mean to hit you that hard." There was a pause. "I didn't think I had hit you that hard. I guess I don't know how strong I am." She laughed, and I couldn't tell whether it was newborn-innocent or grown-up stalker crazy. I could feel blood dripping down my back from where the wood had cut me and suddenly started wondering how bad it was. From the pain, which was fighting with the agony from my left hand, "pretty bad" seemed about right. If I didn't do something soon, I wasn't going to be in shape to do anything.

Abruptly, she stopped. "I should finish up in here. The water's ready, anyway." She laughed again. "I remember how worried you were about the water effects in me and the animations for electrocutions. Well, you don't have to worry. In here, out here, they're just fine."

As she spoke, I slid the card down. With luck, her voice would cover the noise. I could feel the pressure working, could feel the bolt sliding back. Another minute and I'd have it.

Downstairs, the doorbell rang, once and then over and over again with crazy urgency.

"Ryan! What did you do!" Blue Lightning's voice wasn't amused now. She wasn't laughing. I could hear quick steps across the wet floor, each accompanied with a sizzling sound, as she crossed back to where Sarah lay.

"The hell with it," I muttered and shoved the credit card down. The bolt slid back with a click, and somehow I forced my hand into a claw to pull the door open. Downstairs, the bell was still ringing, mixed in with crazy hammering on the door. Someone was shouting out there, a woman, I think. It wasn't important.

The door came open. Inside, one of the women in my life was busily trying to kill the other. Blue Lightning had grabbed Sarah by the hair, which smoked in her grip. She was dragging Sarah over to the tub full of boiling water. Gouts of it splashed here and there, and the floor was a mix of blood and water in pale pink swirls on the tile. Sarah was semi-conscious, waving her arms feebly. Her feet scrabbled and kicked, sliding on the wet floor.

And me, on my knees, in the doorway. There I was, credit card in hand and no goddamned idea of how to stop what was about to happen.

"Stay where you are," Blue Lightning warned me. "This will only take a minute, and then everything will be all right, I promise."

So of course, I launched myself at her. There was no power in my legs, not from a kneeling position. I was hurt and burnt and bleeding and probably would have lost a wrestling match with a stuffed animal at that point, but I threw myself at her anyway.

She didn't hit me. Instead, she dropped Sarah, whose face slammed into the floor with a sound like someone eating a fistful of celery. There goes the nose, I thought, and if we get out of this, she is going to kill me. I stumbled over top of her, throwing myself at Blue Lightning, and succeeded in hitting my creation knee-height with my right shoulder. My left hand went down to keep my weight from landing on Sarah, knives of pain shooting up my arm when the burned flesh of my palm took my weight, but I ignored it as best I could. It was a good hit, the sort that takes out knee ligaments and gets you fifteen-yard personal-foul calls. I was hoping that somehow it would knock her back or knock her down. Then, all bets would be off.

Instead, I just bounced off her. She stood there and took the impact while I looked up, desperately trying to avoid collapsing onto Sarah and the floor in equal parts.

She was nude, I realized, or maybe she'd just become so. Terrifyingly beautiful was the phrase that leapt to mind, that and perfect. Slender, small breasted, perfect skin and lithe strength visible underneath it, and on her mons was a thin stripe of pubic hair, neatly trimmed. Her face was porcelain perfection, sadly disapproving, looking down on me with shoulder-length hair flowing in a breeze of her own creation. I took a slow, deep breath through my mouth, waiting for what was going to come next. It was going to hurt, I knew. It was going to hurt a lot. And she was going to enjoy it. I knew this, as surely as I knew my name or Sarah's favorite flavor of ice cream, because that's the way I'd imagined her. There had been a little bit of sadism in the original vision of the game, a little of *schadenfreude* built into the game mechanics for those moments when you absolutely humiliated your opponent. Now it was manifest and looking at me through bright white eyes.

"I won't say I'm disappointed," she said, and kicked me in the face. My head snapped back, even as my arms collapsed under me. Before I could hit the floor, she'd reached down and grabbed me by the back of my shirt, hauling me up. A spray of blood spewed out of my nose hit her and evaporated, each spot sizzling away in sequence. I could feel the heat of her for that moment, and then she smiled at me.

"I don't *need* to tell you that I'm disappointed. You already know that, because you know me." She cocked her head, and then slammed me against the cabinets. My head hit the fake marble of the countertop and stars exploded across my vision, going from right to left.

She released me, then, leaving me swaying on my knees. I put my hand out on the counter to steady myself, and she stepped over Sarah's body to stand right in front of me. My face was inches from her belly, but this time I refused to look up. I could see the taut lines of muscle under the smooth skin, the beginning of the swell of her hips.

Her hand seized the back of my head. I tried to wriggle away, but she held me there, held me with a grip as strong as the one she'd had on me when she was just an idea and a pile of documents.

She didn't say anything. She didn't need to. Instead, she shoved my head down between her breasts, holding me there, her fingers knotted in my hair. And then my mouth was on her, and the blood coming out of my nose forced me to spread my lips just to get some air, and I could feel her stiffen against me.

"I know what you want, Ryan. I am what you want, or what you think what you want should be. You know what else I know? I know you. I know you want someone else to tell you what to do when things get hard. You want someone to tell you it's all right to want and need and lust, to hate having to share what you've created with anyone else. That's why I'm here, with you. I'm telling you it's OK.

It's always been OK. Want me. Love me. Keep me. Obey me. Give yourself to me, the way you always have."

I listened to her, her words muffled by the pounding of her heart and mine. I listened to her, and tried to find a flaw in her logic, and found none. I listened to her, and wondered what it said about me that this was the manifestation of my creation, the inexorable end product of my imagination.

She ground herself against me, just a little. "Tell me you love me," she whispered. "I already know that you do."

I thought about it, about Sarah on the floor, bleeding. About the additional time I could win for whoever was pounding on the door downstairs if I played along. About how true it might be.

"I love you," I told her. "God help me, I love you."

"I love you too," she said, her voice nothing but gentleness now. "I was always supposed to love you."

I listened to her and nodded and prayed she'd keep talking. And my right hand, the one that had been holding me up against the counter, closed around the only thing I could find—a heavy, ugly porcelain liquid soap dispenser.

Downstairs, something broke, loudly. It was glass from the sound of it. Whoever had been pounding on the door was tired of waiting for someone to answer.

Blue Lighting jerked back, away from me. "Ryan!" she said. "Did you call the—"

I slammed the soap dispenser into the side of her face. She let out a steam-whistle shriek and started toppling over, arms flailing as she tried to regain her balance. In the background, I could hear the sound of the front door opening, and a woman's voice shouting my name.

Shelly, I realized, even as I brought the soap dispenser around for another shot. Blue Lightning was twisting away, bending impossibly as she strove to regain her balance. If she got that, I was dead, Sarah was dead, Shelly was dead…

Like a willow tree in a high wind, she leaned back and twisted. Her hands caught the top of the shower stall, stopping her fall, and then pushed her forward.

She wasn't falling any more.

There were footsteps on the stairs now, doubletiming it up with staccato insistence.

"Shelly! Get out!" I tried to say, but the words weren't there. I swung again, the soap dispenser coming around in a wide arc that she ducked under easily. Before I could stop, Blue Lighting reached up and grabbed me by the wrist. "I don't think so, Ryan," she said, and squeezed. Something crunched under her grip and my fingers were suddenly nerveless. My weapon dropped to the floor, miraculously not shattering, but useless to me now.

Just like I was useless to Sarah.

Who chose that exact moment to wrap her arm around Blue Lightning's ankles and yank, hard.

She didn't make a sound as she went over. Instead, she fell to her right, her waist hitting the top of the tub as she toppled into the scalding hot water. She let go of my hand as she fell, and I staggered to my feet. Sarah stared up at me. "Do something!" she croaked, and I did.

Bubbles were coming out of Blue Lightning's mouth—screams, no doubt, mixed with the still-boiling water. Already her hands were reaching for purchase on the side of the tub. In a second she'd be able to leverage herself back out.

I wasn't going to give her that second.

I put my hand in the water, on the back of her neck, and shoved her down just like she'd shoved my face down a minute before. Her hands slipped off the edge and into the tub, splashing furiously. Drops of boiling water went everywhere, hurting where they hit, but I ignored them the same way I ignored the screaming agony of my hand, submerged to an inch below the elbow in the steaming bathtub.

She felt the pressure and struggled harder, twisting left and right. I could feel her slipping away from me, slipping out from under me. I grabbed for her hair but it came away in my grip, spreading out in the water like dead pine needles floating downstream. Another twist and she was suddenly free and on her back, looking up at me, her arms reaching for me.

I pulled away, but not fast enough. Her hands were claws now, sharp and hard as iron, and they caught my arm hard enough to draw blood. She pulled, and I realized that she was trying to climb out, to use me as a ladder.

Instead, I let her pull me down. The triumph on her face turned to horror and she let go, my face an inch above the top of the water.

But now I wouldn't let her go, wouldn't let her get away, and it was my hand clamped to her wrist.

Suddenly, there was another hand with mine, pushing her down.

Sarah.

I looked at her, her face a mask of blood and rage. "We're going to have a talk, Ryan," was all she said, and then we needed every breath and every ounce of energy to keep Blue Lightning under the water.

It took longer than I would have expected, considering the temperature of the water and the fact that she hadn't had time to take a breath before she went over. Then again, I had no idea if she breathed, so I was prepared to call it even. She gave one last, shuddering effort, her eyes wide and shining, and then it was all over.

I still love you, she mouthed, and then lay still.

I held her there a minute longer, Sarah standing beside me with a look of grim satisfaction on her face.

"Jesus," I said. "Oh, God, Sarah, what did she do to you?"

"I was about to ask you the same question," she said, and tried to smile. "Along with a few others."

"I'll answer them all, I swear," I said. "But first, we've got to get you to a hospital."

"You, too," she said. "Maybe we should—"

"Please tell me this is the amazing makeup sex Ryan is always telling me the two of you have."

We both turned to look then. Michelle stood framed in the bathroom doorway, her hand leaking blood onto the already-ruined carpet. "I'm sorry," she said, "But I just wanted to come over to apologize to Sarah, and then I got this awful feeling, and then..." Her voice trailed off. "I am seeing a naked dead chick in your bathtub, right?"

"Terry's ex-girlfriend," I said, and then I started laughing. I couldn't help it, great racking sobs of laughter pouring out of me. "Oh, Jesus, you were here to apologize to Sarah..."

"It's not funny," Michelle said, visibly annoyed. "Sarah, are you all right? What happened? Did he try to hurt you?"

"Not like this," she said. She sat there, shaking her head. "He didn't do this to me."

"Sarah, I'm so sorry—" I began, the laughter draining out of me.

She shook her head. "I don't want to hear sorry right now, Ryan. I want to go to the hospital and get you and me and even Shelly looked at. We can talk about all this later" She looked up at Michelle, pinned her with eye contact and wouldn't let her look away. "Thank you for distracting her," she said. "I don't know if we would have made it without you."

Shelly opened her mouth to say that she was welcome, but lost the words somewhere along the way.

"I think I can drive," she said. "Do you guys have any Band-Aids? And are we going to call the cops about her?" She jerked a thumb, the non-bleeding one, at the corpse in the tub.

"I don't think so," I said. I could see her losing definition around the edges, pixelating and falling apart, bit by bit. The water fizzed around her edges. Soon, there'd be nothing left. "And the Band-Aids are in the medicine chest."

"Of course they are," Shelly said, and that was the last thing any of us said until we pulled up at the emergency room over at Rex Hospital, half an hour later.

* * *

They took Sarah first, a nurse wheeling her back into the ER in a wheelchair like she was auditioning for the local stock car circuit. Her coworker at the desk alternated between demanding our insurance info and demanding that we call the police. I finally told her that it had been an accident with a light fixture in our bathroom, and that I'd love to fill out the insurance forms if I had a hand that wasn't either well-done or sliced to ribbons. While she was sitting there, her mouth wide in an indignant O, I made the agonizing mistake of pulling my wallet out of my pocket and yanking out the insurance card. Small, crisped bits of skin came with it.

I flipped it to her. "Here. Take what you need. I'm going to go over into the corner and bleed quietly. Let me know if there's anything you need from me to help take care of my girlfriend."

The nurse raised an eyebrow and flicked her pen in Michelle's direction. "Her?"

I laughed, and not in a good way. "Oh, no. Not her. The one you took inside already."

"Oh," Her eyes got big again. "Sit tight, Mr."—she paused to read the insurance card—"Colter. We'll let you know how she is as soon as the doctor has seen her. You go sit down."

I nodded and turned to take the seat next to Shelly, whose hand was mummified in Band-Aids and bloody paper towels. The nurse must have gotten a good look at my back as I did so, because before I'd had a chance to sit down and get the Naugahyde nice and bloody, another nurse—this one short, Asian, and built like a dump truck—came through the swinging doors to pretty much bully me into the patient area in the back.

"Sit down!" she instructed, and nearly threw me onto the bed. "Don't lay down. The doctor will be here in a minute, and he'll want to take a look at your back. And don't exert yourself, or you'll tear it open all over again."

With those final words of admonition, she pulled the drapes shut and left me alone. My little area was one of two tucked into that corner of the ER. It held a hospital bed, a couple of chairs, a few pieces of nicely anonymous medical equipment and a magazine holder bolted to the wall that featured six-month-old issues of *Sports Illustrated* and Oprah's magazine. I thought about hopping down to get one, weighed the pain potential for my back from the jolt, and decided to stay right where I was. Whatever secrets Oprah had for me, they could wait.

So I just sat there and closed my eyes and listened. Phones were ringing, phones were always ringing with harried nurses answering them in tones that were torn between annoyance and compassion. Doctors barked orders, and occasionally nurses barked right back. Curtains and doors opened and closed, and wheels squeaked on the too-shiny floor.

And over in the station next to mine, I could hear someone sobbing softly.

"Sarah?" I asked. "Is that you?"

There was a pause, and then, "Ryan?"

"Yeah." There was a lump in my throat that made it hard to speak. "Oh, God, Sarah, what did I do. I am stupid and selfish, and I would rather have died than let her hurt you."

I heard a sniffle. "That was the ghost you were talking about, right? The one you said Terry…did things with?"

I nodded, then remembered she couldn't see me. Well, the hell with that. Gingerly, I levered myself off the bed and shuffled out of my little area. The curtain on hers was closed, so I drew it back just enough to let me in.

She was barely recognizable. Some of the blood had been cleaned up but not all of it, not by a long shot. Her arms were folded across her chest so I could see the long gashes that Blue Lightning had made, and her face looked like I'd been hitting softballs off it for a week.

"Oh, Jesus," I said, and collapsed into one of the chairs. "Sarah, I don't know what to say."

"Then don't say anything," she said. She slipped her hand off the bed in my general direction. I took it, carefully, and didn't make a noise when she squeezed.

We sat like that for a minute in silence, knowing that there weren't any good places the conversation could go. Finally, she detached her fingers from mine with more gentleness than I deserved. "How long were you awake," I asked, dreading the answer.

"Most of the time," she said.

"Ah. Then you heard."

She nodded. "Most of it." She stopped for a minute. "It wasn't hard to keep my eyes closed for that part."

I thought of a dozen things to say—that I hadn't wanted to, that I'd been trying to buy time, that she's forced me—but none of them seemed even vaguely worthy. "If there had been any other way…"

She turned her head and gave what might have been a half-smile. "I know why you did it. That was hard, but it didn't hurt. The stuff with Michelle, that hurt." She raised her hands. "More than this, almost. And this hurts a lot."

I laughed, which I think is what she intended, but only for a minute. With my feet, I pulled the chair closer to her. "Two different screw ups, both of them mine."

"No. Parts of one big one." She patted my cheek. "Poor, stupid Ryan. You still don't see it, do you?"

"See what?" I asked, not really wanting to hear an answer.

"Any of it," she said. "I'm sorry. I'm really tired, and I'm not up for any more deep emotional moments right now. Besides, the doctor is coming." She closed her eyes and turned her head away from me.

"But—"

Then the curtain was drawn back and the doctor was shooing me back over to my own side of the alcove and that was the last of Sarah I saw for a good long while.

* * *

They let me out of the ER a couple of hours later, with forty-eight stitches in my back, a few more in other places, and a bandage around my left hand that came with a laundry list of instructions as to how to deal with it. The damage hadn't been as bad as it looked, at least not all of it. The nose wasn't broken, the nerves in my fingers were still functioning, and all that good stuff—it could have been a lot worse.

Sarah, they were still working on, and I'd heard one of her doctors mention something about a police report.

As for Michelle, I could see her when I came out the door, reading a not-too-ancient copy of *Discover*. Her hand was bandaged much more professionally than it had been, and her face was the color of the really good paper we put in the color copier at work, but other than that she seemed all right. She looked up over the top of the magazine and saw me.

"Hey," she said.

"Hey, yourself," I replied. "How's the hand?"

She waved it at me, gingerly. "No tendon damage, no nerve damage, no muscle damage. Gloves might be a good idea the next time I do that, though." She tried to smile.

"I don't think there will be a next time, one way or the other." I looked around the room and saw old people, parents, sleeping children, and an entirely different nurse at the desk who somehow managed to look exactly like the one she had replaced. No familiar faces, though, none besides Michelle's.

"Where's Leon?" I asked, figuring the answer would be something like "He's off getting coffee" or something to that effect. Instead, Shelly gave me a brave little smile and dropped the magazine into her lap. "Leon and I aren't really on speaking terms right now. He didn't take the news of our little reunion tour very well."

My stomach dropped like a freight elevator, and it took my jaw with it. "Oh, no. Shelly, don't tell me..."

She waved me off. "No, no, it's all right. If I'd really been serious about him, I wouldn't have climbed back into the sack with you, now, would I? Of course, what that says about Sarah is open to interpretation."

I walked over to where she sat and dropped to my haunches in front of her. Looking up at Shelly was a lot more pleasant, and a lot less threatening, than looking up at Blue Lightning had been. "It doesn't say anything about Sarah. It says a few things about me, and most of them aren't good."

"You were under a lot of stress—" she began, but I waved her off.

"I made that stress. All of that, it was me."

"Some of it was me," she said, softly. "Enough of it."

I stuck my tongue out at her, which seemed like a better option than leaking water out the eyes. She stuck hers back out at me and crossed her eyes on top of it, which made both of us snicker for a moment.

We stopped laughing, and I stood up. She stayed seated, watching me. "I love you, Michelle. I'm not in love with you, but I love you."

Her face got a little grayer, a little sadder. "I know. I love you, too, Ryan. Even though you're a bastard."

I nodded. "Guilty. I'm going to go pay my bill now, and Sarah's. Could you take her home when she gets out? There's something I still have to do tonight."

She sucked in a mouthful of air with a hiss, and I knew right then that she'd figured it out. "What do you have to do?" she asked, but it was a formality, and she sounded defeated when she said it.

"Something at work," I said, and turned away.

Chapter 29

There was one car in the parking lot when the taxi dropped me off at the office. It was Terry's, of course, but I'd been expecting that.

I paid the cab driver and tipped him an extra ten bucks to cover whatever blood he'd have to sponge off of the back seat. He said something that might have been "have a good night" and took off, not that I particularly blamed him. There aren't a whole lot of customers hanging around office parks at midnight.

Five steps from the door I realized that I'd left my keys and my security badge at home. Getting in was going to be problematic. I considered ringing the doorbell to see if Terry would let me in, which took maybe half a second. If he was here, he was here for one reason only, and it wasn't one that was going to make him feel kindly toward me.

Instead, I put my hands on the wall-mounted trash can-cum-ashtray that our building management had foisted on us and yanked. The bolts on one side pulled halfway out of the stucco, and I gritted my teeth to keep from whimpering with the pain. Thank God for cheap-ass construction, but man, I felt bad for all the rent we'd paid for the place. Another pull, and the bolts ripped completely free in a shower of plastery dust. I took that as a good sign and leaned on it, listening to the bolts on the other side pop out one by one.

Then, with all due deliberation, I took the trash can and smashed the glass of the door in.

It took three tries, and a couple of others when my hands just couldn't take. The first time, the trash can bounced off. The second made a satisfying crunch and cracks spider-webbed from the impact in an impressive radius. Third time was the charm, and jagged hunks of glass fell out of the frame to shatter on the ground.

Using the can to shove dangling remainders out of the way, I cleared a safe route under the push bar through the door and into the building. The alarm was whooping, which I had known would happen, but it wasn't like Terry was going to remain unaware of my presence for long anyway. As for the other effects of the alarm going off, they were easy enough to deal with.

I walked over to the keypad by the receptionist's desk and tapped in a code. The alarm died mid-screech, echoing for a moment longer than I would have expected in the empty hallways. I turned, sat down in the receptionist's chair, and waited for part two of the charade.

Two minutes later the main line rang. I picked it up. On the other end of the line, a formal young lady with a hint of a Caribbean accent asked me for the passcode. "Zero-six-six-seven," I told her. "Our boss has a sick sense of humor."

I could hear tapping of keys on the other end of the line and then the voice was back. "Thank you, sir. Is everything all right?"

"Oh, yeah, it's fine. I just didn't close the door properly when I went out to my car." As I talked, a moth flew in through the gap in the glass, fluttering confusedly toward one of the overhead lights.

"Ah. Be more careful next time, sir, please." Her voice was friendly but stern. "And you shouldn't be at the office so late anyway. Go home and get some rest."

"I will," I promised her, and hung up. Then I went to my office and smashed my way in there, too.

I set the trash can down on the floor. It was dented. The glass had been tougher than I thought. "Thanks," I told it, and booted up my computer.

It only took a couple of moments and I was into our versioning database. The active projects were there, Salvador and a couple of prototypes that small teams were working on, but buried a little deeper in was the database that had what I was looking for.

Blue Lightning.

There she was, her file structure spread out before me like a willow tree of data. Animations here, rendering there, mission scripts and text strings and textures, all lined up in neat little boxes, one under the other.

I highlighted them all.

Checked them out.

Moved the mouse over the "Delete" icon.

And I waited, because there was bound to be some sort of last minute drama and I wanted to be sure I faced it on my terms, instead of getting surprised.

Two minutes later, Terry shuffled in.

"Where were you," I asked. "I could have deleted everything ten times over by now."

I looked him over as I said that, and honestly, he looked like shit. He'd either been biting his fingernails or trying to claw his way out of prison, because the tips were ragged and bloody. His eyes were red, the product of way too much time in front of the monitor, and he had a serious case of the caffeine twitchies. His t-shirt, A TeeFury special with a dinosaur, had brown stains down the front. I couldn't tell if they were coffee, cola, or something less palatable, and his jeans had that tell-tale grubbiness at the pockets that said they'd been recycled for one day too many.

He stopped on the other side of the desk and stared at me. "I was talking to her," he said. "She told me what happened."

"That's unfortunate." I leaned back in my chair, careful not to put too much weight on the stitches. "She probably only told you one side of the story, though."

"She told me enough!" His hands clenched into fists, held in front of him like sword and shield. "She told me you hurt her. You lied to her!"

"After she tried to kill Sarah, and—" I looked at him more closely and saw how wide his eyes were. Crazy-wide, my dad used to call it. Not a good sign. "You're really not in the mood to listen to reason, are you?"

"Are you?" he shot back. "Or are you just going to wipe her out?"

I thought about that one for a minute. "I think I'm going to wipe her out," I said finally. "She's done, Terry. It's time to let her go and move on. Besides, did you miss the part where I said she tried to kill Sarah?"

He stared at his shoes, mumbling, "That wasn't her fault."

"The hell it wasn't. Look at me, Terry." He looked away, and I was on my feet, shouting. "Look at me!"

He looked.

"She did this to me, the whole time telling me that she loved me. Sarah's still in the hospital, for God's sake. That's what she did, and that's what she's going to keep doing until I put her out of my misery!"

"Or until she finds someone who will treat her right," Terry said. Suddenly all the anger drained out of him. "She's not just yours, you know. We all made her. We all did. You're not the only one who loved her, either. You can't take that away. It's not right."

I sighed and put my head in my hands. "It's a game, Terry," I said. "It, not a she. And it was only a game."

"You're a piece of shit, Ryan," he said, shoving my big, heavy monitor at me. It toppled over and flew across the keyboard, only to be caught short by the cable and angle sharply downward into my lap. I was already trying to flail my way forward in the chair when it hit, the corner catching me squarely in the package even as my feet kicked up in the air.

"Son of a bitch!" I managed to kick the underside of the desk and use that momentum to bring the seat back to a normal level. I shoved the monitor off my lap. It dangled a minute, then crashed to the floor as Terry yanked all of the cables out of the back of my tower. The mouse and keyboard went clattering, whipping forward like mismatched halves of some insane gladiator's weapon.

"You can't touch her now," he howled, swinging the mouse down onto the floor. Underneath the ugly carpet was equally ugly concrete, and the plastic peripheral didn't stand a chance. It hit with a sharp crack, sending graphite-grey shrapnel in every ankle-height direction. The keyboard he let go, and it sailed across the hall to smash into the wall there.

"Terry, what the hell are you doing?" I threw myself out of the chair just in time to catch the jagged remnants of the mouse across the side of my face, as Terry used it like a whip. It cut me, deep enough to start blood flowing, and I gave an involuntary yell.

He reared back to try again, but this time I ducked to the side and caught the cord as the mouse flew past. It changed its arc immediately and headed for Terry's face. He had to drop his end and duck lest he get the same treatment he'd just given me.

He backed away, and I threw the mouse onto the floor as I came out from behind the desk. "Terry," I said in my most reasonable tone of voice, "I really don't need any of this crap right now." He took a few more steps back, into the hallway, and I followed him.

"I have had a very bad night, Terry. Very bad. And you are somehow managing to make it even worse." I didn't know what he saw when he looked at me, but clearly it terrified him. It was the blood, maybe. Or maybe something else, a certain light in the eyes. Maybe it was something bluish-white; I didn't know. I didn't feel like asking.

I stalked into the hallway. He stood in front of me for a moment, then made some sort of decision and took a swing. It was a wild roundhouse right, made with his elbow locked and no chance in hell of hitting. He might have gotten me earlier, when I wasn't looking, but now that I was ready for him, it was a different story.

I stepped inside his swing and gut-punched him. The pain in my hand was dizzying, but he let out a whumph and folded like he was perforated at the waist. I let him stagger back, then threw a kick at his right knee.

He twisted enough to catch most of it on his shin, but it got him off balance and bought me the time I needed to take one step forward and knee him in the nuts. He sucked in air like a squeaky toy, and I brought my elbow down on the back of his head.

Terry went down. He hit the carpet with a thump that was wetter than it should have been and lay there, moaning.

"I've had about enough tonight, Terry," I said, leaning close, where he could hear. "Our baby girl grew up and did all sorts of naughty things. If I were rational about this, I'd say that we had to preserve her for science, because clearly this is important and groundbreaking and all sorts of other crap. But right now, I'm just pissed off. Correction: I'm pissed off and I'm tired and I'm bleeding, and I'm not in the mood to deal with any more shit from her or from you acting on her orders."

He looked up at me. I could see the tears, but he didn't move, didn't try to get up, didn't try to stop me.

I didn't think I'd hit him that hard.

But there was one shot left I still had to deliver. One more shot and then, hopefully, his part in all this would be over.

Right next to his ear, I whispered, "She didn't love you, Terry. She felt sorry for you. That's all. She told me."

"No! Shut up! Just shut up! It's all your fault!"

I thought about that for a second. "The only thing that's my fault is that you ever met her, and for that, I'm sorry, Terry. Oh, and you want to think about getting your resume up to date. I don't think this is going to be a good place for you anymore."

I balled my hands into fists and brought them down together on the back of his head. Agony sheared through me, running like lightning up my arms. I welcomed it as a small penance, as proof I was serious about what I was doing.

Terry's body went limp, unconscious, not dead. I left him there in a heap, and then stepped carefully over him on my way to reception, where the real challenge was waiting for me.

It was there, in the shape of Dennis' box. I found it in front of the reception desk and scooped it up like it was the baby Moses. "We're going to the server room," I crooned to it. "We're going to the server room, and then this will all be done."

I hadn't taken five steps toward the lab before the lights started flickering and dying. The only steady illumination came from down the long hall, a diamond-bright blaze of blue and white.

The light stopped me. I turned.

"What, are you going to try again? It's not going to work." My voice didn't echo. Instead, it was muffled, swallowed up by the hallway and the heavy ozone in the air. Even as I spoke the words, they dropped into silence.

"No," she said. The voice came from right behind me. I spun, holding the box in front of me like a shield.

She was there. Beautiful. Radiant, even, in every sense of the word. She stood there, the carpet smoking and bubbling around her feet, and slowly clasped her hands behind her back. For a moment she held the pose like a statue, then cocked her head to the side. Otherwise, she didn't move.

That didn't make me feel better. I'd made her. I'd designed her. I knew what moves could come from that stance, what animations and attacks had been built into it.

"Just...stay back, OK? I don't want to fight you anymore." I took a step back, and then another and another, until a soft thump announced that my head had made contact with the wall. I still held the box in my arms like it had my salvation in it.

Blue Lightning did nothing. She breathed, or what passed for it, and small daggers of electricity crawled along her arms, but that was it. She just stood there, watching me, and in return, I watched her. There were no marks from what had been done to her at the house, no sign of the struggle that had written itself so painfully on mine and Sarah's skin. A low hum filled the air around her, the buzz of high-tension wires and overpowered bug zappers. But she said nothing, did nothing.

She just looked.

"What are you doing here?" I finally asked. My arms were aching from holding up the lockbox, while the cuts and bruises and burns on the rest of me throbbed and stung and otherwise inflicted slow-developing agony. I could feel my knees buckling just that first little bit, proof that I'd hit the end of the line. "How did you get here? Why are you back?"

"I never went away," she said. "I'm here. I'm always here. You carried me into your house, Ryan. I didn't go there on my own." She smiled. "And here, I'm just fine. At least, I will be until you do what you're going to do."

I slid along the wall a couple of feet toward the server room. She made no move to follow me, just glowed ever so slightly brighter. "What do you think I'm here to do?" I shouted, finding a last reserve of bravado somewhere. "Huh? Do you think you can stop me?"

"If I want to," she said simply, and vanished.

The hallway went dark; the electric hum disappeared. All over the building, the lights went out. The HVAC died, the thrum of its compressor pushing air through the ducts and vents fading away. One by one, the emergency-exit signs flickered and went out, fading like campfires collapsing in on themselves.

I was alone, and in the dark.

"This isn't going to help you," I shouted. No one answered. "If you're going to stop me, you're going to have to face me, and I'll see you coming! It's kind of hard to hide in the dark when you're glowing!"

Again, there was no answer.

"Well, screw it," I muttered under my breath, and started sliding along the wall toward the server room. It was down the hall, that much I knew, a double door on the other side of the hallway that was usually left unlocked. All I had to do, I told myself, was inch my way down the hallway to the appropriate point, then throw myself into the server room and take care of business.

Two feet. Three. I measured distance by steps, each one a half a cautious foot in the making. Three and a half. Four.

Light flared behind me, enough to blind my dark-adjusted eyes. I squeezed my lids shut and grimaced in pain but didn't look back. Wouldn't look back.

"You're going to the server room," she said conversationally. From the sound of her voice, she was maybe ten feet away, maybe a little nearer, but not moving. Not coming any closer. "You're going to destroy the tape backups, the same way you wiped me from the network."

"Good guess," I told her. Her light flickered out, and she vanished. I rested a moment, to let my eyes adjust and to put the lockbox down on the floor. It felt heavier in my arms than it had any right to be, like it was carrying in it the weight of something of gravity and worth.

Well, hell, maybe it was.

I picked the box back up, the metal warm under my fingers. Another step, then two, then three. The door to the supply closet was smooth against my shoulder as I inched along, then the doorknob caught me in the kidney and I grunted in pain. Damn idiot doors, I thought. Why hadn't we just gone to passcards inside, too?

Down the hall, she flared, nova-bright in the gloom. "Does this make you feel safer?" she shouted.

"Not as long as you can throw lightning," I said under my breath, hoping she couldn't hear me and afraid that she could. If she did catch it, though, she gave no sign.

"The lockbox has the rest of the off-site backups, doesn't it?" she asked, her voice carrying through the empty halls. "You're going to destroy those, too, and then that will be the end of me."

I said nothing.

Her star-bright shape faded away again. My eyes still stung, and all I could see was afterimage, her silhouette burned onto my retinas. I blinked, squinted, and rubbed my eyes as best I could, but it still took a long time to go away.

When it finally did, I blinked a few times against the dark to test what I was seeing. Nothing was visible, no matter which way I turned. I held my breath and counted to ten, to see if she'd come back.

Nothing.

"Good enough," I told myself, and pushed away from the wall with one hand. The other held the lockbox to my chest for fear of losing it in the dark. Back I went, hoping I'd lined myself up straight against the wall, hoping I hadn't overshot, hoping I hadn't undershot.

Another few steps. The hallway seemed infinitely wider than it had in the light. More steps, backwards into the black. Did I aim wrong? I asked myself. Is the wall still here? What if she destroyed it? What if I—

My back thudded into the wall on the opposite side.

I stood there a moment, breathing hard. Nothing moved. Nothing shone. As quietly as I could, I reached out with my free hand, feeling along the wall. The plaster was cool to the touch, the faint bumps and indentations of the paint painfully obvious to my still-battered fingers. Then, abruptly, they hit cool metal.

The doorframe. And beyond it, the door.

Holding my breath, I eased myself forward. My hand dropped to belt height, about where I remembered the doorknob being, and I fanned it back and forth across the door's surface, searching. I could feel the cool of the wood, the grain of it and the almost imperceptible seams where the strips of wood that comprised it came together. Nothing else, though. No metal, no circular base, no doorknob. I raised my hand up a bit, broadened my sweeps, kept searching. Still nothing.

"Come on!" The lockbox fell to my feet as I scrabbled with both hands. She could resurrect herself, she could devour the light, but I prayed that she couldn't make a doorknob disappear.

"Looking for this?" Blue Lightning said, and opened the door from the inside.

"Oh, shit." The light from her was too much to look at. I could feel it on my skin as a physical force, a steady pressure moving me back and away. I turned away as the glow became painful, screwed my eyes shut, and still I could see her. Without thinking, I found myself retreating all the way across the hallway, six feet of staggering backwards and away. My hands went up in front of my eyes to protect them, and still light leaked through knotted fingers. I thought about the lockbox for a moment, but it was gone. Six feet away...but against her, it might as well have been six miles, straight up and into the wind.

"No, no," she said. "This isn't right." The glow faded, but I kept my hands over my eyes, crouched against the wall and huddling against the return of the light. Sounds, I heard. Footsteps. The clank of the lockbox being lifted. And then her voice, very close to my ear. "It's okay. You don't have to look away any more."

Slowly, I unfurled my fingers. Slowly, I opened my eyes.

She was there, in front of me. Her glow was tamped down to a soft blue light, and she dangled the lockbox from her left hand. "You look very silly down there," she said. "Stand up. This is important."

"You're going to kill me now, right?" I asked her, but I shrugged myself to my feet. "You've got the backups. You're between me and the server room. I can't run. You win."

"No," she said, and leaned forward. Her lips brushed my ear. "I'm going to kill myself."

I blinked. "What? Why? You've won. Don't you get it? You've won!" I took a step forward. This time she retreated, gliding gracefully backwards into the room behind her. I followed her. Here, there was still light that wasn't hers—green and red and amber eyes all blinking in syncopated rhythm on all of the server shelves. Against the wall were tape drives, the backbone of the backup system, and stacked in front of them were the actual tapes. These were the institutional memory of the company, the fossilized work of all that had been done in Horseshoe's name.

She turned and laid her hand on them. There was a brief, sizzling crackle, and sparks jumped from box to box to box. The smell of burning plastic and hot metal filled the air. One by one the tapes themselves burst into flames.

I gaped at her. "What are you doing?"

Blue Lightning turned to look at me, and smiled. "What you came here to do, Ryan. I'm destroying everything here that's me."

The fumes from the burning tapes filled the air, leaving my eyes stinging and watering. Lined up in rows on the shelf, they looked like little jack-o-lanterns from the Halloween at the end of the world. Bits of burning tape lifted off and drifted into the air, flaring orange and bright red. And still she stood there, the lockbox loose in her grip and the evidence of her existence disappearing behind her.

I blinked. The fumes were stronger than I'd thought; there were tears in the corners of my eyes that blurred my vision. "But you're killing yourself."

The last of the tapes erupted into flame. Behind it, the tape drives got busy melting themselves into slag. Lightning danced from each to each like a forest fire in the treetops and then leaped to the servers. One by one, those shorted out in a shower of sparks. The red eyes, the green ones and the amber, all began winking out.

"You made this part of me, too," she said, her voice even and low. "You made your choice. I'm just saving you the trouble of putting it into effect."

"Don't you want to live?"

She didn't answer, just looked at me while the servers died and the lights that weren't her went out.

"You made your choice," she said softly, holding up the lockbox, the one thing in the building still holding copies of her. "Goodbye, Ryan. All of me loved you."

The last of the servers guttered out and died.

"Don't," I heard myself say. "Isn't there a way?"

She looked at me one last time. "You didn't give me one."

I looked away, unable to face her. "No. I didn't."

Light exploded from her fingers and danced across the surface of the box. Smoke poured from its corners, and I fell, gasping and choking, to the floor.

Not her, though. She shone, brighter and brighter. And as her light grew, I could hear her singing. Her voice clean and clear, sometimes off-key but always there until the flames consumed the things that held her.

She was singing as she died.

The light from her flared and guttered out. There was an instant of silence, and then the clang of the lockbox hitting the floor. I crawled over to it, but the metal was too hot to touch. It was twisted, too, bent and misshapen by the heat, and on the sides the outline of two hands were clearly visible.

One by one, the burning tapes went out, sagging into ash and melted plastic, leaving me in darkness. And that's where I stayed, huddled on the floor, until Eric arrived.

* * *

It might have been an hour later, it might have been five minutes. I didn't know. All I knew is that I was sitting there, knees to my chest, when he walked into the server room.

"Ryan," he said. He didn't sound happy.

"Hi, Eric," I replied. "I don't think you'll have any more trouble with the black project."

He flicked the light switch in the corner, and, by some miracle, it worked. "Did you do this?" he asked, looking around at the devastation. The fumes were still heavy in the air, and he fought back a cough. "Please tell me you didn't do this."

"I didn't," I told him, without looking up, without standing. My fingers hovered near the lockbox, feeling the heat spill off from it as it melted the carpet it sat on. "I was here when it happened, though. Oh, and I beat the crap out of Terry. I think he's unconscious in the hallway." Then I looked up. "Are you going to call the police?"

He looked at me, looked at the half-melted server farm, looked at me again. "No," he said, a long minute later. "Terry might, but I don't think he will. And when you say you didn't do this, I believe you. She did, right?" He extended a hand to me. After a moment's hesitation, I took it and let him pull me up.

"You saw her too?" It wasn't much of a question.

"It wasn't just your game," he said, and that was enough.

"Yeah," I said, and licked my lips. They were dry and tasted like melted plastic. "I guess it wasn't."

"Come on." He put his arm around my shoulder and helped me out into the hallway. "No sense sitting there breathing that crap any longer than necessary."

I didn't answer. Instead, I concentrated on staying upright and on putting one foot in front of the other. It was enough of a task to keep me busy for a while, or at least until we stopped in front of the door I'd smashed in, a couple of lifetimes ago.

Eric stopped, and I stopped with him by default. "Are you OK to stand up?" he asked me.

I nodded, and slipped myself out from under his arm. "Yeah. I think so."

"Good," he said, and held out his hand. "I hate to do this, but, uh, Ryan? You're fired."

"About damn time," I said, and started laughing.

After a minute, he started laughing, too. But I don't think his heart was in it.

Chapter 30

When I finally staggered outside, there was a car waiting. I rubbed my eyes for a minute before I finally figured out whose it was.

Leon's.

He rolled down his window and leaned out. "You need a ride, man?"

I nodded wordlessly and hobbled to where he sat idling at the curbside. "I thought you were pissed at me."

"I am. Doesn't mean I can't help a brother out. Get in."

Slowly, agonizingly, I made my way around to the other side. He leaned across and opened the passenger door, and I heaved myself onto the seat. I sat there a moment, and then he shot me a crossways look. "Seatbelt. The way your night's going, you need it."

"Yeah, yeah." I strapped myself in. "Jesus. What time is it?"

Leon tapped the clock on the dash. "Coming up on four thirty."

"Is it late?"

"No, it's early." We both laughed for a second, then let it die.

"I'm glad you're here, Leon," I said after enough silence had gone by. "I wanted to say I'm sorry."

"Yeah, well, Shelly told me to get my ass over here. That you might need some help. And pissed as I am at you, bro, she said it was serious trouble, and I don't mess with serious." He looked around. "Course, if I'd gotten here sooner, I coulda been some real help. Maybe I shoulda just called you a cab."

"But then I couldn't have told you what a dick I was to you." I rolled down the window and let my arm dangle. "Take me home, OK? Just take me home."

"I'll take you to your house, man," he said. "I dunno if I'm taking you home."

* * *

He dropped me off in front of the house and made sure I could stand up before peeling out. We'd exchanged promises to sit down and talk, really talk about what happened, but the thought of it seemed insubstantial. What mattered was that I'd admitted fault to him and that I'd told him I was sorry. If there was penance to be borne after that, I'd take it with good grace and appropriate humility.

I watched his car diminish until he turned a corner and vanished. I stared down the street a few moments longer, delaying the inevitable and the climb up the too-steep driveway that went with it.

The door was locked, but the window Shelly had punched out was still gone, so I reached in and unlocked the deadbolt. The door swung open easily. My feet crunched on shattered glass as I entered.

"Ryan? Is that you?" Sarah's voice came from upstairs. She sounded weak but feisty, which was better than I'd hoped for after the evening's events.

"Yes," I said and started climbing stairs. "Did Shelly bring you home?"

"She did." I heard a drawer slam shut and another one open. "She kept apologizing. Which was nice of her, I guess."

I tromped up the last couple of stairs, leaning heavily on the banister. "She feels awful, and considering the circumstances under which…things happened, she's maybe blaming herself more than she should."

"And who should she blame?" Sarah came out into the hallway, and looked at me. She was a mess. Stitches. A big fat gauze pad taped to her forehead. A sling on one arm, and God knows what else.

Then again, I didn't exactly look like a prize at that moment either, and the whistling sound that came out every time I tried to breathe through my nose was equal parts annoying and worrisome.

"She should blame me," I said, hobbling forward. "But maybe not in the way that she thinks. By the way, I just got myself fired."

Sarah nodded. "Good."

I stopped. "Good?"

"Good." She turned around and headed back into the bedroom, talking back at me over her shoulder as she went. "Did you really think you were going to be able to function in that building after what you went through?"

"Well, no," I admitted as I followed her. "Besides, I sort of had to beat the crap out of Terry in order to take care of business. And I wrecked some systems. And a bunch of company property. On the bright side, nobody's going to press charges."

"That's good, too." She sounded like she was going to pin me up on the fridge with a magnet to show off what a good job I'd done. "No matter what, though, I think it's for the best that you're out of there. And not for my sake. For yours."

"You're probably right. I don't know anymore," I said. I edged my way into the bedroom. If anything, it was more of a mess than we were. All of the evidence of the evening's crisis was there in drab, unpleasant detail. Splintered furniture, broken glass, blood spatters on carpet and walls—it gave the room the appearance of a set from the third act of a Scorsese movie. It certainly didn't look like a place anyone would want to spend the night. There was a burned and decapitated teddy bear on the floor. Goodbye, Linus, I told it silently. Thank you for trying to protect her.

And in the middle of the room, on the bed, was the thing that caught my attention. It was a suitcase, and from where I stood, it already looked to be about half full of clothes.

Sarah caught me staring at it, and stared at me in turn until I looked away. "Yes?" she said. It was about as much a question as I was an All-Star centerfielder, which was to say not one at all.

"You're packing a bag," I said, and slid down against the wall to rest on the floor.

"Yes," she said again.

"You're leaving?"

"No." And she crossed to my dresser and pulled open a drawer, then reached in and grabbed a handful of t-shirts. None that I'd gotten from the studio, I noticed. None I'd gotten from trade shows. Just concert tees, an old Carolina Mudcats grounds crew shirt, a souvenir t-shirt from a long-ago trip to Chicago—these she put in the suitcase. Then, and only then, did she turn to me. "You are."

"Ah," I said, and realized I'd been expecting this. I also discovered that I agreed with her. The house, at the moment, was not a place I should be. "Is this a permanent thing, or a temporary one?" I kept the hope out of my voice. Honestly, I had no idea which side of the equation it would have dropped itself on.

"I don't know," she said, then stopped and hugged herself. "God, Ryan, after tonight..." She looked at me for a minute, then tried again. "Look. I know you didn't assault me tonight. I know that you risked a lot, that you did...things that you didn't have to do, that you got hurt trying to rescue me. I know that a lot of couples have come back from a lot worse than what you and Shelly did. But I'm still mad at you, Ryan. You cheated on me. And you may not have hurt me tonight, but it's because of you that I got hurt. That's powerful, Ryan. It's hard to look at you without wondering what's going to happen next. Without being a little afraid."

"There's nothing left," I said, and I meant it. "I'm done, in so many ways, Sarah."

"That doesn't matter," she said softly, and eased herself down onto the floor next to me. "I still love you, Ryan. At least, I'm pretty sure I do. But right now I don't want to be with you. You make me angry and you make me afraid and you make me hurt, and I don't want any of those things right now."

"It's our house."

"After what I went through because of you, I think I'm entitled to it a little more than you are, at least until we figure things out." She wasn't crying, but her eyes were bright, too bright. "Oh, God, Ryan, I told you a hundred times to quit that stupid job. Why didn't you listen? Why didn't you listen?"

I put my arms around her, awkwardly. "I don't know," I said, and meant that, too. "It was just what I did."

"I hate you," she said, and put her arm around me to pull me closer. "You stupid, stupid man. Look what you did to us."

"I know," I told her. "It's my fault. I'm sorry. I'm so sorry."

"It's our fault," she finally said, and then neither of us said anything for a while.

We didn't cry. Neither of us. I'm not sure we had any tears left after what we'd gone through. Instead, we just sat there and held each other until the sun came up and made rainbows on the floor as it danced through the broken glass.

She pulled away finally, slowly. I just sat there and let her go.

"You should get going," she said, and levered herself to her feet. "I'll call you in a couple of days. That will give us both some time to think."

"All right," I said, using the wall to lift myself up. "Do you think I can handle that suitcase?"

She swung it off the bed and dropped it at my feet. "I think you can handle just about anything, Ryan. You just have to decide you want to."

"I love you," I propped the suitcase up on its wheels. She didn't say anything, just followed me as I thumped it down each step in turn. The hard plastic of the wheels did a great job of ignoring the carpet on the stairs and resonating with the staircase underneath.

When I was at the door, she stopped, three steps up. "I know," she said. "That's not enough anymore."

I walked out the door and closed it behind me.

My car was in the driveway. It only took me three tries to get the suitcase into the trunk. Once it was in there, I popped it open. Sarah had been very thorough in her packing, as well as deliberate. Everything of mine that mattered to me, with one exception, was in there, but then again, she was the reason I was going. But books, DVDs, my flash drive—all the things that would make up the lines of a sketch of me, she got right.

Then again, she usually was.

I thought about the flash drive for a minute. Where it had come from, what was on it, whether I'd ever have any need for it again. I thought about dropping it on the concrete of the driveway and grinding it into powder. Blue Lightning had done as much to herself. Surely I could do it now.

In the end, it went back in the bag. Just in case, I told myself. Just in case. And if I saw a little crackle of blue light around it when I tossed it in, well, that was probably just my imagination.

I got into the car and turned the radio on. It was tuned to the local classic rock station, which had been the 80s station, which had been God knows what before that, but for the moment I liked it where it was and what it was playing. It fit my mood, or what was left of it.

I started her up and threw her into gear, backing down the driveway and into the street. Sarah didn't come running out to tell me to stay. She didn't press her face against an upstairs window and gaze out at me longingly. She didn't do anything melodramatic or stupid or grandiose, and that was one of the reasons I'd loved her.

Part of me wished that just this one time, she would have.

But no, she was right. Space was a good idea. Space, and time for healing and for figuring out next steps. She'd call, or she wouldn't, and if she never did I wouldn't be able to blame her.

The song ended. Another one kicked in, Pink Floyd's "Dogs of War." I thought about changing the station, then found myself grinning like a fool and turning it up, until my windows were rattling. "The hell with it," I said, and tore out along the street. The sun was up now, blinding in my rearview. It kept me from looking back.

Really.

It did.

The End

Writer, game designer and cad, Richard Dansky was named one of the Top 20 videogame writers in the world in 2009 by *Gamasutra*. His work includes bestselling games such as TOM CLANCY'S SPLINTER CELL: CONVICTION, FAR CRY, TOM CLANCY'S RAINBOW SIX: 3, OUTLAND, and the upcoming SPLINTER CELL: BLACKLIST. His writing has appeared in magazines ranging from *The Escapist* to *Lovecraft Studies*, as well as numerous anthologies. The author of the critically acclaimed novel FIREFLY RAIN, he was a major contributor to White Wolf's World of Darkness setting with credits on over a hundred RPG supplements. Richard lives in North Carolina with his wife, statistician and blogger Melinda Thielbar, and their amorphously large collections of books and single malt scotches.

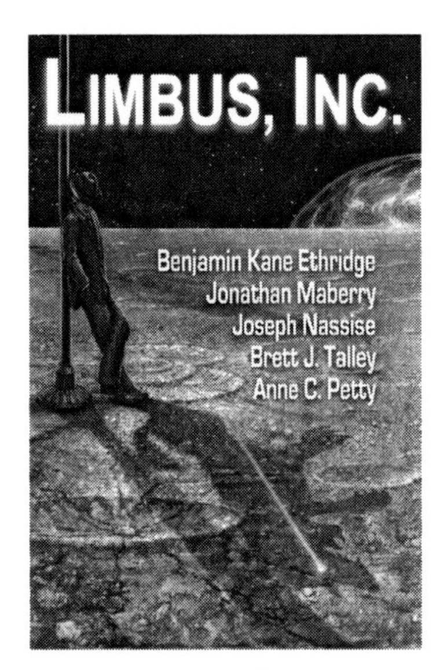

Publishers Weekly - "This shared-world anthology about a mysterious metaphysical employment agency is pleasingly consistent in tone. The execution and intriguing theme leave the reader wanting more."

Are you laid off, downsized, undersized? Call us. We employ. 1-800-555-0606 *How lucky do you feel?*

So reads the business card from Limbus, Inc., a shadowy employment agency that operates at the edge of the normal world. Limbus's employees are just as suspicious and ephemeral as the motives of the company, if indeed it could be called a company in the ordinary sense of the word.

In this shared-world anthology, five heavy hitters from the dark worlds of horror, fantasy, and sci-fi pool their warped takes on the shadow organization that offers employment of the most unusual kind to those on the fringes of society.

One thing's for sure – you'll never think the same way again about the fine print on your next employment application!

Rena Mason proves she is a rising new voice in horror." —**JG Faherty**, author of ***The Burning Time, Cemetery Club, Carnival of Fear,*** and the Bram Stoker Award® nominated ***Ghosts of Coronado Bay.***

William (Billy) Burke and William Hare were two real-life, beer-swilling, fist-fighting lowlifes who managed to stumble their way into infamy in Edinburgh, Scotland in the late 1820's. Step by step, they graduated from the unemployment line to petty thievery, to grave robbing, and then on to cold bloody murder – ultimately becoming Britain's first documented serial killers.
What history doesn't know about, or consider is the possibility that Burke and Hare may not have been acting on their own; and the blame for those heinous crimes might not entirely be theirs. Two mysterious strangers have arrived in the city – an old sculptor and a stunningly beautiful actress – both of which use their money and influence to manipulate the young Irishmen into searching for an ancient artifact rumored to have the awesome power of Heaven and Hell combined.
Seized by the vicious killings of Jack the Ripper, Victorian London's East End is on the brink of ruin. Elizabeth Covington, desperate and failing to follow in her beloved father's footsteps, risks practicing medicine in the dangerous and neglected Whitechapel District to improve her studies. News of a second brutal murder spreads. Elizabeth crosses paths with a man she believes is the villain, triggering a personal downward spiral taking her to a depth of evil she never knew existed. Only she knows the truth that drives the madness of a murderer.

CPSIA information can be obtained at www.ICGtesting.com
Printed in the USA
LVOW11s1550110216

474713LV00002B/490/P